A SHORT ROAD TO LONGBROOK

ALSO BY BETHAN ROBERTS

The Pools
The Good Plain Cook
My Policeman
Mother Island
Graceland

A Short Road to Longbrook

BETHAN ROBERTS

Chatto & Windus
LONDON

1 3 5 7 9 10 8 6 4 2

Chatto & Windus, an imprint of Vintage, is part of
the Penguin Random House group of companies

Vintage, Penguin Random House UK, One Embassy Gardens,
8 Viaduct Gardens, London SW11 7BW

penguin.co.uk/vintage
global.penguinrandomhouse.com

First published by Chatto & Windus in 2026

Copyright © Bethan Roberts 2026

The moral right of the author has been asserted

Every effort has been made to contact all copyright holders.
The publisher will be pleased to amend in future editions
any errors or omissions brought to their attention.

Penguin Random House values and supports copyright. Copyright fuels creativity, encourages diverse voices, promotes freedom of expression and supports a vibrant culture. Thank you for purchasing an authorised edition of this book and for respecting intellectual property laws by not reproducing, scanning or distributing any part of it by any means without permission. You are supporting authors and enabling Penguin Random House to continue to publish books for everyone. No part of this book may be used or reproduced in any manner for the purpose of training artificial intelligence technologies or systems. In accordance with Article 4(3) of the DSM Directive 2019/790, Penguin Random House expressly reserves this work from the text and data mining exception.

Typeset in 12/14.75pt Dante MT Std by Six Red Marbles UK, Thetford, Norfolk
Printed and bound in Great Britain by Clays Ltd, Elcograf S.p.A.

The authorised representative in the EEA is Penguin Random House Ireland,
Morrison Chambers, 32 Nassau Street, Dublin D02 YH68

A CIP catalogue record for this book is available from the British Library

HB ISBN 9781784746018
TPB ISBN 9781784746025

Penguin Random House is committed to a sustainable future
for our business, our readers and our planet. This book is made
from Forest Stewardship Council® certified paper.

For Hugh
and in memory of John Roberts (1943–2020)

It isn't possible to love and to part. You will wish that it was. You can transmute love, ignore it, muddle it, but you can never pull it out of you.

E. M. Forster, *A Room with a View*

PART ONE
Mason Road

2005

Lillian had not meant to go anywhere near Longbrook.

She and her daughter Rachel were on their way from their flat in East Oxford to Abingdon when roadworks sent them on a diversion around the ring road and, to Lillian's horror, right into the village. She tried to think of a way to avoid driving past the hospital, but she knew the village was really just one long road. One long road that led past a church, a row of terraced houses, a pub, and over a railway bridge, as in many other local villages. But this particular road also led to the low wall, the grand gatehouse, the immaculate lawn and the manor-house-like building of the old lunatic asylum. She knew, because as a young woman she'd spent nine weeks inside that place, and, ever since, Lillian had done her very best to forget everything about it. She certainly had not shared anything about the experience with her only and beloved daughter.

Perhaps, she thought, she could ask Rachel something about her imminent departure for university that would distract her. Or she could feign illness and insist they drive straight home; her neck was hot and her mouth felt dry. But no words came. The car seemed to drive itself, inevitably, unstoppably, towards the hospital.

They were across the bridge before Rachel said, 'Wait. Longbrook. As in the Victorian asylum? We did something about it at school once, and it was totally Gothic.'

Lillian managed a 'hmm'.

They were approaching the gatehouse now, and Lillian's

mind scrambled for something to say that would divert Rachel's attention. Then she saw the sign in the driveway:

LONGBROOK LODGE: NEW LUXURY APARTMENTS FOR SALE.

Beneath the letters was a watercolour representation of the main hospital building framed by a blue sky and a lush lawn where a young couple beamed towards their imagined future. Today – another hot August afternoon – the grass was scorched and the sky off-white; there was no one on the lawn.

'Oh my God,' said Rachel, 'that's it!' She laughed. 'Luxury apartments! Who'd actually *choose* to live in a mental hospital?'

Lillian didn't answer. She'd known that the old hospital had closed a few years ago and most of the 'services', as they were now called, had moved elsewhere. But she hadn't known about the housing development. A new fence added to the old wall's height, and across the driveway was a pair of shiny black gates. On the side of the gatehouse was a keypad. Surveillance cameras were angled towards the road and the building itself. The place looked more secure, Lillian thought, than it had when the patients had been wandering around.

She cleared her throat. 'I can't imagine,' she said.

'God, though,' said Rachel. 'I dread to think what happened in there. Especially to women.'

Lillian drove on in silence.

Even before the diversion, she hadn't been looking forward to this visit to Abingdon; whenever she dropped Rachel off at her dad's house, Lillian usually drove straight back to Oxford. But once they were through the shopping streets and had reached the road that ran alongside the Thames, something gave inside Lillian, just a little. The scalded-oat smell from the brewery which had once dominated the town had gone, but otherwise the place had hardly changed since she was a girl. There were the weeping willows, pale in the late summer sun, bending to the riverbank. In the distance was the ancient bridge, beyond which was the weir and the crashing water she'd tried to capture in her sketchbook so many times. She could recall the thrum of it in her feet, even now.

These days, drawing earned her money; not much, but enough for her and Rachel to live on. Lillian worked as an illustrator, picking up whatever she could for children's books, magazines, advertisements, instruction manuals. To Lillian, this career felt a hard-won and precious thing. At fifty-seven, she was still astonished that she'd ever managed to make money from something she loved.

She glanced across to the passenger seat, where Rachel was twisting her wavy hair into a ponytail, one hand neatly catching and securing it with an orange band.

'We could pop in on Dad?'

'Not sure we'll manage that, love.'

Lillian saw her daughter smooth the top of her head then pat the back of her neck, one, two, three times. A recent tic, to add to the others. Lillian had found that, if she largely ignored them, Rachel's tics would disappear – eventually. She'd snapped only once, when Rachel was around fourteen: Lillian had become so worried about her daughter's habit of pulling strands of hair from the side of her scalp that she'd taken her to the GP, who'd explained there were therapies that might help; the waiting list was long, but a unit affiliated to the Longbrook Hospital specialised in child mental health. He could refer them, if she liked?

She'd marched Rachel right out of there and had never looked back.

She wondered what would have happened had she mentioned this to Rachel as they were driving past the place. *You,* she might have said. *And me. We're the kind of people who might live in a mental hospital.*

'Did I tell you Dad wants us to have a family meal, before I go?' Rachel asked.

'You did.'

'You will come, won't you?'

Lillian had yet to agree to this. She felt, in fact, that she'd yet to agree to many of the things that seemed to be happening in her life. Being here in Abingdon to look around Daphne's house, for one. Rachel's leaving for university in a few weeks' time, for another.

It was not that she hadn't been expecting her daughter to leave. Ever since she was little, Rachel had played doctors (never nurses), and when she'd had her appendix removed at the John Radcliffe Hospital, aged thirteen, she'd seemed almost to enjoy the experience. Back then, Lillian had felt a stab of jealousy towards the tidy yet twinkling female doctor whom Rachel had obviously adored. The doctor had given Rachel a real stethoscope and a big hug when it was time for her to go home. Lillian wanted her daughter to follow her ambitions and had encouraged her each step of the way, but ever since the offer from UCL she'd felt afraid. She'd told her friend Gwen that her fears were for Rachel: the degree alone was six years. Then more years of specialist training. Everyone said how much dedication you needed – medicine was more than a career; it was a vocation. But the truth was that Lillian's fears were for herself. She couldn't help feeling that her daughter's departure might cause her to crack so severely that the damage would be irreparable. For years, her daughter's body had been within touching distance. What would she do without it to hold on to? How could she possibly fill that void?

As brightly as she could, she said, 'A family meal. Sounds nice. I'll speak to him about it.'

'He's been thumbing his Nigella. I think it would make him happy.'

'I'm sure it would.'

'You won't be weird about it?'

'Why would I be weird about it?'

'You've been weird about some things, lately.'

'Like what?'

Rachel took a breath. 'You never laugh. You're always staring at me. You don't go out—'

'I've never gone out. I'm too busy looking after you.'

Rachel said, 'Oh, I *see*. It's my fault, then?'

'I didn't say that.'

'You used to go out! You used to see Gwen.'

'I still see Gwen!' Lillian protested, though now she thought about it, she couldn't remember the last time she'd met up with her friend.

'I can just feel you . . . sort of closing in. And I'm worried about you.'

They'd reached Aunt Daphne's house, a three-bedroomed semi with a view of the river and flat fields opposite.

Lillian parked the car, then looked at Rachel with a determined smile. 'I'm fine. Now let's go in and get this over with.'

Rachel studied her mother's face for a moment, then sighed and climbed out of the car.

Lillian followed her up the path, the fierce sun making her squint. The lawn was covered in dandelions, flat and yellow as egg yolks. This whole trip had been Rachel's idea. Lillian had planned to pay someone else to clear the house before selling it and putting the money in a trust fund for Rachel. But Rachel – who'd never even met Daphne – wanted to hunt for photos from what she called her 'family history', to create an album to take with her when she left for university. Lillian, seduced by the promise of a whole afternoon spent with her always-so-busy daughter, had relented.

She slotted the key she'd picked up from the solicitor into the front door. As she pushed it open, sweeping a pile of letters aside, she felt a small thrill of trespass. Inside, the scent of stale sherry and cigarettes still lingered. Daphne's long coat hung on the peg above the telephone table. In a bland tone, the solicitor had informed her that Daphne had been found dead in her armchair a few weeks before. Heart failure. 'Ninety-three,' he'd said. 'If you'll forgive me, that's really not a bad innings.' Lillian had wondered how many times he'd repeated that phrase.

In the hallway, Rachel rubbed her bare arms. 'Why's it so cold in here?'

'It's been locked up for weeks. Look, we'll just see if we can find any photos, then we'll get going, OK?'

Rachel was already opening the door to the front room and exclaiming over the 'cute' furniture. Lillian followed her. Daphne's cardigan was still folded over the arm of the sofa and the leaves of a parlour palm had slumped on the sideboard. Photographs of Ernie beamed from the walls. From the mantelpiece, Rachel picked up a framed picture of Daphne standing on the bank of the river, holding a baby.

'That's her?' Rachel asked.

Lillian nodded.

'And who's the fat baby?'

'Me.'

'Why were you by the river together?'

'I can't remember,' said Lillian. Which wasn't a lie.

'Did your mum take it?'

'I expect it was Uncle Ernie.'

'You look happy,' said Rachel. 'What were they like, Daphne and Ernie?'

'Oh,' said Lillian, 'you know. He was a bit gruff. But nice

underneath. Mostly. And she was—' Where to start? 'I think she had a difficult life. I didn't know her so well.'

While Rachel was studying the photo, Lillian opened the sideboard and found a few half-empty bottles of sherry, a stack of coasters and an ancient tin of shortbread (*Greetings from the Highlands*). There was nothing in the drawers save rubber bands and Co-op dividend books.

But then Rachel said, 'Result,' and produced a photo album from the corner cabinet. It had a plastic cover decorated with line illustrations of fishermen. She read the words printed there aloud: '*Our Family.* Sweet.'

'Give it to me,' said Lillian, snatching it from her.

They sat on Daphne's sofa. Lillian flicked through the stiffened pages, urgently seeking photos of her mother, Winnie. There were photos of Ernie and Daphne's wedding day, and of people Lillian assumed to be Daphne's family and friends. Then there were several pages filled with images of Lillian herself as a baby. Rachel said, 'There's *loads* of you,' but Lillian made no comment, turning these pages as quickly as she could.

She found only one photograph of her mother. In it, Winnie was standing with Ernie, Daphne and another man at the fair. The four of them were dressed smartly, Winnie wearing a dark lipstick, Daphne a pair of high heels. They posed before the waltzers, Ernie gurning at his stick of candyfloss with crossed eyes, Daphne and Winnie laughing. And the man at Lillian's mother's side, who was slight in build, with dark hair and a lopsided smile, had one hand draped across her shoulder, a cigarette balanced between his fingertips.

Rachel was saying that Winnie looked glamorous, and fun, too, but who was the slick-looking guy with his hands all over her? Before Lillian could stop her, she'd tugged the photo from its mount and turned it over. In pencil on the back was written, *Ernie – Daphne – Winnie – Maurice. Michaelmas, 1946.*

'Maurice,' said Rachel. 'A boyfriend, presumably? Did she have many? Did she talk about them?'

Lillian's heart thumped. 'No,' she said, hooking the picture from her daughter's hand. *Maurice.* So there he was. Maurice of the shiny shoes, looking back at her from the photograph as if acknowledging that yes, *of course* he was a man to be gazed upon. There was no surname. But it was clear that this man her mother had so often spoken of was at least real.

Rachel, who seemed to have lost interest in the album, said she'd check the kitchen drawers. While she was gone, Lillian flicked through the pages and found a few loose photos tucked into the back flap. She shook them into her lap. Ernie and Daphne grinning on some prom; Ernie standing before a pond, smoking; and, lastly, her mother, alone. Unmistakably her mother, though as Lillian had never seen her before. Winnie had a hand pressed to her cheek, as though embarrassed but also rather pleased. Her blonde hair had yet to be sculpted into the beehive Lillian remembered. She was standing beneath a willow tree, next to the River Thames. Lillian recognised the exact spot, not far from Abingdon weir. And she was heavily pregnant.

Before everything, Lillian thought. There she is, my mother on the cusp.

And there I am, too.

'Nothing in here. We should look upstairs,' Rachel called.

With a shaking hand, Lillian slotted the photos back into the flap and closed the album. She'd been right to have misgivings about coming here.

Getting to her feet, she told her daughter they would not be going upstairs. When Rachel protested that they'd only just begun, that the really good stuff might be in the bedrooms, Lillian said they'd seen more than enough. They needed to leave, right now.

1965

Lillian was hungry, and she was also waiting for her mother. It was a warm, windless Friday afternoon in September, and the smell outside Trotman's Bakery was enough, as Winnie often said, to make a dying man drool. The queue stretched out of the door and down Ock Street, bulging with school kids wanting something sweet on their way home. Though Lillian felt a vague unease at the prospect of being the only person aged seventeen who'd be standing there with her mother, the promise of a Trotman's bun made social embarrassment worth risking. Trotman's buns were their favourite. Winnie, an excellent baker of sponges, tarts and puddings herself, was always ready to share a treat from Trotman's with her daughter. She was at her happiest with sugar in her mouth and a teacup in her hand. And when Winnie was happy, Lillian was happy, too.

As the queue inched forward, she gazed through the window at the baked goods displayed on steel trays. There were slabs of lardy cake, glistening and fruited; puffy fruit turnovers; ring doughnuts; jam doughnuts; cream doughnuts. By this time of day, most of the loaves had gone, save a few split tins, tops risen and triumphantly parted.

Lillian and Winnie had not long moved to Mason Road, which was still council, but was quieter than Sackville Close, where they'd been before. As Trotman's was now on Lillian's route back from school, her mother had suggested that Lillian meet her outside at four o'clock.

It was now five past. Lillian peered down the street and saw, among the mothers with prams, men with bicycles and old women in overcoats, her mother come battling into view, heels clicking, blonde beehive unmoving. Like Lillian, Winnie was small, but unlike Lillian, she moved as though braced for a fight: head down, shoulders forward, feet taking quick, determined strides.

She gave Lillian a hug. The chemical stench of the Pavlova factory hung around her, despite the whiff of her hair lacquer, but it was always good to feel her tight embrace. With her mother's arms around her, Lillian felt the rest of the world slip away. When she was released, she grinned and said, 'Hair looks nice, Mum.'

Winnie patted the back of her head absentmindedly and gazed at their shoulder-to-shoulder reflections in the shop window. 'I still wish you'd grow yours,' she said wistfully.

The cropped haircut had been an act of great rebellion. Last summer she'd fought with her mother about staying on at the grammar for her A levels. Lillian had pointed out that, with A levels, she'd have a better chance of an office job, which would make marrying someone with money more likely. She'd no idea if an office job or marriage were things she wanted, but in any case the observation did not have the desired effect. Her mother had merely snorted, 'Show me a man wanting a clever wife and I'll show you a pig with wings.' Which had made Lillian smile, if only for a moment. Winnie had made it clear that if Lillian stayed on at school she'd have to bring some money in: the uniform wasn't cheap, and then there were all the school trips she'd no doubt expect to go on. So the next day, Lillian had got a job at Michael John, the hairdressing salon where she now worked Thursday evenings and all day Saturday. After her first shift, she'd asked the owner, Phyllis, for a haircut, having seen a black-and-white image of a woman with a strikingly short style in one of the magazines stacked by the door. She'd sat in silence as Phyllis first gathered her dark hair into a long tail which she sliced from her head, then got to work trimming the rest close around her face. When Phyllis had finished, Lillian was shocked and delighted to see a different girl looking back at her: a girl with a steady gaze and nothing to hide behind. 'It makes you look so . . . *modern*,' Phyllis had said. When Lillian arrived home, her neck newly bare and her ears not unpleasantly sensitive to the breeze, Winnie let out a terrible screech and told her daughter she looked like a boy. There were tears, then, from them both.

But Lillian had won. She stayed on at the grammar, and every so often she stroked the back of her own naked neck with great pleasure. Now, though, she felt it was important – for many reasons – not to upset her mother again.

'Cream doughnut,' Winnie mused, 'or apple turnover?'

For Lillian, there was really no decision to be made. The doughnut, dusted with throat-catching icing sugar, split down the centre and frilled with a line of cream and a stripe of jam, was the queen of the shop as far as she was concerned.

'We'll get two. In case your Uncle Ernie comes.'

Lillian understood that Ernie was not her real uncle but a close friend of the family. Her mother had explained that they'd grown up together: when he was her neighbour in Lockey Court, he'd passed toffees to her through the window; he'd also been good to her when Lillian's dad, Maurice, had slung his hook. It was Ernie who'd got them this new house and the one they'd lived in before. He'd stood by Winnie even when her own mother had turned her back.

Ernie often showed up for his tea after he'd finished at the Pav on a Friday, and always got the best of the meal. His wife, Daphne, never came on a Friday as that was her whist night, and Winnie said that was just as well as the woman was fussy as all hell about what she ate, never mind the rest.

In Trotman's, Lillian marvelled as the woman behind the counter, paper hat perched on the nest of her backcombed hair, expertly assembled a box for their cakes. It was like a magic trick, this making of a three-dimensional object from a single sheet of card, and Lillian stood gazing at it for so long that her mother nudged her. 'Come on, Dolly Daydream. Let's get home.'

Walking along the footpath through Boxhill Woods, Lillian carried the box in her arms so it wouldn't get dented; it felt important to protect the buns from bruising or distress. Winnie chattered about her day. She was a tea lady round the Northcourt Dairy, but to keep up with the raised rent in the new house she'd taken a second job cleaning at the Pavlova leather factory. Uncle Ernie had got her in. She liked the new girls she worked with; they were all wise to which of the men you could trust and which you couldn't. Lillian said little, focused on getting home to unbox her treasure, her mouth watering.

Their new house was halfway along Mason Road. Though at the end of the terrace, number 25 was identical to the other houses in the street: a pebble-dashed two-up two-down, the front door leading straight onto the stairs. The only difference was the curtains, which were a vibrant red. Her mother had got these out of the club book and was very proud of them, but Lillian was aware that they were much brighter than any others in the road. The gate hung loose and scraped along the path as her mother opened it.

Inside, Lillian fetched the best tea plates, decorated with yellow spots, and delicately removed the cakes from their cardboard house, handling them as though they were newborn creatures stolen, or perhaps rescued, from their mother. She sliced the turnover in two, stowing one half in the larder along with Ernie's doughnut. Then she joined her mother on the settee in the front room. Outside, the sun was low in the sky; the room glowed. They had about half an hour, Lillian estimated, before her mother would start worrying over Ernie's whereabouts. Until then, they could devour their treats and share Winnie's favourite stories about Lillian's father. It was often on a Friday afternoon, in the sliver of time between the end of Winnie's working week and before tea, that she would spin a few tales of the love of her life, so handsome that women were known to swoon in his presence – God knows she had, that first time they'd danced together down the Corn Exchange! He'd something of Monty Clift about him! Lillian didn't know whether she believed this or not, and sometimes she questioned whether Maurice was actually her father at all, since she'd never met him – but what did it matter? The idea of Montgomery Clift was much better than a blank space where her father should be, and talking about Maurice always made Winnie happy.

Lillian said, 'Tell me something about Dad.'

Her mother took a tiny bite of apple turnover, put the pastry back on the plate, arranged her skirt over her knees, then said, 'You've heard it all, love.'

Which was what she always said, and it never stopped her. Lillian licked cream from her top lip and waited.

'Well,' her mother said, her eyes shining, 'he had these *lovely* suits. Fitted him perfect. And, do you know, I could see my face in his shoes. I looked down, and there I was! He bought me a smart pair, too. Patent leather with a peep toe.'

Lillian knew these shoes, which were kept in their box in her mother's wardrobe. Sometimes, she was allowed to take them out and slot her own feet into them.

'And he took me to London once. To see where he was from.'

'He took you home? To meet his parents?'

'Christ, no. He took me to the *good* bits. The Albert Hall. Hyde Park. London Zoo. We saw a tiger bigger than your bike.'

Lillian's doughnut was almost gone and she looked at the last nub of it, bite-marked on the jam-smeared plate. One doughnut was never quite enough. Why couldn't she make things last, like her mother?

'What was he doing in Abingdon?' she asked.

She'd asked this before, and had received the same reply as now. 'He was a salesman. Always on the road. He had a car, you see! And a boot full of stuff. This was just after the war, course. But Maurice had the lot. Stockings. Make-up. Hairbrushes. Face cloths. Tea towels. Anything you wanted.'

The room was becoming dimmer. Her mother placed her plate on the coffee table. She'd taken only a couple of bites.

'Course,' she continued, 'my mum didn't like him one bit, on account of him not being from round here. And then he went and slung his hook when I was expecting you. I insisted on keeping you anyway. There was no way I was letting my treasure go!' She opened her arms, and Lillian nestled herself against her. 'Which was why me and Mum fell out,' Winnie continued.

Usually Lillian didn't push things too far, for she knew this conversation could end with weeping. She'd heard it all before: how her Granny Wells, who they never saw, was too stuck up to admit the existence of her unmarried daughter and illegitimate granddaughter.

Then Winnie added something she'd begun saying only in the last few months. 'Now, don't you go falling for some charmer and getting yourself in trouble. Me and Granny Wells had always had our ups and downs but it was my trouble that really did for us. She's a *very* difficult woman, mind. The moods! Sometimes I think my dear old dad went and died just to escape her.' She gave a heavy sigh.

Lillian understood that her mother's 'trouble' was being pregnant, which meant her mother's trouble was *her*. But, she supposed, being her mother's trouble at least meant she was central to her life.

Winnie swiped the turnover from her plate and handed it to Lillian. 'Here. You have the rest, love.'

Lillian, still nestled against her mother, took the turnover and ate it in two bites, cream filling her mouth, pastry clogging her teeth.

'But we're all right, aren't we?' her mother said. 'We're all right together, just the two of us?' She pressed the side of Lillian's face into her chest. Lillian smelled the Pav, heard her mother's heart, and felt, too, the jump of her own. Relentless. Determined. Insistent.

'You're my rock,' Winnie whispered, and Lillian smiled. Being a rock, she thought, might make up for being trouble.

An hour later, she heard the rattle of the Austin's engine. Ernie was parking his car – badly, with one tyre curled into the kerb – out front.

From the window in the front room, Lillian watched Ernie haul his big body from the driving seat, hitch up his trousers and look up and down the street. As he ambled along the gravel path, he kept peering from side to side, as though checking whether he was being observed.

Lillian joined her mother in the kitchen so she could welcome him. Letting himself in the back door, Ernie ignored them both and went straight to the larder, where he levered open the biscuit barrel.

Winnie, who was cutting up potatoes, didn't turn from the sink. 'God. You here again?'

'Must've known you was doing chips,' Ernie said, through a mouthful of biscuit. 'How's my girls, then?'

Winnie tutted in a pleased way and angled her cheek for his kiss. 'All right, no thanks to you.'

Ernie laughed, then headed for the front room, taking the biscuit barrel with him. Lillian followed. He took up her mother's lumpy armchair and munched through another biscuit before asking, 'What's new in the world of books and learning, then?'

'Not much,' said Lillian.

'How about the world of hairdressing?'

'Even less.'

Ernie was rubbing at his bald spot. 'Can't you bring me some offcuts, like I asked? I'm sure your mother could weave me up a rug.'

'I might. You wanted red, didn't you?'

What was left of Ernie's own hair was dark and curled around the tops of his ears and the back of his thick neck. 'Second thoughts, I'll go for blond,' he said. 'What about a mop-top like them boys you see on *Ready Steady Go!*?' He put the biscuit barrel down, then shifted in his seat to fish a packet of cigarettes from his back pocket.

Her mother came through with tea for them both and stood eying Ernie, who didn't move from her chair.

'What?' he asked, lighting up.

'Remind me. Is that your chair?'

He took the teacup from her. 'Can't fit my arse on that tiny settee.'

'If you sat less, your arse'd take up less space,' Winnie said, then disappeared back into the kitchen.

Ernie looked at Lillian. 'She OK?' he asked in a low voice.

Lillian nodded.

'Well done,' he said. 'Good girl.'

For many years, Lillian had lived in fear of her mother succumbing to what Ernie termed an *attack of the nerves*. Lillian could tell when it was about to happen. There were three stages. The first involved a tuning-out from her daughter. Winnie's lips would lift into a smile, but her eyes would remain unfocused, unresponsive, no matter what Lillian said. It was as though she could see something brewing on the horizon, just beyond Lillian's shoulder. The second stage was the declaration of physical pain: a headache or a sprained back. Sometimes she would complain of *everything* aching; she was bone-tired and needed time off. The Dairy would have to manage without her. Lillian could make herself egg and chips, couldn't she, if Winnie were to go for a little lie down? The third stage was the closing of her bedroom door, which would remain shut for days, then weeks. During this stage, Lillian took her mother meals on a tray and was told she'd be better soon: all she needed was rest. After a few days, Winnie would stop saying even that, and Lillian would have no choice other than to wait for Ernie to turn up for his Friday tea, whereupon he'd give Lillian a couple of bob to go round the Co-op for some food. Then he'd get Winnie to Dr Randall; a bottle of pills would appear on her bedside table and, within a fortnight, her bedroom door would open once more and she would go back to work. Ernie always seemed to manage to smooth things over at the Dairy. Lillian had asked, once, what the pills were for, and her mother, lowering her voice, had said they were for *nervous troubles*. Lillian had understood, from the way Winnie looked over her head as she said it, that she was to ask no more questions.

It had been a few years, though, since her mother had suffered such an attack. Lillian had feared her haircut might cause one, but her mother had remained fairly steady then, and now Lillian dared to hope that the new house really would mean the new start Ernie had promised.

Her mother called her to fetch the egg and chips. Ernie put up the drop-leaf, and they sat at the table to eat. Lillian told him, when he asked again about the world of books and learning, that she was currently covering the Darnley Plot in History and the sonnets of John Donne in English. She didn't mention Art, because it was her favourite and she didn't want Ernie to tease her about it. He dabbed at the brown sauce at the corner of his mouth with his hankie and reminded her to show them exactly what she was made of.

Winnie asked if Ernie would be taking them to the pictures later. *Help!* was still playing, and she hadn't seen it yet.

'Can't tonight,' Ernie said, taking a drag on his cigarette.

There was a small pause, then Winnie said, 'Are you taking your wife?'

Ernie shook his head, squinting at Winnie through a trail of smoke. 'Daphne's seen it.'

It was rare for Ernie to mention his wife by name, and Lillian understood this was a warning to her mother. Winnie had told her that Daphne didn't like Ernie coming to their house, because she was a bloody snob, just like Granny Wells.

There was a small pause, then Winnie said, 'I s'pose you really ought to bring her over, Ern, didn't you? It's not right, her never coming here.' Her tone was wheedling, but Lillian knew there was little conviction behind it. It was just a thing she said, sometimes, when she hadn't said it for a while.

Ernie shook his head and picked a hair of tobacco from his lip. 'It's best left. Course, I could take Lillian over to see *her*—'

Winnie sat up straight. 'Without me?'

'She'd like to see her niece.'

'No you don't, Ernie! That's not fair!'

Ernie gazed at Winnie and Lillian saw something close to sorrow cross his face as he said, softly, 'What harm would it do?'

Winnie swallowed and shook her head, wide-eyed. 'Not on your life.'

Ernie glanced at Lillian, who had shuffled her chair closer to Winnie's. The thought of visiting her aunt and displeasing her mother filled her with dread. She blinked at her uncle and asked, 'Why would I go without Mum?'

Winnie put an arm around her and said, 'Exactly. If we was *both* invited it would be different.'

Ernie pushed what was left of his fag into the ashtray. 'You two are impossible. What's for pudding?'

Jim Shepherd had just turned eighteen when Lillian Wells moved in to Mason Road with her mother. The father, Jim's mother pointed out, was noticeably absent. But this wasn't what Jim noticed. Sitting at the table, watching through the nets as the new family moved in across the street, he noticed a girl whose stare was fixed ahead as she walked slightly behind her mother. The two of them were small, but they strode out as though they were entitled to every inch of that pavement. The girl's hair was dark and cut short. She looked, he couldn't help thinking, a bit French. Continental. As though she should be smoking. Jim barely registered the mother, though he heard his own mother's comment – *mutton* – clearly enough.

The doctor had recently advised Mrs Shepherd to reduce, so Monday's tea was a luncheon meat salad. Jim's mother lit a cigarette and pushed her plate away, saying she'd never considered salad an actual meal. She already knew all about this new family, of course. Brian, the rent man, had filled her in last week. The mother in the high heels was Winnie. Two jobs: the Dairy and the Pav. And the daughter was Lillian. She'd stayed on at the grammar, and worked after school at Michael John, the hairdresser on Stert Street.

Lillian. It was spoken with all three syllables, and slight incredulity, by Jim's mother. As if she couldn't believe someone living across the road would dare to insist on such a long and theatrical name. Her own name was Cath, and no one called her Catherine.

'She's an only child,' she added.

'Like me, then,' said Jim.

His mother glanced his way. 'That wasn't my fault.'

Jim's father, who'd suffered rheumatic fever as a child, had died when Jim was two. His mother never spoke about her husband, even now. Not one photograph of him was on display in their house. Whenever Jim asked, she told him there wasn't much to say: Reg had been a good man, but he'd had a weak heart and had been irresponsible never to go to the doctor. Unlike Jim, she added, whose heart was strong and who'd *always* been responsible.

'Anyway,' Mrs Shepherd continued, 'Lillian's situation is quite different to yours, Jim. Her mother's not married. And I hear there's been quite a bit of trouble there. Apparently it's some chap's name on the rent book.'

Lillian. Jim thought about all the *l*s in the girl's name. Almost an obscene amount.

Leaving for work the next morning, Jim slowed his pace as he passed Lillian's house. Lillian's mother had hung gaudy red curtains at the windows. The brass knocker shone, but the hedge was in need of a trim.

Since leaving school a couple of years ago, he'd worked in the Morland accounts office as a junior clerk. His mother, delighted by the appointment, told everyone that her son was a suit-and-tie man at the brewery. 'Your father wouldn't have known what to make of it!' she often said, which Jim thought you could take two ways. Mr Oates, his boss, had his own office, and Jim had plans to be able, one day, to close the door, take off his tie and make personal calls, just as Mr Oates did.

There was a girl, Pam Clarke, who worked as a typist in the accounts office. She wore blouses with collars that looked like the piping on fancy cakes. He'd been thinking that he might ask Pam to the pictures. She often smiled at him and once she'd offered him a chicken and ham paste sandwich from her lunchbox.

But as Jim passed Lillian's house, he began to doubt he'd be asking Pam anywhere.

Every day that week, Jim slowed his steps as he wheeled his bike out of the gate, hoping to bump into Lillian. And every day, the red curtains remained closed and Pam offered Jim another sandwich, which he accepted but didn't taste.

It wasn't until he left earlier than usual, to allow himself time to stop off for Wine Gums at the paper shop, that he saw her.

She was hurrying towards her front gate. Her stare was fixed ahead and it seemed to Jim that, rather than her noticing him, he simply wheeled his bike into her line of vision. She was wearing her school duffel coat and flat shoes, and a large satchel was slung across her body. She frowned slightly as she registered him. His heartbeat deepened, his knees went a little soft, and he was surprised when he managed to get some words out of his mouth.

'Colder, this morning.'

The sky was gently blue but there was, for the first time that month, a chill in the air.

She nodded, meeting his eye for only the briefest of moments, then walked on, leaving him gazing after her.

'You're Lillian, aren't you?' he said, catching up with her.

She didn't stop walking but she did glance at him. There was something unwieldy about her mouth.

'I'm Jim Shepherd. From number 20. Opposite. I noticed you, moving in. With your mother. And I wanted to welcome you.'

He was gabbling.

'I'm on my way to work,' Jim continued into the silence. 'At

Morland. In the offices,' he added, hating himself for this desperate attempt to impress her.

'Oh.'

'Are you going to school?'

'I'm going walking.'

'Walking?'

'Down the river.'

He noticed that her earlobes, too, were cushiony.

They walked in silence for a while, neither looking at the other, Jim registering the pleasant tapping of Lillian's school shoes on the pavement, which seemed to keep time with the ticking of his bicycle wheels.

'So what do you do, down the river?' he asked.

A V-shaped crease appeared between her eyebrows. 'I don't *do* anything.'

'You just walk? At this hour?'

'My mum doesn't like me going there. So I leave for school before she's up, and go on the way.'

'It's a secret?'

'I suppose.'

'Why?'

'She thinks it's dangerous. The weir.'

They'd reached the main road, which was empty of traffic, and they crossed it. He really should leave her here and head to work: his usual route was in the opposite direction. But as he was attempting to form some question that would delay her, she looked at him and asked, 'What's it like at the brewery, then?'

His mind raced: what *was* it like? In that moment, with Lillian gazing directly at him, clearly expecting some truth, he had little recollection of what he actually did all day and no idea whether he liked it or not. 'It's – pretty exciting, actually.'

She raised her eyebrows.

'It's fun, learning about how it all works, the brewing process and that, and all the pubs we have deal with . . .'

'Fascinating,' she said, flatly. But there was a small smile on her face.

'Well,' said Jim, 'maybe not as fascinating as the river. Or as dangerous.'

'Though you could fall into a vat of beer.'

He blinked, then laughed. She raised a hand and walked away from him.

Jim called out after her, 'Maybe I could come to the river with you one day?'

She waved again but did not look back. Jim could only stand and watch her stride away, the blood beating in his veins.

In the yard at break-time, Pam trotted by. It had just rained, and she paused to wipe dirty water from one shoe before nodding towards Jim, who was sitting on an upturned crate, passing his break in the company of Mick Harries. As she walked back into the building, Mick leaned close to him and said, 'She's not half bad. You asked her out yet?'

Mick had been a friend of Jim's since they'd met at Caldicott primary school. Like Jim, Mick had made it to the grammar, but unlike Jim he'd left before taking his exams and was now working in the bottling hall. Mick had always been bigger than Jim and at school he'd offered him shelter from the fists of other boys. They'd discovered, too, a shared passion for the pictures; Mick's sister Ida worked at the Regal and turned a blind eye when they snuck in without paying.

Mick, watching a few of the other bottling lads kick a football about, said, 'It's the fair soon. I reckon Pam'd go through the Tunnel of Love with you.'

Though Mick had something of a reputation as a ladies' man, he was not the type to whistle at women or shout lewd things as they passed and, Jim knew, this was partly why he was so successful with them.

Jim said, 'I can't ask her. That's all there is to it.'

Mick took a swig from his bottle of light ale. Every Morland employee was entitled to help themselves to pop, and those over eighteen had a beer allowance of three bottles of ale per day. Jim never wanted a beer until later in the afternoon, but most of the men drank it steadily, whatever the hour.

'Why the hell not?' Mick asked.

'Because . . .' Jim felt something leap in his chest as he said, louder than Mick had spoken, 'Because I think I'm in love with someone else.'

When he thought about it later, back at his desk, Jim realised that after the initial shock at hearing the word *love* spoken aloud had passed, the look on Mick's face had been one of sorrow. And he understood that by displaying his happiness so blatantly, so bluntly, out there in the yard, he'd somehow wounded his friend.

As she walked home from school through the sodden woods, Lillian thought about Jim Shepherd's mouth, which was wide, with a deep bow in the upper lip. There was something open and welcoming about his face, too. And she'd noticed the way he looked at her. Some men gaped at her like she was a cream doughnut in Trotman's window. As though they couldn't wait to devour her. Jim didn't do that. Jim looked *interested*, she decided. Hungry, yes. But also curious.

She decided his mouth would be a good fit for hers. For a while now, she'd been assessing male mouths to ascertain their fitness for kissing. None of the boys at Wednesday Club seemed to have the right mouth for hers, save Tommy Gray, who was too good-looking even to be considered. Jim Shepherd had a mouth shaped in a way that seemed possible to kiss. She thought it must be important that the two sets of lips should be of roughly the same size and shape. Otherwise there would be too much overlap. Or perhaps too little.

Once, in the school library, she'd read a story in which a male character described how he could always tell when a woman was not just sensual but *ravenous*, not just willing but positively able, by her upper lip. If she had a slightly protruding area of flesh there, this marked her out as being peculiarly sexual. The man could not resist such women, but the story ended badly for them both. (The woman was quite mad; the man narrowly escaped with his life.)

But this ending hadn't been what remained with Lillian. After reading it, she'd examined her own lips in the bathroom mirror and had seen, with a rush of excitement and fear, that her upper lip featured a small bulge. When she pressed it with a fingertip it leapt back. She did it again and again, and every time it insisted upon its springy plumpness.

Perhaps Jim Shepherd's deep bow was a shape into which she could fit. Perhaps, when he'd looked at her the other morning, he'd recognised something *able* in her.

The following Saturday, Jim's mother arrived in the salon.

Lillian, having seen her leave the house opposite her own a few times, recognised her immediately. Mrs Shepherd was wearing what looked like Jim's overcoat, and her hair was hidden by a yellow nylon scarf tied beneath her chin.

As she didn't have an appointment, Lillian suggested Mrs Shepherd sit in the armchair by the window to wait. Perhaps she'd like to watch the men putting up the rides? The Michaelmas Fair, which heralded the onset of winter each year in Abingdon, had been setting up all morning and Phyllis had spent much of the day gazing out of the window as she painted on perming lotion and rolled hair onto curlers, all the while offering Lillian updates on what was being assembled. The Hook a Duck was directly outside the shop. A skinny man with a cigarette hanging from his lower lip and a money belt slung across his hips was arranging plastic bags of goldfish around the top of the circular stall. Occasionally a tannoy would bark into life with the word 'testing' or a blast of Bobby Vinton.

Mrs Shepherd took a seat. When Lillian had made her a cup of tea, she sipped it and commented, 'It's a shame that stall is blocking the window of Ivor Fields's. They've got some lovely wedding photos on display at the moment. Mind you, why those girls go for pastels is beyond me. What's wrong with white? And long, for that matter? No one wants to see a bride's knees.'

Lillian suggested she hang Mrs Shepherd's coat and scarf on the peg.

'I'll keep hold of them, thanks.'

'It's just they'll get all hairy,' Lillian tried.

'I'm having a shampoo and set,' said Mrs Shepherd. 'I won't be shedding a single hair. My son's paying. I think you met Jim the other day?'

Lillian, surprised Jim had mentioned it to his mother, gave a quick nod. Mrs Shepherd continued, 'He wants me to get it done weekly now he's landed himself an office job at Morland's! I won't, of course. I wouldn't waste his hard-earned money on vanities.' She looked Lillian in the eye. 'You'd look lovely in long and white, dear. If you grew your hair.'

Lillian flushed. 'I'm not planning on getting married.'

She wasn't sure about this, but it was true that she'd never daydreamed about a white dress and a train.

Mrs Shepherd narrowed her eyes. Then she said, 'I expect you'll change your mind. Don't take this the wrong way, but you don't want to end up like your poor mother, do you?' She patted Lillian's forearm and lowered her voice. 'Quite a trial for you without a man around, I imagine.'

Lillian gaped at Mrs Shepherd, completely at a loss for how to respond. To her relief, Phyllis appeared and asked what her client wanted doing.

Half an hour later, while Phyllis finished off Mrs Shepherd's hair, Lillian swept round the salon while half-listening to their conversation. In her mind she tried to formulate some devastating response to Mrs Shepherd's comment, but she could only come up with her mother's favoured phrases. *It's easier without a man clogging up the place!* and, *When you're on your own you've only to please yourself.* Which wasn't even true, as Winnie wasn't on her own. She had Lillian.

Then Mrs Shepherd said, 'Did you hear about poor Dolly James?'

Phyllis said she'd heard something but didn't know the details. 'Is it true?' she asked. 'About – you know?'

Mrs Shepherd nodded. 'Longbrook,' she mouthed, barely making a sound. Lillian slowed her broom, fascinated and slightly afraid. At school, there was a warning which was repeated whenever a girl lost her temper or behaved outlandishly: *It's a short road to Longbrook!*

'When they came for her she'd been rocking back and forth for hours in the kitchen, unable even to wash the dishes,' Mrs Shepherd was saying. 'I heard she had to be *restrained*. Imagine it! Being carted off to that place.'

Lillian pictured a Victorian cell, with bars on the windows and a woman in a straitjacket with a bit in her mouth. She'd seen something like it on the telly once.

Phyllis gave a visible shudder. 'Poor Dolly,' she said.

Mrs Shepherd nodded and caught Lillian's eye in the mirror. 'There but for the grace of God.'

Lillian looked away. There was something in Mrs Shepherd's glance that was unnerving. She went back to work, gathering the cut hair into a pile before catching it in the dustpan and taking it out the back to deposit it in the bin. She let the lid bang loudly and stayed there until she heard the door of the salon open and shut. Jim's intentions, she thought, were easy to read. But his mother's were a different matter.

It took her a while to mention Jim to her friend, Gwen Chadwick, who'd recently joined the school and was in Lillian's favourite class: art with Miss Hardy. Unlike many of the other teachers, Miss Hardy was not a nun. She was probably under the age of thirty, her eyelashes were rumoured to be false, and she drove an MG sports car to school. Plus, her art room was always warm and bright; it was housed in a modern annexe and didn't smell of stewed meat and sweat. The art room smelled instead of Miss Hardy's woody perfume, and of paint, and glue, and, occasionally, of the baking coming from the Domestic Science rooms down the corridor. Until a few months ago, Lillian had believed herself neither neat nor exact enough for art, finding it difficult to reproduce a kingfisher or a sunset on the page, always wetting the paper too much or letting her sleeve smudge her charcoal lines. But then Miss Hardy asked the girls to bring something to her lesson on self-portraits – an object, she said, that spoke of some part of themselves. It didn't have to be a possession; they could present a torn leaf picked from a tree, or a passage from a novel. For reference, they looked at prints of Dürer holding a thistle, Rembrandt wearing a beret, Van Dyck with a sunflower, Munch with a cigarette.

Lillian was perplexed. Her mother had given her a portable record player last Christmas, but that was too precious to take anywhere. She decided she would just pick a leaf from one of the willow trees by the riverbank.

Then, before leaving for school that morning, she remembered the notebook she kept beneath her bed and ripped a page from it. Her idea was to write a word there. Something that spoke of some part of herself. Perhaps 'hopeful'. Or 'lonely'. Or – she knew she would never actually summon the courage for this, even though Sister Theresa had seemed to relish reading it aloud when the class were doing *King Lear* – 'bastard'. She would think about it and write the word at break.

As soon as she was in the art room, surrounded by other girls' objects, she realised she'd forgotten to write the word. She sat with her piece of paper, pen in hand, utterly panicked, as the others unpacked their Beatles or Stones badges, their scarves (Gwen's was bright red and knitted), their books (Elizabeth Richardson, always rather pleased with herself, had brought in a copy of *Jane Eyre*). Miss Hardy was already going around the class, exclaiming over the objects. When she reached Lillian, she eyed the piece of paper before her. Lillian was about to explain that she'd meant to write a word there, and had even decided the word should be 'hungry', when Miss Hardy took up the paper and held it aloft.

'Brilliant!' she said.

The other girls looked up.

'Portrait of the artist with a blank page! You're waiting for life's imprint. Excellent work, Lillian.'

And Lillian didn't laugh, or feel ashamed. Buoyed by Miss Hardy's praise, she spent the afternoon painting a portrait of herself with the blank sheet stuck to her chest. She chose garish greens and blues for her face. 'Mysterious,' enthused Miss Hardy. '*Dynamic.*'

Afterwards, Gwen joined Lillian at the sink to wash out her brushes. 'You didn't mean it to be blank, did you?' she said.

Gwen was tall and slender, with sloping shoulders and thick hair the colour of marmalade. Her face was covered in freckles and on her forearms these had spilled over and pooled together to make brownish patches.

'Should I have confessed?' asked Lillian.

'Christ, of *course* not. She loved it. And now she loves *you*. It was a masterstroke.'

Lillian clattered her brushes onto the drainer and smiled.

Gwen had suggested they go to her house after school to do a bit of art homework before heading to the fair. They were to choose and copy one of Van Gogh's pen and ink drawings. Her father had tons of art books in his study, she said; that was one thing he was good for.

Gwen lived on Park Road, the smart, tree-lined avenue that ran around Albert Park, not far from the school. It was a wet

October day and fallen leaves made a yellow carpet all the way to the front door. From beneath her school blouse, Gwen produced a key on a chain and let them inside, where she slipped off her shoes. Lillian followed Gwen's example and walked down the long hall to the kitchen in her socks. The room ran the width of the back of the house and was the size of a small classroom; its walls were painted white and on one was a large framed print of a naked woman with black eyes. There were shelves stacked with spice jars and teapots of all sizes and colours, and a rack above the stove from which copper pans hung.

'Coffee?' asked Gwen.

Lillian, still taking in the size and beauty of the room, managed a nod. She always drank tea at home, but she accepted the rough-hewn mug of brown liquid and breathed in the scent – smoky, bitter, fresh. Maybe it would taste as good as it smelled.

Gwen led the way upstairs and into a book-lined room. 'I'm not supposed to go in Daddy's study when he's not here,' she said, 'but I'm sure he'll make an exception in the name of education.'

Beneath the window, which looked out onto a clutch of apple trees in the garden, was a desk overflowing with papers and open books. Gwen stepped across the white rug, placed her coffee on a stack of papers, then began to trail her fingers along the shelves.

Lillian had read stories in which women went weak with desire, but she'd never felt it herself until now, with steam from her Nescafé wetting her top lip, dust caught in a shaft of autumn light coming through the window, and Gwen's hand on the spines of her father's books. There were so many exquisite and mysterious *things* in this room. The desk was solid-looking, with a leather-lined top of the type she'd seen in the headmistress's office; the chair had curling arms and was covered in patchwork cushions; on the windowsill was a line of tiny bronze hares, each holding a slightly different pose; above the shelves was a turbulent seascape painted in blues and greys. And, among everything, the smell of pipe smoke and damp pages and some sweet, oniony aroma. Lillian took a sip of her coffee and hated its gritty bitterness. But it didn't matter, because she was in this room, with Gwen smiling at her and saying she'd found exactly what she was looking for.

They went into the attic, where Gwen slept in a room much plainer than the study or the kitchen, though it too was gloriously messy. The full-length mirror propped against a wall had so many necklaces and scarves hung over it Lillian could see only slivers of her reflection.

Gwen threw both herself and the art books on the bed. 'Not sure I like Van Gogh an awful lot,' she said. 'Sometimes I think he's only famous because he went mad. Which seems unfair, doesn't it? In France you cut off your own ear and you become a celebrated artist. Do that here and you get carted off to bloody Longbrook.'

Lillian, who did like Van Gogh an awful lot, said, 'I think he did end up in a mental asylum, though.' Miss Hardy had told them this, adding that Van Gogh had completed some of his finest paintings while there.

Gwen raised an eyebrow. 'Poor sod. Still, I bet he didn't get the old electrodes to the head.' She made a buzzing noise, crossed her eyes and stuck out her tongue.

Lillian gave an uncertain laugh, thinking of what Mrs Shepherd had said about Dolly James.

'I'm not sure I even like art that much, to be honest,' Gwen said.

'Why are you doing it at A level, then?' asked Lillian.

'It just seemed like one I might pass,' said Gwen. 'Mummy's keen for me to go to university. You know. Got to take up all the opportunities there are for young women these days. It's all up for grabs, she says. Are you planning on art school?'

Lillian let out a short laugh.

Gwen frowned. 'What?'

'It was hard enough to persuade Mum I should stay on for A levels.'

'Why? Is she jealous?'

Lillian, who hadn't thought of this, said, 'It's more a money thing.'

'But you can get a grant. Everyone's doing it. You could go to London—'

'That grotty place?' said Lillian in an exaggerated Berkshire accent. It was what Uncle Ernie said, whenever someone mentioned the city.

Gwen gave her a puzzled look. 'You're funny.'

Lillian sat beside her on the bed and they both looked at the pages for a while, Gwen tutting at the 'rudimentary colours' and the 'shabby brushwork'. Then she said, 'Do you want to know why we moved here?'

Lillian nodded.

'Daddy had a stupid fling with his secretary. So bloody predictable. Mummy's forgiven him but he's a different person, now. Like a stranger.'

Gwen said all this so easily that Lillian found herself responding, 'My dad left before I was born. So he really *is* a stranger.'

Gwen sat up straight. 'Hell's bloody bells.'

Lillian had never told anyone this before. Her heart was beating hard and she felt close to the edge of something, as though she might say anything at all. Could she tell Gwen the whole truth? she wondered. Could she tell her what she'd hardly dared tell herself – that she suspected her mother's tales of Maurice were fiction, and that Uncle Ernie might in fact be her father? Could she even tell her about the terrible time she'd actually dared to ask her mother about it? She must have been around eight years old. *Is Maurice really my daddy, Mum?* And then, into Winnie's stony silence: *Only, Ernie's always here and he's so nice to me.* Winnie had exploded. *I've told you! Maurice is your father! Don't you think that if Ernie was your dad he'd have the decency to marry me? Why would he be with living with that woman if he was your father?* That had been the first time she'd experienced Winnie succumbing to an 'attack of the nerves'. The thought of provoking another was enough to make Lillian try to suppress even *thinking* about the question of her father.

'I love your hair,' Gwen said. 'The way it allows everyone to see your neck.'

Lillian reached to touch the spot Gwen was looking at. Though she'd touched it many times, it occurred to her now that she'd never really studied this part of her body, even with all those mirrors in the salon.

'I'd cut mine,' said Gwen, 'but Mummy would kill me. Anyway, mine's more like his,' she added, pointing to Van Gogh's self-portrait.

Lillian swallowed. The moment for daring truth-telling about her father had clearly passed, so instead she told Gwen another truth. 'Your hair's beautiful,' she said. 'It's like fire.'

Gwen blinked at her. 'Christ,' she said. 'Thanks. I think.'

To cover her embarrassment, Lillian said, 'You could come into the salon where I work weekends. My boss Phyllis would do it for you. If you wanted.'

'Or,' said Gwen, leaning closer to Lillian and widening her eyes, '*or* we could go to London and I could get it done!' She explained that she had enough money saved; they could get on the bus any time. Her elder sister, Judith, was a student there, and they could visit her.

Lillian confessed that she'd never been to the capital. She didn't mention anything about Maurice possibly living there, though she was already imagining stepping from the bus to find him magically waiting on the pavement, wearing his shiny shoes and beautiful suit. She closed her eyes for a moment, telling herself that this was a stupid fantasy. And it wasn't even hers. It was her mother's.

Gwen had jumped up from the bed. 'We *have* to go! Yes? Yes?'

Lillian let out a laugh. 'When?'

Gwen shrugged. 'Soon.' She checked her watch. 'We should probably get to the fair first.'

By half past six, they'd eaten beans on toast in the kitchen and Gwen had left the pots in the sink. Lillian had forgotten to bring a change of clothes, and, since it was not acceptable to go to the fair in school uniform, Gwen had lent her a violet polo neck and the long scarlet scarf she'd brought to Miss Hardy's self-portraits session. Looking in the mirror, Lillian felt elated, and almost believed Gwen when she commented that the deep colours made her look *irresistible*.

They were in the hallway when the front door opened and Mrs Chadwick appeared. She had a shopping bag full of books hooked over one wrist and was balancing a stack of papers on her other arm. Her hair was caught up in a straggly, greying bun and her eyes were tired. Her voice, though, was loud and bright as she said, 'Hello! You must be Gwenny's new friend!'

'We're just off out,' said Gwen.

Mrs Chadwick gazed at Lillian. 'Isn't that the scarf Daddy bought for you?' she asked Gwen.

'I said she could borrow it.'

There was the briefest of pauses. 'Good! Sharing's what friendship's about, isn't it? Have you eaten, darling?'

'We had some toast.'

'Any sign of Daddy?'

'No,' said Gwen, taking Lillian by the arm and dragging her to the door.

'Thank God,' Mrs Chadwick said. Then: 'Have fun!'

Pop music drifted across the park. On Ock Street, the lights of the Ferris wheel spun through the dusk. They walked deeper into smells of diesel and chip fat. Gwen had five shillings from her father, and bought them both a stick of candyfloss. Lillian tore off hunks of pink fluff that turned solid between her teeth as she chewed. The man riding the waltzers called, 'Take you for a spin, girls?'

'Idiot,' Gwen yelled back.

The coconut shy was hemmed in by men, but that didn't stop Gwen pushing to the front and buying her turn. Four balls for ninepence. Lillian watched as her friend whipped her arm back and chucked the ball directly at the coconut. It took two goes for her to topple it, causing a small ripple of applause from the crowd. She won two prizes, choosing a bottle of pop for herself and asking Lillian what she'd like. Lillian scanned the wall of loot. Boxes of washing powder, tea-sets wrapped in cellophane, bottles of beer and – hung all along the top of the canvas canopy – goldfish in clear plastic bags. When she was little, her mother had told her never to choose a fish. They didn't need another mouth to feed, and, anyway, where would they keep the poor thing? But Winnie wasn't here, and Lillian was soon grasping the top of the bag, holding it up so the fish's little body flickered before her eyes. It opened and closed its mouth, forming a shape like the top of a coal scuttle, and Lillian knew she couldn't offer the creature what it needed. But it felt wonderful to carry that flash of orange life in her hand as she pushed through the fair's crowds, following her friend's fiery hair.

Next came the Hall of Mirrors.

The woman on the door took their pennies and held back

the tent's heavy curtain. Beyond was a space lit by green and pink bulbs and lined with distorting mirrors. Inside, the shrieks from the street were muffled by heavy canvas. 'Whatever you do, do not laugh,' instructed Gwen in a solemn voice, and pressing down their mirth became their game as they walked further in. Their reflected eyes melted into drips, their foreheads warped like paper plates and their thighs flared. They kept their laughter at bay with tensed cheeks and clamped lips, but when Lillian saw Jim Shepherd standing at the exit flap, her amusement exploded in one loud blurt. Next to him was a strikingly handsome man who had one arm draped across the shoulder of a woman with high hair. Jim stepped away from the group and walked towards Lillian with a graceful and determined stride.

She wiped her eyes, sniffed, and cleared her throat of any remnant of laughter.

'Hello,' Jim said, smiling his wide smile. She remembered her decision about his mouth, and then his mother's comment about her looking lovely in white, and felt her cheeks grow hot.

She glanced at the mirror before them, which made them both appear far away, and gave his reflection a little wave. 'Hello.'

He turned to look at himself. 'Oh,' he said, 'tiny, aren't we?'

She was aware of Gwen, who'd discreetly moved to the next mirror, listening in on this conversation.

'You've won something,' he said.

When he looked directly at her, as he did now, the intense curiosity in his eyes made her look away.

'Mum'll kill me if I take it home.'

He bent slightly to examine the creature. 'He looks in good shape, considering,' he said. 'I could take him with me, if you like?'

'You'd look after it?'

'I didn't say that. You'd have to come over to check on the poor beggar, wouldn't you?'

'You coming, Jim?' the woman with the high hair called. 'Mick's taking a turn in the boxing tent.'

Jim stepped closer to Lillian. 'My mother wants to know why it wasn't you doing her hair? She liked you, apparently.'

'She's got a funny way of showing it.'

Jim frowned slightly. 'She can be a bit . . . brisk. But she means well.'

'I don't do hair,' Lillian said. 'Too busy doing my A levels.' To her annoyance she felt herself blush again. She never wanted anyone to think she was a girl with ideas above her station, though that was exactly what she suspected herself to be. 'But I'd love your help with the fish,' she added, hoping to make up for her haughtiness.

She held the plastic bag out to him, and, after gazing at her for a long moment, he took it.

When he'd left the tent, Gwen said, 'Who the hell was that? And why did you give him your fish?'

'That was Jim Shepherd,' said Lillian. 'He's promised to look after it.'

Gwen folded her arms. 'Jim *Shepherd*? Where's his flock?'

'He lives opposite me. He's nice.'

Gwen looked from Lillian's face to her empty hand and sighed. 'We have to get you to London, pronto.'

As Lillian walked to the river, the scent of malt from the brewery became stronger. She breathed in its thick comfort. It was neither bitter nor sweet, smelling more like hot milk than beer, and she loved it almost as much as the smell of the bakery.

That morning, before her mother was awake, she'd snatched up her sketchbook and slipped it into her satchel along with a couple of pencils, thinking she might draw something along the way. Miss Hardy had shown them Leonardo's studies of water swirling and flowing, foaming and falling. Looking at them, Lillian had felt a tug in her core at the movement, as though what was on the page was pulling her with it. Those studies made water something solid, yet they also seemed to *move*. Miss Hardy talked a lot about *mark making*. *Girls*, she'd say, *I want you to make your marks, and think about how you make them, and why*. Lillian wanted to make marks that could capture water.

The bridge across the weir was narrow and high, and the noise of the river as it was sucked in one side and flung down the other was thunderous. She stopped halfway and leaned on the cold metal rail to gaze at the shining muscle of water below. Its surge vibrated through her shoes and up her arms. It was the speed of the transformation – from clear sheet to explosion of foam – that was so thrilling. No wonder her mother never wanted to come here. Winnie often gathered up Lillian's hands, squeezing them tightly as she warned her about the weir. *Anyone might be pulled under, so easily*, she'd say. *And even if I'm there, I can't save you because I can't swim.* This danger was, of course, exactly why Lillian liked it, but whenever her mother spoke those words, her eyes took on a frightened blankness, just as they would during one of her attacks.

Lillian leaned further over, letting the spray dampen her face, then reached into her satchel.

'Morning!'

She hadn't heard the ticking of Jim Shepherd's bicycle wheels behind her, and straightened with a yelp. Over the noise of the raging water, she made out his *sorry*, but not the words that followed. With the book still in her hand, she gestured towards the other side of the weir. He followed her, and they walked together along the bank.

'So what's in the book?' he asked.

Though she wasn't sure what he'd make of a girl with a sketchbook, she risked telling him. 'My drawings.'

'Of the river?'

'Mostly.'

'So you're an artist!' To her surprise, he looked almost triumphant.

'Not really—'

'Will you show me?'

'Maybe.'

'You do look, if you don't mind me saying so, like the artistic type.'

At this, she laughed with delight. 'How's my goldfish getting along?'

'Oh, he's *very* happy.'

'How do you know it's a he?'

'Just a hunch. I think we should call him Gene, by the way. After Gene Kelly. He moves like Gene. As you'll see, when you come over to feed him. Unless you want to call him, I don't know . . . Picasso? Michelangelo?'

She smiled. 'Gene is fine.'

They walked in silence for a while. She watched him as he pushed his bike along. He had large hands, and wore a gold ring on his little finger, which interested her. He hadn't seemed a man for jewellery.

When they reached the town's bridge, Jim stopped and said, 'There's a brewery do at the Corn Exchange Friday night. I don't suppose you'd come with me?'

She looked at his kind face and thought, *Why not?* She hadn't been to a proper, grown-up party before. Those she had been to, at the Wednesday Club, were full of other girls dancing, beakers of warm lemonade, and boys hanging around the exit.

'All right,' she said.

He blinked. 'Smashing,' he said, that smile breaking.

The mini-dress, which Lillian bought in C&A in Oxford, was tangerine, with large pockets and a jumbo zip running up the front. On Friday night, after Uncle Ernie had been and gone, she wore it with a pair of new black tights and was pleased by what she saw when she stole a look in her mother's bedroom mirror.

When she twirled in the front room, Winnie glanced up from the new *Tit-bits* Ernie had left and told her daughter the dress looked knockout. 'Now,' she added, clasping Lillian's hand, 'you'll remember what I said? About not getting in trouble?'

'Mum!'

'From what I've seen he's not too good-looking, which is a point in his favour. He's a solid sort of bloke, is he?'

Lillian squeezed her mother's fingers.

'I told you. He went to the grammar. And now he's an accounts man at Morland. And his intentions seem . . . entirely honourable.'

Winnie smiled. 'No need to show off.'

At half past seven, Jim arrived. He seemed larger in their front room than he had by the river. He was carrying his overcoat across one arm and wore a bottle-green suit. His cheeks glowed. When he looked at her she caught his anxious expression, and she wanted to touch his hand, then, and tell him it would be all right.

'Doesn't she look pretty?' said her mother. Then she added, with a pointed look at Jim, 'Aren't you a lucky young man?'

'She looks smashing,' said Jim.

Lillian pecked her mother's powdery cheek.

As they left, Winnie said, 'Take care of her, then. She's all I've got.'

Jim offered her a small bow and promised to do his best, which her mother received with a short nod.

The Corn Exchange was lit up, its huge window glowing yellow above the open doors. As they approached, she heard music. The band were playing 'You Need Hands'.

Jim rolled his eyes. 'Vernon Whitehead. Needs to move with the times.' He took her hand. At his touch, she realised he was wearing aftershave: a scent like mown grass came at her, and she held on to his fingers as they went in.

The room was full of people. Tables covered with white cloths were arranged at one side, and on the other there was space for dancing. At the far end, the band were on the raised platform, wearing matching emerald jackets and black trousers. The glitter-ball that hung from the ceiling and the flame-shaped wall lights made the room flicker and glow.

Jim led Lillian to a table where two other couples were sitting, staring at the empty dance floor. 'Well,' one of the women said, 'it's Jim Shepherd.'

Jim dropped Lillian's hand and nodded. 'Hello, Pam.'

Pam pulled her fluffy cardigan together and pointed at the man sitting next to her, who had one foot up on a spare chair. 'This is Neville,' she announced. 'My boyfriend.'

Jim shook Neville's hand. Neville looked bored as Jim explained, 'I work with Pam. In the office.'

'Good for you,' Neville said.

'And this is Lillian,' said Jim.

Pam smiled with her mouth only. 'Well, get the poor girl a drink, Jim!' she said, waving him off. 'I'll look after her while you go to the bar. Come and sit next to me, love.'

Lillian did as she was told, but once she'd perched on the edge of her chair, Pam turned back to Neville.

Jim returned with a Babycham for Lillian. She'd tried the

drink before, with Gwen, who'd said it was like alcoholic lemonade, and liked it. They sat side by side, watching the dance floor. There were a few older couples waltzing. Some of the women wore long gowns and gloves up to the elbows, but most were in knee-length frocks with fancy brooches or scarves. In the corner was a gaggle of women of various ages, all smoking. They watched the dance floor eagerly, occasionally breaking their gaze to whisper something to another woman and laugh, nod wisely or stifle a giggle.

'The bottling girls,' said Jim, grinning. 'Completely terrifying.' He didn't sound terrified. 'You can't go through bottling without getting your bum pinched,' he explained. 'Or worse. I've stopped going in there, for my own safety.'

'Can't they resist you?'

Jim put down his pint and got to his feet. 'Obviously not. Shall we dance?'

As she took his hand, Lillian was aware of the bottling girls and Pam looking over.

Lillian had started to explain, as they walked to the floor, that she wasn't good, that she could barely remember any actual steps, but Jim just smiled and, after he'd waited for the band to strike up a new tune, arranged her arm in a strange new position. She'd waltzed before, in school with other girls, and once at a Wednesday Club party with Tony Berriman, who'd no sense of timing. She knew the basics, and as they set off she was relieved Jim stuck to them. His body moved assuredly, one hand placed flat and yet strong beneath her shoulder blade. It wasn't long before he was twirling her beneath his arm, her hand slipping so fast through his she feared she might go spinning to the side of the room, right into the laps of the bottling girls. He was looking past her as they danced, a proud gleam in his eye, but she could feel his breath on her cheek and his thigh on hers as he used it to push her in the right direction.

One-two-three, one-two-three, one-two-three. She had no choice but to go the way Jim was steering. The room span. She began to laugh. *One-two-three, one-two-three, one-two-three.* With Jim to guide her, her body responded to the music. She didn't have to think, she only had to move. She'd never felt this way before – as if she'd left all her thoughts behind, and yet had become completely herself. It made no sense at all, and it was wonderful.

After the song finished, they sat at the table, Lillian feeling dizzy but exhilarated. Neville leaned across to Jim. 'You're good, mate.'

'Didn't you know that?' said Pam. 'I thought everyone knew Jim Shepherd's the best dancer in Abingdon.'

Jim took a long drink, then turned to Lillian. 'Thank you,' he said, 'for the dance.'

When she looked at him, he seemed brighter, somehow. More present. She noticed that ring on his finger again. The deep bow of his mouth. 'I should thank you,' she said. 'I had no idea what I was doing.'

'It's actually better to dance with someone who hasn't already formed bad habits. You're not set in your ways.'

Then he was up on his feet again, holding out his hand. This time, she didn't hesitate. As he led her, he spoke into her hair, his lips close to her ear – *back, side, together, now spin. Smashing.*

On the way home, she could still hear the music in her head, and it seemed that Jim could too, because as they walked down a deserted and damp Stert Street, he took her hand and gathered her to him for another waltz. She watched their reflection in the shop windows as they spun down the empty road, Jim singing the time as they went – *one-two-three, one-two-three, one-two-three.*

As she fell asleep that night, Jim's count sounded in her mind.

It was still sounding when she left the house at eight the following morning, taking her sketchbook with her. She crossed the street and knocked on Jim's door. They'd made arrangements for a stroll in the park on Sunday afternoon but Lillian had decided that was too long to wait, because he hadn't kissed her yet. She needed to see him before going to work at the salon.

Mrs Shepherd opened the door wearing a quilted dressing gown. She peered at Lillian's scarf. 'That's a very red wool, isn't it?'

Lillian looked down, confused. 'Is Jim in?'

Mrs Shepherd tilted her head, seeming to consider Lillian deeply. Then, without a word, she nodded and retreated into the house, leaving the door open. Lillian followed her.

The linoleum in the front room shone dark brown, and she imagined herself skating across it to Mrs Shepherd, who was gazing into the mirror above the fireplace, pressing her hair into shape. 'I wasn't told you were coming at this hour,' she said.

'Jim said I should, to see my goldfish.' Which sounded like a ridiculous statement, now Lillian said it out loud.

Apparently satisfied with the shape of her hair, Mrs Shepherd said, 'I saw that thing in his room. I'm not sure it's still breathing. No life for them, is it, hanging in a plastic bag? I'm not sure how you get over something like that.' She frowned, looking genuinely distressed, then, seeming to recover herself, gave a high-pitched laugh. 'What am I saying? It's only a blasted fish. Jim's still asleep, I'm afraid, but I've been wanting to talk to you. Have a seat.'

Lillian perched on the edge of the settee and folded her arms across her sketchbook, praying Jim would appear.

'How's your mother?' Mrs Shepherd asked, her voice shifting down a notch.

Lillian had left Winnie sleeping off a night at The Anchor. Though her mother never brought a man back to the house – she'd told Lillian that no male other than Maurice or Uncle

Ernie would ever again cross her threshold – she'd plenty of men-friends at the pub. On a Friday and sometimes also a Saturday night she allowed them to buy her as many drinks as they liked. Lillian often spent Sunday afternoons on the settee with her mother, eating the cherry cake they'd made together, listening to tales of how Les Fuller, the daft bugger, had vowed to give up the ale, again, if only Winnie would agree to walk out with him, or how George Trinder had said she was the only woman he really *respected*, which, of course, was because she'd never given in to him and never would, since he looked like a potato. Lillian loved those afternoons, when it was just her and her mother, who'd rejected all suitors so the two of them could eat cherry cake together.

'She's fine, thank you.'

'I see her walking up and down here twice a day. To and fro she goes on those heels. Clickety-clack. *Ever* so busy.'

'She's got two jobs.'

Mrs Shepherd nodded. 'Which can't be easy. But I'm sure you're a great comfort. Jim's a marvel, of course, but I often wish my Reg had left me with a daughter for company.'

Lillian studied the woman's bright eyes. How old was she, exactly? It was difficult to say, but older than Winnie, that was for sure. Perhaps in her mid forties. At sometime around that age, the women Lillian knew seemed to her to collapse into middle age, becoming shapeless and vague, their lives revolving around shopping bags, washing lines and loss. There were a lot of women like that in the street, women alone, bundled into large coats and small hats, their husbands lost to the war or just lost, God knows where or to what.

'And Jim says you're doing so well, at the grammar,' Mrs Shepherd continued. 'A levels and all. What is it you're studying?'

'English, History and Art. I brought my sketchbook along, actually, for Jim to see—'

'Art? You can get a qualification in that, can you?'

Lillian said you could, if you were good enough, and a small silence passed.

Mrs Shepherd cleared her throat. 'What I wanted to say to you, dear, was that I know your mother has been through some troubled times—'

'My mother's fine,' Lillian snapped. 'She doesn't need a man in the house. She's better off without. We look after each other.'

Mrs Shepherd looked startled. 'Of course,' she said quietly. 'I only meant to say that I know . . . I know what it's like, to be a mother alone.'

Were the woman's eyes actually misting over? Lillian looked away, embarrassed and confused. Then, to her immense relief, there was the sound of footsteps on the stairs, and Jim's voice, calling, 'All's well?'

To Lillian's amazement, Mrs Shepherd broke into a smile and called her response in an almost girlish voice. 'Tickety-boo, dear! We're in here!'

Lillian stood up in readiness.

When Jim came in, he was dressed in his trousers and shirt, but was without socks. He stood gaping at her.

'Hello,' he said.

'I came to see Gene,' she said.

'He's upstairs. Come and see for yourself. And bring that sketchbook.'

He held out a hand.

'Now, Jim!' said Mrs Shepherd. 'You can't take the girl upstairs! What would her mother say?'

'Just for ten minutes. She's got to visit her fish,' said Jim, smiling broadly and touching his mother's shoulder. 'I can't disappoint her, can I?' He leaned down to peck Mrs Shepherd's cheek.

'Five minutes then,' said Mrs Shepherd. 'I'm timing you.'

She was smiling, just a little.

Once Lillian was in the room, Jim closed the door. His bed was already made, the eiderdown straightened and his pillow smoothed. She thought of his bare head on that pillow, his body beneath those covers, and deliberately turned her face towards the desk in the corner of the room, which had the goldfish bowl on it. 'I need to get to work,' she said, suddenly panicked at having landed herself in Jim Shepherd's bedroom. 'But I wanted to thank you properly, for last night . . .'

Under the intensity of his gaze, her words dried up.

'Gene's been waiting for you,' he said.

Lillian approached the bowl and peered through the glass. A fish was hiding beneath the plastic bridge but his tail was sticking out, pulsing in the water. Another was gaping at the water's surface.

'Which one's mine?' she asked.

'That's our Gene,' said Jim, pointing at the fish beneath the bridge. 'He's a bit shy. Can I see your drawings, then?'

Part of her wanted to refuse, to keep this special thing all to herself. But a bigger part of her wanted to show Jim what she could do. She passed him the book.

Jim sat on the edge of the bed and patted the space beside him to indicate that she should do the same. Then he began slowly turning the pages. Though she tried to tell herself it didn't matter, that Miss Hardy had already said she had talent, Lillian's heart rate increased. Eventually he turned to her and said, 'These are really good, you know.' He pointed to her sketches of the weir. 'Seems like trouble's brewing, there.'

'Well,' she said, 'that's what it's like.'

'Depends how you look at it.'

There was a pause. 'I should go,' she said. 'I'll be late.'

He put the sketchbook aside and brought his face close to hers so their noses touched. His was a little cold, but as soon as it nudged the side of hers she felt her blood warm. His lips were, as she'd hoped, a good fit for hers, and she took his face in her hands, holding it there so she could concentrate on kissing him.

She began calling for Jim every morning, going up the alleyway to let herself through his back door and into the kitchen where he'd be waiting to go walking with her. She told her mother what she was doing, and Winnie asked if Jim could swim. Lillian answered that he could – though she didn't know this for sure – and Winnie said she supposed it was all right to risk walking along the river if Jim was there. She repeated her warning about not getting into trouble, but added that Jim did seem a solid sort of bloke. 'It'll break my heart,' she added, 'when you leave this house, but at least with Jim you'll only be across the road.'

Lillian thought her mother was jumping the gun, but she said nothing, happy that at least the appearance of a boyfriend – for she supposed that's what Jim was – hadn't brought on an attack of the nerves.

They would part at the bridge with a kiss, and once Jim had mounted his bike, a hand raised in farewell, Lillian would dawdle along the bank, looking for a picture. Every morning, in his kitchen, she'd show Jim her work from the previous day. He took his time studying it, tilting his head and narrowing his eyes as though he were an expert, asking her where exactly she'd drawn it and always pronouncing it 'absolutely smashing'. What she liked most of all was the way that, after surveying her artwork, he would gaze at her with an expression of complete astonishment.

Some mornings that winter the river was jewelled with light, or streaked pink and mauve like a fancy bedspread, and she'd wish she had the courage to set herself up on the bank with a box of paints. She'd balance her sketchbook on the weir's rail, feel the thunder of the river through her shoes, and examine the water's shapes. Alive. Ever-changing. Treacherous. She had a couple of new pencils from Price's, though she preferred the unpredictability of pen and ink. With the smallest amount of pressure (or, sometimes, none at all), the line from the pen would thicken and narrow. The splats and splashes and drips all became part of the picture. Miss Hardy said there were no mistakes – only surprises. And if you didn't think it was a good surprise, then you'd learned something.

On the bridge across the weir, Lillian filled her page with pencil strokes, trying to capture the shape of the river as it moved all the way through the town and past the brewery, where Jim was waiting to take her dancing again.

One night, as they emerged hot and elated from the Corn Exchange, Lillian asked if Jim had heard the town's secret river.

'You mean the culvert?'

'Yes. But have you *heard* it?'

He had to admit that he hadn't, so she grabbed his hand and led him to the archway next to St Nicolas's Church at the top of Stert Street. In the pool of light from the streetlamp, overlooked by gargoyles gurning from the arches, she pointed at a manhole cover in the pavement, then commanded him to kneel.

'Whatever for?' he asked, remaining upright.

'I'll show you.' She dropped to her knees on the pavement and put her ear to the ground.

'What on earth are you doing?'

'Listening.'

He laughed. 'You're listening. To the pavement.'

'I'm listening to the river.'

'But surely you can't actually *hear* it?'

'Shush!'

Watching Lillian kneeling in the street, her school duffel coat over her party dress, one ear to the paving slab, the soles of her shoes scratched and pale in the lamplight, he thought he would never meet anyone like her again. She'd already mastered natural turns, reverse turns and change steps. Her posture was almost perfect: she could extend her spine beautifully, and soon she'd be ready to Fleckerl. But it wasn't just her technique. Jim could tell that Lillian *felt* the music, like him.

Sometimes he snuck a look at her face while they were spinning. Her eyes closed, her mouth slightly open in a loose smile. She glowed. It was all he could do, then, not to lift and carry her outside so they could be alone.

Now he wanted to say: *Show me. Show me how to be the man who loves you.*

Unable to say such words, he joined her. Pressing his ear to the chill of the manhole cover, he listened. After a while, he tuned out from the sounds of the street and heard, not much louder than his own breath, the rush and churn of water below. The river was running its irresistible course, heedless of the town's events.

His face was turned to hers and he felt her breath on his nose, warm in the freezing night. 'Unreal, isn't it?' she said, her eyes shining.

Jim said that was exactly what it was.

2005

Once they were back in the car, Rachel said, 'What's the hurry?'

She was holding the carrier bag of framed photos and the album from Daphne's house on her lap, and she was using her I'm-being-patient-but-really-I'm-pissed-off voice.

Lillian wound down her window to let some air in. Her mind was still on that photograph of her mother by the Thames, on the cusp of parenthood. What had Winnie known, then, of the pain and the glory of being a mother? Almost nothing. Just as Lillian herself had known so little before Rachel was born.

'Mum?'

'Sorry. It was . . . creepy in there.'

'I thought it was cool,' said Rachel. 'That retro fireplace! That *telephone table*! And all those photos of you!' She smoothed the top of her head and patted the back of her neck three times.

Lillian heard the edge in her voice as she turned to her daughter and said, 'Rachel. I'm really worried about that.'

'What?'

'The patting thing.'

Rachel let out a long sigh. 'What's so bad about patting?'

Lillian tried to soften her tone. 'I just wonder if . . .'

Her daughter still had a hand on her neck and was staring back with that fierce determination of hers. '*What?*' she asked, with undisguised impatience.

'I wonder if you're quite ready,' Lillian blurted. 'For uni.'

Rachel's hand dropped into her lap. There was a pause before she said, 'Maybe it's you that's not ready, Mum.'

'What are you talking about?'

Rachel gave a small laugh. 'Well, it wouldn't be surprising, would it? It's been just the two of us for so long. Which is fine, of course. I'm proud of my single mum! But you never *really* let Dad into the picture.'

Lillian told herself that exploding would do no good. No good at all. 'It's . . . complicated,' she said, yanking her seatbelt into place.

'I know. But you're acting weird. I mean, weirder than normal, even? You never really look at me any more. Not properly. Did you know that? You just . . . *observe* me. And you don't talk to me—'

Lillian jabbed the key into the ignition. 'I talk to you all the time!'

'When I asked you about that photo – about my own *grandmother* – you shut me down completely. You never tell me anything about her. Or Daphne. Or Ernie. I mean, why didn't we ever visit Daphne?'

Lillian bought herself time by checking all her mirrors twice before pulling away from the kerb. Eventually she said, 'We were never close.'

'Then why are there so many photos of you in the album? And why don't you ever tell me anything about your childhood?'

'I've told you lots of things!' Lillian said. But there were so many stories that she couldn't tell. Some of them she just didn't know. And some she could hardly tell to herself.

They drove through the town centre in silence until Rachel said, 'I think I'll go to Dad's. I can walk from here. Can you stop?'

'I'll drive you.'

'Mum. Just stop the car. Please.'

Lillian gave in and did as she was told, pulling into the forecourt of a petrol station. 'When will you be home?'

'Not sure. Dad'll give me a lift.'

Rachel held the handle for a few seconds before opening it – another recent tic – then climbed out of the car.

'Call me, then,' Lillian said, and Rachel nodded.

Lillian watched her walk across the oil-stained concrete, towards the path through the woods, and was reminded of Winnie's gait. Each stride quick and determined. A corner of a photo frame poked from Rachel's carrier bag, threatening to split the plastic, and it was all Lillian could do not to call out to her daughter in warning: if she wasn't careful, the bag would break, and there'd be glass everywhere.

Instead, she drove towards Oxford, listing in her head the things she had managed to tell Rachel about Winnie.

1. She loved an apple turnover from Trotman's Bakery.
2. She liked to drink at The Anchor pub, where she had a few male admirers.
3. Daphne and Ernie had been her life-long friends, though she'd secretly thought Daphne stuck-up.
4. She and Lillian had always been very close, as it was just the two of them.
5. She'd said nothing at all about who Lillian's father was, and Lillian didn't much mind because what you'd never had, you didn't much miss.
6. When she died, Lillian had been very sad until Rachel came along.

They were all true, apart from number five.

Her work waited on the big table by the front window. This table, now covered in pieces of paper, trays of gouache, and pots of pens, pencils and brushes, had once been the surface on which she'd changed Rachel's nappy. Both bedrooms were at the back of the flat and didn't get much sun, but here in the main room there was a view of the sky, and the branches of the birch trees which tapped the window pane, and the black lines of telephone wires which bounced when starlings landed or flew away, and all of this had stopped baby Rachel from crying too much when her mother laid her down and exposed her bare bottom. When Rachel was old enough to sit at the table to eat, Lillian had removed all her tools and roughs, placing them on the floor and covering them with an old blanket before sitting down with her daughter. For the last ten years or so it had felt safe enough to leave them where they were, so she'd merely pushed a few things aside and they'd eaten surrounded by Lillian's work-in-progress.

Now she was working on the illustrations for a children's book called *Super Granddad*. She'd already sketched out Granddad, who had a little pot belly beneath his shiny blue skin-tight suit and a comb-over above his superhero mask. Instead of getting on with the drawings that were waiting for her, though, Lillian went into her bedroom to open the window and close the blind. It was going to be another warm night and she may as well attempt to keep the place cool. Then, feeling suddenly exhausted, she lay on the bed in the beige gloom and closed her eyes.

She'd brought a newborn Rachel back from the hospital during a freezing January. Gwen, whose new academic career had just begun to take off, had nevertheless been with her, wearing a lilac silk shirt. Lillian had kept worrying about that shirt, how its square buttons might poke Rachel's face when Gwen held her. So she'd sent Gwen out for nappies and wipes and vegetables. Gwen had come back with a tomato and cheese quiche from somewhere, wrapped in cellophane but clearly homemade. Lillian hadn't known she was so hungry until she ate a slice of that quiche, and could still recall the crumbly, buttery pastry dissolving on her tongue.

Lillian had felt herself in a stupor during those first few

months of Rachel's life. She'd feared she was moving through a routine of caring for the baby without having the energy to actually care about the baby. Gwen suggested that, for the first time in her life, Lillian might have to become a 'joiner'. There must be baby groups, she'd said. Places you can go and be with other mums who're as tired and pissed off as you. It turned out that there were, and – more surprisingly – that Lillian didn't mind going to them. On Wednesdays she took Rachel to Baby Rhymetime at the local library, where they sang songs about monkeys falling out of bunks. On Fridays they went to Tots and Toddlers at the community centre, where she made her own coffee and chatted with the other women while Rachel chewed on the edges of building blocks. Lillian noticed some of the other mums glancing at her ringless third finger. She suspected they pegged her as a *Single Mother*, possibly one who was threatening the sacred family unit and sucking the state dry. Personally, she thought the term inadequate, for no mother was single, not really. Every mother had her own mother, too. Every mother was, in fact, one of many mothers, bound together in a long chain of blood and tears and milk.

Rachel and Lillian had slept and played together in this bed until Rachel was three years old, which was also when she began going to playgroup a couple of mornings a week. Lillian had been grateful for the lightness in her arms, the space that opened up between her hip and her chest – no child to hold! – and also for the time the playgroup gave her, whole hours in which she could look at something other than her daughter: the sky, or her sketchbook, or people in the café at the Museum of Modern Art, where she often went to try to remember that she was someone with a degree in fine art. But by the time those few hours were up, she experienced the lightness as an emptiness, and it was good to have the weight of her girl back on her hip.

She hauled herself from the bed and sat at the table in

the front room. The work was slow-going. She hadn't quite mastered Super Granddad flying through the air. She'd done a few children's books and always preferred the ones about real people to the ones about aliens or talking monkeys. *Super Granddad* was somewhere in between, but she wasn't comfortable with flying people. She'd much rather they were sitting in rooms, sharing meals, pushing prams through parks, or eating in cafés. Or walking by the river.

At six o'clock she rose to stretch and drink a glass of water. It was Friday evening and the scent of barbecue wafted through the window. Lillian threw it wide open and looked out. Down the street, a family sat on the pavement in fold-out chairs, listening to dance music coming from a car stereo.

She crossed the room to check the fridge. Mushrooms, half a tub of ricotta, a jar of capers, another of sun-dried tomatoes. A bag of salad. More than enough for a pasta dinner for her and Rachel. She should be home soon.

Ever since that slice of quiche, Lillian's eating habits had changed. She was careful, at least when with her daughter, to eat three meals a day and to finish everything on her (admittedly small) plate. Rachel had been on the verge of puberty when heroin chic was in vogue. Not long after, the girls in her school seemed to be competing to become the sickest in class. One, Lucy, had ended up in a specialist psychiatric unit which Lillian had known was across the road from Longbrook. Rachel had reported, rather excitedly, that the girls there were rumoured to hide laxatives in their vaginas and hang carrier bags full of their own vomit from their bedroom windows.

So Lillian had been careful all right. She'd been careful to mask her own anxiety by not responding to such stories, never mentioning weight, or dieting, or a girl's size – especially not her own, or her daughter's. Even when Rachel had begun, aged eleven, to grow more fleshy around her middle and thighs,

Lillian had kept her counsel. The words had been right there, waiting to spring from her mouth: *Be careful. Oh! Please be careful, darling girl. Remember to keep yourself in check.* But she'd pushed them down.

She glanced at her watch. Six fifteen.

She sat at the table, but didn't manage to do more than wet her brush before the phone rang. She sprang to answer it.

'Mum?'

Thank God.

'I'm sorry about earlier,' Lillian said. There was a pause. 'Are you staying at Dad's for tea? Or shall I come and get you now?'

'Actually, I might stay a few days. Or maybe a week.'

Lillian took a breath. Since she was around four, Rachel had spent most weekends at her dad's, and had the odd week's holiday with him in Wales or Devon. Once he'd taken her to the newly opened Disneyland Paris, and Lillian had been very grateful not to be there with them. But Rachel had never made the decision to stay longer than her allotted time with her father. Usually, on arriving home from his house, she'd laughingly say he'd driven her half mad with his careful schedules of activities for each day. 'God! Dad's so *organised*! And he's so bloody *literal*! He just doesn't get irony!'

Lillian loved that. Though, privately, she thought Rachel was probably quite literal, too.

'Oh,' she said now. 'A week?'

'Look, it's fine. I'm fine. I'll ring you, OK?'

Lillian thought she heard Rachel's father saying, *Do you want me to talk to her?* and that made the blood beat in her ears.

'I'm coming over,' she said.

'Mum, please don't do that. I'll speak to you tomorrow.'

'I can be there in thirty minutes—'

'I'll call you tomorrow.'

The line went dead.

1966

Jim bought himself a battered but serviceable Riley Elf so he could take Lillian places. She suggested a trip to the art museum in Oxford, and Jim promised they would go there, one day. But he was more interested in places they could be alone together. It was all right going to the Regal – Lillian loved Elizabeth Taylor almost as much as he did – but Jim wanted to get out into the countryside. He wanted to see Lillian's dark hair and pale limbs in the fields, beside hedgerows. At the pictures, Lillian never kissed him for long, saying she didn't want to miss the story. But in the car, she let him kiss the nape of her neck, and she suggested, too, that he could put his hand higher on her thigh, if he wanted. Though that was as far as it went. For months, Jim was happy in the knowledge that Lillian was waiting, if not for marriage, then for his lead. Many times he imagined taking her to some hotel room in Oxford. The back seat of the Elf was prohibitively cramped and wasn't good enough, he felt, for Lillian. He wanted somewhere they could take their time, somewhere he could watch her undress, somewhere they could lie together so he could feel the whole length of her against him. One Sunday in spring he took her to Wittenham Clumps, two small hills that together formed the highest ground in the area. He placed a new tube of Wine Gums in the glove compartment and they set off in the afternoon. It was later than he'd planned – Winnie had kept quizzing him about the brewery gossip – and as he parked close to the gate at the foot of the hills, the sky was already beginning to yellow where it met the horizon. Lillian wore the new blue mac he'd bought for her; she'd also made up her face. It gave him a jolt, to see her eyes so prominently outlined, but he didn't dislike it. He took her arm and steered her around a patch of mud and into the small wood at the summit, away from the other walkers. Once they were deeper in the trees, he pulled her to him and kissed her. Her mouth soon loosened and she pressed herself against him. Kissing wasn't like dancing, though. There were no predetermined moves, no music to lead the way, and Jim was relieved when Lillian was the one to hook a hand around the back of his neck in order to prolong the kiss. Above their heads, the branches tapped together in the breeze.

When he looked at her she said, 'I got an interview!'

It was a strange thing to say after such a kiss. Jim had been ready to gather her up again, and it took him a moment to form a reply. 'What for?'

He heard the pride in her voice, and also the anxiety, as she said, 'Art school. Camberwell. In London, Jim!'

He stepped back and stared at her. She hadn't mentioned applying, though it had crossed his mind that she might.

'There's no need to look like that,' she said.

'Like what?'

'Like I've slapped you in the face.'

He tried to keep his voice mild. 'Well. You have, a bit.'

'I haven't got in yet.'

'You will, though.'

She took his hand. 'Wouldn't you be pleased for me, if I did?'

'Of course I would.' But the idea of her leaving did not please him. He'd already imagined them married, perhaps living on the newer estate on the other side of town once he'd been promoted. He wasn't sure how art school might fit into this picture. 'Promise me something?' he said, drawing her close. 'If you go, you'll come back? I can wait.'

He felt her stiffen slightly in his arms as she said, 'Don't be silly. It's just an interview. I haven't even gone anywhere.'

Sensing her annoyance, he told her he was proud of her and kissed her again, lightly. But her hand didn't fly to his neck as it had before.

They didn't speak much, after that. On the way back to the car, she rested her head on his shoulder and said, 'You'd really miss me?'

'More than you can imagine,' he said, adding that he'd better drive her home; it looked like rain and she did have school tomorrow, after all.

Lillian's plan had been this: she would tell him about the interview, and then she would sleep with him.

Ever since they'd first danced together, she'd felt the joy of responding to his every move. It struck her as being like a conversation, but without the problem of having to actually think about what you were going to say. When they danced together, she felt beautiful, and sure she was doing the right thing. She knew where to put her hands, her body. *That's it, just right, there you go, you look like a bloody film star*, Jim would say, *my Lovely Lillian!* And, her favourite, *You're a dancer now, you know that?* Perhaps sleeping with Jim would be even better than dancing with him. Plus, she was eighteen now, and wanted it over with, despite her mother's warnings. She'd discussed it with Gwen and her friend agreed: it would be much better to arrive at college free of the burden of your virginity. Once she'd done it, she thought, she would step into a new, adult world. She would be ready, then, for London. She would miss Jim and it would be hard to leave her mother, but she didn't allow herself to dwell on either of those thoughts for long.

So when they were beneath the trees at Wittenham Clumps, she'd wanted to whisper to him, *Take me somewhere.* She knew she could never say the words, *I want you to make love to me*, but she felt sure he would understand what her actions meant. His mouth was soft that afternoon and she wanted to unbutton him, to feel the warmth beneath his shirt.

But as soon as the words *art school* were out of her mouth it became obvious her plan would not progress smoothly. Jim had backed away, and his face – usually so open, with a smile waiting there just for her – tightened. His lips closed. He put his hands in his pockets, which she'd learned was a sign of his discomfort, and lowered his head slightly, as though readying himself for the blows.

She couldn't say anything about him taking her somewhere, then.

Lillian didn't tell her mother about the interview.

It was the Easter holidays when she rose early to board the bus for London with Gwen, who said they could easily get the interview done and be back by evening. Lillian had told Winnie that she would be spending the day shopping in Oxford with Gwen and wouldn't be home until late.

Clutching the cardboard folder that made up her portfolio – a gift from Miss Hardy – she stepped out of the back door and stood blinking in the half-light towards the lilac bush at the bottom of the garden. A memory of their old house came to her. She'd hidden beneath a similar bush one summer afternoon, when Uncle Ernie had pressed a penny into her hand and told her not to tell. She'd slipped the money into her skirt pocket and gone into the garden to play with next door's cat. When the cat had slunk into the bushes, Lillian had followed. She remembered liking the cool secrecy of the place, crouching in the cavern between the branches, her backside brushing the soil. Hearing her name called, she'd stayed where she was, watching her mother as she peered behind the coal bunker, then marched scowling up the path, tea towel in hand. Lillian had held her breath, imagining their ecstatic reunion when the time to burst from the bush was right. But as her mother became more exasperated, her voice climbing to a shrill note, Lillian became afraid. So she remained crouched, one sweaty hand grasping the money in her pocket. She didn't know how long she'd waited before reappearing, but Winnie had gone back into the house, so she'd run all the way to the shops on the main road, where she bought a bagful of pear drops with Ernie's penny. Then she ran back and presented the sweets to Winnie, whose face crumpled as she took her daughter in her arms. Holding her tightly enough to hurt, she said, 'Never, ever, run off like that again without telling me where you're going. You can't just disappear! I can't lose you! Promise me?'

Lillian had promised. It had been a long time before her mother had let her go.

Now she gave herself a little shake and told herself that had been the promise of a child who knew no better.

She made her way out of Mason Road, through the town, and across the quiet lawns of Albert Park. The sun was rising, and she felt a lightness in her limbs.

The bus was slow and it was nearly midday by the time they reached the suburbs of the city. Excitement pushed at her chest. Even the grey suburban streets looked vaguely exotic. Gwen pointed out a few coffee shops and pinball bars among the pubs and the branches of Woolworth's and Key Markets. Then the buildings became larger and whiter; columns and flights of steps sprang up; the roads were wider, the pavements busier with people. Lillian spotted a lighted sign for the Underground, royal blue and red, and felt a thrill: they couldn't be far, she thought, from the landmarks her mother had mentioned visiting with Maurice. Hyde Park. London Zoo. She smiled at her own foolishness when she found herself scanning the pavements for middle-aged men in shiny shoes who bore some resemblance to Montgomery Clift.

All the while, Gwen chattered on about what her sister Judith said you could do in the city. You could get work in the offices of a magazine. Or you could work in an actual *boutique*.

You could go to parties with men who were almost actors, or photographers, or pop stars. Judith herself, whose boyfriend shared a flat with someone who worked at the BBC, was apparently getting close to the Jet Set.

The bus dropped them at Marble Arch, where the washed-out underwear shade of the sky did nothing to diminish the colours surrounding her: the vibrant green of the park; the yellow glow of taxi lights; the streak of red buses. Lillian stood and breathed deeply. The air was thick with exhaust fumes, and full of excitement: the smells here were different to the bread and beer of Abingdon. Here there was the unmistakable kick of men's aftershave, the spice of foreign food, the warm stench floating up from the Underground. Gwen looked at her watch. 'Christ,' she said. 'No time for Carnaby Street.'

They caught another bus to Camberwell. On her lap was her portfolio, inside which were her best drawings of the river, some Van Gogh and Leonardo and Dürer studies, and a few self-portraits, including the one with the blank page. Miss Hardy had advised Lillian to have something to say about why she wanted to study at Camberwell. Lillian knew only that she didn't want to do anything else, and had no idea why Camberwell was different to any other art school: she'd applied because Miss Hardy, who'd been there herself, had suggested it. Miss Hardy had also showed her pictures of the work that was being done in London at the moment by young artists – representations of cereal packets and pop groups, and dark canvases ridged with paint so thick it looked in danger of falling off. Lillian had decided to say something about art connecting people with what mattered to them, whether that was pop groups, cereal packets or rivers. She hoped that was the kind of statement that might be appreciated by Mr Fontelle and Professor Goring, who, according to the letter she'd received, would be interviewing her.

They found the School of Painting and Sculpture, where a woman behind a typewriter took Lillian's portfolio and told her to wait in the corridor; she'd be called when the interview panel were ready. Sitting on the hard chair, she felt as though she were waiting to be ticked off by the headmistress. With a worried look, Gwen hissed, 'Absolutely no call to be nervous,' but by the time she was invited into the room, Lillian's mind had gone quite blank and her body felt like a vague presence, slightly disconnected from her brain.

She stood in the doorway. Two men were sitting behind a paint-splattered table with her artwork before them. The room was large, with windows that looked out onto the street. Along one wall were easels and stacks of stools; another was covered in a huge and messy collage of ripped-out pages from magazines and newspapers, beer mats, book jackets, chocolate wrappers.

'Take a seat, Miss Wells.'

The older man, who was pouring soup from a flask into a plastic cup, must be the professor. The younger ground his cigarette into a plate, where two crusts of bread smeared with marg already lay. He gestured towards a stool a good few yards from the table.

'Tell me, Lillian, which works best, of these?' the younger man asked. He was wearing a bright green knitted tank top over a T-shirt and his hair touched his collar.

'The ones of the weir,' she said.

'And why is that?'

She hesitated, knowing the answer *because they seem most like the actual thing* wouldn't be good enough.

'They're dynamic, I suppose,' she said, borrowing one of Miss Hardy's favourite words.

'Are they now?' The man folded his arms across his tank top.

'Well, it's something to aim for.'

Lillian tried again. 'I wanted to capture the shape of the river.'

'And what is a river's shape, exactly?'

'I don't know. I mean – it's always changing, isn't it? Carving its path.'

The professor slurped at his soup and nodded.

'Why do you want to study here?' asked the younger man.

Slightly buoyed by the professor's nod, Lillian decided to be honest. 'I love drawing. It's the only thing I want to do, really.'

'That's all well and good,' said the younger man with a thin smile, 'but we need to know that you're here to work.'

She nodded, confused. What else would she be here for?

'A lot of girls seem to think art school will be terrific fun, but we're not in the business of providing young women with entertainment,' he continued. 'Our course is a vocation, not a vacation.'

The professor put down his cup and dabbed his lips with his hankie. 'You do come with an excellent reference from Rachel Hardy, whom of course I remember well. Lovely little painter. How is she getting along?'

Lillian wasn't sure how to answer that question, either, so she said, 'Very well, thank you.' Into the silence she added, 'She's a great favourite among the girls.'

'What a shame she never had an exhibition,' said the professor. Then he laughed, suddenly and loudly. 'I suppose she's hoping her protégée will do it for her.'

Lillian, unsure if she was also expected to laugh, felt herself blush.

The younger man lit another cigarette and blew smoke in her direction. 'Look,' he said, 'some of your work shows promise. But I'm sick of taking on bits of grammar school fluff who just waste time when they get here. You must be absolutely committed to the course. You must give yourself completely to the work, and the . . . shape of the river.' He smiled again, not unpleasantly. 'Can you do that?'

She thought of her mother, who had no idea she was in this room, and of Jim, who'd said he would wait for her. Giving herself completely would be impossible, clearly. But her work *showed promise*. So what she said was, 'Yes.'

The letter offering her a place came within a fortnight, and for three days Lillian carried it in her pocket, hardly daring to reread it in case the words had changed. It seemed amazing, and still impossible, that she might even consider going to Camberwell. And yet she found that was exactly what she was doing.

She told Gwen first, who said, solemnly, 'Well, of course they want you. And you *have* to go.' Next she told Miss Hardy, who looked briefly tearful, then began helping her with her grant application.

When Uncle Ernie was leaving after his Friday tea, she decided to risk telling him. Her mother was in the back garden, taking down the washing, so Lillian followed him out to his car. Ernie walked, Lillian thought, like a bear, stumping up the path on his thick legs. After she broke the news, he gave her a hug that almost hurt, lifting her from the pavement. 'Good for you!' he said, bright-eyed. 'Clever girl!'

When she told him she was worried about how Winnie would cope without her, he frowned. 'Where is this art school?'

'Camberwell.'

'Where?'

'London.'

'Ah,' he said, smoothing the hair over his bald spot. 'Have you told her?'

'Not yet.'

'This'll need some thinking over. I mean, do you have to go all the way to London?'

'It's not that far,' said Lillian, trying to keep her voice light.

'I'd keep an eye out for her, of course, but . . . you know how she can get.'

Lillian, who'd hoped Ernie would be on her side, felt a flash of anger. 'I'll just tell her. She'll have to get used to it.'

Ernie seemed taken aback by her tone, and there was a long pause. Before getting into the car, he said, 'Break it to her gently, then. We'll take it from there.'

A week passed. Every day, Lillian steeled herself to tell her mother, and every day she failed. After tea, while they washed up together, seemed a sensible time, but if her mother was in a good mood, perhaps singing along with the radio, Lillian wouldn't want to risk shattering it. If she was in a gloomy mood – head low, movements slow and effortful, the need for a sit-down often repeated – Lillian would not want to risk pushing her deeper in.

She waited for when Uncle Ernie returned for his Friday tea, hoping he would help her to soften the blow.

Her mother had made a steak and kidney pie and put a cloth on the table beneath the window. Ernie had fetched a couple of bags of chips. Outside, Winnie's tulips made a row of red and yellow light bulbs along the bottom of the hedge. Ernie had a glass of stout and Lillian poured her mother a cup of tea.

Ernie commented on the loveliness of the flowers, and Winnie said how nice it would be to go to Holland one day to see the tulip fields. The girls at the Pav had been on a trip recently, travelling all the way by coach.

Ernie loaded his fork, scooping up gravy with a knife and smearing it on his meat before aiming for his mouth. 'All day and all night on a bus,' he said, chewing. 'Sounds like a bloody ordeal.'

'Well *I* think it'd be lovely,' said Winnie.

Lillian said, 'London would be far enough for me.'

Ernie looked up, and Lillian willed him to say something that would introduce the subject of art school.

He held a forkful of meat in the air. 'Bet the pie wouldn't be as good in London.'

That wasn't much help. But Lillian ploughed on. 'There are good things, though,' she said, 'in London.'

Winnie, who was picking through her chips, selecting the crispiest ones, looked puzzled. 'What are you two on about?'

'We're talking about London, Mum,' said Lillian. 'About going to London . . .'

Winnie's expression brightened. 'Is Jim taking you? Are you going to see a show? *Half a Sixpence* maybe? I hear it's ever so good. I'd like to see it myself. But I don't suppose there'd be space for me in Jim's car, would there?'

Lillian looked at her plate. 'No,' she said slowly. 'No. I've had a bit of good news, actually. I applied for art school, and I got in.'

When Lillian glanced at her mother she was still picking through her chips, her head slightly tilted. 'Sorry, love, I don't know what you're talking about.'

Lillian took a deep breath. 'I've got into an art school in London. It's not till the end of September. Miss Hardy's helped me with the grant forms. So it won't cost anything.'

Winnie's hands stilled. 'Art school?' she said, moving her mouth slowly around the words as though they were completely foreign to her.

Lillian nodded.

'Whatever for?'

'To study art.'

'And what good will that do you?'

Ernie said quietly, 'If she's really set on it, it might be a good opportunity for her.'

'Thank you, Ernie,' said Winnie, 'for your opinion.' She pushed her plate away and stared, thin-lipped, into the middle distance.

The words were right there in Lillian's mind. *I want to be an artist. That's why I have to go to art school.* But there was no way she could say them out loud. She knew they would only increase her mother's anger and confusion. So she said quietly, 'I don't know what good it would do me.'

'There you are, then!' Winnie said, her gaze snapping back to her daughter. 'Why go all the way to London to study something that will do you no good at all when you could get yourself a nice secretarial job here, just until you're married? What was the point of all those years at that bloody posh school if all you're going to do is fiddle about with paint? And does Jim know about this?'

'He doesn't know they've accepted me yet. But he's said he'll wait.'

Winnie let out a hard laugh. 'I'll believe that when I see it,' she said.

There was a long pause. Eventually Lillian plucked up the courage to say, 'Mum, it won't be a waste. It's what I want to do.'

Winnie shook her head. 'You want to sling your hook and be rid of me, just like my own mother, and your father, too.'

Ernie said, 'Now, Winnie—'

'Don't you Winnie me, Ernie!' Winnie stared at Lillian without blinking, and in that moment Lillian saw the deadness come into her mother's eyes. 'I suppose your mind's made up, is it?'

Lillian heard herself say, 'I suppose it is.'

Her mother poured another cup of tea, then threw in two sugar lumps, letting the liquid slop over the rim. She took one sip before she clattered the cup back into the saucer and stood abruptly. 'I'm sorry,' she said, 'but I just can't have this.'

Ernie and Lillian watched her rush from the room, then listened to her footsteps on the stairs – a heavy tread for such a small woman – and, finally, the sound of her bedroom door slamming.

After a moment, Ernie said, 'Give her time.'

Then he went to the bottom of the stairs and called, 'I'll be off then, gal!'

There was no response.

That night, Lillian heard her mother howling. It was a high, wavering sound – *Ooooh! Oooh-oooooh!* – like a pantomime ghost. As Winnie often hollered in her nightmares, Lillian was used to the noise, but even pantomime ghosts can make your heart thud and the blood pump behind your eyes when they wake you in the early hours of the morning. Usually, Lillian would rise from her own bed and wake her mother gently, telling her it was just a dream and everything was all right. Winnie, startled for only a moment, would pat her daughter's hand and say she was a good girl. But that night, Lillian didn't get up. Instead, she turned on her bedside lamp and reached for the book of Van Gogh landscapes Gwen had lent her. On the flyleaf was a handwritten inscription: *To David, with so much blue – Rebecca.* Turning the pages, Lillian tried to immerse herself in the blues, the yellows, the reds, as her mother wailed on.

In the morning, she came down to a crumbed plate left on the draining board, all the loaf gone and a half-full teacup in the sink, a swirl of grease floating on the cold liquid. Winnie had obviously been down in the night, though her door was now closed. Lillian checked the larder. Two tins of corned beef; one can of peaches; a few eggs in the tray. An inch of milk in the bottle in the squat refrigerator. No butter left in the dish.

She stood at the bottom of the stairs, looking up, as Ernie had done the day before. If her mother called, she would go to her. But there was only silence. So Lillian left the house without checking on Winnie or cobbling together any breakfast. *Let her stew*, she thought.

She wanted fresh air, to be alone. As she walked to work, the spring sun rising, the river shining at her side, the smell of the brewery heavy in the air, she told herself that, whatever her mother said, she would soon be leaving this place for London.

At break-time on Monday she sat in the corner of the art room with Gwen. Outside, the wind was blowing the last of the cherry blossom from the trees, and the large window was dappled with brown petals. The radiators ticked and the strip light hummed. Gwen sat on the desk with her feet propped on the back of a chair and munched through a bag of Salt 'n' Shake. 'You look a bit done in,' she said, offering Lillian a crisp.

Lillian's mouth was suddenly flooded with saliva and she snatched two crisps and ate them as slowly as she could, savouring every salty crunch.

'Have the rest,' suggested Gwen.

Lillian wiped her greasy fingers on her skirt and refused. She didn't know why she said no, when she was hungry. But it felt the right thing to do. Having skipped breakfast all weekend, it seemed a shame to give in, now.

'You on a diet?' Gwen tipped the bag to her mouth and inhaled the last crumbs. 'Judith says all the art school girls are thin. It's *imperative* to look like a ruler, for some reason.' Scrunching the bag in her fist, she added, 'Sounds barbaric, doesn't it?'

Though she hadn't thought of it before, Lillian said that maybe she *was* on a diet. She pictured her kitchen at home, the larder with its few tins of corned beef and the refrigerator with its inch of souring milk. Over the weekend, she'd seen little of Winnie, who'd occasionally crept downstairs to the toilet without saying a word. Lillian knew her mother would expect a tray of food to be presented at her door that evening, just as it had been on Saturday and Sunday, and the thought of it suddenly filled her with rage. She'd have to spend what she'd earned in the salon that week on groceries, and then she'd have to face her mother, who'd retreated upstairs as though it were her absolute right to disappear. As if an 'attack of the nerves' – whatever the hell that actually was – excused everything. A diet would be a way to avoid joining her mother for a meal.

Or maybe there was an even better way to avoid her.

'Can I come to your house after school?'

'Course,' said Gwen. 'Come any time you like.'

All week, Lillian dodged her mother and mealtimes at her own house. She left for school without breakfast, letting the dirty plates stack up. Jim joined her on her walk; they held hands and kissed at the bridge, as they usually did. He'd said little about her leaving, but things seemed to have cooled between them. He'd smiled when she'd told him she'd got a place at the art school, telling her he was pleased and that it was as she'd said they'd still see each other. Of course they would. Then he'd changed the subject. Lillian got the feeling he couldn't quite believe she would actually leave Abingdon. She didn't mention Winnie's reaction. She felt vaguely ashamed of her mother's behaviour and at a loss as to how to explain it to Jim.

She didn't tell Gwen about Winnie's outburst, either. In Gwen's house, the idea that anyone could react so badly to what was clearly good news seemed ridiculous. When Gwen announced to her mother that Lillian had a place at Camberwell, Mrs Chadwick insisted they toast Lillian's success with a small glass of sherry.

After slowly walking home from Gwen's on Wednesday night, Lillian let herself in the back, climbed the stairs and almost tapped on her mother's door. Light was leaking all around the frame, and Lillian rested her forehead on the wooden panel, listening to her mother shifting in the sheets. She imagined hearing her name called, being embraced on the bed, her mother saying she would probably get up tomorrow. She imagined resting her head on her mother's chest, breathing in her scent, hearing her heartbeat and slipping away from the rest of the world.

But no call came, and Lillian went to her room, hungry and afraid. This was the worst attack of her mother's that she could remember, and she wondered if it would ever end.

On Friday, Ernie came in the back door just as she was dropping chipped potatoes in a bowl of water. She'd cleared up the kitchen in anticipation of his arrival, and was planning on feeding him egg and chips, hoping Ernie's presence and the aroma would entice Winnie downstairs.

He gave her a brief smile then looked about, grimacing. 'No sign, then?'

Lillian shrugged, and he headed up the stairs.

She heard his soft tap, followed by his voice, low and coaxing, and, eventually, the door opening and a mumble from her mother. Relief flooded her. Uncle Ernie would deal with this. He'd explain to her mother that art school was a good opportunity. He'd reassure her that he'd be there if she needed him. He'd tell her that Lillian would always come back to Mason Road.

She lit a flame beneath a pan of oil and laid the table for three, not forgetting the bottle of brown sauce that Ernie so liked. Realising this would be the first proper meal she'd eaten for days, she began to feel a little weak. As she waited for the sound of her mother's tread on the stairs, she leaned back on the sink, watching the fat heat up, trying not to think of what she might say to her mother, or what her mother might say in return, but instead about the taste of hot chips, the crispy outside giving way to the fluffiness within, the smack of salt on her lips.

When the fat began to pop she heard Ernie's big body brush past the coats that hung along the stairway. He marched through the kitchen to the bathroom, carrying Winnie's full pot before him. The toilet flushed, the taps ran, and then he reappeared and pointed to the stove. 'Turn that off,' he said, 'and come with me.'

She wanted to cry, *Why isn't she coming down?* and also, *What about my bloody chips?* but Ernie was out of the front door and striding down the path. She hesitated, listening. There was no sound from above, so she grabbed her coat and followed him. By the time she reached his car, he'd started the engine.

They drove through the town in silence. It wasn't yet dark, but the bright windows of the pubs were already fogged with condensation.

'Are we getting chips, then?' she asked hopefully.

Ernie shook his head and looked so serious that she didn't dare ask anything else. He parked along Wilsham Road, next to the river, pulling up the handbrake with a definite creak. Without looking at her, he said, 'How have things been, this week?'

From his tone – careful, expectant – she understood he was wise to her neglect. Ernie knew she hadn't taken her mother food, nor emptied the pot beneath her bed. He knew she hadn't even knocked on the door. Not once. Perhaps he even knew she'd ignored Winnie's nightmares.

She said, 'They've been all right.'

'Don't give me that.' He said it softly, but still he didn't glance at her. 'Has she been downstairs at all?'

'Not when I'm there.' Lillian didn't mention how little she had actually been in the house.

Ernie reached into the glove compartment, fished out his battered wallet and handed her a note. 'Get some food in,' he said. 'I've talked to the Pav, and the Dairy. They're being patient, but it won't last for ever.'

'She might get up tomorrow,' said Lillian.

'I'm not sure she will, love.'

Lillian fought the urge to pound his chest with her fists. 'But she has to get up now!' she cried. 'She has to!'

Ernie looked at her then, his face pinched with dismay. 'The thing is. And I didn't want to have to tell you this. But it looks like I've no choice.' He took a breath, then said, 'There was a time, when you were a baby, so you won't remember, thankfully, but there was a time when your mum had to go away for a bit.'

She almost laughed and said, *But Mum never leaves Abingdon!* Then she saw the seriousness in his eyes and a chill crawled through her stomach.

'She had a spell in . . . hospital, Lillian. In Longbrook. She was very bad then, you see. With her nerves.'

He was watching her now, waiting for her to take this thing in.

Lillian turned her face away and stared through the window. A gentle breeze was blowing patterns on the darkening river. The willows threw shadows across the water. Geese honked. *Longbrook*. The funny farm. The loony bin.

Ernie was talking again. 'What I'm trying to tell you is that it can get – very tricky. I mean, she hasn't been bad for years – not really. She's got you, now, you see.'

On the opposite bank a boy on a bike was signalling to a friend, waving both arms frantically and shouting his name.

'So – I think you should talk to her. She told me that you haven't been in all week. That you haven't said one word to her.'

'*She* hasn't been out. *She* hasn't said one word to me.'

'I know, love,' said Ernie. 'I know it's not fair.'

Lillian continued to watch the boy waving his arms. *Longbrook*. She remembered what Mrs Shepherd had told Phyllis in the salon about the men coming to take Dolly James away. Had that happened to her mother? Had Winnie been *restrained*? It didn't seem possible. Lillian had long known about her mother's attacks, but she'd never linked them with the idea of a mental illness. They were just what her mother did. Winnie wasn't *mad*, surely? Winnie was just her mother.

Then something struck her, and she turned to Ernie. 'Where was I? When she was in that place, where was I?'

'You were with me and Daphne. In our place, just there.' He gestured towards a house across the road. It was more modern and slightly larger than number 25, with a driveway and a front door of frosted glass. The windows were wide and the front lawn was neat. 'It was only a few months.'

'You and *Daphne*? In that house?'

'Of course. Who else was going to look after you?' Ernie patted her hand. 'We were happy to have you! Poor Daphne couldn't get in the family way, so . . .' He trailed off. 'Your mum suffered. But she was lucky. Other ladies lost their children altogether. Specially if they weren't married.'

'Lost them?'

'They were taken away. Adopted, I suppose. But you came to us until your mum was better. And then she had you back.'

He said it as though it were the simplest thing in the world.

Lillian watched the boy on the opposite bank push his bike along the river, no longer waving or shouting.

'How bad was she?' She had to ask, though there was part of her that didn't want to know.

Ernie pressed his lips together, then said, 'I should've kept an eye on her. I didn't know, you see, how bad she was until . . . Well. Maybe you don't need to hear the rest.'

Lillian, who'd begun to shiver, wrapped her coat tightly around her. 'Please. Please tell me.'

Now it was Ernie's turn to look out of the side window. In a flattened voice he said, 'She filled her coat pockets with stones. Walked into the river, right by the weir. The lock-keeper saw her and fished her out.' He covered his face with his hands and his shoulders heaved. For a dreadful minute she thought he might cry, right there in the Austin. But instead he turned to her and grasped her hand. 'First I knew of it was finding you in your cot, screaming the bloody place down. This was in your old house. I'd not long sorted that out for her, after her mother kicked her out . . . What on earth's that woman playing at, I thought, leaving her baby alone like this? But I reckon it was deliberate. It was a Friday teatime, so she knew I'd be coming over, didn't she? Do you see? Your mother knew I'd find you and you'd be all right. She could never have done it otherwise.'

His eyes were searching her face. Lillian swallowed. She said to herself: *I can think about this later. Uncle Ernie has just told me some things. But there's no need to think about them yet.*

'So you'll look after her, won't you, Lillian? We don't want her that bad again, do we? She needs you.'

Lillian nodded, not knowing what she was agreeing to, knowing only that she could not allow her mother to be a woman who filled her coat pockets with stones. A mad woman who ended up in Longbrook.

'And you're to knock on our door, any time, if you need anything. All right?'

Lillian looked again at the house, its perfect square of lawn, its wide windows. Her mother had told her, bitterly, that Ernie's place wasn't council; Daphne actually owned the house, thanks to a well-off uncle leaving her a pot of money. There were neat tubs of daffodils on either side of the doorstep. She heard her mother's voice. *Don't suppose there's much that woman hasn't got. Bloody snob. Thinks she's a cut above.* Should Lillian ever set foot in there, there was no way her mother would forgive her. But, to please Ernie, she nodded again.

'Good girl,' he said, starting the engine.

Before he could drive away, though, a woman appeared in the doorway of the house. Tall, slender, and wearing a long coat that looked brand new. Lillian watched as she strolled down the path, and knew this woman must be Ernie's wife, Daphne, who had never stepped foot inside number 25.

Ernie stopped the engine and wound down his window.

'Hello, Lillian,' Daphne said, bending to peer into the car.

Lillian stared at the woman for a moment. Her hair was dyed a fierce shade that she was sure was Miss Clairol's Cherry Silver, and her intense eyes were outlined in black kohl. It was difficult to look away.

'You've been a long time,' Daphne said. Her voice wasn't posh, exactly, but it was clear. Confident. 'Is everything all right? How's Winnie?'

'Not good,' said Ernie. 'And Lillian's a bit upset. I had to tell her . . . some things.'

There was a pause. Lillian wished Daphne would go away so she could go home and cry. Or scream. Perhaps both.

Daphne said, 'Why don't the two of you come in for a cup of tea? I can make you a sandwich if you're hungry?'

Lillian shook her head. The last thing she wanted at this moment was to betray her mother by going into the house.

'I'd better get her home,' Ernie said.

'Then I'll have to come to you,' Daphne said, and she climbed into the back seat.

'Daphne—'

'Don't fret, Ernie. I just want to make sure Lillian here's all right.'

She leaned forward and laid her hand on Lillian's shoulder. Lillian felt its warmth, but did not look round.

'She'll be fine,' said Ernie. 'I just had to fill her in on . . . her mother's spell away and that. You know. The river. On account of her mother being bad at the moment.'

In the rear-view mirror, Lillian saw Daphne frown sympathetically. 'And do you understand, love? About what happened to your poor mother? Poor woman! Being *deposited* in that place!'

'No need to go on about it,' said Ernie.

Lillian blinked at Daphne's reflection. 'The girl has a right to know, Ernie. Do you have anything you'd like to ask me?' Daphne said. 'About anything at all?'

Lillian couldn't think of how to phrase a single question, so she shook her head and said, as determinedly as she could, 'I think we should get back to Mum.'

Daphne dropped her hand. Ernie, sounding relieved, said, 'Good idea.'

As Daphne opened the door, she said, 'If you need anything, Lillian, you know where I am.'

Once they were back at number 25, Ernie took off his jacket, rolled up his sleeves and said, 'Go and see her. I'll get these chips on.'

She trudged upstairs.

Her mother's room was in darkness. Without looking at the bed, Lillian flicked on the light and crossed the room to close the curtains. Then she turned to face her mother, who had the blankets pulled to her chin and her eyes tightly shut. Without her teeth, her mouth looked small and sunken.

Lillian tried to steady herself. This was her mother, who had been in Longbrook. Her mother, who had walked into the river.

'Ernie's making chips. Are you coming down?'

Winnie's hand crept over the eiderdown and batted at the air. Lillian understood the gesture perfectly, and, after a minute, she clasped Winnie's clammy fingers.

'Come here,' her mother said, and Lillian found herself collapsing onto the bed. Her mother pushed herself into a sitting position, and took Lillian into her arms. Lillian placed her head against her mother's flattened chest, listening to the determined beat of her blood. She waited for the rest of the world to slip away, but it didn't, quite.

'Sorry, Mum,' she said, clinging to her. 'I'm so sorry.' Once Lillian had started to cry, she found she couldn't stop.

Her mother held her. 'It's all right, love. Don't take on so. We've got each other, haven't we?'

It was a relief to embrace the old routines. She would be a good daughter, her mother's rock. For the next fortnight, she went straight home from school to cook the tea and take it to Winnie on a tray. Winnie was now sitting up in bed, teeth in, looking brighter. Lillian would perch on the edge of the mattress and chatter about her day, being careful never to mention her art class. Winnie ate daintily, pushing at least a third to one side and placing her knife and fork over the leftovers, which Lillian would eat later, instead of her own meal, once she was back in the kitchen.

Ernie brought a couple of bottles of pills over on the first Friday and, after a few days, Winnie was dressed and sitting downstairs when Lillian arrived home. But there was a slower quality to her mother now. She moved deliberately, and there seemed to be a delay between what Lillian said and her mother's reaction. She rarely laughed. There was that blank deadness, Lillian thought, in her eyes. As though she wasn't really registering what was going on around her. But the important thing was that she didn't weep, or wail. The nights were long and silent.

In the kitchen, Ernie took Lillian aside and told her that the Dairy had employed someone else, which was maybe just as well as two jobs would clearly be too much for Winnie, but she had to go back to the Pav. He'd persuaded Brian the rent man to let them go into arrears for the next couple of weeks, but he wouldn't be able to keep it that way for long. That meant, he said, that Lillian might want to think about taking on some extra shifts at the salon after school. And certainly in the holidays, when Winnie's family allowance would come to an end.

No one mentioned London, or art school.

No one spoke of Longbrook, either.

When Gwen asked Lillian why she no longer came to her house after school, Lillian said her mother had a bad dose of the flu and needed looking after.

For two weeks in a row, she said the same thing to Jim when he asked if she'd like to go dancing at the social club on a Saturday night. But she couldn't refuse a third invitation.

The club was busy when they arrived. The pool table and the pinball machine had been shoved into a corner, and the music was already going. It was Vernon Whitehead's band again, scaled down this time and without the matching jackets.

Jim's friend Mick signalled to them from the bar.

'Here's old Twinkle Toes!' he said, clapping Jim on the shoulder. 'And the gorgeous young Lillian.'

Mick reached to touch her cheek and she smelled the tobacco

on his fingers. 'I see you've grown more gorgeous since I last saw you. How is that possible? Ain't she, Jim? Ain't she grown more gorgeous?'

'Every day,' said Jim.

'But I hear you're too good for us!' Mick continued. 'Jim tells me you're off to *college*.'

So Jim had told his friend. Perhaps he did believe she would leave, after all. Which was more than she did, at this moment.

'Poor old Jimbo!' Mick continued. 'How will he ever cope?'

Jim, who was trying to catch the barmaid's eye, gave a mirthless laugh.

Mick leaned close to Lillian and whispered, 'He'll be *destroyed.*'

She excused herself, saying she needed the lavvy. Jim raised his eyebrows in a gesture of, *So soon?* but she pretended not to notice. All the way to the club, she'd been too preoccupied by her worries about her mother to listen to his chatter about his job. Winnie had been watching the wrestling when Lillian left, and had told her daughter not to be so silly when she'd suggested she cancel her arrangement with Jim and stay with her. *Don't leave a good man waiting*, she'd said. But there was, still, that deadness in her eyes. Would she get up in the morning, having been left alone?

As Lillian walked towards the Ladies', one of the men clustered around the dartboard let out a long, low whistle. Lillian knew it wasn't just her who had to go through this; some women, though, seemed to know how to feign complete indifference, and others even seemed to enjoy the experience, flipping a comment over a shoulder as they swanned past. All Lillian could do was duck her head and scowl. As she scurried on, she overheard one of them say, 'Foxy bird.'

In the toilets, she looked in the mirror and felt strangely satisfied. Regardless of whether she managed to make it to art school, her body was changing. She had *made* it change, just as she'd done when she'd cut her hair. She'd reduced herself to a new person. She was a foxy bird. The phrase made no sense at all; she knew that. But she'd been noticed.

When she got back, Jim was at a corner table with Mick and his current girlfriend, who kept one hand on his thigh, even while sipping her shandy. Jim tapped his foot in time with the music, ignoring the conversation around him. Lillian knew he was itching to get up. But she kept picturing her mother alone, hearing her whispery voice, thinking of the bedroom door that, if it closed again, might stay that way for who knew how long. And her coat. It was a grey mohair thing, itchy to the touch, and she knew Winnie couldn't have been wearing it that night. But that didn't stop Lillian picturing it, the pockets bulging with stones. She pushed the image away. She pushed away, too, the image of the river and the weir. Those things were out of bounds now, even in her imagination. And she'd told herself that she must never even think of the word *Longbrook*.

Perhaps she could check Winnie was all right, then return. She bent to Jim's ear and hissed, 'I'll have to go, soon.'

Jim glanced at his watch. 'It's only half eight.'

'I'll just check on Mum. And then I'll come back.'

'Why? She seemed fine when I picked you up.'

'She's not herself at the minute.'

'What does that mean?'

Lillian shook her head, unable to begin to explain. Jim stood, then, and held out his hand. 'Let's dance,' he said. 'You worry too much about her.'

He led her to the floor. As usual, Jim was the first up, and Lillian was aware of the assessing eyes of others. She tried to move through the music with him, letting the melody lift her and the rhythm ground her, as Jim had advised she should. He smiled that ecstatic smile of his, gazing over her shoulder at some invisible loveliness, and she felt the pressure of his leg, guiding her. But by the end of the song she was apologising and pulling away from him. She grabbed her coat from the stool and hurried for the double doors, ignoring Mick's cry of, 'Leaving us so soon?'

The evening was fresh with recently fallen rain. She jogged down Ock Street, glad of the cool air kicking into her lungs. Hearing Jim call her name, she increased her pace. The long street was alive with Saturday night. Piano notes scattered from the open window of Mr Warwick's Arms; the beat of the jukebox leaked through the doorway of The Crown. Jim's voice had faded and Lillian ran on, gaining momentum now. She was light and fleet as she passed the Regal, and she didn't stop until she reached the High Street. When she looked back there was no sign of Jim. She pressed on, up Stert Street, past the salon, and along the Vineyard. Outside The Red Lion a woman she didn't recognise staggered towards her and said, 'You're the little sweeper at the hairdresser's!'

Lillian jogged past her, towards home.

Number 25 was quiet. Winnie's plate had been washed and placed on the drainer. On the pull-down shelf of the kitchen cabinet an opened packet of malted milk biscuits spilled crumbs.

Still in her coat, Lillian rushed upstairs. Hearing soft snores before she'd even made it to the landing, she exhaled. The door was a little ajar so it took no more than a gentle push to let herself into the room. She stood, still in her coat, breathing in time with her mother to calm herself. On the glass top of the bedside table, there were two bottles of pills beside the pot in which Winnie kept her teeth, and a paperback with a red-haired woman swooning in a dark-skinned man's arms on the cover. Lillian had seen the pills before, but now she snatched up a bottle and read the label carefully. *Carbrital. Take TWO at night for insomnia and ONE up to THREE TIMES a day.*

The small Westclox ticked loudly. Lillian read the label again, twice, before beginning to understand the words.

Downstairs, in the weak light of the kitchen, she emptied the malted milks into the biscuit barrel and pressed the lid to make sure it was firmly shut. Then she swept the crumbs away with one hand and pushed the cabinet closed with the other. *Carbrital. TWO at night for insomnia.* These were sleeping tablets. Tranquillisers. Lillian had read stories in her mother's *Daily Mirror* of people killing themselves by overdosing on tranquillisers. The details were always unclear but there was usually a reference to bottles left abandoned around the body, by the bed, or on the floor, and also to the 'shock and disbelief' of those left behind. *I knew she wasn't herself*, they might say (it was often a woman), *but I had no idea she was that bad.*

Lillian placed the biscuit barrel on the larder shelf and looked around. Tomorrow, she could have half of the grapefruit she'd bought for breakfast. If she sliced it now and sprinkled it with sugar, it would be crusty and sweet by the morning. Half a grapefruit meant there would be no need for toast.

She prepared the fruit, then turned off the lights. The thought of breakfast was in her mind as she locked the back door and, finally, removed her coat and hung it on the hook on the stairs. She kept it in mind as she undressed, shivering once she was barefoot on the linoleum. It was there, too, as she lay in bed, blinking into the darkness, listening for her mother's moans. Whenever the bottle of Carbrital slid back into her thoughts, she replaced it with half a grapefruit, encrusted with sugar.

Winnie was in the bath, having not long emerged from her room, and Lillian had eaten her grapefruit, slowly, with a small spoon, when Jim came to the door.

After bolting last night, she'd expected anger from him, and hurt pride, but as he stood on her doorstep and asked what on earth had happened, all she witnessed was his concern. Jim's brow furrowed. He put a hand to her elbow and clasped her at arm's length, as if trying to get her into perspective. He was attempting, she realised, to understand something she did not quite understand herself. She suggested they go for a walk.

Something seemed to have shifted in the weather as they strolled to the end of the road and into Boxhill Woods. The air was gentler and the horse chestnut leaves had relaxed into splayed fingers of green. Jim took Lillian's hand and led her down to the stream, where the smell of warming soil came at her.

He blurted, 'Have you met some other bloke? If you have, I'd rather you just told me now.'

He looked so stricken, and grasped her fingers so hard, that a small, surprised gasp escaped her.

'I won't be angry,' he said, his voice very low. 'Please. I just need to know.'

So she told him. She told him how, after she'd broken the news about art school, her mother had taken to her bed with an attack of the nerves. She explained how her mother had done this before, but never for as long. She told him, too, what Ernie had said about the river. While she spoke, Lillian had the sense that she was telling a story about herself without quite knowing whether it was true.

'She had to go away, once, when I was a baby,' she said. 'She had to go to hospital.'

'What hospital?'

Lillian closed her eyes for a moment. 'Longbrook.'

Jim didn't exactly flinch, but he took in more air, and seemed to hold himself in a different way – less stiff, perhaps, yet more self-conscious.

Her mouth was dry and her limbs felt light. It was as though saying the word had sucked the energy from her. 'I need to sit down,' she said.

They found a log so Lillian could sit. Jim paced back and forth, and she watched the edges of his polished shoes become rimmed with mud.

'I'm so worried about leaving her,' she said, her tongue loosened now. 'Ernie says she needs me, and he's right! How can I go to art school?'

Jim nodded, still pacing.

'And if I leave, and she's only working at the Pav, there won't be enough money—'

Suddenly, Jim knelt on the ground before her and looked into her face. His eyes were bright. Taking both her knees in his hands, he said, 'So marry me.'

She stared at him in disbelief.

'Think about it! It makes perfect sense! I'll be promoted soon. I can look after both you and your mum. And you can have your own life. You can have your own life, with me.' He squeezed her knees. 'I'll worship the ground you walk on. For the rest of my life, that's what I'll do.'

She smiled, then, at the ridiculous hope in this statement. Jim gave a small smile, too. She looked at him for a long time, registering the expectation in his expression, and she understood that this was what he'd wanted all along. She was tempted to give it to him. To say that easy word, *yes*. To surrender herself to this good man who loved her.

'What would we do, if we were married?' she asked.

'What do you mean, what would we *do*? We'd be married. That's what we'd do.'

'But what about art school, Jim?'

'What about it?' He tilted his head, as though slightly amused. 'I don't think married women go to art school, do they? I mean, you'd be my wife, not an art student.'

She nodded, and looked away from him, into the trees. 'Then I can't,' she said.

Gwen's mother opened the door. She was wearing an embroidered dressing gown, and held a mug of coffee.

'Goodness,' she said, startled. 'Gwenny's not up yet. But how lovely to see you.'

Lillian, who'd run all the way from the woods to Park Road, realised that she needed to cry, very badly. At the sight of Mrs Chadwick's hopeful smile, her face crumpled and she put a hand to her mouth.

Mrs Chadwick said, 'Oh, you poor dear. Want to come in? I'll wake her.'

Lillian nodded and stepped inside.

She leaned on the wall and took some deep breaths, managing to swallow her tears, wishing she could follow Mrs Chadwick upstairs and hide in that room of exquisite and mysterious things belonging to Gwen's father. She could lie on the white rug, a mug of Nescafé steaming beside her – though she didn't like it much, it might be improved by a few sugar lumps – and gaze at the shelves of books and know that the garden was stretching away outside the window.

Gwen came thundering down the steps in her pyjamas, gathering a cardigan around her shoulders. She peered at Lillian, frowned, then hugged her, yawning loudly. Lillian felt her friend's jaw shudder on the top of her head and smelled her sweat. Without speaking, Gwen gestured for Lillian to stay where she was as she ducked into the kitchen. When she came out, she was holding two slices of brown toast. Handing one to Lillian, she said, 'Let's go.'

They crossed the quiet road and walked along the gravel beneath the trees, patches of sunlight warming them now and then as they munched. Lillian's toast was cold and soggy but the salty butter and claggy bread provided some comfort.

'Tell me what's going on, then,' Gwen said, licking her fingers.

'Jim asked me to marry him.'

Gwen stopped walking. She'd never joined Lillian and Jim when they went dancing and knew little of him, saying she'd rather expire a virgin than play gooseberry. Even so, what she said now was, 'I thought he might.'

'Did you?'

'He looked serious, to me, that time at the fair. Like he had plans.'

Lillian saw that Gwen was right: Jim did have plans, always. And his plans were usually carried out.

They had come to a halt close to St Michael's Church, where they could hear the congregation struggling through 'He Who Would Valiant Be'.

'So what did you say?'

When Lillian didn't answer, Gwen's expression darkened. 'Wait. You don't *have* to marry him, do you? Because if you do, my sister knows someone who can take care of things—'

'No,' said Lillian. 'It's nothing like that. I said I couldn't marry him because of art school.'

Gwen nodded and began walking again. 'Good.' Then, after a pause, she asked: 'So you're not in love with him?'

Lillian thought about it, and thought that she couldn't be, if she had to think about it. In the novels she'd read, love was a kind of chaos, something that struck you down with its intensity of feeling, rendering you incapable of thought. It wasn't like that with Jim. She looked forward to seeing him with a pleasant kind of pain, and when they were together she felt entirely safe. She loved dancing with him, she was sure of that.

She thought he might love her, though he'd never said as much. To have her every move and syllable anticipated and welcomed by Jim, on and off the dance floor, was – bar the pleasure of drawing something well – the most wonderful feeling she'd ever experienced. But was that enough?

She said, 'I'm not sure.'

'Then you aren't,' said Gwen, linking her arm through Lillian's and leading her off the path and across the sunny lawn. 'Which is good, because you want to be free when you get to Camberwell.'

'The thing is,' Lillian said, 'I'm still not sure I can leave Mum.'

'For God's sake!' said Gwen, stopping and throwing her hands in the air. 'She's a grown woman, isn't she?'

Lillian looked at her friend, whose cardigan had blown open in the breeze and whose pyjama trousers were wet around the hems from the damp grass. A trail of sleepy dust was encrusted on Gwen's cheek, making her appear younger, but she placed her hands on her hips and sounded absolutely certain, and almost convincing, as she said, 'Your bloody mother will manage without you.'

Lillian laughed, then, though she didn't believe it was true.

2005

With Rachel at her father's, Lillian tried her best to keep busy. On the Saturday morning, she met her friend Scott for coffee at a new place with leather armchairs, grey walls and tables made from salvaged wood. Since becoming a commissioning editor at a children's publisher, Scott was always in vintage-looking suits. Today he wore a tweed jacket and a linen shirt, despite the heat, and he smelled of something zesty and expensive. The *Super Granddad* work had come through him. When he asked about Rachel, Lillian said nothing about the phone call, or about her daughter's various tics and obsessions. Instead, she spoke of how they were both nervous but excited about her starting university. As she was saying this, she realised it was a lie and her coffee soured in her mouth. She felt no excitement, and she didn't know, exactly, how Rachel felt. There had been many conversations about Rachel's plans, but none about how her daughter might cope with leaving home.

Scott asked if she was all right, and Lillian insisted she was fine.

'Fine as in fine, or fine as in just about hanging in?'

'Fine as in *fine*.'

Scott looked doubtful. 'So fine as in it's none of my bloody business?'

She tried to smile. 'Fine as in my only daughter is about to leave me.'

Scott, who had no children of his own, patted her hand. 'It's bound to be a tricky transition. But we all have to do it, don't we? Fly the nest and all that. Up, up and away.'

What if your wings don't work? thought Lillian, a lump coming to her throat.

On the way back to the flat, the lump swelled. Her daughter, who was leaving in less than two weeks' time, was spending the weekend with her father and she, Lillian, could do nothing to fetch her home, where she belonged. Telling herself she would have a good conversation with Rachel about uni as soon as she could, Lillian bought two bunches of lilies. Back at the flat, she tidied every room, mopped all the floors, then arranged the flowers in her best vase – a blue glass bowl-shaped vessel which Gwen had given her for her fortieth birthday – and placed them in Rachel's room.

She texted her daughter. *Sorry if I overreacted. Call me? Mum x*
It took Rachel over an hour to reply. *No worries. Speak soon x*

Rachel's first physical tic had appeared long ago, at primary school. Aged seven, she'd begun pulling on her bottom lip while she watched TV or turned the pages of a book. At first Lillian dismissed it as a harmless habit that helped her daughter concentrate, but soon the pulling caused a red mark to appear above Rachel's chin. Then Rachel's teacher, Miss Winch, bustled up to Lillian in the school playground at pick-up time, saying she'd noticed Rachel's habit and was everything OK at home? The public humiliation of being singled out by Miss Winch, who had a green fringe and pink DMs, made Lillian stand straight and fix her smile. She wasn't about to be one of those parents who were always getting called in for a 'quick chat' after school, even if she was a *Single Mother*. She knew that term would be clearly printed on Rachel's file. Doubtless Miss Winch had already assumed Rachel faced a difficult home life and had been denied a relationship with her estranged father.

She'd assured the teacher that she would speak with Rachel but as far as she knew everything was fine. Perhaps, she enquired, keeping her voice smooth, there might be a problem at school? Miss Winch had smiled rather coyly. She'd keep an eye out, she said, but things in the classroom were going *so* well. Rachel was such a good girl! Bright and so very determined. And though she had few friends, they were lovely ones.

As soon as they were home, Lillian had asked her daughter, 'Is someone bullying you?'

'No,' said Rachel, pulling her lip tight.

Lillian had to stop herself from physically removing Rachel's fingers from her mouth. 'Do you like Miss Winch?'

Rachel dropped her coat into Lillian's waiting hands. 'She's OK.'

'What about Milly? Is she being nice to you?'

Rachel nodded.

Milly was Rachel's friend, and Lillian privately thought her to be a difficult child. She refused to eat the pasta Lillian made unless it had tomato ketchup on it, and whenever she came to the flat to play, Lillian would hear Milly ordering Rachel about. *You be the nurse!* Rachel resisted that one, of course, wielding her beloved toy stethoscope, but she gave in to every other demand. 'Miss Winch says she's noticed you pulling on your lip,' said Lillian, hanging their coats on the back of the door. 'She's worried about you.'

Rachel was already standing on a chair and searching in the cupboard above the sink. 'Can I have a biscuit?'

Lillian placed a hand on her daughter's leg to steady her. 'I'm a bit worried, too, Rachel. It looks quite sore. Does it feel sore?'

'I can't find the KitKats.'

'I'd like you to try and stop doing it, all right?'

'What?'

'Pulling on your lip.'

'OK.'

There was a small pause, during which Rachel pulled on her lip.

Lillian grasped Rachel's fingers and gently removed them from her face. Then she lifted her from the chair, kissed her head, and found her a biscuit.

The lip pulling had stopped eventually, but a few years later it was replaced by Rachel picking at a spot on her scalp, just above her right ear, until it became infected. That had been the catalyst for the visit to the doctor who'd uttered the word *Longbrook*, which had only increased Lillian's determination to deal with the problem alone. If any doctor thought she would let her daughter anywhere near that place, they could think again. She'd kept applying antibiotic cream to Rachel's scalp, hoping it would pass. And it had. Just as Rachel's next habit of encircling one wrist with the fingers of her other hand had eventually passed. That one had chilled Lillian when she'd seen it, as it perfectly echoed one of her own habits from long ago. But she'd said nothing. What could she say? *I notice you're holding on to your own wrist?* She'd bitten her tongue, and it had passed.

But now, just as her daughter was about to leave home, Rachel had not one but three new tics. The patting of her neck. The holding on to handles. And the deliberate blinking. *One, two, three.*

On Monday morning, Lillian finally received another message from Rachel. *Meet me in the Abbey Meadow at 4?*

Going out of her way to avoid the diversion through Longbrook, she drove to Abingdon. She waited in the shade of the poplars, next to what had once been the paddling pool but was now a sprinkler system for children to play in. She watched toddlers and older kids running in and out of the water jets. A girl of around five, with sweaty hair and only her bikini bottoms on, slipped on the wet grass. She didn't make a sound as she went down, and remained silent when a woman, whom Lillian assumed to be the girl's mother, slowly approached then carefully inspected her legs for damage. The girl merely stood, waiting for it to be over, then ran off to play again. The woman folded her arms and watched her go. No tears, no drama. A triumph, Lillian thought.

Then her own girl walked down the grassy slope towards her, wearing a strappy sundress and green sandals, hair scooped in some sort of knot, sunglasses on, looking shockingly like a young woman. Had she grown over the last couple of days? It had been at least a year since Rachel had surpassed her in height. Her shoulders, too, were wider than Lillian's, her feet and fingers longer. Her daughter had, Lillian reflected, greater *reach*.

Rachel raised a hand to pat her neck. It was hotter than yesterday, and Lillian wondered if that neck had any sun lotion on it.

'Hi.'

'Hi.'

They embraced. Lillian held on for a few seconds longer, relaxing into the moment of holding her child; that brief, wonderful moment when all was safe and all was well.

'It's so good to see you again.'

'Mum. It's been two days,' said Rachel.

'Three.'

'Maybe two and a half? At most?'

Lillian allowed Rachel to draw back.

'How's your dad?'

'The usual. You know.'

Lillian nodded.

'Should we walk, then?' Rachel asked.

Lillian smiled. Her daughter was like her in this respect: always wanting to get on with things.

They walked along the riverbank. Lillian had avoided bringing Rachel here in the past. Despite walking here so many times, as a girl and young woman, she hadn't returned to this spot since Ernie had told her about her mother walking into the water. There was a defined gravel path, now, following the line of the river. As they walked, she heard the low roar of the weir, though the view of it was obscured by the bend in the river and the trees. She told herself that though the place might be much the same, everything else was different.

Once they'd rounded the bend, Rachel stopped and sat on a bench. From here they had a view of the iron structure of the weir to their left, and of the opposite bank. Foam from the crashing water gathered in ungainly clumps around the reeds, but the river before them was calm and deeply green. This, she thought, must be the exact spot where her mother had filled her pockets with stones and waded in, the water quickly flooding her shoes and making her coat balloon, then sink, around her. Bending its shape to take her in. Would she have even been aware of the cold that must have slammed into her body with every step? How deep would she have gone before the lockkeeper saw her?

But she couldn't think about that now. She had to think of Rachel. Turning to her daughter, she asked, as gently as she could, what was going on.

With her eyes on the water, Rachel said, 'It's a big step. Moving away. Lots to think about.'

Nothing followed, so Lillian said, feeling her heart lift a little in hope, 'You know, it's fine if you're not ready. You can defer. Stay at home for another year while you think it over—'

Of course this was the answer! Rachel should delay her departure. It had been staring her in the face all along!

'But I *want* to be ready. I want to be ready *now*.'

Lillian sat on her hands. She wondered if this was going to be one of those circular conversations in which she tried to draw conclusions from her daughter but Rachel brought everything back to where they'd begun.

Rachel patted the back of her neck. *One, two, three*. Then she said, 'Dad said this thing about needing to understand your past if you want to move on with your present.'

This was so outlandish that Lillian let out a laugh. But Rachel frowned.

Lillian said, 'Sorry. That just doesn't sound like something your father would say.'

'He's been seeing a counsellor.'

Lillian blinked. Perhaps this wasn't going to be one of those circular conversations after all. 'Your father is seeing a *counsellor?*'

'Uh-huh. He likes it.'

'But what's wrong with him?'

'Nothing. It's actually a thing people do now?'

'Is he having a mid-life crisis?'

'Does he have to be?'

'Christ.'

'He said I should talk to you, actually.'

'What about?'

'He said you had counselling, too, once. He said you had some . . . mental-health problems, and you saw a doctor.'

Lillian's thoughts were racing to keep up with the words that seemed suddenly to have stained the air. She'd assumed Rachel's father would have kept his mouth shut. It was what he usually did, after all.

She said, 'Your father had absolutely no right to tell you that. Not without talking to me first.'

'He thought I knew.'

Lillian pushed herself up from the bench and walked to the place where the earth met the lip of the river. She dragged the toe of her sandal through the mud, wetting her foot. How many stones had Winnie crammed into her pockets? Had she planned the whole thing, stashing piles of them somewhere, so she'd be ready? Or had she just made do with what was near by?

'Mum? Dad did apologise. He seemed surprised that we hadn't talked about it.'

It wasn't that Lillian minded people knowing. It was that she minded her daughter knowing. If Rachel knew about Lillian's *mental-health problems*, as she'd put it, then Rachel might also begin to understand what obstacles were in her own way. How easy it was, as a girl, as a woman, to stumble. Lillian had been determined that her daughter wouldn't have to contend with any of it. Unlike her, Rachel wouldn't have to be a good girl (though she was). She wouldn't have to be thin (though she was). She wouldn't have to fear leaving her childhood home (though perhaps that's what this was about).

Rachel came to stand quietly by her side. On the opposite bank, a lone fisherman sat still beneath the shade of his umbrella.

'He'll never catch anything,' Lillian pointed out. 'It's too hot.'

Rachel said, 'What Dad said didn't come as that much of a surprise—'

Lillian cut her off. 'I did have some problems. Everyone does! But it's all behind me now. And what's important is that you go and become a doctor.'

'A surgeon.'

'A surgeon. It's what you've always wanted, isn't it? To make people well?'

Rachel patted the back of her neck. 'You're not listening to me. We were talking about *you*—'

'But you said, just now – it's what you want. You *want* to do this, don't you?'

'I want to. But I'm afraid.'

'Of what?'

Rachel looked directly at her mother and Lillian saw panic in her eyes as she said, 'Of leaving you, Mum. I mean – will you look after yourself, when I'm away? Because I'm not sure you will.'

Lillian's heart caved in then.

She stood, motionless, for a few seconds. Rachel couldn't leave home because she was anxious about her. Just as she, Lillian, had been worried about her own mother. Had nothing changed? Would nothing ever change?

She touched her daughter's forearm, feeling the heat of her skin. 'I am so sorry,' she said.

Rachel nodded. She seemed to be holding her breath.

'So tell me,' Lillian said, as gently and carefully as she could, 'what I need to do to convince you that I'll be fine? Because I will, you know. You'll go away, and I'll be fine, because you'll always come back—'

'Isn't it bloody obvious?' asked Rachel. 'You need to start being honest with me. Opening up. So that I can understand. And so that I know you'll be OK when I'm not here. Because at the moment you do not seem OK.'

Lillian let go of her daughter's arm. 'What are you talking about?'

'I know you have a thing about food . . . and I get it, Mum – what woman doesn't? But whenever I try to talk about it you just fob me off with some platitude. *Things were different when I was your age, Rachel.* Or, *I got out of Abingdon and I never went back.* But I have no clue *why* you left.'

There was a pause.

Lillian wondered how long her daughter had carried this weight around. Had Rachel always known? Despite her care to cover the tracks of her own anxieties, had her daughter seen them all too clearly?

Then Rachel said, slowly and rather patronisingly, 'I appreciate it's not easy. But I need to know you'll be OK. I need to know you'll eat properly when I'm gone, at least. And, I mean, I'd like to support you.'

Lillian turned away, unable to look at Rachel's determinedly even expression for any longer. That expression had served her daughter well, Lillian knew. It had got her through many exams and difficult situations at school. It was what would make her a good medic. Lillian herself had been pleased when she realised that Rachel had this strength in her. But sometimes she hated it.

Rachel sighed. 'Will you at least think about it?'

Lillian dragged her sandal through the water again, letting the mud coat her bare toes. Her mother must have planned it, she thought. Had the pile of stones ready. If she'd been deliberate enough to pick her time – Friday teatime, so that Ernie would be visiting, as he'd said – then surely she would have planned other things. What to wear to give herself maximum weight. How many stones it would take.

Rachel said, 'I'd better get back.'

Lillian shook herself. Then she faced her daughter. 'You're not coming home?'

'I told you. I'm staying the week with Dad. I said I'd make dinner tonight.'

'You're *cooking*?'

Rachel had never cooked before. Not once.

With a little smile, Rachel said, 'Dad's teaching me. I've got to learn sometime, haven't I?'

Then she stooped slightly to peck her mother's temple, reminding Lillian of her superior height, said she'd be in touch, and walked away.

1966–1967

Following her refusal, Jim tried his best to pretend Lillian didn't exist. This wasn't easy. Whenever he spotted her shape at the opposite window he turned away, and if he saw her approaching in the street, he steeled his jaw, locked his gaze on the mid-distance, and crossed the road. Making a conscious decision to plough his energies into the brewery, he volunteered for overtime and began quizzing other suit-and-tie men on what it was they did, exactly. After he got off work, he often met Mick in The Crown, where he stuck to the story that Lillian had suddenly decided it was over, as she was sodding off to college. Mick raised his glass and proposed a toast to *all the other pretty creatures in the river.* Jim said he wasn't sure there were any pretty creatures in the river that ran through their town.

Every evening before bed, he sprinkled a pinch of fish food into Gene's bowl and relived the details of Lillian's refusal. She'd failed to say any more than, *I can't.* He'd knelt before her, clasping her knees and searching her face, but she'd only repeated the phrase. She hadn't even added an apology. Eventually he'd got to his feet and walked away, leaving her sitting on that log by the stream. He'd walked to the town where, with muddied trousers, he joined the early lunchtime crowd in The Crown and drank three whiskies, then allowed himself to weep quietly on the way home.

Ever since, the word that kept coming back to him was *Longbrook*. She'd said her mother had been in that place! What on earth had happened to Winnie? Lillian had gabbled something about her mother trying to drown herself by the weir, but Jim could hardly believe the woman would do such a thing when she had a baby to look after, so he dismissed it as an exaggeration. But. Longbrook! When he pictured it he saw endless corridors, barred windows, women in dirty clothes, rending their hair and howling.

So he tried not to think about it. He even tried to tell himself that he was better off: sometimes these things ran in families.

It was a couple of weeks before his mother asked why Lillian hadn't been round lately. She was washing up after Sunday lunch, and Jim was poised with the tea towel when she dropped Lillian's name into the conversation. He polished a couple of knives to a good sheen as he outlined a slightly different tale to the one he'd told Mick. The decision had been mutual, he said: they'd agreed to give things a rest, as Lillian was leaving for art school.

'She's a bit of an odd girl, I can't deny that. But you did seem happy,' his mother said. 'And, I'm sorry to say this, Jim, but to me you don't seem very happy now.'

He crossed the room and clattered the knives into the drawer, trying to work out how to respond. 'It's better this way,' he said.

His mother paused her scrubbing and turned to him. 'And you're letting her go that easily, are you?'

They stared at each other. Jim was uncomfortably aware of the crack in his voice as he said, 'There's nothing easy about it, Mum.'

She offered him a hot, sudsy hand, which it took him a moment to grasp. 'Oh, my poor boy,' she said quietly. 'You love her, don't you?'

In late June, Jim received a small promotion which meant a move to a more private office. He shared it with the large, untidy and often smiling Malcolm Jones, who was charged with the task of training Jim up to be a Junior Sales Manager. Two doors away, Pam Clarke carried out her secretarial tasks, many of which involved looking after Malcolm and the other Sales Manager, Dave Peasemarsh. Ever since Jim had failed to ask her to the do at the Corn Exchange, taking Lillian instead, Pam had been quiet with him, hardly catching his eye when he nodded in her direction. But on his first day in his new job, Pam fetched Jim a coffee, black with two sugars. She'd remembered that he never drank tea. 'So sophisticated of you,' she said, with a tinkle in her voice that Jim was unsure whether to interpret as fond teasing or dismissive barb. She'd arranged two Nice biscuits in the saucer, and as she stooped close to place the coffee before him, she asked if he needed anything else.

Jim, who'd been admiring the expanse of mahogany veneer that was his new desk, the shine of the telephone, the heft of his Rolodex, said that he couldn't think of anything at all.

Whenever he and Malcolm returned to the office after a sales meeting with a pub landlord, Pam would be there with his coffee. Jim liked reporting their successes to her, though he was careful to be only quietly confident when she asked how it had gone. 'Pretty good,' he'd say. 'We'll see. But I think we're in with a chance there.'

It was all a good distraction from the memory of that morning by the stream.

One afternoon, after he'd been in the new job about a month, he was late getting back to the office. He and Malcolm had sealed a deal with The Three Cocks in Gorsehill. Malcolm had already headed over the road to The Crown to celebrate, but Jim went back into the office to pick up his jacket; it had been a sweltering day and he'd left it hanging from his chair. As he walked down the corridor, he was surprised to spot Pam still behind her typewriter, and found himself calling to her, 'It's a done deal, Pam!'

She appeared in his doorway. 'I knew you'd do it!'

He couldn't help but smile. 'It was Malcolm, really . . .'

Pam shook her head. 'You're too modest by half.' Then she said, 'How about a little drop of something, to celebrate?'

Jim, already buoyed by the pint he'd had in The Three Cocks, agreed. Pam put her finger to her lips, closed Jim's office door, then pulled a bottle of Bell's and two sherry glasses from Malcolm's desk drawer. 'He'll never know,' she whispered.

How Pam herself knew, Jim didn't ask.

She filled the glasses. Jim held his aloft and proposed, 'To Morland.'

As he took a drink, he looked at Pam and remembered that she was attractive, with rounded cheeks and a dimpled smile. When he asked how Neville was doing, she pressed a hand to her chest, her silky orange blouse shifting under the pressure, and said, 'Your guess is as good as mine, Jim.'

This was uncharted territory. Jim had never asked Pam any personal questions at all, and the look on her face made him wish he hadn't now. Pressing her lips together, she said, 'He ended it. Said he just didn't have time for me at the moment.'

Jim tried not to glance at the clock on the wall, knowing it was already gone six.

Pam took another sip of whisky.

Jim said, 'He's busy working, I suppose.'

He hoped she'd agree and they could pass on to other subjects, but she gave an incredulous snort. 'Too busy with all his other girls, more like.'

Her breathing had become a little uneven, and her hand was still at the silkiness of her blouse, as though she were holding something back. Jim noticed she'd stuck a balled-up paper tissue just inside her cuff; a few strings of its damp material hung over her charm bracelet, and he guessed that she had spent at least some of this day, his day of triumph, in tears.

There was a pause, during which Jim wasn't sure whether he wished she wouldn't cry, or whether he hoped she would, so that he could at least try to relieve her distress. He knew he wanted Pam to feel better, and wished he had the power to make her do so. He attempted to think of something to say – something comforting but not too intimate. In the end, Pam saved him the trouble. Slotting the Bell's back in Malcolm's drawer, she offered him a sad smile. 'You know what would cheer me up, Jim?' she said. 'Some dancing lessons.'

'Pardon?'

'Only, there's this wedding I'm going to in a few weeks. A cousin. Neville will be there, and I can't help thinking, wouldn't it be great if he could see me gliding across the floor without a care in the world?'

Jim swallowed. 'That would really show him, Pam.'

'It would, wouldn't it?'

There was a pause, then she said, 'I don't suppose you'd teach me? Everyone says you're the best in town.'

Jim couldn't help but smile. 'I don't know about that—'

'Just a couple of lessons. I've got the basics.'

It was very hot, he realised, in the office. In order to escape across the road for another pint, he said, 'I don't see why not.'

She sniffed. 'Thank you, Jim,' she said, her voice wavering again. Then, from the doorway, she added, 'You know, I was always telling Neville I wished he was more like you.'

Jim sat for a while after that, patting his damp brow with a handkerchief and listening to the doors of the building slam shut, wanting to make quite sure Pam was gone before he ventured outside.

Many other men, including married ones, had their favourites at the office: women who provided comfort and reassurance while at work, and perhaps a few thrills beyond the domestic sphere. Women who made the men's days a little brighter, their working hours slightly shorter. Jim liked to think of it as a kind of dance, a flirtation, and also a working system. But he also understood that there were men who took it too far, whose wandering hands were known to the women. He found it all very unsavoury, but what could he, Jim, do about it?

He could be nice to Pam, he decided. He could at least do that.

And that was what he told himself he was doing, when he agreed to hold the lesson one lunchtime. Pam lived with her parents in a modern block of flats between the church and the brewery, so it would be convenient, she said. She didn't want to put Jim out. They could be done in half an hour and be back at work. Her father would be at the factory over in Cowley and her mother was on the check-out at the Co-op Monday and Thursday lunchtimes, so they'd have the place to themselves.

The morning of the lesson, she leaned across his desk and slid a piece of paper with her address on it in his direction, whispering that it would probably be better if they arrived separately so that people wouldn't get the wrong idea.

At lunchtime, he gave it five minutes before following Pam out of the office and across the courtyard, past the bottling hall and the line of trucks ready for that afternoon's deliveries. Jim was aware of Mick watching as he strode across the cobbles with his carrier bag of records, but he didn't pause to wave. He hurried out of the gate and along the lane, past the old brewery workers' cottages, and onto Pam's street.

The double doors into the block were open and he jogged up the concrete staircase, the smell of furniture polish and boiled veg becoming stronger when he reached her floor. The sound of the lunchtime news drifted from someone's radio. Outside Pam's door, which was slightly ajar, was a mat with the word 'Welcome' printed on.

As Jim pushed the door open, he suddenly became aware that anything at all might be behind it, and his stomach contracted. What was he doing at this woman's flat? And what was *she* doing in there? Undressing? Waiting for him on the bed, perhaps?

Then a fully clothed Pam appeared at the end of the hallway, a plate balanced on one hand. 'Sandwiches now,' she asked, 'or after?'

'There was no need.'

'It's just a few cheese and pickle.'

'Afterwards, then.'

Pam smiled and showed him into the front room, where she placed the plate on a low table. On the wall behind a ridged settee were several framed photographs of a man in fishing gear, holding up his catch. Pam caught Jim's eye and said, 'Dad's mad on carp.'

'No one else home?'

Pam shook her head. He held up his carrier bag. 'I brought some records.' He'd selected carefully: 'Perhaps, Perhaps, Perhaps' by Doris Day for a cha-cha and 'Moon River' for a waltz, in case they got that far. Making the selection the night before, he'd remembered that he hadn't danced with anyone since Lillian. He hadn't even listened to a record since she'd turned him down.

He deposited the bag on the armchair. 'We'll need a bit of space,' he said, and, without waiting for Pam's approval, he shunted the settee to the wall with his knees. 'We'll just walk it through, first.'

They stood opposite one another on the carpet. There was a wide window all along one wall of the room, through which the sun landed in a pool at their feet. He'd left his shoes on but he noticed, now, that Pam had removed hers; her painted toenails were visible through her stockings.

'All right, then,' he said. 'First we rock – one, two, three;

then we step to the side – one, two, three; then we close – one, two, three.'

She giggled as he went through it again, this time demonstrating. 'That *looked* easy,' she said.

'Have a go.'

She mirrored his movements, and he enjoyed having her watch him so closely. He could see straight away that she had it. 'You know that already,' he said.

'I told you I could do a bit.'

'Time for some music, then.' He put the record on, then took her hands in his and counted them in.

The song was different – he and Lillian had never danced to 'Perhaps, Perhaps, Perhaps' – but as he led Pam it was easy to imagine she was Lillian. Pam was a similar size and shape to Lillian, and Jim found himself closing his eyes, overwhelmed by the sensation of having her back with him. It was Lillian's hand he held, the small of Lillian's back he touched as they swayed – *cha, cha, cha* – and rocked on Pam's carpet. In an effort to distract himself he led Pam in an open promenade and then an underarm turn, thinking she would stumble. She performed perfectly, which made him drop her hand and clutch at his mouth. Pam asked if he was all right, and every part of Jim wanted to say yes. Instead, a small sob broke from his chest and he found himself leaning his head on her shoulder.

She gently rubbed his back.

'Sorry,' he said.

'No need to be.'

She didn't ask him what the tears were about, though Jim had a suspicion she knew well enough. She kissed him lightly on the cheek, once, and when she did it again he turned his face and found her lips. They stood in the puddle of light, kissing. He didn't know if he was kissing Pam merely to overcome his embarrassment, or to make it up to her in some way; he only knew that the kiss eased his pain, so much so that Jim didn't want it to stop, and soon he was leading her to the ridged settee. She said no one would be back for hours, so he slid a hand up her skirt and found her soft thigh, and she lay back and let him do with her all the things that he'd long dreamed of doing with Lillian.

That summer, they escaped to Pam's flat most lunchtimes. When she produced a plate of sandwiches and balanced them on Jim's naked stomach with a laugh, they devoured them and Jim thought nothing had ever tasted so good. He didn't invite her to the pictures or even to go dancing – her cousin's wedding was never again mentioned, and he wondered if she'd invented it. But at the weekend he found himself looking forward to Monday, when he might spend his lunch hour with Pam. They didn't bother with the dancing, going straight to the settee. What he loved most of all was the feeling of just *feeling*.

At work, Pam was very discreet. When she fetched his coffee she often placed an extra biscuit on his saucer, but that was the only sign of her ardour. Jim himself would have liked to open her collar and plant a kiss on her neck, right there in the corridor, but she never seemed to linger long enough for him to do so. While he flipped through his Rolodex, he fantasised about bending her over Malcolm's leather chair and sliding into her.

But the extra biscuit was all he got, in the office.

During these weeks, he was able to let Lillian fade into the background of his thoughts. Still, he deliberately looked away from her house when walking out of his gate. He also took to cycling everywhere, so he would be able to pass her without pause, should she spot him. And he asked no questions about her, even when his mother mentioned that she'd seen Lillian in the town, and wasn't she looking slim these days? He reassured himself with the thought that, any day now, Lillian would be enrolled at her art school and safely out of both his and his mother's sight.

When, after they'd made love one lunchtime in early September, Pam turned to him and said she thought she might be expecting, there was a part of Jim that was relieved. Now he could be who he knew himself to be: strong of heart and always responsible. He sat up, pulling down his shirt. Then he reached for Pam's blouse and held it out so she could put it on. He heard himself telling her that everything would be all right, and they'd better get married, now, hadn't they?

Tears came to her eyes, then, and Jim put his arms around her, finding it enormously comforting to comfort her.

Lillian sat and passed her exams, but school no longer seemed very important. That summer, her only task was to keep her mother alive.

She no longer went walking by the river, fearful of catching even a glimpse of the weir. Before her mother woke, she headed in the opposite direction, past Northcourt Farm and out over the fields towards Sunningwell village. Winnie was subdued and often in bed early, and the pill bottles remained on her bedside table, but she did keep working. Though Ernie hadn't managed to persuade the Dairy they should take her back on, he'd sorted out another cleaning shift for her at the Pav. Every Friday he came round for his tea – the only meal Winnie made, now.

Once she didn't leave the house early enough, and saw Jim wheeling his bike out of his gate. She froze on her doorstep, hoping he'd look over. Just as she was raising a hand, he pedalled off, as though she were completely invisible. For a second she felt sick. Then she admonished herself. Well, what had she expected? She was the one who'd rejected him. She'd have to get used to it.

One Saturday at the salon, she received a letter, which she opened while she was alone in the back room.

Dearest Lillian,

I've written to you many times over the years and it shames me to say I've never had the courage to send those letters. But I cannot be silent about this. Ernie tells me you have won a place at art school.

This is wonderful, and you should take it up. I know you'll be worried for your poor mother, but you cannot live your life for her.

Please don't mention this letter to Ernie, who would accuse me of meddling.

Daphne

She folded it and kept it in the pocket of her tabard, turning over its contents in her mind as she swept the floor, hung up coats, washed hair and made tea. What was Daphne up to? Who did she think she was? Perhaps she meant well, but Ernie would be right to accuse her of meddling. It was the term 'poor mother' – Lillian remembered Jim's mother using the same words with pity and condescension – that finally made her screw the thing up and toss it in the bin, along with the piles of cut hair she'd collected in her dustpan.

As soon as she arrived home, she wrote to Professor Goring, explaining that she regretted she was unable to take up her place due to unforeseen circumstances. It seemed the only possible thing to do.

But one afternoon, after taking Winnie some tea and toast, she went into her bedroom and indulged herself in packing her suitcase, as if she were getting ready to leave. She looked about the room: what would she take with her? She'd once been proud of the doll made of shells that she'd bought on her Sunday School outing to Southsea. Now it stood dusty on the sill. Her *Picturegoer* annuals – which she'd spent hours poring over as a little girl – were piled, long unopened, on the shelf. Eventually she selected her tangerine dress and the book on Van Gogh that Gwen, who was leaving to study English Literature at York University in a few weeks' time, had said she should keep, together with a photograph of her three-year-old self sitting in her mother's lap on a picnic blanket in the Abbey

Meadow. The sun had bleached half of her mother's face, but Lillian was clearly reaching out, one hand and arm blurred. 'You never sat still,' Winnie would say fondly whenever they looked at the photo together. 'Always wanting to get hold of the blessed machine.'

Lillian tucked the photo into the pages of the Van Gogh book. Then she closed the case, sat on the mattress and allowed herself to wonder what it might be like if her mother was dead. What if she were to wake up tomorrow and Winnie had simply stopped breathing? She could take Daphne's advice. She could pick up that suitcase and do as she liked. Get on the bus to London. Or anywhere at all. She could be whoever she wanted to be. She could be free. Perhaps, once she was in London, she could invite Jim to meet her in some coffee bar. She would wear the tangerine dress. Away from the town, he might begin to understand that she was happy in her new life. He might even want to be a part of it.

It took only a few seconds, though, for Lillian to begin to feel the crushing weight of her imagined loss. Appalled by herself, she shoved the case beneath her bed and took her mother another round of tea and toast.

At the salon, Phyllis said business was booming and offered her more hours if Lillian agreed to train up as a full-time hairdresser. She could be on ten pounds a week, with tips, by Christmas. Plenty for the Regal and whatever else she fancied.

Lillian tried to focus on Phyllis's lessons in rolling, trimming and blow-drying, telling herself that this was artistic, too. The heads she coiffed were not unlike sculptures, and it was up to her to produce something of beauty, even with the most unpromising raw materials.

One afternoon, while she was giving a new customer a trim, she overheard Mrs French filling Phyllis in on the latest about Dolly James, the woman Mrs Shepherd had said was in Longbrook.

'I hear she's back home,' said Mrs French.

Lillian heard herself asking, 'What was wrong with her, exactly?'

Phyllis and Mrs French exchanged looks.

'It was her nerves, dear,' said Mrs French.

Lillian wanted to ask, *But what does that mean?*

'She's home now; that's what matters,' said Phyllis.

'Did they cure her, though?' Lillian asked.

Mrs French licked her lips. 'Well, she's home. But I dare say she'll never be the same.'

Lillian was about to ask how Mrs French knew this when Phyllis said, 'How about we put a cream rinse on today, Mrs French? I think it'll do wonders,' and led her to the sinks.

Work meant that she didn't see much of Gwen over the summer, but the night before her friend left for university, Lillian went to Park Road and spent the evening sitting in the kitchen.

After a glass of sherry each, Gwen asked, 'Can't you just tell your mother you're going to art school, and that's it?'

'Maybe I should've married Jim Shepherd,' Lillian said.

Gwen pulled a face. 'He seems sweet enough. But he's so . . . I don't know. Orderly.'

So am I, thought Lillian, looking into her lap. That's what I am. Not mysterious or dynamic, but *orderly*.

'Maybe you could marry some rich old man!' Gwen said. 'One of those tycoons who just, you know, want something lovely to look at. You'd have your own private flat in London. Then I could come and visit.'

'Would I be part of the Jet Set?'

'You'd be *beyond* the Jet Set.' Then Gwen looked serious. 'Promise me you'll try, though?' she said. 'To go to art school?'

Lillian considered telling her friend, then, about her mother and Longbrook. Despite her fears, she would just say it. *Begin anywhere*, she told herself. But when she opened her mouth, what came out was, 'I'll miss you.'

'I know you will,' said Gwen.

With Gwen gone, Lillian decided it was time to face Jim. She wouldn't put up with him ignoring her. Instead, she would tell him that she wasn't going to art school and was staying in Abingdon. She'd apologise for hurting him and say that she hoped they could at least be friends. There was no need for them to avoid one another! She wasn't sure they'd be able to pick up where they'd left off, exactly, but she thought perhaps Jim might begin to forgive her refusal. He was a generous man. A kind man. She allowed herself to imagine dancing with him again. After all, Jim must hate being without a dancing partner. If she could position herself in his arms and allow him to lead her across the floor, things would surely develop.

It was a Sunday afternoon. The morning's rain had eased and steam was rising from the road. Lillian peeled off her cardigan and let the sun warm her shoulders as she crossed the street to Jim's, picturing herself falling into his arms. She would have to say that what she'd meant by *I can't* was *I might*. She felt her heart lift. They would be dancing together again in no time.

She rushed down his path and rounded the corner of the house. She would remind him who she was: Lillian Wells, who had no need to knock on the front door. His Lovely Lillian, who could march up the alleyway and let herself in the back way.

She glanced up at the kitchen window as she passed, and returning her gaze through the glass was a young woman. Lillian paused. It took a second to remember Pam from the brewery dance, and when she did she stood and stared. Pam's mouth had fallen open, too. A moment of utter confusion unfolded. How could Pam be in Jim's house? But in the time it took for Pam to fill the kettle, twist off the tap and turn her back on Lillian, everything became clear. While Lillian wasn't looking, Pam Clarke had entered Jim's house through the back door.

She was no longer Jim's Lovely Lillian, and there would be no more dancing.

She turned and fled back to number 25.

Not long after that, her mother informed her that Jim was married. 'Shotgun job,' Winnie said. 'His secretary, apparently.'

'He doesn't have a secretary,' Lillian responded. 'She's more of a general typist.'

Winnie raised her eyebrows. 'Well, she's his wife, now.'

Though the wedding was arranged in haste, to Jim's surprise, his mother seemed pleased. One Sunday afternoon, Pam had visited the house and taken an interest in the dahlias. Afterwards, mother and son sat together in the back garden, the rooks squabbling on the rooftops, and Mrs Shepherd said, 'She's on our wavelength.' Then she told him that she'd dreamed of a child. 'She was down the bottom of the garden, by those gooseberry bushes!' she said, patting his arm. 'Imagine it! Just like my mother told me, when I asked where babies came from!' She giggled, almost girlish. 'Oh, don't take any notice of me, Jim. I'm going batty.' But in the next breath, she added, 'Pam's a *marvellous* girl.'

In his front room on the morning of the ceremony, Jim presented a royal-blue tie to Mick, who was to be his best man. They'd been drinking in The Crown the night before, and Jim's eyes were gritted, his stomach roped.

Mick stretched the tie between his hands. 'You know,' he said, 'it's not too late to change your mind.'

Jim, who was squinting into the mirror above the fireplace to knot his own tie, hesitated. Mick's expression was serious, and Jim remembered that day in the brewery yard when he'd told his friend he was in love. Mick was the only person he'd ever told, he realised. He hadn't even told Lillian herself.

'What are you talking about?' Jim said.

'You could do a flit.'

Now Jim laughed.

'I've got a mate,' Mick continued, 'up in Coventry. He'd get you a job in the brewery there. You could just . . . disappear. Stay with him for a bit.'

Jim flipped the end of his tie twice over and through the knot, tightening it into the crease of his collar. 'Don't be a daft bugger,' he said eventually.

'Well, if you're sure this is what you really want—'

Jim looked Mick in the eye. 'Isn't it about time you grew up?' he said, louder than he'd intended. 'People don't do *flits*. They stay where they are and they face things. That's what they do. Now put that bloody tie on. We're going to be late.'

No more was said, but throughout the ceremony Jim was aware of Mick's face, pink and slightly raw-looking, as though it had been slapped.

After the wedding, Jim and Pam lived with his mother until December, when a house came up along the road. Number 6. His mother visited them there on Christmas Eve, bringing with her a bag full of treats and the news that Lillian was still working in the salon. She'd been told by Phyllis that Lillian had got a full-time job instead of becoming a student. As his mother related this to Jim, unpacking the box of Viscount biscuits and the tins of mandarins she'd bought with her Co-op dividends, she beamed. 'The girl's come to her senses!'

'What's that supposed to mean?' Jim asked.

'She always did have ideas above her station.' Mrs Shepherd grimaced. 'And look what's come of it. A job as a hairdresser.'

'What's wrong with being a hairdresser?'

'I'm just saying, Jim, that you're a married man with a promotion. And she's given all that up to work there.'

Jim opened his mouth to tell his mother Lillian Wells was so much better than that; that she deserved more than a suit-and-tie man like him; that she should have left Abingdon for art school; that she was too beautiful, too clever, too complete a human being for his mother even to *comprehend*, then he shut it. He knew that if began to speak of Lillian, he might never stop.

After a moment, he said, very slowly, 'Let's not mention Lillian Wells ever again.'

Mrs Shepherd patted his hand and said, 'Good idea.'

One January evening, Lillian arrived home from the salon to the smell of her mother's home-baked cherry cake. It sat, fragrant and glistening, on the table. Lillian's mouth watered. As she bent to inhale the cake more deeply, her mother's voice came from behind.

'That's for you,' Winnie said. 'Because you're my rock.'

Straightening up, Lillian saw her mother standing in the doorway. To her astonishment, Winnie was wearing lipstick, a tight skirt and a fussy blouse. On her feet were the peep-toe shoes bought by Maurice, and her beehive was taller than it had been for some time.

'You look nice,' Lillian said, watching as her mother fetched her good handbag with the silver clasp from the cupboard. Into it Winnie dropped a compact and a comb. She then opened her purse and shook it, peering into its emptiness. 'Lend us a few bob, would you?' she said. 'I'm off out.'

Lillian was so surprised by this statement that it took her a moment to ask where.

'Pub,' said Winnie.

Lillian, shocked, didn't respond.

'Well,' Winnie said, 'it's Saturday night, ain't it?'

Lillian asked, 'But what about tea? I was thinking we could have those sausages.'

Winnie, swaying slightly on her heels, approached and touched her daughter's shoulder. 'I'll get a cheese roll down The Anchor,' she said softly. 'Why don't you get some of that cake down you and go out yourself? It's not good, a young girl like you being at home all the time.'

Lillian looked at the cake and then back to her mother, still catching up with what was going on. Was she actually *going out*?

Winnie clucked her tongue and smiled. 'You're not still mooning over that Jim Shepherd, are you?'

Lillian let out an exasperated noise. 'If you remember,' she said, 'it was me who said no to him, not the other way about.'

Winnie studied her. 'Why on earth *did* you turn him down? I've never understood it. Such a steady bloke.'

Lillian gaped in disbelief. 'Mum, how can you even ask me that?'

'Sorry, love?'

'How can you ask me that?'

Winnie looked bewildered.

'I couldn't leave *you*!' Lillian cried.

She knew there was more to it than that, but it felt good to release her anger, to blame someone, and good to see her mother, in that fancy blouse and those high heels, shrink in pain and confusion.

'Is that what you think?' Winnie asked quietly.

'How could I go and get married when you wouldn't get out of bed?' Lillian was shouting now. 'Who else would've made sure you were still bloody breathing?'

A long silence followed, during which Winnie clasped her purse shut and slotted it into her handbag. 'Well,' she said, 'I'm sure I'm very sorry to be such a burden to you.' She turned on her heel. 'Don't eat all of that cake. And don't wait up.'

After her mother had left, Lillian took off one shoe and threw it against the door.

Most evenings that week, Winnie went to the pub while Lillian sat on the settee, telling herself she should be happy that her mother was up and about. But she couldn't help feeling betrayed. If her mother had decided to live again, where did that leave *her* life?

She passed the time by writing to Gwen. Since leaving for university, Gwen's letters had been sporadic, but they were always full of new language. York wasn't London, she wrote, but it was a blast. She had digs in town now, and she'd met tons of men who wanted to sleep with her, but they were mostly creeps. There was a particularly dreamy one named Terry who she was doing her best to avoid because his reputation preceded him. Mostly, though, she wrote about her new friend, Sheena. Sheena was so inspiring, and Lillian would adore her, Gwen wrote, but Lillian felt only a stab of envy towards Sheena, who, according to Gwen, was probably going to start a revolution. She wrote for a radical magazine. Gwen suspected that sometimes Sheena slept with Terry, but only, she added, for kicks.

In her letters, Lillian tried to be similarly chatty and upbeat, to fill her friend in on the goings-on in the salon. A new girl, Rita, had arrived. She had a habit of talking over the customers, and was always trying to get Lillian to the Regal with her on a Friday night. Lillian found herself writing the line, *I haven't forgotten about art school*, but on rereading it decided it sounded too grandiose, and started again.

One night, after arriving home around eleven, Winnie sat on Lillian's bed and drew her in for a tight hug. Lillian, who'd been attempting to read, despite straining to hear evidence of her mother's return, bristled. But Winnie was warm; her cheek powdery; she smelled of hair lacquer and stout, and eventually Lillian's shoulders relaxed a little. When Winnie said, 'You know I appreciate everything you do, don't you, love?' Lillian balled her fists, digging her nails into her palms to stop herself crying out in frustration, and also relief.

It was very nearly an apology.

The following week, Lillian agreed to Rita's suggestion of

a Saturday night at the pictures, meeting her on the steps of the Regal. The night was damp and chilly. Lillian wore her old duffel coat from school, and had the red scarf Gwen had given her wrapped several times around her neck. When Rita saw Lillian, she asked, with a fond shake of her head, 'Why are you dressed like a blimmin' student?' Before Lillian could answer, Rita looped an arm through hers and led her up the steps.

Gambit was playing. Lillian hadn't been to the pictures since things had finished with Jim, and felt a rush of joy at the sound and colour of the film, but Rita kept glancing round the auditorium, keeping Lillian abreast of who'd just arrived and who was canoodling in the back row. She'd bought a bag of Revels which she ate noisily, spitting the peanuts into a hankie after sucking off the chocolate and assuring Lillian, who'd refused all her offers of a sweet, that they would have chips later.

After the film, Rita and Lillian were pushing through the crowd in the foyer when Rita yanked on Lillian's upper arm, hard, and hissed in her ear, 'Over there! Look who's ogling you!'

Standing by the lit kiosk was Jim's friend Mick Harries. He was wearing a maroon sweater and had a tweed overcoat slung across his arm. He was, of course, still handsome, his lips full like a girl's and his dark hair curling up at the neck of his sweater. As he made his way over, Lillian suppressed an urge to laugh at the serious intent in his hooded eyes.

Rita nudged her. 'Making. A. Beeline.'

'The gorgeous young Lillian,' Mick said. 'I've been hoping to bump into you.'

'Well, now you have.'

His brow furrowed in an amused frown. 'But you look sad. Where's that beautiful smile gone?'

For Lillian, *beautiful* was something of a magic word. No one had ever applied it to her – not even Jim, who'd often said she was pretty, lovely and smashing, but never *beautiful*. It seemed a word he reserved for dances, landscapes and Elizabeth Taylor.

She looked Mick in the eye and asked, 'Did you like the film?'

He shrugged. 'I liked Shirley MacLaine.'

Rita interjected, 'I *loved* Michael Caine.'

Mick didn't take his eyes off Lillian as he replied, 'I'm sure he loved you too.'

Rita ejected a humourless *huh* and tugged on Lillian's sleeve. 'We'd best get to Windsor's before they run out.'

'See you again, then,' Mick called, grinning, as Rita pulled Lillian towards the exit.

Winnie's better mood continued. She still went to the pub most evenings. She also rekindled the tradition of an end-of-the-week-treat from Trotman's, which Lillian ate instead of dinner. When Ernie asked why she'd left most of what was on her plate, her mother said, 'She's reducing. You men don't know what us girls have to go through,' to which Ernie shrugged and helped himself to Lillian's food.

One evening they were sitting side by side watching *Coronation Street* when Winnie said, 'That man there looks just like my friend Ron.'

Lillian glanced across at her mother. 'Who's Ron?'

'Just a bloke who sometimes buys me a drink down The Anchor.'

The man on the screen was cradling a pint while raising his eyebrows at the new blonde barmaid. Lit by the glow of the television, Winnie gave a thoughtful *hmm* and said, 'Oh, he *does* put me in mind of Ron.'

Lillian heard the hope in her mother's voice. Winnie spoke that name as though it were not shared by the many thousands of Rons all over the country, but something quite unique and precious.

★

A few days later, Mick Harries was waiting for Lillian after work. He was standing beneath the striped awning of Hedges' butcher's shop, sucking on his cigarette and squinting down the street. He kept his hands jammed in his pockets as he announced, 'I've come to take you for a drink.'

Winnie would be out by now. At home, Lillian would have to lay a fire herself and eat alone.

'All right,' she said. Her mother had decided to live, and so, she thought, should she.

Mick smiled and walked briskly ahead, leaving her to follow the small clouds of smoke trailing after him. Like running after a train, she thought, noticing the width of his shoulders and the way his neck was pinking in the cold of the January evening. On the market square he paused and looked over his shoulder. 'Get a move on,' he said, holding out a hand, which she took. His fingers were warm and they clasped hers tightly. Lillian pressed down a memory of dancing along this same street with Jim, reminding herself that he was a married man now.

Even at this time, there was a gurgle of chatter in The King's Head and Bell. Mick pointed to the snug, where the fireplace was large enough to stand in and a couple were sitting by the window, sharing a bag of crisps while taking it in turns to sip one pint.

He bought her a rum and ginger wine, saying it would warm her cockles. She took a large gulp. It was thickly sweet with a burning aftertaste.

'Good girl,' said Mick, which made her gulp down the rest and announce she wanted another.

Halfway through her second drink, a hot, liquidy feeling grew in Lillian's chest, and she said, 'My friend Rita told me to steer clear of you.'

'Did she now?'

'She said you *love 'em and leave 'em*.'

It was actually Jim who'd said this, but Lillian didn't want to mention his name.

Mick hid his smile in his pint. Then he said, 'Do you want to know what my friends say about you?'

She'd been enjoying playing the game of being the cheekily flirtatious one, but now she floundered. 'Not really,' she said, gazing into the fireplace.

He leaned close to her. 'They say you're an *enigma*,' he said, his nose almost in her ear. 'And I have to say that I agree.'

She was reminded of Miss Hardy's words about her artwork – *mysterious*, *dynamic* – and also of her own estimation – *orderly* – and she kissed him on the mouth. It took a moment for him to respond, but when he did the liquidy feeling spread all along her jaw, down her spine and into the place between her legs.

'Let's get out of here,' he whispered.

Outside, cold air slapped her face and she swayed, realised she was drunk, and laughed out loud. Mick laughed too, swept an arm about her shoulders, and propelled her over the road. 'Off we go,' he said. 'This way to paradise.'

As they walked across the flags beneath the Town Hall, her limbs seemed to move faster than her brain and she stumbled. 'You're all right,' Mick said. 'Hang on to me.' She did as he suggested, aware of the strength of his arm, the grip of his fingers around her ribcage, very close to her breast, as he scooped her along. Feeling as though her feet were barely brushing the pavement, she made a decision: she would sleep with this man. She was nineteen, and had waited long enough, and, she thought, if she slept with Mick something essential within her might change. She might become what he said she was: enigmatic. She might forget all about dancing with Jim Shepherd. She might find it easy to tell her mother she had to try for Camberwell again. Or some other art school. Now that Ron was on the scene she might be free to go.

It was cold inside his flat. Rita had informed her that Mick's father had not long moved out, taking up with his fancy woman across town, but Lillian was still taken aback by the fact that it was just the two of them. No lights on, no fire in the grate. She perched on the settee, listening to him crashing crockery in the kitchen.

He appeared with two steaming mugs, which he placed on the floor before sitting beside her. Nescafé, like at Gwen's house. Feeling very small next to his big body, she took a sip of the scalding coffee. It was improved by the sugar Mick had added.

'You're all alone here?'

'Not now.' His arm was around her neck and he kissed her on the nose, then the cheeks – one, two. Tobacco and soap. 'Let's take this off,' he said, unbuttoning her coat. She shrugged it from her shoulders and he slid a hand down her back and into the waistband of her trousers, his fingers inching past her knicker elastic. Her pulse jumped, and as his hand went lower a sound came from her. Though she still had the sensation of her brain being slow to catch up with her vision, everything sharpened as Mick pulled her jumper over her head and put his mouth to her side.

Up until that moment, she'd felt herself a little removed from the scene. *This is me*, she'd thought, *losing my virginity to handsome Mick Harries in his empty flat*. She'd been aware of the faint thump of music from someone's television in the room above, the smell of hair oil on the settee's antimacassar. But now her breathing thickened. Mick unbuttoned his shirt and shrugged it off, and she saw his skin, so pale it glowed, the pleasing curve that ran from his shoulders to his arms, and she found herself kissing his neck.

They stayed on the settee a long time, kissing, Mick undressed to the waist, Lillian in her bra, until he said, 'It's getting late.'

She glanced at her watch. A quarter to ten.

'I'd better walk you home.' He was slipping his arms back into his shirt.

She blinked at him. 'But I thought we—'

'Oh, yes,' he said. 'Yes. But we should wait. Shouldn't we?'

Lillian thought she might cry with the disappointment and the shame. Mick's voice was light with amusement as he said, 'It's better this way. Trust me. We don't want to have everything at once, do we?'

He kissed her on the hand and she managed to smile and nod, though that was exactly what she wanted. *Everything at once* was exactly it.

On Thursday, Mick was again waiting beneath Hedges' awning. It was icy on the pavements and he held her about the waist as they walked quickly to his flat. This time there was no drinking, and little talking. He lit the gas heater in the bedroom. A spider-plant hung from the ceiling, and it brushed her hair as she stood next to the bed, gazing at him. He undressed, and she kissed his white skin, grazing her teeth on his nipple, collarbone, neck, earlobe. When he reached into her waistband she helped him by undressing herself and climbing between the cool sheets.

Mick swallowed and said, 'Will you let me do something for you?'

Before she could reply, he drew the covers over his head and began kissing his way down her neck, breasts and belly. She tightened the sheet over her mouth and squeezed her eyes shut, not quite believing what he was doing. When he reached her pubic hair, he rearranged his body between her thighs. And then his mouth was on her, and she couldn't think of anything except the exquisite pressure building then releasing in a rush of pleasure.

When he'd finished, she lay panting, stunned by the way

Mick had enabled her to leave the room entirely. His smiling face bobbed back into view.

'Thank you,' she said.

When they weren't in bed, they went to the pictures. Like her, Mick would sit through anything, and if he liked something he'd watch it over and over. One Saturday they saw *One Million Years B.C.* twice in a row, and when they emerged into the dark the town felt unreal, its sounds muted and toneless, its colours rinsed grey. Sometimes they pretended they were in a film. Bringing her cups of coffee in his flat, Mick would provide a voice-over for the trailer: *It was a long, cold afternoon. A beautiful woman had just popped out for milk. How could she know what was waiting for her between her lover's sheets?* But it felt to Lillian that their games always ended once they were in bed, and what unfurled between them there became the joy of her life.

Then one murky Sunday in March, Winnie's friend Ron came for tea.

It was Lillian's job to make the trifle, and she spent a pleasant half an hour heaping cold Bird's custard and sterilised cream on the jelly. She ran a fork through the cream to make a wavy pattern, thinking all the time of Mick's fingers trailing her back and belly after they'd made love. She'd been to his flat twice that week, telling Winnie that she was going to the Regal with Rita, and was planning to go again that evening. It seemed simpler to keep Mick to herself. If she wanted her own life, she might have to keep it from her mother. She remembered Winnie's warning about not repeating her mistake with Maurice by *falling for some charmer and getting yourself in trouble*. But Mick was always prepared, telling her they could avoid any 'little mishaps' with the French letters he used.

Standing at the nets, watching Ron prop his bicycle against the wall, Lillian murmured, 'He hasn't got a car.'

Winnie raised her eyebrows. 'Can't I enjoy myself?'

Lillian was in a good mood, so she said, 'Of course you can,' and she kissed her mother's cheek.

Winnie smiled. 'Will I do?' she asked, doing a little twirl to show Lillian her new frock.

'Knock-out,' said Lillian.

Ron came in the back door without knocking – *Already*, Lillian thought – and Winnie took his coat and hat, handing them to Lillian. Though both items were smart and un-darned, there was a whiff of mothballs about them.

Winnie had laid out a cold tea: slices of luncheon meat, home-made Scotch eggs, pickled onions. Ron rubbed his hands. 'Looks like a feast, love,' he said, and Lillian saw her mother blush.

At the table, Winnie exclaimed over the length of Ron's limbs, marvelling that he was too big for their little room. 'Not a bit of it,' said Ron, looking pleased as Winnie heaped his plate with food. 'This place has more than enough room for me.' Lillian took a few celery sticks and some crackers and ate in silence, her mind still on her lover's bed with its cool sheets and shaded lamplight. Her lover. She smiled to herself at the thought of that word.

Holding up a pickled onion, Ron glanced around the room and said that a bit of new wallpaper would really cheer the place up. He knew someone, he added, at Aubrey Smart's, and could get them a good deal. He could even paste it up for them, one weekend.

'That would be lovely!' said Winnie. 'Wouldn't it, Lillian? You get fed up, waiting for the council to do it.'

Ron crunched on his pickle. 'Unless you'd like to do it,

Lillian? Being a painter and all? You could get your brushes out, couldn't you?'

For what seemed like the first time, Ron looked her full in the face. She noticed a blob of butter on his moustache.

'I'm not really that kind of—' she began.

But he cut her off. 'Just pulling your lovely leg,' he said, a gleam in his eye. 'You don't mind, do you? You're not a girl who can't take a joke?'

'Of course she isn't,' said her mother, rising to clear the plates.

Lillian said she would help, but Winnie pressed her shoulder and insisted she stay put.

When they were alone, Ron fixed her with a stare and said, very quietly, 'Your mother tells me you turned a good man down not long ago.'

She swallowed, trying to think of a way to respond.

Ron continued, 'No need to look so shocked. Your mother does tell me things, you know.' He planted his elbows on the table. 'It's your business, of course, who you marry. But I want you to know that should you have any . . . *misgivings* about that whole issue, your Uncle Ron is here to help.'

'Misgivings?'

He gave a small smile. 'What I'm saying is, sometimes it takes a man of the world to show a girl what's what.'

Something pressed into her knee and she yelped and pulled her leg away, but the something caught her knee and held fast. There was a pause, then, while she tried to understand what was happening. Why was Ron grinning at her as though they were sharing some kind of secret joke?

'There are some things,' he said, his fingers now on her inner thigh and reaching higher, 'you can't share with your mother.'

Lillian leapt from her seat. In her hurry to escape the room she collided with Winnie, who was carrying the trifle. 'I almost dropped your masterpiece!' said her mother, regaining her balance. Then, seeing Lillian's face, she said, 'Whatever is it, love? You look like you've seen a ghost.'

Lillian stood, staring at her in silence.

'Lillian? What's happened?'

'He touched me. Under the table,' Lillian said. 'He tried to—'

Lillian heard Ron speak in a flat, bored tone. 'I patted her knee, that's all.'

'He put his hand,' Lillian said, as steadily as she could, 'on my thigh.'

'Whatever are you on about?' Winnie's voice was incredulous, but a look of doubt passed over her face as she glanced at Ron. 'Ron? What's she on about?'

Then Ron was on his feet, his hands on her mother's shoulders, and Lillian dropped her eyes to the trifle.

'Now,' he said, with a laugh, 'this is all a storm in a teacup. I think what we have here is a little case of daughterly jealousy.'

Winnie eyed Lillian. There was a quiver in her voice as she said, 'Is that what this is about, love?'

Ron said, 'Must be difficult for her, seeing her mother so happy with a man when it's been just the two of you all this time.'

Lillian focused on the lines she'd made on the top of the trifle. They were almost perfect.

'Don't be too hard on her, Winnie,' Ron was saying. 'It's understandable, when a girl has such an attractive mother. She's bound to feel a bit put out.'

Lillian backed away from them both. Winnie called her name, but she grabbed her coat and was out of the door, running for Mick's flat.

★

She'd been used, of course, to the unbidden touches of men. On the bus to Oxford, there were often men who, when it was busy (or even when it wasn't), stood too close, bumping their groins against her spine, or brushing any soft part of her with a hand. She'd learned long ago that it was fatal to react: if you turned to face them and tried to scold, either they'd wink and say it was an accident or they'd accuse you of being an uptight cow. In the public library, there'd been a youngish man in a striped blazer who'd asked her if she knew where the play scripts were – he was searching for something by George Bernard Shaw. Delighted to have appeared like someone who would know such a thing, Lillian had led him to the corner stack, where he'd smirked and reached across her for the Shaw, letting his fingertips brush her breasts. She'd whacked his arm with the book in her hand and got away, but he'd only laughed and called out after her, 'I like them with a bit of spunk.'

She'd assumed, though, that she was safe in her own house. She'd also hoped that losing her virginity would somehow help her deal with the leers, the brushes, the grabs; perhaps once she'd been touched in a way she liked, in a way she'd *invited*, she might be able to shrug off the other sort of attention. In fact, as she steamed across the bridge to Mick's flat, her outrage only increased: now she understood there was this other kind of touching, she also understood what these men were doing when they squeezed, patted, lifted and grasped without permission. They were taking something from her. They were stealing.

But after Mick listened to what she said about Ron, he seemed to conclude that something had been stolen from *him*. Immediately, his face flushed a rude pink.

'What do you mean, he touched you?'

She blurted the words she couldn't have said to her mother. 'He almost had his hand in my bloody knickers!'

Mick inhaled. Closed his eyes. They were standing together in the hallway. She was still in her coat. She'd known that if she didn't say it straight away, she wouldn't say it at all. As it was, she was breathing unevenly, gripping her cuffs.

'Did you say anything?'

'Of course! He just denied it. Said I was jealous. And Mum just stared at me, like she couldn't believe a word I said.'

Then she knew: she wanted Mick to hit Ron. She wanted Ron pushed to the ground. She wanted that hand, that stealing hand, stamped on until it could never steal again. So she looked Mick in the eye and said, 'He was talking about how he could show me things only a man could.'

'Dirty fucking bastard,' said Mick. 'Stay here.'

Once he was gone, Lillian stood, looking out of his living-room window onto the stream and the houses beyond. It had begun to rain, large drops clattering on the panes. She paced the flat, sweeping toast crumbs from the kitchen table, drinking two glasses of water in order to avoid eating a biscuit, plumping the settee cushions.

He'd have reached number 25 by now. Gone round the back and called to Ron, who would've stridden to the door. Mick might invite him outside, and there, between the water butt and the coal bunker, his fist would meet Ron's face, breaking open his tobacco-stained skin. Ron was a tall man, but Mick was muscular, younger. The force of the second blow would knock Ron to his knees. There might be blood on the concrete path, a tooth spat onto Winnie's back step. Ron would stagger to his feet and Mick would bring a knee to his chest, felling him again. Winnie might come running, but it would be too late. Her man would have been taken apart, and it would serve him right. He was a thief – not only of that touch, but also of her mother.

★

She wasn't sure if she slept, exactly. Mick got back around eleven, the smell of The Crown on him, crept between the sheets and told her he'd 'dealt with it'. Then he promptly fell asleep. He took up most of the mattress and Lillian found herself clinging to the bed's edge, blinking into the darkness, imagining her mother's grief and rage at the sight of Ron's bloodied face. Mick didn't stir when she rose at six. She dressed quickly in the icy bathroom and let herself out of the flat. Though she had no wish to face her mother, she needed a change of clothes.

It was a damp morning and the scent of the brewery was heavy as she crossed the bridge and entered Mason Road. She had a good hour and a half before she'd need to get to work but still she hurried round the back of number 25, where she stopped. Propped against the wall was Ron's bicycle. Her heart jumped and her fists clenched. Clearly Mick had not done enough. There was no blood on the concrete slab between the coal bunker and the water butt. No splintered wood panels in the back door. No broken window panes. With her fingers on the back-door handle, she paused. She could be in and out before Ron rose. All the curtains were drawn; they would still be in bed. She could grab some clean clothes, retrieve her front-door key and her sketchbook and be out of there in minutes. Maybe she could leave a little message for Ron. A blob of spittle on his shoes. A smear of snot on his coat sleeve.

But when Lillian put her shoulder to the door it didn't move. She tried again, not quite believing she was locked out of her own home. It didn't budge.

She crept to the front of the house, where she toyed with the idea of knocking on the door. Across the road, Mrs Shepherd's curtains were already open. If she were to emerge, not only Jim but the whole street would know that Lillian had stayed out all night and had been locked out of the house by her mother.

There was nothing for it. Lillian shoved her hands into her pockets, kept her head down, and strode back to Mick's.

When he rose, he didn't seem surprised that she was in his kitchen, frying bacon and eggs. She'd made a pot of tea and had his plate warming under the grill. He stood behind her, hanging his arms on her shoulders, and yawned into her neck. 'You're still here.'

She scraped food onto the hot plate. 'Mum locked me out.'

His arms stiffened. 'She did?'

She turned to face him. 'What if she doesn't let me in again?' She was holding out the plate, the rim scalding her fingers, but he didn't take it. Instead, he thrust out an arm, dramatising his version of a husky-voiced film trailer. 'She was destitute, with nowhere to run, until *he* took her in . . .'

Lillian hung her head, and Mick gently took the plate from her and placed it on the table. 'Come back to bed,' he said, touching her elbow.

She sniffed. 'I've got to get to work.'

'Well, come back to bed when you get home.' He kissed her cheek then sat down to eat, concertina-ing strips of bacon onto his fork before dipping them into his egg yolk.

She moved to leave the room, but he reached for her hand. 'You can stay here as long as you want, you know,' he said. 'I like protecting you, Lilybud.'

It took only a few hours for Winnie to appear in the salon, carrying Lillian's suitcase.

Lillian understood from her mother's posture – shoulders high, body bundled into her best coat, hair stiff and upright – that she was in big trouble. She was finishing Mrs Mortimer's shampoo and set, and, balancing the mirror between flattened palms, was showing the woman the back of her head. Mrs Mortimer was reaching to touch her own skull, as if surprised that this part of her anatomy actually existed, when her mother bustled in, dropped the case and approached her daughter in three long strides. She grasped her by the shoulders, turning her so roughly that the mirror fell to the floor, where it smashed.

They both looked at the shards, which had skittered across the tiles into all corners of the salon.

Winnie grunted. 'Seven years,' she said, dropping her hands. 'Serves you right. You and your bully-boy boyfriend.'

Lillian opened her mouth to speak, but Winnie held up a hand. 'Ron's really opened my eyes to what's been going on. You've been mucking about with that Mick Harries behind my back. I know all about it! I told you, didn't I? I told you not to go falling for some charmer. If you get yourself in trouble you've only yourself to blame.'

'I'm not in trouble—'

'And then to go accusing Ron! When all he wanted was to help!'

'I was going to tell you about Mick—'

'Ron's poor face! He didn't deserve that. What were you thinking? What was *he* thinking?'

'I told Mick what Ron did. That's all.'

Her mother held her gaze for a long time, then sniffed, patted her hair, and said quietly and with great sadness, 'You always did overreact. You're too sensitive by half.'

After Winnie had stalked out of the shop, Mrs Mortimer picked up a sharp chunk of glass, handed it to Lillian, and said, 'That's just a superstition, dear. I wouldn't worry too much about it.'

In their new bed, Pam gave off so much heat Jim had to throw the covers from his own body. He lay listening to his breath, wondering if the rhythm of it matched Lillian's where she lay, not far up the street. Had she also woken, like him, from a dream of clawing her way out of the woods at the top of Wittenham Clumps? Often he rose at four in the morning, chastising himself for such thoughts, and went to sit downstairs with a cup of tea and yesterday's *Daily Mirror* in an attempt to escape them. As he flicked through the stories about wage freezes and the conflict in Aden, inhaling the new paint he'd slapped on all the skirting boards, he tried to turn his thoughts instead to the baby. Sometimes Pam guided his hand to her stomach, saying she could feel their child roll around, or kick, or even, she said, hiccup – though this idea seemed very fanciful to Jim. His fingers met her flesh a second too late, every time. 'Can't you feel it?' she'd ask, and he'd have to shake his head. A couple of times he pretended he could, just to please her.

When the baby was born in May, he saw how impossible it would have been to prepare for any of it. The sleepless nights, which went on and on; the drudgery of feeding and changing this helpless being who could do nothing by herself except breathe. In those first few months, Pam, confined to the house, grew pale, hollow-eyed, and often livid. She blamed him for the mess of her days. He was at least able to go to work, where her replacement, Jenny Cole, served him coffee. If Jim mentioned Jenny, Pam held up a hand and said she did not wish to hear one thing about the woman who had stolen her job and was now free to walk about the office all day as she pleased, picking up phones and typing out memos, chatting with other adult human beings, while she was stuck here on this bloody settee with only the baby for company.

Jim had been unprepared, too, for the love he felt for his daughter.

They called her Meg, after Pam's grandmother. It had been a long labour, during which Jim had become very familiar with the layout of the hospital, having walked around it so many times. Eventually he'd collapsed into a chair in the waiting room and dozed intermittently until he was called in by the Sister who'd told him to go home the previous morning. Or was it afternoon? Jim couldn't remember. On the ward, Pam, limp but smiling, handed him a bundle of flesh wrapped in a green blanket. Sister was right behind him, reminding him to support the head, and Jim held his breath, anxious about dropping it, but as soon as he saw the baby's face, wrinkled and topped with a tuft of soft black hair, he knew she was *his*. His daughter blinked back at him, her eyes reflecting his astonished gaze. She was his, yet she was also already herself. He almost gave a hoot at the wonderful shock of it, and it took him a moment to find his actual voice. 'Good grief,' he said softly. 'There you are.'

Lillian had slipped out of the salon during her lunch hour and was queuing at the Woolworth's delicatessen counter, where she was after a pie for Mick's tea. The shop was busy with women clutching nylon bags and children to their sides. This being a Saturday, there were also a few men, who were generally either studying the packets of seeds at the back of the shop or greeting other men also subjected to a shopping outing with the family. Lillian was almost at the front of the queue when she saw Jim Shepherd's straight back. The unmistakable shape of his head, the pink tips of his ears. He was striding down the aisle towards the doors, lightly swinging a shopping bag from his fingertips. She took a moment to scan the area for signs of Pam. Finding none, she slipped from the queue and went after him.

Ordinarily, she would have stayed put, averted her eyes, and congratulated herself on successfully avoiding Jim, to whom she hadn't spoken for over a year. But that morning in June, a rebellion rose in Lillian. She'd been living with Mick for a few months now. Handsome Mick, who brought her cups of tea in bed and told her she was beautiful. Who took her to the pictures every Saturday night. And while she might not have managed art school, she was no longer a schoolgirl but a hairdresser. Beneath her tabard she was wearing a mini-skirt, not just because Phyllis preferred no trousers in the salon, but because she'd lost weight and Mick had told her she had great legs. She was wearing more make-up, which Mick said made her look *foxy*. She still considered that a ridiculous term but had learned to enjoy its connotations. If you were foxy you might at least be sleek and fast, with plenty of bite. And it was a kind of magic trick, seeing Mick jump to attention when she wore those things – black eyeliner, mini-skirt, lipstick. Perhaps she could make Jim Shepherd jump, too.

Outside, the High Street was filled with the sound of a baby crying. It was coming from a blue pram parked beneath the tree near the shop, and was relentless as a siren. Lillian hesitated in the doorway, distracted by the din. Jim also stopped, so she stepped to his side and tapped him on the shoulder, suddenly shy of saying his name aloud. As she did so, he bent over the pram and scooped the crying child from within. When he turned to her he flushed deeply, but it was difficult to tell if this was due to Lillian's presence or the stress of the baby yelling in his face.

She'd been ready to smile and act buoyant; to joke about him catching her in her hairdressing tabard. She'd been ready, too, for his full attention. For one mad moment, she thought that Jim was rescuing someone else's child. Perhaps he'd heard the baby's distress call and had responded, hoping the mother wouldn't be far away. She knew, of course, that Pam had given birth to a baby girl: she'd seen Jim's wife pushing the pram down the High Street a few times. But she'd never seen – or even imagined – Jim himself with the baby.

Jim looked away from her towards the child, who was still shrieking. 'I'll have to walk her round a bit,' he said. 'Don't suppose you'd push the pram for me?'

Lillian wished she'd kept her place in the queue for the pies.

'Just to the park?' Jim pleaded. 'If you've got five minutes?'

She took hold of the pram's handle and followed him along the crowded pavement. The sunshine lit the long windows of the bank opposite. An old man coming out of the Beehive pub stopped and flat-out stared at Jim. Several women slowed their steps to watch this man walking down the street with a baby at his chest. Many looked concerned at the sight, but they saved their deepest frowns for Lillian, pushing the empty pram. She walked faster, wanting to shout: *It's not my fault! I'm not the poor beggar's mother!*

Jim strode ahead, gently patting the baby. As they neared the end of the street, her siren became fainter, and by the time they'd reached the archway by St Nicolas's Church, it had ceased altogether. The river rushed silently beneath the pavement but Jim pressed on, showing no sign of remembering how they'd knelt there together that night after the dance at the Corn Exchange.

They walked through the shadows of the Abbey ruins, Lillian grappling with the pram's handle as she shoved the carriage over the bumpy ground. Jim crossed the lawn quickly and waited for her on a bench overlooked by the statue of Queen Victoria. As she toiled towards him, she wondered who he was, now, this man with a baby sleeping on his chest. She didn't think he'd put on weight, but he appeared more substantial. His hair was shorter, and he'd removed the ring he used to wear on his little finger.

Jim bent his head to kiss the top of the child's knitted bonnet.

'What's her name?'

'Meg.'

He said it in a manner similar to the one adopted by Winnie when uttering the name 'Ron'.

'Short for Megan?'

'No. Just Meg.'

The child's bottom lip hung open in sleep, spit bubbles forming on its inner pinkness. Her fists curled lightly on her father's chest. Jim lowered her into the pram, his upper body shielding her from the air as he placed her gently onto the mattress. It was as though he were lowering the child into a cold pool of water, braced for the shock of her entry. Once she was down, there was a long moment where he seemed to stop breathing, one hand still on the baby. Lillian experienced a terrible pang of yearning for Jim's love. If she'd have married him, would he have shown her such care and attention?

Only when he seemed satisfied that Meg was truly asleep did Jim perch on the seat next to Lillian. 'So,' he said, eyes still on the baby, 'how have you been?'

'Smashing,' Lillian said.

He flicked a glance at her. 'You certainly look . . . smashing.'

She nodded, determined to take the compliment as her due. 'How's life as a married man, then?'

'Good,' he said, after a pause. 'Keeps me out of mischief.'

She gazed past him, towards the Victoria statue. Squat, serious and jowly, the queen was mildewed in the creases of her sturdy skirt and the orb she held was crusted with pigeon droppings.

'Why are there no statues of young women?' Lillian mused.

'What?'

'There aren't, are there? They're always old.'

Jim seemed to give the question some thought before replying, 'I suppose you've got to get a few years under your belt first. Even if you're a queen.'

She realised, then, that she'd missed the way Jim talked to her. It wasn't the same with Mick. Since moving in with him, she'd started sketching again while waiting for him to come home from The Crown. When he'd seen a couple of her pictures of the view from the window, he'd said it was good she had a little hobby. But he'd offered no word of praise or criticism beyond that.

'I didn't think it would be Pam,' Lillian said.

Jim peered into the pram, though the baby was quiet. Then he said, 'I thought it would be you.'

Lillian gripped the scissors in her tabard pocket. She hadn't really dared look Jim full in the face until now, and when she did he returned her frank gaze and said in a low voice, 'I hear you're with Mick now.'

She straightened her back. 'We're living together.'

'I heard that, too.' There was a coldness to Jim's tone that she hadn't heard before. 'I have to say, I was surprised. I didn't think . . .' He trailed off and shrugged.

'What?'

'I just didn't expect it of you, that's all.'

'Why not?'

'To be honest, I thought you'd do better.' He flicked her a smile. 'What happened to art school? I expected you to be doing great things with paint by now.'

Lillian, pierced with anger and shame, rose from her seat. 'Your *expectations* don't matter to me, Jim.'

He looked at her, taken aback. 'I only mean – I thought you'd at least be with someone who respects you.'

'Mick respects me!'

Jim only shushed her, gazing into the pram again, his hand hovering over the baby's head.

Lillian turned and walked away without another word. And when Jim called her name, she walked faster.

Not long after that, Mick took a new job at the MG factory. It would be more money than the brewery. After he told her the news, he added, 'I think it's about time we got married, too.'

They were in bed, and instead of answering she kissed him. Then one thing led to another, and no more was said.

In the morning, she wasn't sure if he'd even asked her, officially. All week she waited for some further declaration. A ring, perhaps. She was slightly relieved when it didn't come, as while she knew she wanted Mick, she wasn't sure she wanted marriage.

She decided she must write to Gwen and let her know about the proposal. It was months since she'd heard anything from her friend, and it suddenly dawned on her that Winnie couldn't have been forwarding her post since she'd moved in with Mick. So on Thursday morning, when she had a half-day off from the salon, Lillian marched over to number 25 for the first time in four months.

It was a bright July day, warmer than Lillian had anticipated, and she felt the hot hand of the sun on her head as she crossed the bridge. A couple of kids crouched in the shallows below, scooping mud from the stream's bottom and chucking it at one another. Fearing she might bump into Pam and the baby, Lillian looked straight ahead and walked briskly along Mason Road.

Ron answered the door. It took him a second to smile. 'I was wondering when you'd turn up,' he said. His string vest was tucked tightly into a pair of pyjama trousers. 'If you're looking for your mother you're out of luck. She's at work.'

Lillian could hear the radio playing behind him and a smell of eggs frying came at her. He'd obviously settled in. Despite her mother's vow that no man would ever again cross her threshold, this man was living at number 25. Which meant that her mother, who had once walked into the river and ended up at Longbrook, whose *attacks of the nerves* and bottles of pills had prevented Lillian taking up her place at art school, could actually manage without her. Evidently, Lillian was no longer needed in this house.

She made her decision. 'Can you give her a message?'

'Anything for you.'

'Tell her I'm marrying Mick.'

Ron raised his eyebrows. 'Up the duff, are you?'

'No.'

'Too uptight, I suppose. Well. High time he made an honest woman of you. Course, I'm not sure your mother will want to come to the wedding, what with your . . . behaviour. And you might want to tell that fella who was always sticking his nose in – Eric, is it?'

'Ernie.'

'That's him. Nice enough bloke but he was round here way too often. I had to put my foot down, there. So you might want to tell him. About your nuptials.' He paused. 'I understand he's got a right to know.'

This was too much. What on earth had Winnie told him? More than she'd told her, clearly. 'You do know,' Lillian said, fighting an urge to slap him, 'that she's unstable?'

Ron squinted at her, then shook his head. 'What are you on about?'

Lillian paused, feeling slightly dizzy. All along, she'd been wrong, it seemed. She'd failed to be a good daughter. Despite her efforts, she was not her mother's rock. She was merely her trouble.

'My mother,' she said, 'is not a well woman.'

'What the devil does that mean?'

'It means that she's mentally ill.'

'Don't be ridiculous.'

'She was in Longbrook.'

She saw the impact of the word on his face, which, for the briefest of seconds, fell into an expression of absolute shock. Then, recovering himself, he gave a mirthless laugh. 'You're lying.'

'She tried to kill herself.'

Ron's eyes swept the length of her body before he grabbed her roughly by the wrist and brought his face so close to hers that she smelled the sourness of his breath. 'You're a meddling little hussy, aren't you?' he hissed.

Lillian didn't flinch. Now that she'd said it, she could say anything. 'Why don't you ask her? Ask her about Longbrook.'

Yanking her hand free, she turned away from number 25 and headed for Mick's.

PART TWO
Longbrook

2005

Lillian took the iron steps onto the narrow bridge across the weir. It was busy that afternoon with kids on bikes and mums wheeling buggies, which meant she had to push through a crowd to reach the middle. Once there, she leaned on the railing, the heat of it burning her stomach through her T-shirt, and peered at the thick ribbon of water rushing into the river below, trying to still her thoughts. Encircling one wrist with the fingers of her other hand, she held on to herself and leaned over as far as she could, inhaling the cool spray. As a girl, she'd always loved the freshly metallic smell of it. Since she'd heard Ernie's story about Winnie all those years ago, she'd felt unable to come here. But she should have had the guts to show Rachel this place. She should have let Rachel stand here, lean into the spray, and feel the vibration of the river's force through her shoes.

'You all right there, love?'

There was a tap on her shoulder and, looking behind her, she saw a man and woman, both elderly, wearing matching beige trousers and sunhats, peering at her.

'You were quite far over, there,' said the man, half-smiling, and the woman in the matching hat nodded. 'Your feet weren't touching the ground!' she added.

'OK,' Lillian said, looking back at the water, hoping they'd go away.

They did not. 'We thought you might be about to do something silly!' said the man. 'You never know what people are up to. And that's quite a drop, right there. You could easily get in real trouble—'

Lillian straightened up. Though she knew there was nothing to be gained from snapping at this couple, she said, 'Why don't you mind your own business?'

The couple shared a puzzled look. 'You can't help some people,' the man muttered, and they walked on without another word.

'I was just looking at the water!' Lillian yelled, louder than she'd intended.

When they didn't look back, she was unable to stop herself from adding, 'I'm not planning to kill myself!'

Once she'd peeled her body from the railing, she walked slowly to her car, trying to steady her breathing. The steering wheel and the seat were almost too hot to touch, but she made herself sit inside with all the windows and doors open to think about what Rachel had said. Not the request that Lillian should be honest about her own difficulties – her mind refused to dwell on that. It refused, too, to contemplate what Rachel had said about Lillian 'opening up'. Instead, it was caught on the fact that Rachel's father was teaching her to cook. That man! Who hadn't made one meal until he was past forty!

She took a swig of the now-warm water she'd left in the car. She'd have to intervene in some way. But how?

She started the engine with no idea where she was headed, and found herself driving through town towards Daphne's house. She told herself she'd simply park outside, sit on the riverbank where it was quiet, and try to come up with a plan.

She'd always prided herself on presenting wholesome, balanced meals to her daughter, never relying on anything ready-made or take-away, and never discussing any of it with Rachel. She didn't want her daughter to have to think about such dull, domestic and yet potentially explosive things. She wanted her daughter to think about other, better things. Her schoolwork. Her friends. The world around her. Not carbs and sugar and protein and fat. Especially not fat.

Lillian had been glad of the weekends she'd had to herself while Rachel was at her father's, not only because they afforded her vital hours in which to work, but also because they gave her time to prepare batches of meals for the week ahead. She would turn the radio on and let the flat fill with steam. And the meals – a vegetable curry; a pasta sauce; a lentil soup; a bean chilli – would be prepared, boxed, labelled, and placed on the table until they were cool enough to slot into the freezer. It had probably seemed to Rachel that her dinner just magically appeared, perhaps made by the freezer itself. Rachel's job was to wash up. Rachel, Lillian reflected, had always been very good at washing up. She even seemed to enjoy it: there was, after all, something surgical about the snapping on of latex gloves, the scrubbing of implements, the spraying of surfaces with Flash.

It wasn't that Lillian had never wished to cook with her daughter. She could picture it, right now as she sat in a traffic jam on the High Street: they would bake a cake. Just as she had done with her own mother. Of course. She could see the big porcelain mixing bowl. The fresh aprons tied around their waists. The flour dancing in the air as Rachel sifted it. Her daughter weighing the sugar and pouring it into the bowl, ready for Lillian to cream, stir, and fold the mixture. The yellow sponge rising perfectly in the oven.

But there was a problem: what would she do with so much cake? One slice each – and then what? Either it would go stale or Lillian, sitting at her table trying to work while Rachel was at school, would have to stop herself from eating slice after slice after slice until it was gone.

So that had been out of the question.

There had, however, been a weekly treat. Most Fridays after school, right up until Rachel had joined the sixth form, they went to the Nosebag Café in the city centre, where Lillian usually had a flapjack while Rachel devoured a wedge of cheesecake and a hot chocolate. Lillian had told Rachel that she'd done something similar with her own mother, but that no cake nowadays could ever hope to be as good as a Trotman's cream doughnut. It had seemed safe to speak of her appetite for Trotman's inside the musty café with its dark tables, each lit by a shaded lamp, the windows almost concealed by Laura Ashley curtains, low music – Mozart or Bach – coming from the stereo. They always sat at the same table, tucked in the far corner of the room. When Rachel was old enough to keep still for more than five minutes, Lillian began bringing her sketchbook along so she could draw her daughter chasing crumbs around her plate with a finger or licking cream from her hot chocolate. Then, for Rachel's entertainment, she began to sketch the other customers looking bored or greedy, stuffing their mouths with cake or sipping timidly at soup. 'Mum!' Rachel had said, when she'd first done it. 'Are you *allowed* to do that?'

'Of course you are!' Lillian said. Then she leaned close and whispered in Rachel's ear, 'I've done it for years. But it's best not to let anyone catch you.'

Rachel's eyes widened.

'It's my research,' said Lillian with a shrug.

'Like an experiment?'

'Kind of.'

'What are the results?'

Lillian considered this. 'I'm not sure it's about results, exactly,' she said.

'All experiments are about results. Why do them, otherwise?'

Lillian said, 'Then I suppose the results are what's on the page. The picture itself.'

Rachel looked at the drawing. It was of two women sitting by the door, one feeding a bowl of ice cream to the spaniel at her feet. 'It's good, Mum,' she said. 'You're really good at that.'

Lillian had felt such a surge of pride at her daughter's admiration that it had been difficult not to weep.

But, she reflected as she turned into Wilsham Road, she should have taught Rachel to cook something. Anything. How could she have failed her daughter so utterly?

She parked in the spot where Ernie had told her, so many years ago, about Longbrook. Even now, a sick feeling crawled through her at the memory. *You're to knock on our door, any time, if you need anything*, he'd said, pointing to his house. The house she was peering at through the car window. The house that Winnie would have hated her to step foot in. The house that now belonged to her.

She remembered the letter Daphne had sent to the salon. *You cannot live your life for her.*

She fished in the glove compartment and found the keys. Then she took another swig of warm water, got out of the car, and walked through the heat towards the front door.

1968

They came to take her on a Monday morning in September. Lillian stood at what had been her mother's bedroom window wearing only an old shirt of Mick's, watching a woman in a loose mac clutching a folder to her chest as she walked up the path to number 25. A beefy young man with short red hair was waiting by her car. At the sight of the woman, Lillian dived back into bed, pulled the covers over her head and breathed into the sheet, aware of the dungy tang of her own breath. Which was terrible, obviously, but also good, because it meant she hadn't eaten anything since yesterday lunchtime. Yesterday had been a very good day. Two oranges, three cups of black coffee and one slice of toast, no marg. Reaching beneath the shirt, she checked the sharpness of her hip bones. They jutted upward in two peaks, as they'd done the day before, and the day before that, and on the many days since her mother had died.

Since she'd caused her mother's death, Lillian reminded herself.

She listened to Mick answering the door, his murmured greeting met with a bright *Good morning!* He'd bunked off work in order to 'see her off', as he'd put it. She felt her ribcage, and it was like trailing her hand along a wooden xylophone at primary school. The woman downstairs was asking, loudly, if she should slip off her shoes. Lillian couldn't remember anyone asking such a thing on her doorstep before. Mick, clearly flustered, seemed to be agreeing that she should.

Lillian tapped her ribs in time to the sound of the woman's footsteps on the stairs, counting off each one.

There was a knock at the bedroom door, and the woman's voice again. 'Mrs Harries? May I come in?'

Lillian remained still. Breathed. Tapped.

'I'm Dawn,' said the woman, cracking the door open. 'Will you let me help you?'

'I don't need help,' said Lillian, into the sheet.

It was what she'd been saying to Mick for months. Every time she said it, he looked a little angrier, but she kept saying it anyway, even though there was a small part of her that longed for someone to relieve her of this fight.

'Let's get you up.'

'I've changed my mind.'

'Come on, love. Help me out, eh?' Dawn said, looming over the bed and peeling back the edge of the coverlet. Lillian attempted to snatch it back, but Dawn held fast. Curly-haired and fat-cheeked, she wore a sad smile. Her glasses had a smear of make-up on one lens. Lillian hoped her terrible breath was reaching this woman's little nose, and that she was recoiling, inwardly, at the sight of Lillian's proud collarbones and sunken chest.

'If you want my advice,' said Dawn, 'I'd suggest not putting your husband through it.'

'What?'

'Well. It's either you get dressed and walk out of here with me, or I send Big Alex in to carry you out. Which is it to be?'

Lillian turned on her side. Facing the wall, she said, 'I've changed my mind. You can't make me. No one can.'

'So you said. But the forms have been signed. And everything's arranged. Think how disappointed your husband will be, if you kick up a fuss now.'

Lillian stared at the massive purple flower on the wallpaper next to her nose. Mick had decorated both bedrooms when they'd moved in after her mother died, saying the place needed an update, and she'd never liked it. He'd also insisted they use

Winnie's old bedroom, as it was the larger of the two, and had laughed at her reluctance, calling her superstitious. What, he'd asked, did she believe? That Lillian's mother could see her in bed with her husband? Did she think Winnie was *spying* on her from the afterlife?

I wouldn't put it past her, Lillian had thought.

'Lillian? Is it Lillian? Or Lilly? Or do you prefer Mrs Harries?'

'Lillian.'

'Should I send Big Alex in? Or give you five minutes to get yourself out of that bed?'

After a moment, Lillian mumbled, 'Five minutes.'

She listened to Dawn tapping lightly down the stairs, then hauled herself into a sitting position and glanced around the room. Mick was not an organised man, but last night he'd suggested that she lay out some clothes, ready for the morning. Lillian had ignored him, not quite believing that the morning would arrive. Besides, what did you wear for your first admittance to Longbrook Psychiatric Hospital? Nothing fitted any more, though the trousers she was in yesterday could be cinched with Mick's old belt. She'd made extra holes in the leather with his boring tool whenever she lost half an inch from her waist. Those holes were records of her successes, like notches on a bedpost.

As she unbuttoned the shirt, she heard Dawn downstairs, asking Mick if he'd spoken to the salon about his wife taking time off. Mick was saying that Phyllis was a good boss who understood Lillian was poorly and needed help.

Poorly. It was the term her mother used to use, when Lillian needed a day off school. Closing her eyes, she felt her mother's warm hand on her forehead. *Dear me. You are a poorly girl. Stay at home today.*

'And you, Mr Harries?' she heard Dawn ask. 'You'll manage without her?'

Her husband replied that he'd be just fine.

There was no point in the bra, really, but she hooked her arms into the straps and fastened it. Trousers on and belt tightened, she dragged a brush through her hair and gazed at the suitcase in the corner of the room, the same one she'd once packed for art school. Mick had shoved a few things in there: underwear, nighties, a couple of changes of clothes. Lillian noticed that he'd chosen the tangerine dress she'd bought for the brewery dance with Jim, which would be huge on her, now. But she didn't remove it from the case. She added the Van Gogh book, the photograph of her and Winnie in the Abbey Meadow, her sketchbook; then carried the case downstairs. She was light-headed, dry-mouthed, stiff-backed. But this was how she usually felt. She knew she just had to get through each minute at a time. It was like when her mother had suffered the heart attack: you had to move through the moments without thinking, because there was no choice. The terrible thing was going to happen, whatever you did, and your task was simply to get to the end of it, even if the end was only the beginning of something more terrible.

Mick and Dawn appeared in the hallway.

'All set?' said Dawn, with a tight smile. 'I'll wait for you in the car.'

The doctor had referred to Longbrook as a 'unit', which Lillian thought made it sound less like a prison and more like a cupboard. A temporary holding place. Or somewhere to hide. He'd said he knew it sounded alarming, but he'd heard the unit had a good record of success and had been thoroughly modernised. Lillian hadn't asked if she would be force-fed, or if electrodes would be put to her head. But something in the doctor's assured manner, his flickering smile as he spoke, seemed to prohibit such questions.

When she was outside, Mick gestured towards the case and said, 'You should have let me carry that for you.'

Then he touched her arm. She felt it through her blouse, the warmth of her husband's fingers on her elbow. During the last few months he'd shrunk from her, and she'd learned to avoid physical contact, fearing his inevitable wince and half-concerned, half-exasperated frown. Once, on touching her wrist, he'd recoiled, thumped the settee, and cried, 'I don't understand it! All you've got to do is eat!' She'd felt herself go cold – she was often cold, but this was a deep chill that came from her chest. She'd looked at him and said quietly, 'I don't have to do anything.'

Now her husband said, 'Thank you for doing this, Bud.'

Four months earlier, Lillian had taken her usual walk across the fields towards Sunningwell, stopping to sketch cow parsley as tall as her waist. Catkin seeds floated through the air, catching on her sleeves, her hair, her mouth. It was Thursday, her half-day off. Earlier that morning, she'd failed to look over the Situations Vacant in the *Herald*, despite her husband's plea that she find a new job. Desperate to escape his cramped council flat, especially now that his father was threatening to move back in, Mick had suggested she find something better paid than hairdressing. Wouldn't she like to get a nice little job at the library, or maybe something in the offices at the carpet factory? She'd gone to that posh school and passed exams, after all: it should be easy for her.

Lillian didn't say that the only thing she'd like to do was draw.

She slipped her sketchbook into her satchel and raked the seeds from her hair. When she reached the town, she bought a loaf from Trotman's to take to her mother.

She'd patched things up a bit with Winnie. Her mother hadn't attended her wedding – a small ceremony at St Michael's Church in November – but Ernie had surprised her by turning up at the last minute, without Daphne, to walk her down the aisle. She hadn't seen him since she'd moved in with Mick. Lillian thought there were tears in Ernie's eyes as he squeezed her hand and said, 'I did my best. I know it wasn't much. But Mick'll look after you now, gal.'

He'd disappeared as quickly as he'd appeared.

Lillian still didn't know if her words to Ron had prompted him to clear out of number 25, but whatever the case, her mother had turned up at the salon the following spring, asking for a cup of tea and opening her arms for a strong embrace. Winnie was pale and had lost weight; even her hair seemed to take up less space. Sitting in a chair by the window, she gave what Lillian guessed was a positive version of events, saying she'd got the measure of Ron and had turfed him out with a flea in his ear. She apologised for missing the wedding, adding that she was glad Mick had finally made it official. There was no mention of what had happened at the dining table with Ron, and no mention, either, of what Lillian had told him about Longbrook.

When Lillian asked her mother if Ernie had been round, Winnie gazed out of the window. 'I don't suppose he'll bother so much, now you're not there.'

'Why not?' Lillian asked. Friday teatimes without Ernie at number 25 were unthinkable.

Her mother put down her teacup and said, 'Truth is, I 'spect Ernie was doing his duty by me.'

There was a long pause. Was this the moment, Lillian wondered, when her mother would finally tell her that Ernie was her father? Right here in the salon? Now Lillian was married, maybe Winnie would feel able to speak the truth.

Nothing came. So Lillian asked, slowly, 'What does that mean, Mum?'

Winnie gave her a distant smile. 'Daphne's interfered, most likely. But I'm sure he'll drop by now and then.'

'Shall I go over and ask him? Let him know Ron's gone and you'd like to see him?'

Her mother looked her in the eye and spoke very clearly. 'No need for that. You know how I feel about you going to that woman's house.'

Afterwards, Lillian understood two things.

One was that not knowing whether Ernie was her father or not was a relief of sorts. If she knew for sure, she reasoned, she would have to face Ernie as this new person, a person she might expect things of. And how would he respond? He might still deny it, and that would be worse – much worse – than evasion. Knowing the truth about Ernie might also lead, she thought, to her mother speaking of Longbrook, which would be unbearable. If she spoke of it, Winnie might fall into another attack of the nerves. And then where would they be?

The other thing Lillian understood was that now her mother was alone, she was needed once more at number 25 – which was also something of a relief.

So she made it her business to drop by regularly, which was what she was doing when she opened the back door, hung her satchel on the larder hook, then placed the loaf on the kitchen shelf. Usually, at this time, Winnie was making herself a lunchtime sandwich before her shift at the Pav began, but the kitchen was tidy and there was no sign of her in the front room.

'Mum?' Lillian called. A small moan drifted from above.

Lillian went upstairs. The bedroom curtains were still closed but Winnie was sitting up in bed. 'Thank goodness you've come,' she said, rubbing at her chest. 'I've such a pain. Right here.'

'Indigestion?' offered Lillian. Winnie often suffered. 'Why don't you take something?' She looked at the pill bottles lined up on her mother's bedside table. Plenty of Carbitral, but no Rennies.

Winnie grasped Lillian's hand. 'I've such a pain,' she repeated.

Lillian gazed at her. Her mother's face was a little grey, but she hadn't been sleeping well for weeks. Lately, Winnie's ailments had multiplied: she battled not only indigestion but also headaches, back aches, strange tremors in her face, dry patches on her scalp and around her middle, unexplained episodes of nausea and dizziness.

'Why don't you come down?' Lillian said. 'I'll find you some Rennies, then we'll see how you are.'

Downstairs, she found the box in the bathroom cabinet and set the kettle on the stove. Familiar sounds came from above – the creak and crack of the bed as Winnie heaved herself out of it, her heavy tread as she shuffled to the door. Then there was a pause so long that Lillian went to the bottom of the steps and peered upwards.

Seeing her mother standing on the landing, gripping the handrail and swaying slightly in her dressing gown, Lillian suddenly realised how much Winnie had aged, and she took a couple of steps towards her, meaning to meet her halfway. 'Careful,' she warned, holding out a hand.

Winnie, having taken a few steps down, smiled a little. And then she fell.

There was a series of terrible whacks followed by a long cry. Her dressing gown billowed open as she crashed from step to step, finally managing to clutch at the coats hanging on the rack.

Lillian scrambled to her mother's body, now heaped across

the bottom three steps, one foot beneath her backside and the other at a strange angle as she gripped the remains of a torn mac, her face screwed into a mask of pain, breathing loud and hard, as if doing so was taking everything she had.

'It's all right,' said Lillian, more to herself than to her mother. 'Let's get you up. Can you move?'

Winnie shook her head.

'It's all right, Mum.'

But it wasn't. Without opening her eyes, Winnie let out a long, terrified moan, which turned into a coughing fit.

Lillian tried to think. Mick was at work. She couldn't possibly move her mother on her own.

'Stay there,' she said, not sure whether her mother could hear anything over the noise of her own coughing. 'I'm going to get help. Back in a tick. All right?'

Winnie groaned, which Lillian took for a yes.

There was no reply from either of the immediate neighbours when Lillian hammered on their doors, so she ran to the phone box at the end of the street, worrying all the while that someone would appear, find Winnie, and assume Lillian had left her own mother alone to cough out her heart on that narrow stairway.

Once she was inside the booth and had the calm and decisive voice of the emergency services operator in her ear, Lillian almost relaxed. Then the voice told her to stay with the patient, keep her warm, and the ambulance would be with them soon, which made her panic return. Leaving the receiver dangling from its flex, she sprinted back to number 25.

As she ran, it was all she could do not to cry out for her mother and beg her forgiveness for ever leaving her alone in that house. How could she have been so selfish? So stupid? She should never have left! She remembered Daphne's letter. *You cannot live for her.* But why not? What else did she have to live for?

When she made it to the garden path, she heard coughing and knew Winnie was still there. Still grey, still sprawled, but still breathing and still there. Mrs Shepherd had appeared beside her, and was trying to cover Winnie's bare legs with the dressing gown but it was caught beneath Winnie's back. It didn't seem right to step over her in order to fetch a blanket from upstairs, so Lillian yanked the torn mac from the peg and tucked it around Winnie's body.

'Whatever's happened?' asked Mrs Shepherd, who was now hovering in the front doorway.

'I don't know. She fell.'

Lillian sat on the bottom step of the stairs, holding her mother's hand. Winnie breathed. Coughed. Breathed. Lillian knew she should offer comforting words, but could think of none. Mrs Shepherd, too, was silent.

Together, the three women waited.

Lillian expected a siren, or the screech of wheels, but there was just the sound of the engine and the squeak and scratch of the gate. The ambulance man was pasty-faced and stout. A young lad stood behind him, avoiding Lillian's eye. The man spoke to Winnie loudly, holding her wrist as he asked how she was feeling, but Winnie only moaned. He listened to her chest, took her blood pressure. Then he turned to Lillian, removing his cap as he said he'd have to take her mother in, just in case.

The lad had his arms hooked beneath Winnie's before Lillian could object. Winnie cried out in pain as she was manoeuvred onto a stretcher and down the path, Lillian following. Once they had Winnie in the back of the vehicle, the man slammed the doors shut and suggested Lillian follow them to the hospital, if she could get a lift? Maybe her husband would drive her? They could take her, but it wouldn't be a comfortable ride and she'd only be stranded at the other end. Mrs Shepherd touched Lillian's shoulder and said she could call Jim: he'd be happy to give her a lift and could easily slip out from work. Morland were very good that way. Lillian said there would be absolutely no need for that. Her husband could do it.

She ran to the phone box once more and got a message to Mick, who came home. In the car, he tried to persuade her it was unlikely to be an emergency: Winnie was only in her early forties, and was always exaggerating her symptoms. Lillian pressed her hands into her thighs and didn't respond. Not wanting him in the way, she told Mick to wait in the car when they reached the hospital; she'd check on Winnie and would be out in a while.

While Lillian gripped the desk, the hospital receptionist made a call, then asked her to wait for the doctor to come down. Would she like a cup of tea, perhaps?

Lillian began to tremble, then. A cup of tea couldn't be a standard offer; it must be reserved for dire situations. She thought about going to fetch Mick, but she didn't want to risk missing the doctor, so managed to sit for a few seconds on a low chair. She was soon on her feet again, pacing the reception area. The woman behind the desk offered her a sympathetic smile but said nothing. Lillian's teeth were chattering by the time the doctor appeared, his tie butter-yellow and shining. He asked her name and her mother's name, then showed her to a room with a vase of plastic roses and a box of tissues on the table. When they were both seated he said, very gently but without pause and never once varying the tone of his voice, that regrettably her mother had suffered another heart attack in the ambulance and there was nothing they could do; by the time they reached the hospital she'd passed away. It had been quick, he said, which he knew wasn't much comfort but it was something. Her suffering would have been short-lived. Lillian was welcome to sit there for as long as she liked, of course, and he'd get a nurse to bring her a cup of tea, but was there someone he could ask his secretary to telephone? Her husband, perhaps?

Lillian blinked at him. As he'd been talking, she'd thought only of how difficult it must be to tell someone such news. To have your silk-tied day of life-saving interrupted not only by death but by the need to announce it. How did he stand it?

'Mrs Harries?' he asked, and she realised she must have been staring at him for quite a while.

'Can I see her?'

He swallowed. 'I would recommend waiting until your husband arrives. It's not easy to do these things alone.'

Lillian got to her feet. 'I'd like to see her now, please.'

Minutes later, she was in a white room with no windows or pictures on the walls, at the centre of which was a raised hospital bed where her mother lay. The doctor said he would be just outside, if she needed anything. Lillian stood at the foot of the bed, trying to comprehend the sight of Winnie, who was no longer in her dressing gown but still wore her nightie, the neckline of which had been cut and pushed to the side, revealing her collarbones and the sunken skin of her neck. A single sheet was pulled up to her chest. It was chilly in the room and though Lillian glanced around for a blanket she understood this was a useless idea, because clearly this was not her mother on the bed. She stepped a little closer. The woman's hair had fallen away from her forehead and the bones in her face protruded. Her skin was the colour of dried cement. Her mouth gaped, revealing the ridges of her dental plate. Where had her face gone? It seemed to have been replaced by something more like a landscape than human features. Something craggy and monumental.

Lillian turned away and opened the door, feeling no remorse: though this was her mother's body, this was not her mother. Winnie was elsewhere.

In the corridor, the doctor asked, 'Did you say goodbye?'
'No,' said Lillian.

When she woke in the early hours of the following morning, she knew what she had to do.

She crept from the bedroom and into the kitchen, where she slipped her coat over her nightie and pushed her bare feet into her shoes. As she was about to leave the flat, Mick looked around the bedroom door, his hair sticking up from his forehead.

'What's going on?'

'I need to look for Mum.'

Mick seemed to wake up fully, then. He moved down the hall and reached for Lillian's hand. 'You've had a shock, Bud. Come back to bed.'

She glanced at him, thinking she would need, later, to take a good look at this man she'd married and work out why she was living in this flat with him and not at number 25 Mason Road. But for now she had more urgent things to do. She yanked her hand away from his and opened the door.

'Lillian! It's two o'clock in the bloody morning!'

But she was already gone, taking the concrete stairs two at a time.

Outside, the rain punished her uncovered head and soaked her collar. Her feet began to slide inside her wet shoes as she marched across the bridge to Mason Road. She pushed Winnie's gate open and let it screech shut behind her.

Inside, she called for her mother. There was no reply, but Winnie's teacup was on the draining board, next to a box of Rennies. Her apron hung, together with Lillian's satchel, from the larder door. The loaf was on the shelf in its paper bag. Lillian poked her head into the front room, where her mother was not, then made her way upstairs, stepping over the mac strewn on the bottom step.

In Winnie's bedroom, she stood by the wardrobe, looking wildly about. The bed was unmade but there was nobody in it. On the floor were Winnie's slippers, misshapen from her bunions. Lillian marched into her old bedroom and flicked on the light. Her *Picturegoer* annuals were still stacked on the bookshelf, and the doll made of shells from Southsea was perched on the sill. But there was no Winnie.

At the top of the stairs she had a strange urge to let herself lean forward and fall all the way to the bottom. She closed her eyes and waited for it to pass. When she opened them, she wasn't surprised to see her husband, standing on the doormat below, rain dripping from his jacket.

'I can't find Mum,' she said.

When Mick spoke, his voice was strained. 'She's not here, love. How could she be?'

Lillian made her hands into fists and closed her eyes again. Perhaps he would go away.

'Come on, Lillian. Come down. Please.'

'Where is she?'

'They took her in the ambulance. You must remember. They took her to the hospital.'

Lillian opened her eyes. 'We'd better go there, then.'

Mick stared at her, one hand grasping his hair. She noticed he was wearing his pyjama trousers. 'But she's not there either, is she?' he said.

'Then where is she?'

There was a small pause before Mick replied, 'She died, love. I'm sorry. But your mum's dead.'

At this, Lillian's body flinched.

Mick took the stairs. It seemed pointless to shout at him to stop right there. To get out of her mother's house. She stiffened as he put his arms around her waist, and waited for him to let go.

'Lillian,' he said, 'we should get to bed. I've got work in the morning.'

'Where's she gone, though?' Her voice was loud but she could hear a waver in it. It was, she thought, a logical enough question. Winnie might very well be dead. But where had she *gone*? Where was she, *right now*?

'It's time to go home,' Mick said.

Now she did shout, right into his face. 'I am home!'

Then she went to her mother's room and slammed the door behind her.

After a while, Mick got tired of tapping on the wood and pleading with her to see sense. Lillian waited until she heard him leave the house, then she curled herself into her mother's sheets, where she stayed until the following afternoon.

Mick said they had to face the facts, but Winnie's death didn't seem like a fact that Lillian could recognise.

For many nights after her mother died, she left her bed and walked across the bridge to number 25. In the early hours of the morning, Mason Road was quiet and dark enough for her to imagine Winnie everywhere. Passing the hedge, Lillian saw her mother leaning from her bedroom window, waving to her daughter as she walked home from school. At the back of the house, she saw her standing on the path, tea towel in hand, frantically calling her name. And Lillian also saw her mother being carried to the ambulance, one hand flailing to the side of the stretcher.

Inside, she rooted through Winnie's bedroom. Mick had already been down the council and arranged the transfer of the house to his name. He said it was a good idea to sort through everything before they moved in. Lillian wasn't sorting anything, though; she was on a hunt for clues. In her mother's chest of drawers, she delved into never-used handkerchiefs; chipped pomanders; letters from the council about the rent; ribbons and lengths of elastic. In the bottom of the wardrobe, she found a wooden box of mismatched buttons and a stack of romantic novels. She examined each item, turning it in her hands, smelling it, bringing it to her cheek or running it across a lip before placing it carefully back where it had come from. The only things she threw away were a man's mac that she assumed belonged to Ron, her mother's spare set of false teeth, and the dozens of empty pill bottles she found in a plastic bag beneath the bed. Perhaps Winnie had been too worried about the bin men spotting this evidence of her weakness to throw them away herself.

The satchel, with the sketchbook inside, she left hanging from the larder door.

After two weeks of this, Mick said they may as well move into the place right now, since Lillian spent most of her time there anyway.

Ernie had wept quietly as Winnie's coffin was lowered into the ground. It was a warm, bright afternoon and Lillian squinted into the sun, glad to be momentarily blinded. She reminded herself that the body she'd seen in the hospital had looked nothing like her mother. The vicar had spoken of a hardworking woman who'd be remembered by all who knew her as a kind soul. He'd said her mother's full name – Winifred Eliza Wells. Lillian couldn't remember anyone ever saying those three names together, and they sounded to her like a different person entirely.

The wisps of Ernie's hair fluttered in the wind as he sobbed. Lillian tried to focus on that movement, keeping her eyes averted from Daphne's intense, questioning gaze and the box going deeper into the mud.

Once the dirt had been thrown into the grave, Ernie grabbed hold of her and she buried her face in his chest. He told her he was sorry, and asked whatever would they do now? Lillian had no answer. Eventually, Ernie gently prised her away. Drawing back while still holding her arms, he looked her up and down and said, 'Where've you gone to, gal? There's nothing of you.' She couldn't help but feel pleased by that.

When Mick suggested they come back to the house, where his sister had made sandwiches and a cake, Ernie glanced at his wife and said they couldn't. Daphne had a terrible headache and they needed to get home.

'But you should come to us, whenever you like,' Daphne said, her eyes searching Lillian's face. 'There's no reason not to, now, is there? And you'll always be welcome—'

Ernie put a hand on his wife's shoulder, silencing her. 'Lillian's aware of that,' he said.

Lillian knew, then, that Ernie wouldn't visit her at number 25 like he used to. With her mother gone and another man in the house, there was no need. She understood, too, that he wouldn't want to risk being alone with her, because she might ask him anything now.

'Pop over to see us some other time, then,' Mick said.

Ernie nodded, but made no promises. Daphne continued to stare, as though she were drawing something essential from the sight of Lillian.

Dawn drove and the redheaded lad, Alex, sat up front, his shoulders spilling over the seat. The car had a chemical smell that made Lillian nauseous, but this was a good distraction: if she could concentrate on inhaling deeply through her nose and swallowing the saliva trickling into her mouth, she could avoid thinking about leaving Mason Road. She closed her eyes so she wouldn't have to watch her house disappear. Inhaled. Swallowed. Dawn spoke of the traffic and how she loved to see the leaves turning at this time of year. It was her favourite, she said. All that change. Lillian swallowed. Inhaled. Gripped the door handle. What would happen if she were to pull on it when they stopped at a traffic light? She pictured herself calmly boarding a bus home. Or she could walk it. Five miles a day wasn't unusual for her. She often completed two and half miles at night and another two or three during the daytime, pounding the same path to Sunningwell and back. She could head towards Boars Hill, tramp through Bagley Woods. It was a dry enough day and she'd make it back after lunchtime. She could reward herself with half a Digestive and be done with food until Mick was home. She swallowed. Inhaled. Gripped the door handle.

'Lillian? Did you hear what I said?'

'Pardon?'

'I was asking about your husband,' said Dawn. 'Where is it he works?'

'The MGs.'

'Shame he couldn't accompany you today.'

When the doctor had suggested Mick drive Lillian to Longbrook himself, Mick's face had greyed and Lillian had spoken up: she would go alone. The doctor said the hospital liked to involve the patient's family as much as possible, but Lillian insisted there was no reason for Mick to take time off work. She knew he wouldn't be able to face telling his boss what he needed it for. While she didn't want him to be ashamed, she'd also no wish for Mick to be involved in this thing. It was hers, and hers alone.

Dawn was talking again. 'He'll be able to visit, when you're settled.'

I do not mean to settle, thought Lillian. *Settling is not my intention.*

'You're lucky: you'll have your own room. Did I say you'll be looked after by Dr Will? Everyone likes him. He's not been with us long but he's already changed a lot of things.'

The car had slowed. Lillian opened her eyes and willed the traffic lights to turn red.

'You're not to call him *doctor*,' continued Dawn. 'He doesn't like it. Wants everyone to call him Will.'

The car stopped. Lillian yanked the handle but the door did not budge. She pulled again, pushing at the window with her other hand. In the rear-view mirror, Dawn caught her eye, raised an eyebrow, and spoke in a sad but unsurprised tone. 'We've had those fixed.'

The lights changed. Lillian slumped back in her seat.

The car took a right into a tree-lined road. They passed a clutch of terraced houses, a church, a pub, then crossed a railway bridge. Dawn turned into a wide gravel driveway and drove through an open pair of iron gates. Everything in Lillian clenched. Though there was no sign, she knew this was the place. There were stone pillars either side of the gate, topped with lichen-splattered spheres. As they drove past an ivy-covered gatehouse, manicured lawns opened up before them, and a huge biscuit-coloured building which looked more like a stately home than a hospital loomed ahead.

This, then, was where her mother had been *deposited*, as Daphne had said. She remembered Mrs Shepherd talking about Dolly James in the salon. *I heard she had to be restrained.* How had Winnie survived the experience? And why had she never passed such essential information to her daughter?

Dawn stopped the car and walked around to open Lillian's door. Leaning into the fresh air, Lillian vomited, spraying the gravel and Dawn's shoes with watery bile.

There was a pause. Lillian spat on the stones and wiped her mouth with the back of her hand. At least she was purged. Not that she'd eaten since yesterday lunchtime. Glancing down the drive, she saw there was no way she could make it to the gates.

'Alex will bring your case,' Dawn said, holding out a hand. 'Let's get inside and fetch you a cup of tea.'

Lillian straightened up. Swallowed. Inhaled.

'It'll be perfectly all right, Lillian. Everyone here is really tremendously kind.' Dawn pointed to a modern-looking, square building to the left. 'Look. That's our patient canteen and shop.'

On the lawn, a few old people were sitting in deckchairs, drinking tea. It looked like a postcard Ernie had once sent of the tearoom at Pontins, except here there were no children playing and no Guinness adverts in the windows.

'Dr Will wants to meet you.' Dawn took her elbow and led her to a doorway at the side of the building. Inside were rows of chairs covered in blue and green tapestry fabric and long windows running floor to ceiling. A fish tank gurgled on a low table. A radio played softly. The front of the reception desk was decorated with orange diamond-patterned wallpaper, and behind it sat a man with a small moustache.

'Morning, Dawn, my angel!' he chirped, waving to her as though she were royalty.

'Nigel. I've got Lillian Harries, and we're turning left.'

'Very good,' he said. 'On you go.'

Still holding Lillian's elbow, Dawn pressed on, through the door in the corner of the room and into a different world. The smell hit Lillian first. It was a stronger version of the scent in the car: like the chemical aroma of a swimming pool, mixed with paraffin wax and urine. She covered her nose and mouth, almost vomited again.

'You'll get used to that,' said Dawn.

The corridor stretched ahead. The green and white floor tiles shone, despite being chipped and gouged here and there. The white walls were lumpy and unplastered. They passed a girl dressed in a baggy cardigan and long skirt, hunched over a huge polishing machine just like the ones Lillian had seen used in the corridors of her school.

Swallow. Inhale.

'Morning, Isobel!' said Dawn, and the girl nodded, her eyes sliding over Lillian's body.

'We ask patients, as part of their recovery, to get involved in the upkeep of the place. So good to keep busy and have a sense of responsibility.' Dawn marched on.

On both sides of the corridor were numbered doors, each with a shatter-proof glass square at the top. All were closed. Lillian heard a shout and a crash that sounded like metal objects being hurled to the floor. She whipped her head around, but saw only Isobel's hunched figure, guiding the machine at a glacial pace. Dawn ploughed ahead, unflinching.

Swallow. Inhale.

When they reached a door with a number 7 on it, Dawn peered through the window before turning to Lillian and saying, 'Right. There's no one in this one. In you go. Dr Will will come and see you in a bit.'

She dropped Lillian's elbow in order to hold the door open,

but Lillian could not move. Why had she agreed to this? They were going to imprison her. They were going to restrain her. There were going to clamp electrodes to her head. They were going to fry her brain and force food into her. They were going to make her obese. She could feel it already. Lumpen flesh would sprout all over her body.

Dawn lowered her voice. 'You're bound to feel nervous. But it'll just be you and Dr Will in here.'

Lillian held on to the doorframe. Swallow. Inhale. She couldn't seem to see into the room.

'Come on, Lillian. We're going in now.'

Dawn had her fingers on Lillian's arm, but Lillian was still grasping the doorframe. She tipped her head back. Swallow. Inhale. On the ceiling was a large stain the shape and colour of a potato. A hole in the tiles with a bunch of wires dangling from it. If she reached up, would she be able to pull the whole ceiling down?

'Just take a look with me, OK?'

'No.'

Dawn increased the pressure on Lillian's arm. Lillian yanked herself away. They stared at each other for a moment. Dawn's lips were pursed but her eyes had a bored sheen. She said, 'Don't make me fetch Alex.'

Lillian ran.

It was very hard to say when it had all begun.

A few years ago, after meeting Jim, she'd slimmed down a bit – probably all that dancing – and he'd encouraged her by commenting that she was lighter everywhere now, not just on her feet. Following her mother's attack, she'd begun to skip a few meals, and her regulars in the salon had congratulated her on her new slenderness. But it wasn't until the death of her mother in the spring that Lillian realised quite how much weight she'd lost. Mick noticed, and told her she was already 'lovely and slim' and she shouldn't 'take it too far'. At the salon, she saw her reflection in the mirrors and liked how she took up less space. She began to try things on in every clothes shop, regardless of whether she could afford to buy them, just for the feeling of fitting into things, of being the right shape, and, later on, the sensation of fabric swimming around her. What a triumph it was to be too small! There was power in it, and also pleasure. Going into Woolworth's, she was aware of other women's eyes on her and felt elated because this enabled her to forget, for hours at a time, that she'd abandoned her mother, leaving her alone with those bottles of pills at number 25, and that now she was dead. Lillian could forget, too, that she'd failed to go to art school and was married to Mick Harries, who increasingly seemed like a stranger, while Jim Shepherd cycled past her front gate twice daily and pretended not to notice her. She was able to forget all this, to hold her head up, to feel the sun on her face.

She did everything she could to keep that feeling close. She began writing lists in an old exercise book. *Breakfast: 1/2 grapefruit, black tea. Lunch: 1 slice toast, Bovril. Apple. Tea: 1 slice luncheon meat. 2 boiled potatoes. Peas. Weight: 6 st 11 lb.* She also began baking. She stood in the kitchen, sifting, creaming, folding, just as she had with her mother. She found it was possible to make a Victoria sponge without eating a slice (she reserved a third for Mick and took the rest into the salon), and also possible to spend all day thinking about food, planning meals, shopping for food, preparing food, and not take more than a few bites. Somewhere in the back of her mind she knew this was not a good thing to do. But if her mother's old scales showed a loss, she was close to that elated feeling. And so she carried on.

Phyllis noticed. She told Lillian she looked like Jean Shrimpton and asked if she was taking diet pills. Lillian shrugged, delighted, and said she just hadn't felt very hungry, since her mother had passed.

But she was hungry. So hungry that it woke her in the night, gnawing at her insides, squeezing her mind into one single thought: food. She must have it. But she must not have it. What would be left, if she gave in? Sometimes she made a bargain with herself: she could have a glass of milk and a biscuit now if she made up for it tomorrow by cutting out breakfast altogether. Or lunch. Or both. Other times she lay there, Mick sleeping at her side, imagining Trotman's window display: the trays of doughnuts sequinned with sugar, the softly folded Chelseas, the cream-stuffed apple turnovers. Still other times, she rose from the bed and sat in the front room (the kitchen was too risky) where she pored over the details of the most wicked entries in the recipe books she'd borrowed from the library: coq au vin, beef Wellington, salmon en croute. There was one close-up photograph of a hunk of glistening pork crackling, tiny cubes of salt visible on its surface, which felt vaguely pornographic. She salivated, then hid the books beneath the settee.

She lost more weight. Phyllis told her to be careful, saying that Mick might miss having something to get hold of. Lillian didn't want to displease Mick but she hated the thought of herself as some kind of comforting pillow. And she'd liked it when he'd mentioned her weight loss, one night in bed. 'Look!' he'd said. 'I can almost get my hands right around your waist!' He'd demonstrated, clasping her middle with both hands, seeming shocked, but also – undoubtedly – pleased. Her thought had been: Only *almost*? And she'd silently vowed to make herself so small that she could slip away from him. It frightened and exhilarated her, that idea of sliding free.

Not long after her mother died, she decided to pay Ernie a visit. As she'd suspected, he'd failed to come to number 25 since the funeral, and she wanted to punish him for that by putting him on the spot. She imagined saying it in a chirpy, offhand way. *Not that it matters now, but is it you, then, Uncle Ernie? Are you my father?* To do so would no longer hurt her mother. And if Ernie was going to disappear anyway, she might as well know the truth.

It was a dull, warm Saturday afternoon when she walked across town to Wilsham Road, and all the way there she experienced an invigorating sense of purpose. Despite the threat of Daphne's piercing gaze, she was going in search of what was rightfully hers. She'd always told herself that she didn't need a father, that her mother was quite enough to be going along with. But now her mother was gone, there was all this . . . What was it? Loss. Longing. But also nothingness. Space. Space into which she could surely ask this one question.

She remembered the house all too well, though she hadn't walked by it since that evening Ernie had driven her there to tell her about Longbrook. The perfect square of lawn was looking a little brown, but everything else was the same.

When Daphne answered the door, it occurred to Lillian that it might have been better to telephone first.

'Is Uncle Ernie in? I need to ask him something.'

There was a moment of silence as Daphne studied Lillian with her kohl-rimmed eyes. 'It's you,' she said.

It had begun to rain, sending an earthy smell up from the lawn.

'He's not here, but come on in.' Daphne turned and walked along the hall, leaving the door open.

Lillian had little choice but to follow her into the front room. Though it was June, the electric fire was going and the place smelled of cigarettes and perfume.

'Now. Tea? Or how about something stronger?'

Lillian declined and Daphne gave a resigned grimace. 'Suit yourself. I need a sherry.' She reached for a bottle and a glass from the sideboard, poured herself a drink then settled in the armchair next to the fire. 'Have a seat, dear. It's so lovely to see you.'

On the mantelpiece was a framed photograph in which a young Daphne stood on the riverbank, holding a plump baby in her arms. The baby gaped at her face, surprised.

Daphne said, 'That's you, of course. When you were living here with us.'

Lillian nodded.

'Why don't you have a drink?' Daphne was already pouring another measure, which this time Lillian accepted. 'So what was it you wanted to ask?'

'It's – personal.'

Daphne looked at her steadily, then said, 'You know, when we brought you back here we were so *happy*. Chubby little thing you were, then. You settled down a treat. I thought to myself: She fits right in. And you never cried. Not until we had to hand you back to your mother, when you went stiff as a board. Bright purple, too.' As Daphne spoke, she stared at the photo on the mantelpiece, as though recounting the tale to her younger self. Then she suddenly stood and said, 'Stay there. I've something to show you.'

While Daphne was out of the room, Lillian got to her feet, swaying slightly. She'd skipped lunch, and the heat and the alcohol made her light-headed. She decided she would make an excuse to leave as soon as Daphne reappeared. She couldn't ask this woman anything. For her mother's sake, it had to be Ernie himself she questioned. But when Daphne returned, carrying a large cloth bag with wooden handles, she was already talking. 'Here we are. Some keepsakes from that year you were with us.'

Lillian used a hand to steady herself against the wall. 'Year?'

'It was a year and fifteen days before your mother was in a fit state to have you back. And even then . . .'

'Ernie said it was a few months.'

Daphne was busy digging in the bag, laying out items on the settee. 'I expect he wanted to save your feelings. I mean, it's not nice to think about, is it? Your poor mother! Electric shock treatment and all! Imagine it! Being *restrained*. And the *pain*. Awful!' She shuddered, then continued laying the items on the settee.

Lillian closed her eyes. *Your poor mother.* She did not want to hear any of this. She needed to get out of this place. She should never have come.

When she opened her eyes she saw a yellow lacy cardigan. A knitted hat and booties. A dress with roses embroidered around the hem and sleeves. Smoothing the dress, Daphne said, 'You looked a picture in that one.'

Lillian stood staring at the items. Then she found herself asking, 'Shock treatment?'

'Oh dear. Didn't she tell you?' Daphne reached for her hand, but Lillian put it in her pocket.

'I'm sorry, love. I didn't realise you didn't know—'

'She never spoke about it.'

Daphne nodded. 'I suppose she wouldn't.' She sat back on her haunches. 'It was quite a new thing, back then. Ernie told me she said it just made her forget. She couldn't remember a lot of what happened in that place. Which was probably a blessing, don't you think?'

Lillian, who had no idea what she thought, said, 'She was in there for a year?'

'Thereabouts. Her own mother wouldn't fetch her home! She just . . . deposited her there. Imagine! Of course, she'd already thrown her out on account of her expecting you. Ernie said she'd taken up with a new fella after Winnie's dad died and that was it. End of story. Having an unmarried mother for a daughter was bad enough, but an unmarried mother who'd been taken to Longbrook . . .' She trailed off. 'Anyway. Ernie got Winnie out of there in the end, thank goodness, and into another house . . . By that time I didn't want to give you up, but Ernie insisted we had to let your mother try again. He was so soft with her, even after all she put him through. Fancy doing such a thing, with a beautiful baby to look after!'

Lillian sank into the armchair, trying to take it all in. Daphne was stroking the booties, still talking. 'Ernie promised me we'd see you. But it was all so . . . difficult, with your mother. I suppose she had to claim you for herself, didn't she? But it broke my heart.'

She glanced up and seemed to brighten. 'But – look! You're here now! Which is wonderful. And aren't these pretty? Why don't you take them home? They're yours, after all.'

Lillian swallowed. She'd heard more than enough. Nothing in this house was *hers*! She had to stop Daphne talking. So she said in a clear, loud voice: 'I hoped Ernie might be able to tell me something about my father.'

Which did the trick. Daphne was silent.

'Do you know anything about him?' Lillian asked. 'Anything at all?'

Daphne put the booties down and said carefully, 'You'll have to ask Ernie. I promised him long ago that I wouldn't get into all that.'

'Mum used to say he was from London,' said Lillian, with a short laugh. 'She told me he was called Maurice. He sold stuff out of the boot of his car and he looked like Montgomery Clift.'

Daphne raised her eyebrows. 'Did she, now?' She stretched one of the dresses out and examined the stitching. 'Why don't you at least take these with you?'

Lillian stared at the dress. It was hard to believe her own body had ever been contained by it.

'I'm just sorry you didn't get to stay here, with me and Ernie,' said Daphne. 'I can't help thinking it would've been better all round. Sometimes a woman just isn't cut out for motherhood. No fault of her own, but there it is.'

Lillian got to her feet, trembling with rage and confusion. 'If you're going to insult my mother, I think I'd better leave.'

Daphne flapped a hand. 'Now, don't be silly, love! . . . I've got cake out in the kitchen. Stay at least until Ernie gets in. Then you can ask him your question.'

But Lillian had left the room and was heading for the front door.

'You know you can come here any time, don't you?' she heard Daphne call after her.

The thud of boots on the perfect lawn. Rasping breaths. She hadn't even reached the gates before she knew they would catch her. She stopped and turned to face the men. Alex and an older brown-skinned man, who wore a turban and had a thick beard. The older man said, still panting, 'Want to come back for a cup of tea, love?'

Unlike Alex, he looked at her directly, and while he didn't smile, his voice was calm. His eyes were also very beautiful. Dark, framed by thick lashes.

'No,' she said. 'I want to go home.'

In the distance, a lawnmower started up.

The man rubbed his beard. 'Dr Will would like to talk with you,' he said.

How many times had this man stood on this lawn, very politely saying this sort of thing to some poor woman running towards the road?

Alex was gazing over her head towards the gates, as though he, too, wanted nothing more than to run through them.

'And there's bingo later!' Beautiful Eyes said. 'Housey-housey!'

She smiled a little at that, more in confusion than approval, and this was their cue to grasp her by the elbows and lead her back to the hospital. Lillian, suddenly feeling terribly tired, hung her head. She let herself be led.

They marched her through the door to ward 7, where a man in a suit was perched on the end of a bed.

His red socks peeked from between the hems of his trousers

and the pair of white plimsolls on his feet. His hair, which he now swept across his forehead, was the colour of bread crusts and long over his ears. His collar was open and he wore no tie. She thought he was probably around forty, and she didn't begin to believe he was a doctor until he spoke.

'You must be Lillian,' he said, standing and holding out a hand. 'My preference is to be called Will but most people here seem to insist upon Dr Will.'

His voice reminded her of all the priests who'd spoken during school assemblies. Deliberately subdued. Lofty. Correct. She said nothing, keeping her arms folded.

Dr Will dropped his hand. 'Alex, Akal, you can leave us, thanks,' he said. 'I think the dayroom might need some attention.'

The two men retreated, Akal whistling softly as he went.

'Shall we sit?' the doctor asked, walking towards the high-backed chairs lined up by the French doors. She followed, perching a few chairs away from him.

'I want to welcome you, Lillian, and to explain a few things about how it all works here.'

'I've changed my mind,' she said. 'I want to go home.'

Dr Will nodded. 'But I wonder if you can consider: is going home what you really need at the moment?'

She stared at him, uncomprehending. He was wearing an expression of lightly amused patience.

'We all have *wants*, don't we? For example, I want a new briefcase. But I don't really need one in order to live a satisfactory life. Can you tell me, Lillian, what *you* might need in order to live satisfactorily?'

'To get out of here.'

He smiled at that. 'Quite so. And that's ultimately what we want, too: to help you live a normal life beyond this hospital. We're always working towards our patients' home-goings. But can you tell me what will enable you to do that?'

It was like doing an oral exam in a foreign language. What the hell was a *home-going*? Surely he meant *homecoming*?

'I need money for the bus.'

He laughed, once. When she scowled at him, his amused expression faded. 'I understand from your GP and your husband that you've stopped eating properly. Is that right?'

'I don't know.'

'Let me help you. Are you eating three good meals a day? A few snacks in-between?'

'I suppose not.'

'And you've lost an enormous amount of weight over the last year, is that correct?'

An enormous amount. Yes, that was correct. And good. She nodded.

'So much weight, in fact, that you are now seriously emaciated. Nurse Dawn will pop you on the scales in a bit but there's really no need. I can see with my own eyes that you are dangerously underweight.' He paused. 'Can you tell me how food – the thought of food – makes you feel?'

Oh! she wanted to cry. *Like I could burst with hunger and shame!*

'A bit . . . uncomfortable,' she said.

'And can you say why that is?'

Why was he asking questions with such obvious answers? 'I don't want to get fat.'

He nodded. 'And do you think that's a problem, considering that you are clearly morbidly underweight?'

But it's my problem, she wanted to say. *Mine. And what would I do without it?* 'I don't know,' she said.

He crossed and uncrossed his legs and frowned, apparently considering his options. 'Lillian, don't you *want* to get better?'

'Not here.'

'I'm wondering, then, if you can tell me what getting better might mean – here or elsewhere?'

She should have kept on running earlier, when she'd had half a chance. She glanced towards the doors. They were closed, but were they locked?

'Lillian?'

Outside, a man rode past on a lawnmower, waving at the window. Dr Will gave a small wave back. 'Our head gardener. Wonderful chap. Lots of our patients find it very rewarding to work in the gardens here. And many women work on the wards, organising and preparing meals, cleaning – just as they would at home.' Focusing once more on her, he asked, 'What do you need to do, to be well? Can you tell me that?'

'Put on weight, I suppose,' she said, hoping this answer would be good enough to prompt the end of the conversation and the doctor's exit.

'Excellent. But not quite correct.'

'Put on enough weight?' The doors didn't *look* locked.

He smiled. 'Well, yes. But more importantly, I think you need to *believe it's all right* to put on weight.'

Dr Will rubbed at the knee of his trouser leg as though it were stained, which it wasn't. 'I know this is all very difficult, Lillian. But I'd like to strike a bargain with you, if I may. I have a form of treatment which I think works very well for your condition. Would you like to hear about it?'

He leaned closer, examining her face. She could smell mints on him. It was clear that he wouldn't leave until he'd told her. So she said, 'All right.'

He clasped his hands together and settled back into his chair, apparently more relaxed. 'You go to a special room, your own room, where you get round-the-clock care from our best nurses. To help you, they'll administer a medicine which will make you feel very calm, and much more *positive* about eating. And, once you approach a more healthy weight, you'll join the others on the ward for something called group therapy. It's quite a new thing, and I think it works most marvellously well.'

The idea of feeling positive about eating brought tears to her eyes, but she wasn't sure whether they were of longing or fear. What would that be like? It was impossible to imagine. To hide her emotion, she asked him a direct question. 'Will you force me to eat?'

'Not unless your life is in grave danger.'

She gazed into her lap, picturing her mother strapped to a table with electrodes jammed to the sides of her skull. 'Will you give me . . . electric shocks?'

'We won't administer ECT without your approval.'

She took a breath, then looked up. 'So I just have to take this medicine?'

'And eat every meal that you are given. We usually find that, once ladies reach a good weight, they feel much better about eating generally. When the body is healthy the mind follows. And then we can work towards your home-going, can't we? My hope is that you will get better and be home within six weeks with this treatment.'

The lawnmower moaned past the window again, the gardener still waving, but this time Dr Will did not raise a hand. Instead, he looked Lillian in the eye and said, 'If we don't manage to get your weight increased in the next month or so, your internal organs will start to shut down. And once that happens, things get very grim indeed. There's only one ultimate outcome to starvation, as I'm sure you understand.'

The doctor tipped his head in a way that suggested he might have enjoyed giving his little speech.

She'd heard something similar, albeit more directly expressed, from Mick. *You'll die! That's the only way this ends! With you starving to death!* Those words had done nothing to weaken her resolve. Lillian had thought him ridiculous. Hysterical. But this doctor sounded quite logical. Maybe she could meet him in the middle. Agree to what he wanted but flee before the treatment started.

She swallowed. 'All right.'

'Good. So we'll start today.'

'Today?'

'We've no time to lose, have we?' he said, getting to his feet. 'I'll send Dawn to help you prepare.'

Mick had cried. He'd put his big, handsome head in his hands and wept. Lillian hadn't believed her husband capable of such a thing, but there he'd been, on the edge of their bed, sobbing. She'd made a mistake, and allowed him to see her naked form. Usually she made sure he was at work or in the garden before she performed her twice-daily examination from every angle in the bedroom mirror, but on that Saturday she hadn't heard him creep back up the stairs and he'd caught her, completely naked in front of the glass. She'd been half-smiling at herself, pleased that her elbows were still angular, her wrists prominent, her thigh bones visible from hip to knee.

Mick clapped a hand over his mouth, as though suppressing a sudden urge to vomit. Then he sank to the mattress and gaped at her.

'What?' she asked, grabbing at her dressing gown.

He shook his head.

'What?' she asked again, tying the cord tight.

Perhaps her stare had been too strong, too defiant. Because that's when the shouting started. He couldn't go on like this, he yelled. He didn't know what the hell was wrong with her, but he couldn't take it any more. She had to get to the doctor. Now. It was either that or he would leave.

She said he should calm down. She'd just lost a bit too much, that was all. She hadn't meant to.

And he shouted that he'd been calm all summer. He'd tried to remain calm and talk reasonably to her about this. He knew this was deliberate. But she had denied everything, every time.

And now she looked like a concentration camp victim. How could she be so fucking stupid? Didn't she realise she'd never get pregnant like this?

Lillian realised it well enough. But she said nothing.

On Monday, before he left for work, Mick informed her that he'd booked an appointment with the doctor and he would take her down there himself as soon as he got in.

Where could she have gone, if she'd refused? Her mother was dead. Ernie hadn't contacted her, and she had no wish to set foot in his house again, after Daphne's comments about her mother. Gwen was living in her student digs in York.

And she couldn't leave number 25. She couldn't lose that, too.

There was also a part of her that wanted it known: she was unwell. She needed help. *Look how ill you have made me!* she wanted to cry. Though to whom, exactly, was less clear to her.

Lillian was disappointed when Dawn didn't flinch at the number on the scales. The nurse took her blood, examined her ears and throat, then showed her to the bathroom. Its metal soap dispensers, hair-clogged shower drain and fumes of pine disinfectant reminded Lillian of the school changing rooms. She was glad there was no mirror, so she couldn't watch herself shedding her clothes. She stood beneath the tepid water, shivering, then scrubbed herself dry with a greying towel. Hanging on the back of the door was a large nightgown, high at the neck with what might once have been a pattern of daisies on the bib, the lace edging on the sleeves washed to softness. As she stepped into the nightgown, she felt an odd relief. All her clothes had been taken from her and her body was about to be placed in the hands of others.

Back on the empty ward, her teeth chattered as Dawn handed her a pair of pink slippers and told her not to worry; she was going to give her some medicine to help her. If she took this, she would be able to eat. Just a little at first. They would take it slowly. Wouldn't that be good? She held out a spoonful of liquid, and, remembering her mother's bottles of pills, Lillian opened her mouth to ask what, exactly, she was taking. But before she could speak, the spoon was in her mouth and she swallowed.

'What was that?' she asked, panicked.

'A little something to help you relax.'

'A tranquilliser?'

Dawn put her head to one side. 'Think yourself lucky,' she said. 'Lots of people would pay good money for that.'

Lillian watched her own body walk down the corridor. *Slap. Slap. Slap.* The slippers kissed her heels and clapped the tiles. Like a countdown. The nurses led her, carefully. One was the woman who came this morning. Dawn. So appropriate. The other was Beautiful Eyes. Akal. It was a mistake, Lillian knew, to confuse beauty with tenderness. But beauty was not nothing, and she was grateful for it.

Slap, slap, slap. Such a regular rhythm. 'You're doing really well,' Akal assured her, and she thought of Jim Shepherd holding her elbow in the Corn Exchange as they walked to the dance floor, just as Akal was doing now. *I like the way you dance*, Jim had said, before correcting himself: *No, I* love *the way you dance.* That had been the only time he'd used the word in relation to her, but she'd felt he really meant it. It was offered simply as a piece of true information. It had been, she saw now, a gift.

Beautiful Eyes opened the door to a room with blinds folded across the windows. It was modern, like the reception area. A picture of lilies on the wall. A bed, its sheets a blank white lozenge. The quiet was punctuated by Lillian's own breathing and a steady ticking sound. Another nurse was sitting by the bed, wearing a neat pink dress.

The slapping was replaced by a muffled thump. Sweat formed on Lillian's top lip, beneath her armpits, between her toes. A heaviness landed on her chest. She wondered if she'd stepped into some sort of waiting room for death. The nurse sitting by the bed was knitting. Something pale blue draped across her knees.

'Lillian,' said Beautiful Eyes, 'we need you to lie down, please. Complete rest, now.'

She knew this to be true. She really must lie down. What other choice was there? She was so tired. Her limbs leaden. Her breath slow. But her body rebelled, pulling away from them. Beautiful Eyes caught her with his large hands and Dawn was at her side and suddenly she was held – so easily – and the floor disappeared from beneath her feet. She was airborne. The lace edging on her sleeves dangled and there was a great noise which seemed to come from her own mouth. The other nurse was on her feet. The knitting needle became a syringe plunging into Lillian's thigh – it felt cold, more than painful. And then she was theirs.

She was coming to the surface of something. All she wanted was to stay in the blissful nothing of the warm, light place where every part of her was relaxed. But her eyes flickered open. A ticking noise. A bright room. The weight of her body. Her limbs so heavy she couldn't lift them. Her stomach roiling. Her nightgown – was it hers? – wet with sweat. Where were her hands? Her feet? Her eyelids closed. She willed the blissful nothing to return.

'How are you feeling, Lillian?'

Beautiful Eyes. Then she remembered. The hospital. Longbrook.

She should scream. Try to run. But her body seemed stuck to the bed, and all she could manage was a growl. Beautiful Eyes wiped her face with a damp cloth, offered her water through a straw. She sipped. His fingertips were on her wrist. She remembered his name. Akal.

He smiled. 'You've had a good long sleep. You'll be groggy for a while but you'll be fine, don't worry.'

She stared at him. It was the strangest thing. She knew she was frightened but her body had no response to this knowledge.

Her limbs remained weighted. Her eyelids drooped. Akal slid out of focus.

'Good,' he said. 'Sleep a while longer.'

Awake again. She could move her fingers, then her whole arm. She checked her middle for flesh. Slick with sweat. But flat. She traced the angle of her hipbone. The keys of her ribs.

She opened her eyes.

'Oh,' said Akal. 'Hello. How are you feeling?'

Her tongue was thick, her throat scratchy.

'I'm going to get you a nice drink, all right? Just drinks today. That's all you've got to do, Lillian. Keep drinking.'

Her eyes closed.

Two women were standing over her. They wavered and merged into one, then back into two, then one. The woman grasped a pair of knitting needles.

'You caused a right racket,' she said, 'the other day. Nearly knocked poor Dawn flying. You feeling all right, now?'

The woman blurred and became two again. 'Yeah,' she said. 'You'll be OK.'

Akal stepped close with a tray.

'I was just saying, she's calmed right down now.'

He drew a table across Lillian's bed and balanced his tray on it.

'You *were* naughty,' said the nurse, grinning.

'Thanks, Jenny,' said Akal. 'I can take this from here.'

Jenny disappeared.

Akal closed the curtain around the bed. The two of them bathed in a sea of green light. Warm and smelling faintly of chlorine. Swimming pools. If she closed her eyes, perhaps she could sink into the water. She heard her mother's voice. *You could get pulled under, and I can't save you.*

Akal squeezed her hand. 'How are you feeling, then?'

A noise came from her mouth.

He nodded. 'Drink up. Then you can sleep again, if you like.'

He propped up her pillows, helped her to sit. His hands were firm, strong. He held out a plastic beaker. 'Just some milk.'

She thought of the warm bottles handed out at primary school. The smell alone made her feel sick.

'It's nice and sweet,' said Akal, angling the straw towards her mouth.

She took a sniff. Not much to smell. But when she sipped, it was buttery and rich on her tongue. She drank half of it straight down. It sat heavily in her stomach. She closed her eyes. Sleep should come, now.

'You're doing really well,' said Akal. 'A good rest was exactly what you needed. One step closer to getting out of here, yes?' The drink had been replaced by a spoonful of clear medicine, which he tipped into her mouth as he spoke. 'This will help you back to sleep.' He wiped her lips. 'And when you wake up, I'll be here, and you'll have another nice drink. Very simple, yes?'

She nodded. Swallowed. Slept.

How many times was this repeated? Every time she opened her eyes, it was the same. She was dragged from the blissful nothing, into the swimming-pool-green. Her mother's voice. *I can't save you.* Two smiling Akals becoming one. *Very simple, yes?* The sweet clag of the drink. The bitter kick of the medicine. How many times? She never remembered to count until her eyelids were drooping again.

Then one day – she'd no idea which day, or even if it was day at all – she awakened not to the drink but to a tray of food.

She smelled it before she saw it. Savoury and fresh. Fish in white sauce, mashed potatoes, peas. Something custardy in a green bowl. It was difficult to remember exactly why she shouldn't eat. Her body felt weighted, as though covered in warm sand. An alarm went off in her brain but her body didn't respond to it. Saliva flooded her mouth. Her stomach gurgled. Smiling Akal helped her sit, leaning her forward to prop the pillows behind her. He positioned the table over her legs. She was aware of a new softness to her middle.

But she could float above all this. She watched herself take up the fork and eat a few mouthfuls.

All the while, Akal talked. He said, 'You are doing really very well.' And, 'I'm so proud of you.' And, 'What a champion you are, Lillian!'

She liked that.

She liked his accent, too. It danced over words like 'champion'. No one with skin the colour of Akal's had ever spoken directly to her. It made her feel as if she had stepped out of her usual world.

She ate everything. Even the stewed prunes. The sweet fruit and silky custard were calming in her mouth.

Then a buzzing sensation pushed through her veins and her breathing quickened. A hot flush ran through her body. Her limbs jerked from the warm sand, sloughing off its weight. As she pushed herself from the bed her arms gave way, as though made of paper straws. Sweat bloomed across her face. She yelled the word *no*. She had eaten so much. She must move. Purge herself somehow.

Akal had the syringe in her leg. He told her it would all be all right in a jiffy. Then he held her hand. Smiled. 'Breathe with me now,' he said. 'Just breathe. Very simple, yes?'

She did as she was told. The warm sand covered her again.

When she woke, Akal spooned in the medicine.

★

How many times was this repeated? She never remembered to keep count until her eyelids were drooping.

A blistering whiteness. A man in a suit was sitting on the edge of the bed, talking to Akal.

She registered the word *weight*. She knew this word had a siren in it, though her body didn't seem to feel it.

The doctor turned to her. Swept his hair across his forehead.

'Hello, Lillian,' he said. He had been here before. On her bed. Legs crossed. Rubbing at an imaginary stain on his knee.

Akal's hand was on her forearm. 'I was just telling Dr Will that you're doing wonderfully well.'

Dr Will beamed. 'As I knew you would. How are you feeling?'

Like shit, she thought.

'Akal here is doing a super job of looking after you. I'm very pleased with how you're doing. Only a week more of this treatment, and then – if you continue to progress – you can get up and about. After that we can think about you going home. How would that be?'

She could not think what this word *home* meant.

'Your husband will be pleased,' said Dr Will.

Jim's hand on her elbow.

The blankets lightened, and the doctor was replaced by a meal. Meat pie, roast potatoes, gravy, carrots, peas. A bowl of syrup sponge. Her stomach growled. Akal smiled. 'We're on the last stretch, now.'

She positioned herself above her body. Then began to eat.

Once she was out of here she could put things right.

Into the blissful nothing, her mother came again.

She was waving from the bedroom window. Waving and calling her daughter home. *I've made a cake*, she said. *Hurry. It's waiting for you.*

But as Lillian moved closer, Winnie's calls grew frantic. Instead of waving, she was clutching a tea towel and screeching her name. Lillian sprinted to the house, but when she reached the front gate, her mother had disappeared from the window. And when she opened the back door, there was no one in the house. Her satchel hung on the larder door, useless and abandoned.

'So what do you think?' asked Dr Will. 'Ready to transfer to the ward?'

Lillian was sitting in a chair, her legs covered with a blanket. The bitter medicine still came three times a day, before meals. It wasn't lost on her that this medicine must have been similar to the one her mother had taken. Or that she'd ended up in the very same place as her mother. But she couldn't think very hard about this. She couldn't think very hard about anything at all.

Dr Will, perched on the edge of the bed, swung one foot over his knee and grasped his laces, leaning towards her. 'Your body is healing itself, Lillian. What we have to work on now is your mind. And that starts with getting you back on your feet, and with other people.'

It was so comfortable sitting there! The medicine keeping her body beneath that layer of warm sand that pushed most thoughts away and allowed her to get on with the business of eating, the business of sleeping. Both of which seemed a little safer, because the hospital was a temporary holding place. A unit. Akal told her eating and sleeping were necessary to live, yet she had been in danger of giving them up altogether. Which would have been a tragedy. Lillian wasn't sure she agreed. But it was good to see the kindness in his eyes when he said it.

Dr Will was talking. 'In the morning we all work together. So you'll be helping to keep the ward clean and tidy. And in the afternoons, there's all sorts going on. Basket-weaving. Bingo.

And we have a party whenever there's an excuse. Sometimes even if there isn't one.' He flicked a smile her way.

'I think Lillian likes art,' said Akal. 'Is that right?'

Lillian stared at him. How did he know, when she herself had forgotten?

'And I believe there's an art class, isn't there, Will?' Akal said.

'Oh yes,' said the doctor. 'Of course. Every Thursday afternoon.'

Akal winked at her. 'Shall we sign you up for that, then?'

She nodded.

The doctor slipped out through the curtains.

'I'll come and visit you on the ward,' said Akal. 'You'll be on Gresham. You'll have a bed right by the window. There's a lovely garden out there, you know.'

She remembered sprinting across the lawn, chased by him.

'Magnificent cedars of Lebanon,' Akal said, as he smoothed the covers on the bed. 'Glorious rose bushes. Geraniums. Dahlias. Hydrangeas. The lot.'

'How did you know I liked art?'

He sat on the mattress and studied her, looking a little surprised. She realised this was the first sentence she'd spoken to him.

'Call it a lucky guess,' he said eventually. 'This illness seems to affect the arty girls. Don't ask me why.'

She tried to make sense of this information. What was her *illness*, exactly?

She felt pleased to be an arty girl. But did this mean she must starve herself? Art didn't seem like something that would starve you.

She asked, 'Is this an illness, then?'

'Of course. Didn't you know that?'

She looked at the soft creases in his shoes. Was she supposed to know that?

'Lillian,' he said, 'why do you think you're here?'

'Because I was so thin.'

'You have *anorexia nervosa*. Do you know what that means?'

She shook her head.

'*Anorexia* means lack of appetite. But *nervosa* means nervous. Of the mind. A lack of appetite, coming from the mind.' He tapped his forehead and smiled.

Lack of appetite? That couldn't be right. Though she longed for such a thing.

'But I stopped eating,' she said. 'It's something I chose to do. So how can it be an illness?'

Akal crossed his arms and tilted his head to the side, thinking. 'Your mind made the decision. But that doesn't mean it was your fault.'

He looked at her for such a long time that she had to drop her gaze once more. Then she said, 'Has my husband been to see me?'

'Not yet.'

'I thought he might have come when I was asleep.'

'He didn't. I'm sorry.'

She'd suspected Mick would avoid visiting Longbrook. And there was relief in the anger she felt. Now she could blame him, when he'd seemed almost innocent before.

'Maybe it's good he didn't see me like this,' she said.

Akal shrugged. 'You could talk about that when you start your group therapy. It's good to talk through your problems with someone who understands.'

'What if I don't have any problems?'

'Then you are a rare person indeed. Or dead, perhaps.'

'I could make it up, I suppose,' she said, thinking, *That's what Gwen would do*. She had a sudden longing for Gwen's open freckled face and her loud laugh. Her way of throwing straight and winning prizes. After marrying Mick, Lillian had stopped writing to her friend for reasons she could now barely recall. Something to do with shame, she thought.

'Can I send letters from here?'

'Of course,' said Akal. 'You want to write to your husband?'

'No,' she said.

He brought her paper, a pen, an envelope.

Dear Gwen,

I hope you're having fun in York. I'm sorry I haven't written for ages. It's a long story but Mum and I fell out for a while and I ended up married to Mick Harries. Did you know that?

I am in hospital. I'm not sure how it happened but after Mum died I got really thin. Apparently I have something called 'anorexia nervosa'. Have you heard of it? They tell me I'm getting better now but I have to stay for a while longer.

Anyway, there's a lot to catch up on, so please write to me. It would be so good to hear from you.

She could remember most of Gwen's address, which she wrote on the envelope. Akal said he'd post it straight away.

There were four beds on either side of Gresham Ward. In the space next to Lillian's, a woman sat in a chair, frowning at a jigsaw on a tray-table. Lillian judged her to be around sixty. The woman picked up a jigsaw piece, slid her spectacles down her nose, and held it close to one eye to examine it. Then she tossed it back in the box, leaned towards Lillian, and said, 'It gets easier. You get used to it.' Her eyes were huge behind her glasses. 'I'm Joan. What's your sentence?'

'Pardon?'

'When can you go home?'

'I don't know. They haven't said. A few weeks, I think.'

'I been waiting for months, you know. I keep telling Doc

Willy, I'm absolutely fine! And when I'm not fine, I'll just come back here for a little holiday!'

Beneath her lipstick, her teeth were grey. On Joan's bed was the lid of the jigsaw's box, with the words *Scenic Oxford* printed over a picture of a man standing on a punt, beaming into the overhanging willow trees. For a moment Lillian was back by the river in Abingdon, walking towards the weir. She flicked a look towards the ward door and saw it was open. It was pointless to run, though: she had no idea how to get out of this place, and her limbs were too heavy to move fast.

She slid her suitcase from beneath the bed, lifting it onto her lap and opening it. Every item was out of place: the Van Gogh book and the sketchbook were on top of the photograph. Then she remembered Akal saying her clothes had already been put away in the cupboard. Someone had riffled through the case. *Lillian likes art.* So that was how he'd known. She felt in the lining for the bottle of laxatives she'd hidden before leaving. Nothing.

From the bed opposite, a woman with a severe fringe lit up a cigarette.

'Not supposed to smoke in here, are you, Anna?' said Joan.

The woman ignored her, taking a long drag while squinting at Lillian.

'Dayroom's for smoking,' said Joan.

'My advice is this: do not listen to that woman's prattle.' Anna pointed her cigarette at Lillian. 'Want one? They won't come round for another ten minutes.'

She was almost as thin as Lillian, with huge, yellowy eyes. The skin on her neck and hands looked baggy.

A nurse, her rectangular-shaped body encased in a navy-blue dress, strode in.

'Put it out, please, Anna,' she said smoothly. Unlike the other nurses, she wore a uniform: her short sleeves were decorated with gathered white cuffs and a white cap was tightly gripped to her hair. 'We don't want to have to take all your cigarettes away, do we?'

Anna ground the cigarette into a saucer by her bed, staring at Lillian all the while. 'What are you in for?' she asked.

'She's coming with me,' said the nurse. 'Lillian, I'm Sister Barbara, and I'm taking you to lunch.' She handed her two pills and a plastic beaker of water.

'Thought so,' said Anna.

Sister Barbara watched Lillian with steady eyes. Without the pills it would be very difficult to eat anything at all. And she wanted the warm sand feeling. So she swallowed them.

'Good girl,' Sister Barbara said. 'Follow me.'

'Enjoy your lunch,' Anna called after them.

Through the canteen window, the sun touched Lillian's face. Her breathing slowed. Sister Barbara delivered two plates of food to the table and sat opposite. 'What a lovely day!' she said, tucking in to her lunch.

Lillian watched her own hand as it lifted the fork and speared a chip. She looked at the glistening potato for a moment, aware of Sister Barbara's eyes on her. So this was who she was, now. Tranquillised, like her mother. Drugged, and eating chips. What would happen if she were to throw the fork to the floor and scream?

'You're doing so well,' said Sister Barbara.

Lillian chewed. Swallowed. Chewed. Through the window, she watched the cedars shiver in the breeze.

'Good girl,' said Sister Barbara. 'Carry on like that and you'll be out of here in no time.'

When she dreamed, it was always of her mother.

Winnie moaning like a pantomime ghost. Or screeching with a tea towel. Or waving from the bedroom window.

Whatever her mother was doing, Lillian could not reach her.

It was early October.

Every day the routine was the same. Breakfast at seven, followed by chores. Lillian was in 'Home Group' and it was her duty to clean the ward windows. Pills and lunch. Rest. Time outside or a class in handicrafts, needlework or flower-arranging. Pills and dinner. Television in the dayroom. Bed at nine thirty.

Whenever a feeling of panic rose – it began in her stomach, a tightness that made her breath quicken and her hands clench and her thoughts turn to how she must escape, how the days that were left were too many and she must get out of this place and stop her body expanding – it was stifled by the pills given to her by Sister Barbara. Lillian found it hard to comprehend who she'd been, before. A hairdresser. A wife. It seemed particularly impossible that she'd been a wife. She had no desire for Mick to visit her. If he were to turn up and see her like this, fat, medicated, surrendered to this system, the whole thing would become completely intolerable. And though she knew it was what he'd begged her to do, she could not believe it was what he'd really wanted.

She was, too, a daughter. Though she winced at the idea of following in her mother's footsteps, there was a strange comfort in imagining her mother in this place before her, moving through the same routines. There was comfort, too, in the idea of being reunited in the place her mother must have longed for her.

Group Meeting.

Lillian understood from Akal that this was the therapy he'd

spoken of. The patients sat in a circle in the dayroom, and Dr Will, perched on a table, one foot balanced on the opposite knee, played with the laces of his plimsoll as he waited for someone to speak. Anna smoked and tapped her slipper. Isobel, the woman Lillian had glimpsed in the corridor on her first morning, slumped in her chair and stared at the doctor. Joan held a jigsaw box on her knees, rapping at the picture. Sister Barbara, Dawn and Akal sat together near the door.

Joan said, 'I want to ask the doctor when I can go home.'

'Christ. Not this again,' said Anna.

To Lillian's surprise, no one admonished Anna for speaking in this way.

'Any thoughts on whether Joan is ready to go home?' asked Dr Will.

'I want *your* thoughts, Doctor!' said Joan.

Isobel said, 'The thing is, Joan, the thing is, you say you're ready to go home but you just come back again, don't you?'

Lillian glanced at Dr Will, who said nothing.

'But that's all right!' said Joan. 'That's perfectly all right, because this is my holiday home.'

Anna groaned.

'It isn't all right, Joan!' Isobel was almost shouting. 'It isn't all right because what's the point of going home if you only come back again?'

'Most of us have done that,' said Ivor quietly. 'Haven't we? This is my third time here.'

Ivor was the only man on the ward. He had a scar on his cheek the size and colour of a teabag. Once he invited Lillian to touch it, saying that he did it to himself one day when the voices told him his face was evil and he should cut it off.

'The doctor knows,' said Joan, her smile fixed, her speech becoming more rapid. 'He knows I'm well, don't you, Doctor? So why can't I go home?'

There was a pause. Dr Will said, 'Any thoughts, Lillian?'

Lillian stared at him, speechless.

'The issue,' the doctor said, letting his plimsoll go so he could gesture with both hands, 'is this: when is a patient ready for their home-going? How do we judge that? Does the patient himself know?'

Lillian tried to understand what was going on. It was as though Dr Will wanted some kind of classroom discussion, but the patients just wanted to air their grievances. She decided it was safest to play the doctor's game.

'It depends,' she said, 'on what you mean by home.'

Dr Will nodded seriously.

'I know exactly what *I* mean,' said Joan. 'Bicester! Home sweet home, Bicester.'

'But Lillian has raised an interesting point,' said Dr Will. 'What is home, do you think? What defines it for you? Anyone?'

'That's obvious!' said Joan. 'It's where you grew up, isn't it? Where your family is.'

Then Anna spoke, and each word was slow, low and stretched. 'Not. For. Me. I wouldn't call that place home if my life depended on it.' She ground out her cigarette, then shook a new one from the packet up her sleeve.

Dr Will gripped his plimsoll lace again. 'Anyone else feel that way?'

Isobel put a hand up, then pulled it down.

'There's only one home for me,' said Joan, cleaning her lenses with her handkerchief, her voice whispery, 'and that's where my dear old mum is.' She put on her glasses and closed her eyes, as though imagining her mother before her.

Lillian found she was unable to stop herself doing the same. Winnie was sitting beside her, holding out her arms. The cakes from Trotman's were on the spotted china plates. The fire was lit. The tales of Maurice were about to be aired. Closer, now. Her mother's powdery cheek. Lacquer and stout. That relentless, determined, insistent heartbeat. She felt Winnie's warmth. Heard her breath. The world slipped away.

Her throat swelled and her eyes pricked with tears. She found herself moaning as she sobbed. Anna rose from her chair, kneeling before Lillian and grasping her hand, hard. 'Poor girl,' she said, through a blue plume of smoke. 'Poor girl.'

2005

The cool inside Daphne's house was a relief after the heat of the late afternoon. Shutting the front door behind her, Lillian wasted no time looking downstairs. She and Rachel had already combed the front room and it was unlikely there would be anything in the kitchen, except the mouldy remains of whatever was in Daphne's larder. She felt an urgent need to find something – anything – of her mother. Despite Winnie having never stepped foot in this place, there must be some trace of her. Perhaps Ernie had kept a letter. A card. A photo. Some doctor's notes, even. Maybe he'd mentioned Winnie in a diary. At home, Lillian had a few photos, together with the peep-toe shoes bought by Maurice. But she could see now that these had never been enough. There were so many things she didn't know. She'd never known – beyond what Daphne and Ernie had said – what had really happened to her mother in Longbrook.

The runner on the stairs was worn to a shine and she almost slipped in her haste to reach the top. There were three bedrooms, two at the back of the house and one at the front. Looking in the first, she saw nothing save a single bed, neatly made, an empty wardrobe, and her own reflection in the wall mirror. For a moment she paused, frowning. Her hairline was damp with sweat, her face flushed, her T-shirt creased and smeared with a line of dirt from the weir's rail. It was a shock to see herself, so clearly a middle-aged woman in the grip of a crisis. She turned away and continued her search.

In the front bedroom, which was the biggest and must

have been Daphne and Ernie's, she threw the wardrobe doors open. Daphne's dresses rocked on their hangers, and a smell of mothballs and talc came at her. There was a real fur coat and several pairs of high heels, but nothing else of interest. Lillian's heart leapt when she found a small hard-backed notebook in the bottom drawer of Daphne's vanity table, but there was nothing on the pages save some scribbled addresses and a set of directions to a guest house in Torquay.

She moved on.

At the open door of the third bedroom she stopped, the breath taken from her.

It was a baby's room. Bunnies in flowered hats danced across the curtains. A frilly coverlet nestled inside a wooden cot, together with an array of stuffed animals: a duck with an umbrella beneath its arm, a blue bear with buttons for eyes. Lillian leaned on the wall for support, then, when that wasn't enough, sank to the floor, legs splayed like a doll's, trying to take it all in. On the pink walls hung framed prints of Noddy and Jesus. On the chest of drawers was a glass tray containing a rusted tin of zinc and castor oil cream and a bowl crammed with cotton wool balls. Though it was musty, the room appeared clean and dust-free. Daphne must have kept it so. Like a museum. Or a shrine.

This was obviously where Lillian had slept as a baby, yet everything here was foreign to her. She'd been looking for her mother, and had found instead this room.

Lillian covered her face with her hands as she began to understand how Daphne must have yearned for her, the girl who was in her arms for a year and then was gone. She'd yearned so hard that she'd kept everything in place, just in case the girl ever returned. Lillian had always felt Winnie had loved her, despite their problems. Until now, she hadn't known that Daphne had loved her too.

After a few minutes, she got to her feet and lifted the toy duck from the cot. It was flattened and faded, and made of some sort of flannel material. Bringing it to her face, she brushed it against her cheek, her lip, inhaling its slightly medicinal scent, and remembered the soft cloth clown that Rachel had as a toddler. Rachel couldn't be without Clownie, sleeping with her face pressed against him, reaching for him on waking, crushing him in her fist when upset. Once, after weeks of a virus which had made Rachel's tonsils flare, her nose stream, her lungs fill with a crackling cough, and had kept her and Lillian awake every night and sealed in the flat all day, Lillian had put the toy in the washing machine. Rachel had been inconsolable. 'Clowie!' she'd cried. *Clow-ie!* She couldn't yet form the 'n'. Nothing would comfort her – not Lillian's embrace, not milk, not even the distraction of her favourite *Postman Pat* video, which Lillian switched on mid-morning, breaking her own rule. Rachel, strapped into her bouncy chair, screamed and screamed, her face purple with rage. Eventually Lillian had screamed, too. She'd wanted to throw the beaker of milk right at her daughter, who'd kept her awake for God knows how many nights, who'd refused food, who'd made her a prisoner here in this flat for weeks. Instead, she chucked the beaker across the room, milk splattering the wall, and yelled, *Shut up! Just shut the fuck up!*

There'd been a second when Rachel had stopped screaming, utterly shocked, but then she'd started again, louder, almost choking on her own cries, and Lillian had crumpled to the floor and cried with her until her throat became sore. When they'd both run out of steam, she'd cradled Rachel, and they'd sniffled together. Lillian had rocked her daughter until Rachel's rigid limbs went limp and her moans became snores.

After that, Lillian had kept two spare cloth clowns in the drawer, just in case.

Now she pressed the toy duck to her cheek and wondered

how many times her own mother had screamed when she'd been a small baby. Like her, Winnie would have screamed alone. But, Lillian realised, Winnie'd had no one else to help care for her baby. Who would have come to her aid, even if she'd screamed long and hard? Not her own mother, who'd refused to see her. Not Ernie, who was married to Daphne. At least, Lillian thought, she'd had Gwen, who'd come over after she'd screamed at Rachel, and had listened, and told her she was not a bad mother; she was just run ragged.

Placing the duck back in the cot, it came to Lillian what she must do. Record it. Get it down on paper. Right now.

She went downstairs to the kitchen, where she gulped water straight from the tap. Then she left the house and fetched the sketchbook and pencil she always kept in the boot of her car. She would draw the room, and everything in it. The frilly coverlet. The toy duck. The tin of zinc and castor oil cream. Once she had it all down she'd do what she'd always done in times of trouble: call on Gwen.

1968

Jim's daughter Meg was just beginning to walk and Pam was expecting again when he learned of Lillian's fate.

On Sunday mornings he'd take Meg to see his mother, allowing his wife a lie-in. If it was fine they'd head through the woods to the swings in the Abbey Meadow, and this was where they were going when Jim's mother asked, 'Did you hear about what happened to Lillian?'

Jim was allowing Meg to totter on the reins while his mother steered the empty pushchair, and it was a shock to hear Lillian's name. To cover his confusion he lifted his daughter's reins, making her airborne, and let her dangle for a moment. She gave a small sound of delight, so he did it again.

'What happened?' he asked, keeping his gaze focused on Meg.

His mother lowered her voice. 'They took her away. To Longbrook.'

Jim frowned. Then it came to him. His mother was in a muddle. 'You're getting her mixed up with Winnie.'

'Winnie's dead, Jim!'

'I know that. But she's the one who went to Longbrook, when she was young—'

'She did?'

'Apparently. But don't go repeating that.'

His mother tutted. 'I did hear something, years ago, about poor Winnie and her trials. Apparently her own mother threw her out—'

'So you've got this mixed up, then.'

'There's no mix-up, Jim! This is *definitely* Lillian. No one knows why. But they do say it runs in families. So I suppose it all makes sense, in a way.'

Jim tried to understand what his mother was telling him.

'Mind you,' she continued, 'you only had to look at her to know something was wrong. She'd got so thin.'

'Don't be ridiculous,' said Jim. 'You don't go to the funny farm because you're thin.'

'Whatever the reason, that's where she is.'

They were directly in front of number 25 now, and Jim stopped and grasped his mother by the elbow. 'Who told you?'

'The hairdresser.'

Jim considered this. Maybe there was some truth in the story.

'Poor Mick,' said his mother with a glance towards number 25.

'Poor *Mick*?'

'It must be very hard on him.'

'What about poor Lillian?'

It was the first time he'd spoken her name for months and it changed something. The image of her on Mason Road was clear to him once again, right on the spot where they'd first met.

'Did he put her in there?' he demanded.

'I don't know anything more about it.'

'I bet he'd had enough of her and he put her in there.'

'You're upsetting Meggie.'

His daughter was twisting and moaning on her reins, so Jim gathered the girl to him and pressed his cheek against hers, breathing in her scent in an effort to calm himself. His mother shifted from foot to foot. 'Come on,' she said, 'let's go to the swings, shall we, Meggie?'

'That's not her name!' snapped Jim, unable to hide his irritation.

'Give her to me,' said his mother, sternly.

Jim, who was gazing at the closed curtains of number 25, allowed his mother to strap Meg into the pushchair. Being free of his daughter seemed only to further unleash his fury.

'I'll bloody kill him,' he muttered.

'Jim! It's none of our business! *Jim!*'

Ignoring her, he strode up the path and rapped on the door. For a long time there was no reply. He glanced back to where his mother was hovering at the gate and saw her pleading expression. But Jim knocked again, only slightly less determined to give Mick Harries a piece of his mind. The two of them had barely spoken since Mick had taken up with Lillian. Jim had been glad when Mick left the brewery for the MGs and he could stop worrying about how to arrange his face when he was forced to greet him. Now, though, he felt a confrontation was long overdue.

When Mick opened the door, he looked as though he'd just got out of bed. His chin was shadowed with stubble and his too-long hair seemed to have exploded at the back of his head. He folded his arms and stared directly at Jim. 'All right, mate?'

'I heard about Lillian.'

'Oh,' said Mick. 'Yeah.'

'What the hell happened?'

Mick examined Jim's face, as though weighing up whether his old friend had the right to ask such a thing. Eventually he said, 'She's – not well.'

'What does that mean?'

Mick dropped his voice. 'They say she's got something called slimmer's disease. Ever heard of it?'

'No, but—'

'Me neither. Doctor thought the hospital the best place for her and I'm sure he was right.' He paused, then asked, 'Anything else I can help you with?'

Jim's hand twitched. He'd never hit anyone before, but now

he wanted to. He wanted to draw his fist right back then drive it into Mick's stupid, bleary, gawping face.

Mick sniffed and said, 'Nothing for you to worry about, mate. Looks like you got enough on your plate already.' He nodded towards Jim's mother and the pushchair, in which Meg was beginning to keen.

'There was nothing wrong with Lillian,' Jim stated. 'Not one thing.'

'Yeah. Well. Who knows what goes on in women's minds?' Mick attempted a laugh, but it came out flattened and short, more like a gasp, and Jim saw a look of bewilderment pass across his face. He saw, too, that Mick's jaw was clenched hard.

Jim swallowed. 'When's she getting out?'

'Oh, it won't be long. It's not like she's actually *ill*.'

There was a pause. Then Jim asked again, almost of himself, 'What the hell happened?'

'She was always . . . sensitive. And what with her mother dying . . .'

'But *Longbrook*.'

'It'll blow over,' said Mick, with a fixed smile. 'Has to.'

Cramming his fists into his pockets, Jim turned to go.

'I'll tell her you were asking after her,' Mick called.

At the gate, Mrs Shepherd handed Jim the pushchair and he stalked away from her. Meg screamed all down the street, arching her back and thrashing her legs, but Jim just marched on, his heart slamming.

Meg had quietened a little by the time they reached the woods, and Mrs Shepherd took the opportunity to call to her son. 'Jim! Wait! Please!'

He paused beneath the yellowing leaves and looked back. She was puffing as she hurried towards him. 'For pity's sake!' she said, stopping just short of touching him. Her tone was urgent but not unkind. 'Whatever's got into you?'

Feeling a sob rise in his chest, Jim suppressed it with a shout. 'Bastard! That bastard! What did he do to her? She was fine – she was *perfect*! And now – she's in the bloody funny farm! How in hell did that happen?'

Mrs Shepherd stood, shaking her head. Then she lifted the still crying Meg from the pushchair and held her, patting her back and kissing the top of her head. It was as though, Jim thought, his mother were trying comfort him – or perhaps herself – through the body of his daughter.

'I should have let him have it,' he said.

'And I am so glad you didn't.'

'But I have to do *something*!'

'Yes,' said his mother. 'I can see that.'

'I should have looked after her. I should've—'

'You tried. It wasn't what she wanted.'

'I've got to sort this out.'

Meg was whimpering. Jim knew she would sleep soon, that it was too late for the park. He looked at his mother, who held his gaze as she said, 'Then go and see her.'

Jim took a breath. 'Pam won't like it.'

'Well,' said his mother, 'does Pam have to know?'

Even before Lillian had told him about Winnie, Jim had been aware of the place; but since the day of her refusal, he'd done his best to push the word *Longbrook* from his mind. Nevertheless, it had a tendency to pop up when he least expected it. Not long after he'd married Pam, for example, there'd been Ian Thornhill, an accounts man at Morland who'd stopped speaking. Never a good thing, for an accounts man. One day Pam had found Ian, crouched, sweating, trembling, moaning, in the corner of his office. She'd called the ambulance but they'd found nothing wrong and it had been Ian's wife, Nessa, good-humoured but rueful in her tightly knotted headscarf, who'd turned up to take him home. The management called it a mild heart attack and Ian had taken early retirement. When they were alone, Pam informed Jim that in her opinion it was an attack of the nerves rather than the heart, though she had to admit the two were closely linked. It wasn't long before she also told Jim that Ian had ended up in Longbrook. Jim thought this unlikely, as he'd only heard of women being taken there, but Pam had insisted it was true. What? she'd asked. Did he really believe that men never went mad?

He'd wondered about that afterwards. It did seem to him that men rarely ended up in mental hospitals. When he imagined men who were mad, Jim pictured them rampaging through the streets, embarking on killing sprees, setting light to buildings or fields of crops, crashing cars, throwing themselves from the railway bridge, drinking until they ended up in a ditch. Not inside the four walls of the funny farm, where they slowly but safely expired.

The next day, Jim waited until most of the other men were out for lunch, then closed his office door and telephoned the hospital to enquire about visiting hours. A woman with a measured voice told him he could come on Wednesday afternoon, or at the weekend.

Wednesday. Two days away. It would be easy enough to leave the office: his trips around the brewery's pubs were so frequent that no one would ask where he was going, and if someone did he could say he was visiting a client.

On Tuesday night, with Pam and Meg asleep upstairs, Jim sat in front of the television news and allowed the idea of tomorrow's visit to swell in his mind. Would she be locked up? Imprisoned with a gaggle of disturbed and unpredictable women? Perhaps there would be violence. Gnashing of teeth. Screams echoing down the corridor. He told himself not to be so melodramatic. Surely things would be different, nowadays. And surely Lillian herself was neither disturbed nor unpredictable? She would be on the ward with women well on the road to recovery from nervous breakdowns of some kind. They had pills for that sort of thing now. She might be sitting up in bed, thin but beautiful.

His reverie was disturbed by the sound of his wife in the kitchen. Meg was still in the habit of waking around two in the morning, so Pam often had a late-night snack, saying you needed more meals when you were awake for more hours. She called to him, asking if he wanted anything, and Jim called back that he didn't. When she popped her head around the door, her face prettily flushed, he said she should come and sit with him, but she said she was tired and would head back up. She waddled across the room to plant a kiss on the top of his head. Her huge belly touched his nose and he smelled washing powder and sweat. 'I won't be long,' he said. 'Don't wait for me.'

'I won't,' she said, backing out of the room with a biscuit between her teeth.

Jim had never actually been to Longbrook – it wasn't the sort of place you visited unless you really had to – but he'd seen the road signs to it often enough. It began to rain, hard, when he left the brewery, big drops hammering on the roof, which made his drive frustratingly slow. He'd anticipated a fit of the jitters about lying to Pam – though he hadn't quite lied yet, he reminded himself – but instead his mind slid into a sort of automatic blankness and he was surprised to find he felt no inclination to turn away from his mission. He felt only the need to reach Lillian.

It was one thirty when he arrived, and he still had half an hour to wait. Even in the driving rain the place looked rather grand. Jim was shocked by the size of it – the low brick wall around its perimeter, overhung by mature trees, went on for what felt like the best part of a mile before he reached a gatehouse. Here he slowed, half expecting a uniformed member of staff to check his credentials before he entered, but there was no one about, so he drove on through the gates. The hospital looked, Jim thought, like a vast Victorian school. Turreted hexagonal towers flanked either end of the main building. He was relieved to see that the small-paned windows had no bars.

He parked facing away from the building, then cracked open the window. His was the only car in the visitors' bays. The rain had eased a little and ahead of him were neat lawns and two huge cedars. To the right was the dome of a chapel. A couple of men who didn't look in the least mad were heading up the path, holding umbrellas and chatting.

It was only then he remembered he'd meant to buy flowers. He checked his watch. Probably there was enough time to drive into the village to pick up a bunch of something, but having made it this far he didn't feel he could move an inch backwards. He wished he smoked, so he could light up in order to pass the minutes and subdue the tremble in his chest. He fished in the glove compartment for a couple of Wine Gums. As his mouth filled with sugary goo, he felt again the pain of his failed proposal. It wasn't just that she'd refused him. He'd failed, too. Failed to be patient about Lillian's 'I can't'. Failed to swallow his pride and ask her to reconsider, or at least explain. Realising that her explanation about Winnie's past and the word *Longbrook* had scared him, he found himself letting out a noise – something between a laugh and a growl. None of it made any sense at all. That he must see her was the only thing of which he was sure.

Two more cars arrived. Looking in the rear-view mirror, he watched a woman in a Rain Mate, a box of Roses cradled against her chest, walk towards the double doors, leaving a man sitting in their car with a newspaper propped before him. From a newer vehicle two young women who looked like sisters emerged, pausing twice to check a letter before daring to approach the entrance.

Jim gave it a few more minutes, not wanting to engage in conversation with any of these women. Then he side-stepped the oily puddles in the car park and pushed open the door to the reception area. A radio was playing at low volume. There was a whiff of Pledge. The room was overheated and he felt the itchiness of his polo neck and heard the squeak of his best shoes as he walked across the parquet.

Jim told the man behind the desk that he was here to visit Lillian Harries. The man suggested Jim take a seat while someone fetched her.

There was a coffee table with a spray of newspapers arranged on top, together with a trolley on which sat a tea urn, a pile of cups and saucers, and a plate of biscuits. In the far corner was a tropical fish tank. The room was rather like the reception areas he'd seen in Morland small-town hotels – places that were supposed to appeal to businessmen and their wives.

No sooner had he sat than the tremble in his chest forced him to his feet once more to circuit the room, hands in pockets. Now the moment was so close he began to feel slightly hysterical, as though he might suddenly have to shout or laugh in order to purge his nerves. The radio was playing a different tune, and Jim focused on that – he didn't recognise it but it was upbeat in tempo and would have suited a cha-cha-cha – and he found himself stepping around the parquet in time to its rhythm. *Five, six, seven, eight.* In his pocket, he snapped his fingers. It had been a long time since he'd danced. He'd taken Pam to the brewery social club when they were first married, but once her pregnancy had started to show she announced herself not too keen on jigging about. Jim realised, now, that he'd missed this feeling of moving through music. He'd missed it terribly.

And then a man wearing a turban led Lillian into the room.

Jim stopped moving and stood, rooted to the floor. The man nodded towards Jim, and, taking Lillian by the elbow, guided her to where he was standing, next to the fish tank. She wore a saggy skirt and large jumper, but was clearly very thin. Jim saw to his immense dismay that she walked without that determined stride she'd once had, though her head still tilted to one side. Nearing him, she held one tiny wrist encircled in the fingers of her opposite hand, as though measuring its width. Or perhaps holding herself together. She looked – and Jim didn't know how this was possible – both younger and older. He noticed, too, that the skin on her face was dry and flaking, and he had to stop himself from reaching out to brush her cheek with the back of his hand.

The turbaned man was speaking to her, asking if this was her visitor. Lillian nodded. The man held out a hand and said, 'Akal.'

It took Jim a few moments to realise he must introduce himself. Akal told Jim he was pleased to meet him. 'I'll leave you to it,' he said. 'I just wanted to say hello, since I have been looking after Lillian here. And I wanted to tell you that I have been most enormously impressed by how she is doing.'

Throughout all this, Lillian was staring at the floor. Akal patted her shoulder. 'Why not take your . . .'

'Cousin,' said Lillian.

'Why not take your cousin for a walk around the gardens? It's stopped raining, I believe.'

It was only then that Jim noticed Akal was carrying the blue mac he'd bought for Lillian when they were first courting, which he now held out for her to slip her arms into. The coat swam around her. She shoved her hands into its pockets and headed, quickly, for the glass doors. She had yet to meet Jim's eye.

Jim followed her outside.

They walked in silence, shoes scrunching on the wet gravel, Lillian a little ahead. She led him away from the hospital building, towards the chapel. It occurred to him that she might try to run from the place – he was a little surprised that she was allowed to wander the grounds without the supervision of a nurse. But she showed no sign of bolting. He searched his mind for something to say. Even 'How are you?' felt too intimate, too dangerous.

'Cousin?' he asked, eventually.

'I thought you wouldn't want them to get the wrong idea,' said Lillian.

The wrong idea. Was that what he had?

'Where are we going?'

'To see the dahlias,' she said, cutting across the lawn towards one of the cedar trees.

His mouth was dry and his legs felt a little weak. He said the next thing that popped into his head. 'Is that Indian fella looking after you all right?'

'His name's Akal,' Lillian said. They'd reached the tree. She stopped and looked at Jim with the same quizzical expression she'd worn when he'd first spoken to her at the gate of number 25. He clasped his sweating hands together, trying to press some sense back into himself, trying to decide if he did indeed have entirely the wrong idea.

'Are you all right?' she asked.

'I have to sit down.' To Jim's horror, his head felt both light and terribly heavy, and it was quite difficult to get his lips around the words. 'Is there a bench?'

She frowned, then removed her coat. 'Use this,' she said, placing it, lining-first, on the damp ground beneath the tree.

It was either allow himself to sit or fall to the grass. He sat.

'Put your head between your knees,' Lillian instructed. 'Take some deep breaths.'

He did as she suggested and, after a minute or so, the thump in his chest returned to a tremble and he was able to look up again. Droplets fell from the low branches of the cedar. The sky was brightening in patches, casting the immense hospital building in a yellowy glow.

'Sorry,' he said. 'I felt a little light-headed. I forgot to eat lunch.'

'You're as bad as me, then.'

He looked at her and was relieved to see she was smiling, just a little.

She knelt beside him. 'Why did you come?'

'Your skirt,' said Jim, 'it'll get muddy—'

'Doesn't matter. Why did you come, Jim?'

Her face was shaded by the tree's arms, but he found it hard to return her direct look as he said, 'I was so worried about you. I had to.'

She nodded. Then she said, 'Do you remember I told you about Mum being here, before?'

'Of course I do.'

'I keep seeing her, on the ward.'

'You do?'

'I just can't help imagining her here. And I wonder: Why didn't she warn me?'

She was looking at Jim with real curiosity, as if he might know the answer, and he found himself saying, 'I don't suppose she could talk about it.'

'No,' said Lillian. 'I suppose not.'

'It would be difficult. A thing like that.'

There was a short pause before she said, 'Maybe it was fate, me ending up here, like her.'

Jim felt this was very wrong indeed, so he said, 'You mustn't think like that.'

'Why not?'

He really didn't know how to answer that. So he asked, 'Does Mick come to see you?'

She shook her head.

And Jim felt both furious and delighted.

'How about Ernie and his wife?'

'Not yet.'

And Jim felt only furious.

'I hope Mum at least had a visitor,' she said.

He felt the weight of her sadness then, and he said, 'You've got me. I'm here.'

She stood and held a hand out to him. Taking it, he allowed her to help him to his feet.

Lillian took Jim to the allotment, to see the last of the dahlias. 'Look,' she said, cupping the full redness of tens of tiny-tubed petals in her hand. They were grown by the long-term male patients and were sometimes sold in the village. Akal had shown them to her the week before, suggesting she could draw them. She hadn't, yet, but standing there with Jim, examining the perfect shapes and colours of each bloom, Lillian felt that she might. 'Look!' she said. 'Jim! Isn't it so beautiful?'

When she turned he was looking at her with raw need. No one had looked at her that way for a very long time. During the recent months of her marriage, Mick had barely glanced her way. When he'd finally seen her, it was with an expression of fear and disgust. Since then, everyone who'd looked in her direction had needed nothing from her. They'd reviewed and analysed her body without requiring her response. And now here was Jim, clearly needing her to somehow answer his gaze.

She looked back at him as fully as she could.

'Yes,' he said. 'It's very beautiful.'

The low sunlight came through the windows in the reception area, lighting Lillian's hair. It had grown longer and Jim fought the urge to tuck it behind her ears. She balanced her teacup on the arm of her chair without taking a sip and looked towards the door through which she'd appeared. He noticed that she'd developed a new habit of holding the back of her neck, as though it hurt.

'I didn't think there'd be a fish tank,' he said. 'Is there one on your ward, too?'

Suddenly she turned to him and asked, 'What happened to *our* fish?'

So she remembered. He opened his hands. 'Gene died, I'm afraid.'

She looked so crestfallen that Jim immediately added, 'I'm sorry.'

'No,' she said. 'Of course he did.'

'You can't expect anything that starts life in a plastic bag to live for ever.'

He didn't tell her that he'd taken the fish with him to his new house and fed it daily. Or that he'd sat dumbfounded on the bed for half an hour when he'd discovered the thing floating on its side in the bowl, like a dropped petal. Pam had offered to buy him another, but Jim had refused, saying it was silly to bother about a goldfish when they had a baby to feed and clothe.

'Poor Gene,' she sighed.

Jim sipped at his metallic-tasting coffee. 'So do you think you're . . . recovering?'

She squinted at him and said slowly, 'Jim, do you know why I'm here?'

He put his cup on the floor. 'Do you want to tell me? Why you're here?'

'What are people saying?'

'I don't know. They're not saying anything.'

She raised her eyebrows.

Jim sighed. 'Well, I did speak to Mick.'

She leaned forward. 'You spoke to *Mick*?'

'Mum told me you were in – here. But she didn't know why. So I knocked on your door and asked him. I was worried. I thought perhaps he'd . . . I don't know. Put you in here. You know. For his own sake. You hear stories like that, don't you?'

Lillian nodded, her eyes wide. Jim wished he'd hit Mick, then, so he could tell her that, too.

'So what did he say?'

'He said you had slimmer's disease.'

'Do you know what that is?'

Jim had to confess that he'd never heard of it until the words came out of Mick's mouth. He'd asked his mother about it, and she'd said it was something that happened when girls took dieting too far and couldn't stop. Which she couldn't understand at all, because she'd been overjoyed when her diet ended.

Carefully, he asked, 'What's it like?'

Lillian hesitated, pressing at the back of her neck with one hand. 'I know I need to eat. But it seems . . . dangerous to me.'

He waited for more, but none came.

'But why?' he asked.

She looked to the floor. 'I don't know.'

'Aren't you hungry?'

She shrugged.

'But the food seems . . . sort of scary?'

'Sort of.'

To Jim, who once, as a child, had become afraid of the buttons on his school shirt, this made a kind of sense. He knew he shouldn't push her, but he couldn't help but ask, 'And have they cured you, Lillian, do you think?'

Again, she said, 'I don't know.'

'Well,' he said, reaching for her hand. 'You look OK to me. For what it's worth. You look – smashing.'

Lillian didn't remove her hand as she said, very quietly, 'Thank you, Jim.'

It was after four when Jim drove away, and the traffic was building. He had to tell himself, out loud, to pull himself together. He slapped the steering wheel and shouted the words. As soon as he was on the road he knew he couldn't head straight back to the office, and he certainly couldn't go home: he needed time to gather himself, somewhere quiet. So he turned towards Sandford Lock.

He pulled into the small parking area alongside the trees that lined the bank and sat listening to the birds. Slumping in his seat, he closed his eyes and felt again her tiny hand – and every bone in it – clutching his as she helped him up. She was thin, far too thin, he could see that; but the way she'd looked at him when she asked questions – so direct, so interested in his answers! Her intensity was undimmed. It was like it always had been, he thought. She expected and would settle for nothing less than the truth. She invited him to do better. Which, he remembered now, was why she could be exhausting.

When he recalled that he'd told her he was there for her, he winced. How could he promise such a thing, when he was married to Pam?

He got out of the car and walked to the wooden fence by the lock. Opposite was The King's Arms. One of Morland's pubs. Suddenly it came to him. That would be the story, he thought, of his afternoon. When Pam asked how his day had been, he could answer her, truthfully: he'd visited The King's Arms at Sandford Lock and they really should go there together, in the spring. The beer garden was lovely.

But he already knew that next Wednesday he would be at Longbrook again.

That weekend, Lillian had two more visitors.

   Gwen looked altogether too large and healthy for the reception area. She arrived at three, when the room had emptied of other visitors, who'd already escaped for their Saturday-afternoon outings. Gwen almost knocked over her chair when Lillian came in, such was her rush to embrace her friend. She had her hair caught in a low bun, from which ginger curls were struggling to be free. She wore no make-up but in her ears was a pair of hoops that looked like brass curtain rings. Her brown coat was fluffy all around the edges, making Lillian think of Highland cattle. Lillian fell into her embrace and held on for a long time, her cheek nestled in the softness of Gwen's coat, which, though it looked like an animal, smelled of beer and perfume. No one had embraced her since she'd been in the hospital, and she held her breath, trying not to weep with relief.

   When Gwen pulled away, she held Lillian at arm's length to look at her. 'Hell's bloody bells,' she hissed, her eyes wide. 'I mean – what *happened*?' Her expression was so full of curiosity and surprise that Lillian was flooded with shame.

   'I'm sorry,' Lillian said.

   Gwen put her hands to her hips. 'What on earth for?'

'All this.'

'For Christ's sake. There's no need for *you* to apologise.' Gwen glanced around the room. 'Are you allowed out? I mean, could we go into town or something?'

'How?'

Gwen smiled. 'I thought we might walk out of the door and get into my car.'

'Your *car*?'

'I borrowed it from Mum.'

'I didn't know you could drive.'

'Mum insisted I learn, over the summer.'

'I just have to tell Sister Barbara—'

'Sister Barbara? What is this, school?'

'It's sort of similar.'

Gwen's car was a dirty white Mini. She reversed out of her parking spot and pointed the car towards the gates. She'd told Sister Barbara they'd go somewhere quiet; perhaps a nice tea-room. Sister Barbara had said that was fine, so long as Lillian was back by five thirty. But now Gwen turned to Lillian and asked, 'Pub?'

'Anywhere.'

Being driven by Gwen felt like flying. The car rattled, the seat was low and lumpy, and Lillian's feet were freezing in the draughty footwell, but she was elated as they sped noisily towards the city. After the white walls and shining linoleum of the hospital, the streets leading into Oxford that Saturday afternoon appeared joyfully complex. On the pavements were crates of unidentifiable fruit and vegetables (knobbly roots, prickly leaves, bulbs of bright purple and green and yellow); dented dustbins and red phone boxes; launderettes and fishmongers and churches and pubs and chip shops. And *people*. All kinds of people, some shuffling with shopping bags or paused to chat while children tugged at their sleeves; some running awkwardly in high heels; old ladies with dogs; dogs without leads; a priest in a stiff cassock; and two girls with matching white hairstyles and boots, arm in arm.

Gwen crunched through the gears as she talked. She talked for the entire journey. About her friend Sheena, mostly, who had abandoned the old radical magazine and started a new one that was really working for proper change.

Lillian nodded, amazed such things were still happening in the world outside Longbrook.

Gwen parked on St Giles and they ducked into the narrow doorway of The Eagle and Child. Lillian had never been there before but Gwen seemed familiar with the pub. It was panelled in dark wood and not very busy. On the bar was a glass dome, beneath which were a couple of bits of French stick and a wedge of cheese.

'It'll do,' said Gwen. 'You get a seat. I'll get the drinks.'

Lillian sat by the unlit fireplace and Gwen fetched them two halves of cider and a couple of packets of Golden Wonder. Lillian stared at the crisps. 'Oh,' said Gwen, sitting opposite her, 'is that all right?'

Telling herself she would think about it later, Lillian opened the packet and ate a crisp. Its salty crunch was delicious.

'So tell me about what happened.'

Lillian took a couple of gulps of cider. It was the first alcohol she'd drunk for months, and its sweetness dropped heavily into her stomach.

'I don't really know.'

Gwen took a sip.

'Mum died.'

'I heard. I'm so sorry. I would've come to the funeral if I'd known when it was. You should've told me.'

'I was . . . distracted.'

'Of course you were. It was a heart attack?'

Lillian said quickly, 'She fell down the stairs. I think she'd taken too many tranquillisers.'

'She was on tranquillisers?'

Lillian hesitated, then decided she couldn't yet face sharing her mother's story – or, at least, what she knew of it – with her friend.

'It's a long story. I'm not saying she meant it, but I should have been there, to stop her.'

'But you were married by then, right?'

Lillian nodded.

'And I'm presuming you were being a good wife and were at home, looking after hubby?'

Lillian thought back to how she'd been walking and drawing the morning of Winnie's death. 'Sort of.'

'So there it is. You can't be in two places at once. And after that?'

'And after that . . . I just couldn't eat. I mean, I knew I should. But I felt I shouldn't. And I got really thin.'

She waited for Gwen to ask, *How thin?* And was slightly disappointed when her friend said only, 'Go on.'

'At the end of the summer, Mick said I needed to see the doctor.'

'And what did the doctor say?'

'He said he thought they could help me at the hospital.'

'And what did Mick say?'

'That I looked like I'd been in a concentration camp and I should get help or he would leave me.'

Gwen put her glass down. Then she asked gently, 'Why on earth didn't you tell me?'

'I didn't tell anyone.'

Gwen nodded. 'So have they helped you? In the hospital?'

'It's – I mean . . .' Lillian thought about the swimming-pool-green room, the warm sand covering her body. She couldn't tell her friend that she'd been so ill that she'd had to be drugged in order to eat. That seemed like the height of stupidity. So she said, 'The doctor says I'm near a healthy weight now.'

'You're still thin,' said Gwen.

Lillian let out a breath. 'Am I?'

'God, yes! But you'll be out of there soon?'
'I think so.'
'What will you do? When you're out?'

Lillian gazed at her shoes. *Lose weight*, she thought. 'Go home, I suppose.'

Now Gwen grasped her hand. 'You can come to me, if you'd rather. I mean, there's no spare bed or anything but there's a big settee.'

Lillian laughed. 'Don't be daft.'

'I'm serious.'

'What would I do in York?'

'Sign on. Or get a job in Betty's. Or at a salon. You can be a hairdresser anywhere, can't you? And then you could reapply for art school.'

Lillian sat back in her chair, relishing the fantasy of joining Gwen in her student digs. She'd take up smoking. Go to pubs with Gwen. Wear a coat that looked like an animal and talk about *change*. But, she realised, she hadn't opened her sketchbook in she didn't know how long.

Gwen was grinning. 'What do you think?'

'It sounds . . . fantastic—'

'Doesn't it?'

'But I'm married.'

Gwen drained her glass and slammed it down. 'I suppose that is a complication.'

'And I haven't done art in ages.'

'Then for God's sake start.' Producing a pen from her coat pocket, Gwen wrote a number down on her beer mat and handed it to Lillian. 'Phone me any time you like.'

The following day, Ernie came.

He embraced her strongly but briefly, then, still in his heavy overcoat, plopped himself in an armchair in the reception area.

With a glance at the tea trolley, he declared himself parched. 'I'll take a couple of them biscuits, too,' he instructed.

It was just like a Friday teatime at number 25.

Lillian fetched him his drink, then sat next to him.

'Well,' he said, dipping his bourbon into his cup, 'you *look* OK, gal. When are they letting you out? Can't be long, can it?'

Lillian, who was trying to think of a way to formulate the question she must ask, said she didn't know.

'I should've come sooner,' Ernie continued. 'Daphne kept telling me to.' His eyes darted around the room. This being Sunday afternoon, it was full of other visitors, mainly women carrying gifts: boxes of chocolates, bunches of flowers, puzzle books. 'Truth is, I didn't know you were here. That Jim Shepherd told me.'

'*Jim* told you?' She'd assumed it was Mick.

'I got off work the other day and he was waiting in the street. Took me a minute to think who the bugger he was.'

So Jim had remembered where Ernie worked, and bothered to seek him out.

Lillian said, 'Did Daphne tell you I went to your house?'

'She mentioned it.'

Because she had little to lose, and because she knew, now, that Jim was on her side, Lillian asked, 'Why did you lie to me?'

Ernie stirred his tea. 'About what?'

'You told me I lived with you for a few months. Daphne said it was over a year.'

'It was all a long time ago. I don't remember the details.' He took another slurp of tea.

'How's Mick getting on?'

'I don't know.'

'He must be missing you, at home.'

Lillian blinked. 'I haven't heard from him since I got here.'

Ernie sucked in a breath. 'Oh. Dear me. Well, can't be easy, coming over here.'

She was about to say, *It's a lot easier than staying here*, when she saw Ernie's serious expression. She shrugged and looked away.

'Should I have a word?' Ernie asked. 'Tell him to buck his ideas up?'

She imagined Ernie knocking on the door of number 25, swallowing down his sorrow at Winnie's absence, having to wait on the step for Mick to answer when he should have been letting himself in the back door. It occurred to her that, even if Ernie were to venture up the path of number 25 and face Mick, he would remain polite and respectful. He might gently chide him, but would go no further because, in Ernie's estimation, Mick was, like him, the husband of a difficult woman.

'Lillian? I could speak to him. If you like.'

'No need, thanks,' she said.

Ernie nodded, looking relieved, then fished in his inner pocket and produced two brand-new pencils wrapped in a five-pound note. 'I brought you these,' he said. 'Not much, I know. But I thought you might need something to do. And a little something extra to spend in the cafeteria or whatnot.'

As she took the gift, his head dipped and his shoulders gave a great heave. A moment passed. Lillian touched his sleeve and thanked him. Ernie's breathing was laboured but his shoulders had stilled. When he looked up, his cheeks were florid. 'I'm so sorry, gal. I should've kept an eye on you. Whatever would your mother have said?' Then he grasped her hand tightly. 'I did what I could, for Winnie. It was my name on the rent book, you know – at least at first. I sorted all that out for her. I never wanted the two of you to suffer. But I couldn't do more. You can see that, can't you?'

Lillian looked away from him, towards the fish tank, where she could see the flash of a gold tail.

'Did you come here, before?' she asked. 'To see her?'

'Course I did.'

'What was it like?'

It took him a few seconds to answer. 'I'll be honest with you, it was bloody terrible. I knew I had to get her out. Whole place stank of piss. And they had her drugged up to the eyeballs.' He felt in his pocket for a hankie and blew his nose. 'And any fool could see that she needed to be with you. Nothing else for it. She told me so herself. *Where's my little girl?* she kept saying. *I want my little girl.*'

Lillian swallowed. 'And what about you?'

'What about me?'

'Didn't you want to be with me, too? And for all those years afterwards?'

She searched his face, her heart pounding. He looked back at her and for a moment she thought he would finally admit the truth, but then he looked away. 'Like I said, I did what I could. And I'm sorry.'

Lillian felt her body become very heavy. She closed her eyes.

With forced brightness, Ernie said, 'But she got home, didn't she, your mum? Just like you will. And you've got things she never had, ain't you? You're a married woman with someone waiting for you.'

When she opened her eyes, he was looking at his watch. 'Better get off. The missus will start to wonder.' He stood and pressed her shoulder. 'Take care of yourself. Let me know if you need anything. You'll be all right, gal.'

Lillian helped herself to one of the last of the dahlias on the allotment. Having been in hospital for two months, now, she felt entitled to take a little something without asking.

Carefully, she carried it to the dayroom, where she sat at a table by the window to draw using Ernie's pencils. Outside it had started to drizzle, and the window was framed with condensation. The after-lunch and after-medication murmur of women making raffia mats made the room feel quite cosy. A woman named Maria came in on a Thursday afternoon for the art class – one week, she'd had them cutting up newspapers and sticking the pictures on old lampshades, and another she'd helped them model ashtrays out of clay.

Maria seemed pleased when Lillian set up the dahlia on the table before her. 'I see you have your own project,' she said. 'Well done.'

Lillian tried to concentrate, but her attention slipped from the dahlia to thoughts of Ernie. He hadn't denied he was her father, but he was obviously not willing to say it out loud, either. She told herself to focus, but the petals seemed to multiply before her eyes and she couldn't keep track of which one she was looking at. She remembered that she must merely start again, look once more. Perhaps it was a bit like with Ernie, she thought. If she could only look harder, comprehend the shapes, see the light and shade, she might understand. But she was tired of trying to work out exactly what Ernie was to her, and it had been so long since her hand had made any marks on paper that she soon felt close to despair.

Then Anna leaned across and said, 'That's much better than my raffia mat.' Sitting down, she helped herself to a pencil and asked Lillian to rip a blank page from her sketchbook. 'This looks more fun,' Anna said, and began to draw. They sat in silence, heads bent, pencils moving. Anna's pencil broke several times and she spent a lot of time sharpening it.

After a while, Anna said, 'You won't come back in here, will you, once you're out?'

'Why?'

'Cos that would be stupid.'

'It's not *that* bad in here,' said Lillian.

'That's no reason to stay.'

Anna was still looking at her piece of paper, and Lillian saw that she hadn't drawn the flower but a woman with a huge head whose hair flowed to all four corners of the page.

'She's . . . interesting,' Lillian said.

'You do know,' Anna said, ignoring her, 'that Joan has been in and out of here five times? And Isobel – Isobel never goes home.'

'Why not?'

'Nowhere to go. And some of them upstairs have been here since they were girls.'

Lillian knew the long-term patients were upstairs, but she rarely saw them. Occasionally they went out into the grounds, where they were herded around by nurses, or sat in the deckchairs outside the canteen. Many of them were old, or looked so.

'Some of them have had lobotomies, of course. So they can't really go anywhere anyway. Poor cows.'

Lillian put down her pencil. 'But they don't still do that.'

'Not much,' said Anna. 'Not here, anyway.' She grimaced. Her eyes, though dark and shadowed, seemed to dance, briefly. Then she took up a yellow pencil and began to shade in the woman's hair. 'You're an anorexic, aren't you?'

She said it lightly, as though confirming Lillian's star sign.

Lillian gave a vague nod.

'Thought so. So what did they do to you?'

No one had asked this before, and Lillian realised that she had no name for what had happened to her behind the swimming-pool-green curtain. So she said, 'They – kept giving me medicine, which made me sleep. I think it went on for a few weeks.' What she remembered, most, was the feeling of not wanting to wake. Of being dragged to the surface against her will.

'Same as me. The last few times, anyway,' Anna said.

Lillian asked, 'How many times have you been in here?'

'This is my fifth,' said Anna, with a small smile. Lillian noticed her teeth were stained, and a couple were missing. 'I put on enough weight to get out. Then I lose it and come in again. I managed a few years, this time. But, well . . .' She reached for an orange pencil. 'It's such a waste of everyone's time, I know that. But I just can't seem to get out of the habit. It's like an addiction.'

The cords in her neck protruded as she spoke. What confused Lillian was that Anna sounded almost proud of her experience.

'Course, the treatment's not nearly as bad now, though it's still as useless. It used to be an insulin coma, when I first had it. Not here. At another hospital.'

'It used to be what?'

'Insulin *coma*.' Anna grinned and moved her head closer to Lillian's. 'They do the tranquillising thing with the Largactil, but they also give you enough insulin to almost put you into a coma, which is supposed to make you hungry.' She lowered her voice. 'Very dangerous. A woman died once. Or so I heard.'

Lillian's mouth dried. She stared at Anna, who met her gaze steadily. How old was she? Forty-five? Fifty? Lillian suddenly imagined herself sitting in this room thirty years from now, telling some younger woman not to be like her.

'Someone died?'

'Apparently. So be grateful they didn't do that to you.'

'But – how?'

'Dunno. Maybe they gave her too much. Heart couldn't take it. Maybe she was weak already.'

'But she died? They *killed* her?'

Anna glanced over at Sister Barbara, who was looking in their direction, and hissed, 'Keep your bloody voice down.'

Lillian pushed her drawing away. 'Why should I?'

'Listen to me,' said Anna. 'Don't get agitated. Just get out. And then – try to kick the habit. Don't come back again.'

Sister Barbara was approaching, and Anna repositioned her page so Lillian could see her drawing. 'What do you think, then?' she asked loudly.

It looked pretty amateur to Lillian – the proportions were all wrong, and the woman's features seemed tiny in her massive face. But, aware of Sister Barbara standing behind her, she said, 'I like her hair.'

'It's on fire,' said Anna.

Sister Barbara, glancing at the drawings, murmured, 'Poor thing. Keep up the good work, ladies.'

The following morning, Lillian fetched a bucket of cold soapy water from the bathroom, together with the sponge and a dry cloth, in order to begin her work washing the ward windows. Anna had said, when she'd first shown Lillian how to carry out this chore, that it wasn't a bad job as you got to gawp at the view. Looking now, Lillian saw that the garden had changed since she'd arrived. It was late October, and the drive was littered with fallen leaves. She pictured Jim Shepherd sitting beneath the cedar tree. She'd felt pleased, when he'd visited, that for once she seemed to know more than he did, and she'd led him around the gardens like an old-hand. But she realised now that she'd known nothing. She hadn't even known the word for her own medication. No one had thought she needed to know. Just like she hadn't known her own father. Or what had happened to her own mother, in this place. No one had told her the truth.

She drenched the sponge in soapy water and slopped it at the window, suds running into her sleeve. She did it again. And again. She pounded on the window pane, each time a little harder, until her arm was wet, the front of her skirt damp. She became aware of Isobel, leaning on her mop to watch. And then of Joan, yelling for Sister Barbara.

When Lillian felt a pair of arms around her, she half-expected to be lifted and for a needle to find her thigh, as when she'd first arrived, and she struggled to be free. But in her ear was Anna's voice. 'No need to smash anything,' she said. Anna's hand grabbed hers, stilling the dripping sponge. They stood together, swaying slightly, Lillian breathing hard.

Sister Barbara had arrived. 'What's all the commotion? Lillian? Anna?'

'She was thumping the window!' Joan, now standing on her bed in her excitement, squawked. 'I'm surprised it's not broken!'

'Get down, Joan,' said Sister Barbara. 'Now. What on earth is going on?'

Anna, keeping a tight hold of Lillian's hand, said, 'We were playing. She was washing the windows, and I said she should throw the sponge at me. It was a game.'

Sister Barbara crossed her arms. 'Is that true? Lillian?'

Lillian managed to return her gaze as she nodded.

'And no one's hurt?'

'Of course not,' said Anna, letting Lillian go and producing a packet of cigarettes from her pocket. She shook one free. 'It's only a bloody sponge.'

Sister Barbara said, 'Go to the dayroom if you want to smoke, please, Anna.'

Anna stayed where she was, unlit cigarette perched between two bony fingers, watching Lillian. Lillian's hand clenched, squeezing the sponge dry so it leaked water onto her shoes. Sister Barbara frowned at the puddle on the floor, then prised the sponge gently but firmly from Lillian's hand. 'You too,' she said. 'Off to the dayroom. Have a cup of tea. You can finish this later.'

Lillian looked at Sister Barbara. One of the shining hairgrips that secured her smart little hat had come loose and was lodged at a strange angle.

'Lillian?' asked Sister Barbara. 'Did you hear me?'

Lillian swallowed. *Someone died!* she screamed, silently. *Why did no one tell me someone died?*

Anna brushed her wet hand lightly with her own. 'Come on,' she said.

Afterwards, she walked alone to the allotment. As soon as she stepped outside, she smelled smoke. In the corner plot a metal brazier was full of fire. Five men stood around it, their faces glowing. Two were nurses – one of whom was Akal – and the rest Lillian assumed to be long-term patients. The head gardener she'd spotted that first day was also there, beaming in a knitted hat, a camouflage jacket and a pair of wellington boots. She hung back, watching the group, who all seemed happily mesmerised by the flames. One man, short and bald, kept turning himself around, lifting up the flaps of his coat to warm his backside and laughing.

Spotting her, Akal raised a hand, then took his turn feeding the fire. Lillian wondered why there were no women. It was always the men who were outside, digging, cutting, burning, while the women remained indoors. Ivor was the only man on the ward and also the only patient in 'Work' group. Every morning he left to carry out his tasks in some shed or other while all the women stayed on the ward to clean, weave raffia mats or assist in making meals. Just like they would at home, as Dr Will had said. As if they were housewives.

She thought of her marriage to Mick. How the payment for her enjoyment of his body had been the making of his meals, his bed, the cleaning of his house, his clothes. Would it have been different, if she'd married Jim? She doubted it. Why had Jim's only solution to her predicament been marriage? If he hadn't asked her, she wouldn't have needed to say those words – *I can't*. And perhaps they could have carried on. Perhaps they could have loved each other.

Her breathing remained steady, though her body felt hot and strangely light as she approached the brazier, scooped up an armful of dried leaves and dead branches from the pile, and, wedging herself between Akal and the short man, dumped them onto the flames. The fire crackled and spat, and dark smoke rose, making her cover her eyes with her arm.

'Lillian,' said Akal, 'you should wear gloves, please.'

Ignoring him, she picked up another pile of garden waste and tossed it in.

The short man said, 'She shouldn't be here! Love! You shouldn't be here!'

The gardener, exchanging a look with Akal, said, 'She's made a mistake, that's all.'

'No mistake,' said Lillian. 'I want to burn stuff.'

'All right,' said Akal, touching her shoulder, 'but, please, wear gloves—'

She shook him off, scooping up another handful of leaves. It struck her that the leaves could have been left to compost. They didn't even need to be burned. It was all an excuse for men to stand around a fire.

When she turned to dump more waste into the brazier the head gardener stepped in front of her, blocking the way. 'I think you should go back inside,' he said.

'Why?'

Again, he glanced at Akal, who said nothing. 'You're not – trained.'

'Is there training,' she asked, 'for chucking stuff on a fire?'

Akal said, 'It's not that, exactly.'

'What is it, then?'

A man who hadn't spoken yet, his face greasy with smoke

and sweat, said, 'Suits you, darling. Being angry. I love a bird with a bit of spunk.'

The short man laughed, very loudly, and the gardener smirked. And Lillian was back in the library with the man asking about the Shaw, and at the table with Ron feeling her thigh. She blinked at Akal, who dropped his eyes.

'Fuck the lot of you,' she said, throwing the waste into the gardener's face. He stood, a damp leaf stuck to his cheek, staring at her in shock. There was a moment, then, when all the men's expressions changed from amusement to something darker. But Lillian said it again, louder, clearer. 'Fuck. You. All.'

Then she turned and marched towards the hospital. As she strode across the grass, she heard a wolf whistle, then Akal's voice, saying that was enough, now.

The following morning, she was taken to Dr Will's office.

He was sitting at a desk by the window. Shelves of books took up one entire wall, and on another was a swathe of red and purple material, decorated with embroidered circles and squares and inlaid with tiny mirrors. It looked like a bedspread. The doctor crossed his legs at the knee, grasped a shoeless foot in one hand, and invited Lillian to take a seat in the armchair.

She braced herself for a ticking-off. So far, no one had mentioned the incident at the brazier, and Lillian hadn't spoken of it, even to Anna. She'd simply gone back to the dayroom, where she'd resumed her drawing.

'Lillian,' Dr Will said, 'how are you feeling?'

'All right.'

'You're at a good weight, aren't you? How does that feel?'

It felt to her like a temporary situation, one she could remedy when she was out of this place, but she knew she could not say this.

'Do you feel your appetite has returned?' the doctor asked.

'A bit.'

'And the medication? How are you doing on the lower dose?'

'All right.'

'I hear you were upset yesterday.'

She focused on his hair while waiting for him to continue.

'Do you want to tell me what happened?'

She arranged her skirt on her knees and said, 'Akal was there. He can tell you.'

'I'd really like to hear it from you.' The doctor steepled his fingers and added, 'You're not in trouble. I'm just interested.'

She hesitated, then said, 'I was told I wasn't allowed to put leaves on the fire. So I lost my temper a bit.'

'Go on.'

'It just seemed so – unfair. It's always men doing the burning. Never the women.'

'So you wanted to be one of the boys, was that it?'

She held his gaze. 'I wanted to throw leaves on the fire. So I told that gardener to fuck off.'

She felt her face grow hot, but the doctor didn't flinch. There was a long pause before he said, rather cheerfully, 'How would you feel about going home?'

She gaped at him.

Dr Will continued, 'You've reached a healthy weight. And you're displaying signs of – more independence, I think is how I'd put it. Presuming things don't change, we could prepare for your home-going. We'll give you a prescription, of course, and I will be recommending that you come back to visit us every week for a month or so, for a follow-up appointment. What's your view?'

'On going home?'

'Precisely.'

She pictured number 25 without her mother in it. She pictured Mick's handsome face, his clever hands, and his vague expression whenever she opened her mouth to speak. She didn't want to go home. She knew that, now. But she did want to get out of here. She swallowed. 'I think that would be good.'

'Excellent. I'll telephone your husband, shall I, to let him know?'

Lillian said, 'We haven't got a phone at home. But I can get a message to him. I can phone a neighbour and they can pass it on.'

'He hasn't been to see you, has he?'

'He's been busy,' said Lillian. 'At work.'

'Could you tell him I'd like to speak with him, quite urgently?'

'Yes,' she lied. She didn't yet know where she would go after being discharged. She only knew she didn't want Mick involved.

'And you'll need someone to fetch you. I can't let you walk out of here alone.'

'That's fine,' she said quickly. 'He'll do that.'

'All right, then. Let's give it a few more days. Just to be sure. But we'll aim for next Wednesday afternoon.' The doctor leaned towards her. 'I do so hope you feel we've helped you, Lillian.'

He was waiting, it was clear, for her to thank him. Lillian was just as clear that she wasn't about to do that. 'Can I ask something?' she said. 'About the treatment I had.'

'Please.'

'Was it dangerous? I mean, could it have been?'

Dr Will sucked air through his teeth. 'Well,' he said slowly, his face taking on a blank expression, 'no medical procedure is without risk. But in my assessment, Lillian, what was really dangerous was how underweight you were. And look at you now! You're a healthy weight and about to go home. I call that a success, don't you?'

'Only,' she said, her mouth dry, 'I heard that someone died. Having treatment a bit like that.'

For the first time, the doctor looked away. When he looked

back his voice was clear. 'I assume you're referring to insulin therapy, Lillian, which was not what you had. That practice is no longer condoned by most psychiatrists—'

'Anna had it.'

Dr Will said, 'As I'm sure you'll appreciate, I cannot discuss other patients with you—'

'And it didn't even work,' Lillian persisted. 'That treatment. She told me she's been in here five times.'

Dr Will cleared his throat. He took up a piece of paper and a clipboard from his desk and scribbled something on it. 'These are your discharge papers, which I've just signed. And I think – if you'd like to go home – you should sign them too, don't you? Then we're all ready for next week and we'll waste no more time.' He turned the page towards her, tapping a dotted line. 'Just there.' He held the pen out. 'Unless you have any other questions for me, of course?'

Lillian had so many questions. But what was the point in asking them? The doctor would always have the same smooth and not-quite-true replies. And all she wanted, now, was to get out of here. She picked up the pen, and she signed.

On his way over, Jim had stopped by the tropical fish shop off the Cowley Road to choose the fish, which was larger than Gene, with a fancier tail and black markings on its orange side. Now he sat in the reception area and lifted the plastic bag so it was level with his face. The fish looked solemnly back at him. *Keep an eye on her for me, will you?* he asked it, silently.

When Lillian appeared, he rose and held the bag out. She was wearing the same strange outfit but this time the man with the turban wasn't there. Coming closer, she saw the fish and laughed out loud. Hearing that sound, Jim felt himself a little lighter.

'I bought him for you. To say sorry about Gene.'

She accepted the bag and examined the fish. 'Hello there,' she said, 'you poor little thing.'

'Why poor?'

'Being stuck in a polythene bag.'

'It's not for long,' Jim said. 'I checked with the man on the desk. He said you can keep it here, in the tank.'

'You are funny.'

'Am I?'

Her answer was a light peck on his cheek. He touched the place her lips had been and gazed at her, but she was still focused on the fish. 'He looks posher than Gene. I take it you didn't win him at the fair?'

'I didn't go this year,' said Jim. 'Shall we put him in the tank?'

'We could. But I'm getting out next week, so I won't be here to feed him.'

'Next week?'

She smiled and nodded.

Jim couldn't help feeling a little disappointed. He'd imagined a whole string of afternoons with Lillian, here in this strange place where they could exist without acknowledging the rest of the world. He'd imagined them watching the progress of the fish who, in his mind, he'd already named Bertie. A sort-of offspring of Gene. Now she'd go home to Mick. She would be a different creature, back on Mason Road. As, he reflected, would he.

'That's wonderful news,' he said. 'Good for you.'

Lillian walked over to the tank, opened the bag and let the fish flop – rather carelessly, Jim thought – into the water. It twitched, rolled, and swam beneath a plastic bridge, where it hid.

'I wanted to ask a favour, actually,' said Lillian, suddenly turning to face him.

'Anything,' said Jim, delighted.

'I don't suppose you'd pick me up?'

'From here?'

'Yes.' With the empty bag still in her hand, she watched him.

'Pick you up and take you home, you mean?'

'Yes.'

He couldn't resist asking, 'Is Mick not able to do that?'

'He can't take the time off.'

Jim tried not to grin. 'Well. I'll need to check.'

'Of course.'

'But I don't see why not.'

She smiled. 'Thank you, Jim,' she said, pecking him on the cheek once more.

They walked the leaf-streaked path to the chapel. It was colder now, and the rounded bell tower shone in the low sun. They sat together on the stone bench by the door, both looking back at the hospital's blank windows. Lillian didn't shiver, but her closeness made Jim feel as though his skin was about to jump through his clothes.

From the squat shed behind the chapel came the sound of music. A transistor radio was playing. Nothing Jim recognised, though Lillian tapped her foot.

'Won't Mick mind if I pick you up?'

'I doubt it.'

'He still hasn't visited?'

She sighed. 'I didn't really expect him to.' Then she asked, 'Are you still dancing?'

'Not really.'

'Not at all?'

'Not since Meg.'

'Don't you miss it?'

'Oh,' he said, 'more than anything.'

He hadn't meant for this truth to come out of his mouth, yet there it was.

She turned to face him and said, 'I miss it, too.'

Jim had to sit on his hands to stop himself reaching for her. Blood flooded into his chest, as if his heart had been squeezed, hard. He returned her gaze, which was open and frank, and tried to form the words he knew he should say. *I'm sorry. I should have been more patient. I wish it had all been different.*

Then 'All I Have to Do Is Dream' by the Everlys came over the radio, and they smiled at one another. Jim stood and held his arms out, waiting.

Lillian knew where to put her hands, her body. Jim held her for a second, one hand between her shoulder blades, the other lightly clasping hers. Then they were off, turning in circles on the damp lawn, Jim with his head in exactly the right position, gazing beyond her, smiling. What a relief it was to know the steps. To move in time, as they'd so often done before. She felt her body become both more alert and relaxed as it responded to Jim's. It was wonderful, this forgetting and remembering. She could forget – almost – her body's need for food and her need to deny it, and remember instead its ability to dance. She extended her spine and neck. Jim told her she was a natural. 'Look at you,' he said. 'Look at you, dancing.' The ground was slightly slippery beneath her shoes, but Jim was more than capable of navigating the bumps while keeping time. He danced her beneath the almost-bare branches of the plane trees to the side of the chapel. Basic walking step, corner step, side-sway, promenade.

When the music stopped he didn't let go. Instead, they swayed together and he spoke into her hair. 'I'm sorry,' he said. 'I should have waited.'

She let go of his hand and stepped back. 'For what?'

'For you to say yes.'

She closed her eyes for a moment, understanding that he was serious. The transistor was playing another tune. She said, 'I wish you hadn't asked me, Jim. If you hadn't asked me, I wouldn't have had to say *I can't*.'

He frowned. 'What does that mean?'

She let out an exasperated breath. 'You only gave me one choice! I needed your help, and you gave me . . . a proposal.'

Now he looked stricken. He ran a hand down his face. 'Lillian,' he said quietly, 'I asked you because I loved you. I still love you.'

He was looking at her again with that raw need. After a moment, she found her voice and said, 'I know.'

Because she had no more words to offer, she kissed him. He drew her in, tightly, and she kissed him again, with softer, more open lips. As he held her she was aware of the ridges of her spine, the hooks of her hips digging into his belt. She was reminded, too, of how much she liked kissing Jim Shepherd.

'Wednesday?' he asked.

'Wednesday,' she replied.

The week passed slowly. Each day Jim told himself that he wasn't sure what to do, that tomorrow he'd decide one way or the other. But deep down he suspected nothing would stop him driving to Longbrook on Wednesday to open his passenger door to Lillian Wells, despite having deliberately folded the memory of dancing with her and the words they'd spoken into a far corner of his mind.

All his wife wanted, now, was to eat or sleep. She ate whole bricks of ice cream almost as soon as Jim had slotted them into the freezer compartment, then woke in the early hours, wanting more. One night, when he told her there wasn't any left, she'd cried, and Jim had held her, feeling the fierce heat of her belly through her nightie.

At the weekend, he took Meg to his mother's while Pam rested. Mrs Shepherd sat on the settee with Meg on her lap. She'd recently bought her granddaughter a fat baby doll made of unbending plastic. Sprouts of synthetic hair were injected all over its scalp; its mouth was a sculpted orange smile, and its unblinking eyes, glassy blue, were framed with lashes thick as draught-excluders. Jim thought it a hideous thing, and at home Meg had been ignoring it, but Jim had brought it along so his mother would see her gift was appreciated, or, at least, acknowledged. When he handed it to his daughter, she gazed at it for a moment before letting it drop onto the settee.

'Doesn't she like it?'

'She's tired.'

Mrs Shepherd smoothed Meg's wispy curls from her forehead and crooned, 'Have a lovely nap on Granny.'

Pam had given Jim specific instructions not to let Meg sleep, as she'd already had a short nap late morning and another might mean she wouldn't sleep tonight. So Jim picked up the doll and waved it close to his daughter's face. 'Meg!' he said, in a bright tone. 'Don't you want to play with Fifi?'

Meg twisted her head away, slumping further into the softness of her grandmother's body.

'Fifi?' his mother asked. 'It said Victoria on the box.'

'Pam thought she looked like a Fifi.'

'How can a doll look like a *Fifi*? Surely that's a dog's name.' Mrs Shepherd gave a rueful laugh. Then she lowered her voice. 'I've been meaning to ask you, Jim. Have you seen . . . *her*?'

He'd hoped his mother had decided not to enquire about Lillian. She must have been waiting for her chance to pry.

'Once,' Jim lied. 'I went once. Just to check on her.'

His mother's eyes lit up. 'And? How was she?'

'All right. She's getting out soon, I think.'

'That's good.'

'Yes. It is.'

Meg's eyelids fluttered and her breathing thickened.

'I'm not supposed to let her sleep,' Jim said, relieved to be able to change the subject. 'Pam wants a good night tonight.'

'Oh, poppycock!' said Mrs Shepherd. 'Look at her. You said it yourself: she's tired out.'

A bubble of saliva formed then popped on Meg's lower lip.

'So did you find out what it was all about?' Mrs Shepherd persisted, encouraging Meg's head into the crook of her arm and rocking her slightly.

Jim, playing for time, said, 'What what was all about?'

'Lillian's . . . *problem*.'

'It was like you said. Slimmer's disease.'

Mrs Shepherd clucked her tongue. 'And *that* put her in hospital?'

Jim nodded.

'Good grief.' There was a pause, during which Jim tried to think of a way to distract his mother. He was just about to snatch the dozing Meg from her lap when she said, 'Poor Lillian. Still. She didn't have a chance, did she?'

Jim sat back. 'Meaning what, exactly?'

'Meaning, Jim, that there was no father around. I'm not saying anything against Winnie – she worked hard, we all know that, and she had her troubles – but it can't have been easy for either of them.'

'There was no father around for me, either.'

Mrs Shepherd waved a hand before her face. 'That's different. Your father *died*. And, anyway, you were always so responsible. The man of the house. It's different, with girls.'

Jim glanced at his daughter, who was now fully, blissfully asleep, her legs slack and her fists uncurled. Useless to try to rouse her. He thought of Lillian's fatherlessness. They had never once discussed it. But they had never discussed his own father, either. Jim had barely discussed him with his mother. Irked by her comments, he suddenly demanded, 'Why aren't there any photos of Dad in the house?'

Mrs Shepherd blinked, then looked away. 'There are. In the album.'

This was true. There was one photo of Reg on his wedding day. In it, he was beaming from ear to ear, showing a gap between his front teeth. He looked, Jim had always thought, a rather jovial man. And Jim's mother, wearing a hat the shape of a plate, also appeared delighted. Her laughing face was slightly turned, which had blurred the photo, but you could clearly see that she was held tightly about the waist by her new husband.

'He's safer,' Jim's mother continued, 'in the album.'

'Safer?'

Mrs Shepherd nodded, dipped her chin to kiss the top of Meg's head, and kept her gaze lowered as she said, 'I just couldn't stand to have him on the wall, that's the truth of it.'

'Why not?'

With a determined edge to her voice, she said, 'It was more than I could bear, to see him looking back at me all the time when he was . . . gone. Gone and never coming back. So I put him away. I kept him safe.'

Jim couldn't help the thought, *You kept him from me*, from popping into his mind. But he heard the tremble in his mother's voice, and saw her face was pale and flattened with pain. After a second, he grasped her hand, understanding for the first time that she had grieved, secretly, searingly, for all these years.

By Tuesday night he'd decided he would tell Pam about picking Lillian up the next morning. He'd mention it off-handedly, as he left the house for work. He would say that Mick, whose car was being repaired, had asked him to do it. Of course, he didn't *want* to do it, but how could he refuse? The poor girl couldn't catch the bus home from Longbrook, could she? Perhaps he wouldn't say those words, *poor girl*. *Woman* might be better. Less vulnerable.

As he lay awake he imagined a smiling Lillian handing him her suitcase to toss onto the back seat before they drove to Sandford Lock. There'd be no hurry to get her home. They could walk along the bank of the river, maybe feed the ducks, and discuss how to arrange their futures. He couldn't imagine exactly how this discussion might unfold, however.

At four in the morning, he was woken from a light sleep by Pam squeezing his hand. The sheet beneath him was wet. 'Jim,' she said, her voice more excited than urgent, 'we need to get to the hospital. The baby's coming.'

While the rest of the women did their chores, Lillian packed her case. From the other side of the ward, Joan repeatedly informed Lillian how fortunate she was to be going home. 'You lucky bugger! It'll be my day soon, mind! Doc Willy's promised!'

Lillian was wearing her tangerine dress. It was too big, but it didn't drip from her bones or slip from her shoulders, for which she told herself she should be glad. She'd already rolled the trousers, doctored belt and shirt in which she'd arrived into a tight ball and thrown the lot into the bin of fabric scraps in the dayroom.

The previous night, Anna had presented her with an open packet of cigarettes. 'Fags are very useful,' she'd said, 'in all sorts of situations.' They'd embraced, but neither spoke of keeping in touch, or of what was to come. Before bed, Lillian had looked inside the carton and found an address written on a slip of paper. Now, as she slid the packet and the address into the lining of the case, alongside the beer mat with Gwen's number on it, her hand found the photograph her mother had given her. She peered at the image of herself and Winnie sitting in the Abbey Meadow, and tried to find the answer to what was next. In the picture, Winnie's hand clutched her daughter's elbow as she strained from her lap towards the camera, and Lillian found herself welling up at the thought of evading her mother's grip. Her mother's things waited for her at number 25. The lumpy armchair still by the fire; the yellow spotted plates in the kitchen; the peep-toe shoes bought by Maurice.

She pictured each of them in turn and felt again their shapes and textures. But she knew they were only things. Her mother was not in that house; she was not in those things. Her mother was no longer anywhere at all.

Perhaps she should go back to Mason Road, if only to tell Mick she was leaving him. But once her foot was over the threshold, would she have the strength to remove herself from the house? Mick might persuade her, in bed, that it was a good idea to stay.

She pushed the clasps of the case shut.

Joan was still talking. 'You lucky bugger! Going home! I'd give my eye teeth to be driven away from here!'

Perhaps that was it. Perhaps there was no need to think beyond the moment she'd be driven away in Jim Shepherd's car. After all, that was one place she knew she'd like to be. Sitting beside him while he pushed through the gears and steered them elsewhere.

After lunch, Akal walked her to the reception area, carrying her suitcase as they strode in silence along the corridors. When they'd reached the reception door, he held the case out and she took it.

'I think you're going to do very well,' he said, with a tilt of his head.

Somewhere a polishing machine droned and a woman let out a yelp. Whether of pleasure or pain it was difficult to tell.

'Just look at you now! The treatment has worked!'

She kept her voice steady and low as she said, 'Anna told me, about the woman who died having insulin treatment.'

A moment passed. 'That may be true. But many others recovered.' He showed her his palms. 'It's the nature of medicine.'

Then he held out his hand and she took it. 'It was such a

pleasure,' he said, 'to watch you throw leaves onto the fire. I want to wish you the best of luck.'

Aside from Nigel behind the desk and the fish in the tank, the reception area was empty. The transistor was playing a Tom Jones song and Nigel was singing along under his breath. He looked up when he saw her. 'Going home today?' he asked, grinning. 'Good for you!'

To avoid having a conversation with him, Lillian walked across the room and stood close to the tank to wait. Jim's fish was swimming to and fro, seemingly energised by the music, its tail undulating like a dancing girl's headdress. The tank gurgled. She wondered if the fish was female, and whether Jim had given it a name. She suspected he might bring a plastic bag along, so he could take it home with him.

She checked her watch. Five past two.

She sat by the window with her case at her feet, so she could watch the car park, which remained empty. Jim was never late. It must be the traffic. An accident, maybe.

The transistor was crackling with the announcer's insistence on the weather forecast: blustery showers. Nigel whistled tunelessly. She touched her case. Then she put on her mac, to be ready.

It was a quarter past two when Lillian heard a car's engine, the sound of tyres on gravel. She stood abruptly and, picking up her case, walked to the exit.

Nigel raised a hand in farewell. 'Good luck, then, poppet.'

Opening the door, she saw it wasn't Jim's car parked on the gravel, and for a moment she thought he must have borrowed Mick's car. But then her husband climbed from the driver's side and strode to the bottom of the steps, where he stood looking at her. He ran a hand through his hair. He was clean-shaven, and wore his smart jacket and trousers, as though he were off to the pub on a Friday night.

'Is that my Lilybud?' he asked, reaching for her case.

She held on to it. Mick gave her a questioning smile. 'What? Don't you want to get out of here?'

The bite of cold in the breeze made her eyes water. She hesitated, watching the cedars pulse. In the distance, the gardener was raking leaves, gathering them together, then dumping them in his truck. There would be another fire, later.

Mick said, in his film-trailer voice, 'She was a young woman beset by problems so great she ended up in a mental institution! Then *he* came to take her away, and together they were dynamite!' He put his hand on hers, and she let him gently remove her fingers from the case's handle. He winked, then trotted to the car and threw the bag in the boot.

She glanced up the drive. No other cars were on the horizon. Her watch said twenty past two. Why hadn't Jim come? And why had Mick actually turned up, after all this time? She hadn't even contacted him. In her confusion, she turned to face the reception doors.

'Wrong way, Bud!' Mick called.

Lillian closed her eyes. Breathed. She didn't want to go back through those doors. But neither did she want to return to number 25.

Because there was no other way out, she got in the car. It smelled of leather and aftershave. There were a couple of laundry bags on the back seat. Presumably her husband had been saving up his dirty washing for her while she'd been in hospital.

Mick put a warm hand on her knee and said, 'You look better. Do you feel better?'

'Sometimes.'

As soon as they were out of the gates, he lit a cigarette. 'Well, there's more of you. Which I like.'

'I wasn't sure you'd be here.'

He laughed. 'Don't be ridiculous. I wouldn't *abandon* you, would I?'

'You didn't visit. Not once.'

He shifted in his seat. 'Well, you didn't write. First I heard from the place was a letter from a doctor, saying you were being discharged.'

She gazed out of the window, trying to think. It was a while before she realised that he was taking the same route as Gwen had: not towards home, but towards Oxford.

'Where are we going?'

Mick blew a long stream of smoke to the side. 'I've been thinking.' He took another drag. 'I'm sorry I didn't come to see you. The truth is, I wasn't sure I could go inside that place. Gives me the heebie-jeebies.'

She folded her arms.

'But it made me realise. What we need is a fresh start. Somewhere new. Away from your mother's house.'

Lillian stared at the side of his face in disbelief. There he was, her husband. His profile still beautiful. His lips, curled around his cigarette, still full, like a girl's. But her time away from him had put him in perspective, and a coldness – even a revulsion – crept through her. Did this man really think that her mother's house was the problem here?

'What's wrong with my mother's house?' she asked.

'Listen. I've got this new job. With a brewery in Coventry. Mate of mine got me in there. It'll be better money.'

It was as though he expected her to carry on as though nothing at all had happened.

'What the hell are you talking about?' she said, her voice rising.

Mick didn't take his eyes off the road. 'He's offered to put us up, until we find our own place. It won't be a palace, but it won't be for long.' He glanced at her. There was something sheepish in his expression as he said, 'It's a new start, Bud. For both of us.'

'When?'

'Right now. Job starts Monday.'

She turned to look again at the bags on the back seat, and noticed within them not only clothes but the outlines of a few pots and pans.

Panic pulsed in her chest. They were on the outskirts of the city, but she had no clue where. She didn't know, either, how far it was to Coventry.

'Where's Mum's stuff?'

'I gave a lot of it to my sister. You can always get it back off her, when we visit—'

'And what about Mum's house?'

There was a pause before he said flatly, 'I gave the rent book back to the council yesterday. It was never *her* house, really, was it?'

A noise came from Lillian's throat.

'I know it's sudden, but I wanted it all sorted for you, so you wouldn't have to worry and we could go straight there—'

'Why would I want to go to bloody *Coventry*?'

'It's not that bad,' he said quietly. 'And it's a good job.'

She wound down the window and gulped at the fumey air. They must be near the centre, she thought, because she could hear the chime of college bells. They came to a halt in the traffic. A bus shuddered beside them.

Mick was talking, saying something about doing it for her benefit, saying that things would be better in a new place.

Lillian pulled on the door handle.

This time there was no locking system and she stepped out, right into the stalled traffic. A horn blew. A wolf whistle came from somewhere. She heard Mick's voice, calling her name, as she opened the boot to retrieve her case. The traffic began to move, but she felt nothing but light as she dodged honking cars to reach the safety of the pavement. Someone shouted, 'Stupid bloody woman!' When she looked back, she saw a little girl on the bus gazing at her, nose pressed to the glass, open-mouthed. Lillian raised a hand, and the girl waved back. Then she began to run.

PART THREE
The River

2005

By the time she'd got through the traffic in the city it was almost six o'clock, but it was no cooler. Lillian drove the last mile to Gwen's place with all the windows down, fanning her sweating middle with the loose cotton of her untucked shirt. She negotiated the speed humps along Gwen's street, her sketchbook bouncing on the passenger seat. Inside were her drawings of the room in Daphne's house. Spending an hour or so deeply focused on the shapes of the toys, the lines of the cot, the way the tin of zinc and castor oil cream sat atop the glass tray, had calmed her a little. Now the evidence of Daphne's care was right there, on paper. She slotted her Corsa between two much bigger cars, using their substantial bumpers to help her squeeze into the spot, feeling pleased by her dexterity.

Gwen had bought the bottom floor of a Victorian villa on the north side of the city not long after she'd secured a permanent position lecturing in English Literature at Oxford Brookes. She lived there alone now, though for a while she'd shared the space with a man named Matthias, a heavily bearded, mostly jovial, alcoholic poet who had ended up back with his ex-wife. More recently, there'd been an American woman named Chrissy who also worked at the university. Lillian had liked Chrissy: she'd helped Rachel with her UCAS application, and always asked Lillian, with a genuinely curious look, how the *view was from her world*. While Chrissy and Gwen had been together, the flat had been spotless. Labels had appeared on all the jars and drawers in the kitchen. Coats and shoes were hidden in a cupboard Chrissy built along the hallway. When they'd split the previous year, Gwen had explained that Chrissy really deserved someone more committed to domestic bliss who'd be capable of doing her the very basic favour of resisting sex with another woman. Lillian had held Gwen as she'd cried and cried, and for months afterwards she'd kept a close eye on her friend, meeting her most weekends for coffee or a trip to the cinema. But Rachel was right: over the last few months, she'd let things slide.

She made her way around the house, inching past Gwen's bicycle, which took up most of the narrow alleyway leading to the back garden. She knocked briefly on one of the patio doors before sliding it open and letting herself into the kitchen. The room smelled of Gwen's dog, a lurcher-cross called Nettle, who was slumped in sleep under the bench. There was a pile of washing-up in the sink and an overflowing recycling bin by the door.

Calling Gwen's name, Lillian walked through to the front room, where it was dim. Gwen's Birkenstocks lay abandoned on the rug.

A voice came from behind her. 'At bloody last.'

Lillian span around, and there was her friend, messy hair to her shoulders, chipped polish on her toenails, a pen tucked behind one ear. 'I was napping,' Gwen explained. 'This heat . . .'

They embraced.

'Sorry,' Lillian said. 'I'm all sweaty.'

Gwen held her at arm's length. 'It's been ages.'

'Sorry.'

Lillian was aware of Gwen examining her face, and she looked away, not wanting to cry. Not yet.

'Go and sit in the garden. I'll bring us a drink out. Wine? Or what?'

'Wine,' said Lillian. 'And water.'

Though she didn't much care about interiors, since buying the flat Gwen had become a gardener. A meandering wood-chip path led Lillian past flowering shrubs of all kinds, dozens of roses, which were Gwen's favourite, and finally into a wooden gazebo which Chrissy had built. The roof was strung with fairy lights and the bench was padded with cushions. Lillian sat, head in the shade and feet, still muddied from the river, in the sun. She inhaled deeply. A sweet, green scent came from the clumps of salvias near by, all of which Gwen could name but Lillian could only smell.

Gwen came out with a tray, which she placed on the grass.

'Water first,' she said, pouring two glasses before sitting beside Lillian.

Lillian gulped hers gratefully.

They spoke for a while of Gwen's work, which was, she said, hellishly busy – which Lillian understood to mean very successful indeed – and of Lillian's. Gwen laughed at the idea of *Super Granddad*. 'For God's sake,' she said, 'does such a being exist?'

'Not in my experience,' said Lillian.

Then Gwen began to talk about her mother. Mrs Chadwick – Rebecca – had been suffering from dementia for a while now, but lately things had become unmanageable. 'I visit every weekend, and a lovely woman called Tasha comes in every other day to keep an eye on her,' Gwen said, 'but it's not enough. Last week Mum left the washing basket on the hob and somehow managed to turn it on. Bloody thing melted. Horrible mess. And the stench!' She grimaced. 'Anyway. I've made a decision. I'm going to move back into Park Road.'

Lillian gaped.

'Well, I can't have her burning the place down, can I?' said Gwen.

'You're going to *live with your mum*?'

Gwen groaned. 'Yes! I am going to live with my bloody mother. Back in bloody Abingdon.'

Lillian didn't know what to say.

Gwen gave a long and theatrical sigh. 'It'll be *fine*. Probably. I can still commute to work. I'll get Tasha to come in when I'm not there. And we'll take it a day at a time.'

Lillian took a mouthful of wine. She'd never imagined Gwen would end up as her mother's carer; both women had always seemed too independent for that. And now here Gwen was, stepping in to save Rebecca. Which was what Lillian should have done for Winnie. She closed her eyes, waiting for the familiar feeling of guilt to pass.

'And,' Gwen continued, 'Chrissy's agreed to look after this place and Nettle-sit while I'm not living here. Mum can't stand dogs.'

'Chrissy? Are you two getting back together, then?'

Gwen gave a shy grin. 'We'll see. But then I thought: God! How stupid! I should have offered it to you first.'

Lillian blinked. 'What?'

Gwen looked a little embarrassed. 'Well,' she said, 'your place isn't exactly massive, is it? And the kitchen here would be perfect as a work room: so much light, view of the garden . . .' She trailed off.

'But I don't need it,' said Lillian. 'I've got my own place.'

'Yes. No. Of course not. And I suppose you've got Daphne's house, anyway, right? If you did want to move somewhere bigger.'

Lillian said, louder than she intended, 'Why would I move to a bigger house when my daughter is about to leave home? Why would I do that?'

A short silence followed.

'It was just an idea. No need to bite my head off.'

Gwen touched her shoulder, and Lillian exhaled. Then it all

came out. She told her friend about Rachel disappearing to her father's. About him teaching her how to cook. About the tics and obsessions she'd noticed. About the room she'd found in Daphne's house. The only thing she did not tell Gwen about was Rachel's plea for her mother to be more open.

'I should've taught her how to cook!' she said. 'How is she supposed to leave home when she can't even feed herself?'

Gwen put down her glass. The sun had slipped a little lower and they were completely in shade now. Lillian took off her sandals and dug her toes into the cool grass, trying to slow her heartbeat.

'I'm presuming she told you that she came to see me a couple of weeks back?'

'What?'

Gwen tutted. 'I *told* her to tell you.'

'Rachel came here?'

'She was worried about how you'll cope when she leaves. She thinks that if she goes away you might not eat . . . Did you tell her about your eating disorder?'

Lillian, who had never even uttered the term out loud, shook her head.

'Well, she knows. And she's frustrated that you won't talk to her. She was asking me about it. I said she should talk to you. And I told her she had to go to uni, of course,' Gwen continued, 'and that you'd be fine, because I would look out for you and, anyway, she isn't your parent.' She crunched on a crisp. 'I hope I did the right thing? I know how much it means to you, Rachel becoming a medic.'

'A surgeon.'

'Right.'

There was a pause. Gwen said quietly, 'But I also know you're bound to find it difficult, when she's gone. And Rachel's right. Unless you open up, we can't help you.'

Lillian took a deep breath. She fixed her gaze on Gwen's salvias. Such rich blues. 'What if she can't take it?' she said.

'Take what?'

'Who I am! All the . . . shit, and the rage! And the . . . madness! Just like I couldn't take my own mum.'

'But that was different—'

'We were both in Longbrook, weren't we? And I left her, Gwen. I abandoned my mother and she *died*. What if Rachel does the same?'

Then she clapped a hand over her mouth and let out a sob.

Gwen put her glass down and took her into her arms. It felt so good to be there that Lillian let herself cry on as Gwen rocked her.

When she was cried out, Gwen said, 'Listen. I won't state the obvious. I won't say that you didn't *abandon* your mother, because you were there for her all along and, anyway, she was an adult. I won't say that Rachel may be going away but she's not dying, and neither are you. She'll come back. I'll just pour you some more wine.'

Lillian placed a hand over the top of her glass. 'I'm driving.'

'Stay here,' said Gwen. 'The bed's all made in the spare room. Has been since Chrissy left.'

A light came on in the flat above Gwen's, and together they watched as a young woman, singing along to a Dolly Parton song, produced a frying pan and began dancing around her kitchen with it.

Lillian blew her nose. 'Does she live there alone?'

'As far as I know. Loads of gorgeous young things coming and going, though.'

Lillian smiled.

'So what was Daphne's house like?' Gwen asked.

'A bit . . . creepy. A lot of ghosts. You know.'

'Rachel liked it?'

'She enjoyed the idea of a telephone table.'
'Isn't it right by the river?'
'Yes.'
'And a big garden, too, I'll bet?'
'Big enough.'
'Three bedrooms? Two receptions? Close to the town centre.'

Lillian gave Gwen a sideways look. 'Stop it. I'm selling it so Rachel can have the money later. She'll need it to get through all her training, and then she'll need a deposit for a house – no one can buy anywhere, these days . . .'

'What about you, though? What about you, *right now*?'

Lillian thought about this. She'd be lonely, without Rachel. Terribly lonely. But moving would feel like an added problem, rather than a solution.

'I mean, I know you like where you live, and it's nice enough, but . . . think about it,' Gwen was saying. 'At Daphne's you'd have plenty of space for when Rachel comes home from uni and wants to bring someone else with her . . . And you'd have a whole room to work in! A room of your own!'

'I told you. I'm selling it.'

'*And*,' Gwen said, throwing her hands in the air, spilling wine down her arm, 'you'd be just down the road from me!'

Lillian laughed. 'Like old times.'

'Like old times,' said Gwen, 'but better.'

Lillian's phone pinged. It was a text from Rachel's father.

Rachel and I are doing the family dinner tomorrow night. Please come.

She turned off the phone and slid it into her pocket. Then she refilled her glass and told Gwen she'd like to stay the night.

1983

No one living on Mason Road was divorced.

There were widows, and also women whose husbands were a bit part-time. Stan Thomas, for example, seemed only to turn up at Jim's neighbour Nina's house a couple of days a month. Tom Bridges worked away a lot and never hurried home. But no one, to Jim's knowledge, asked questions about these men.

Jim wasn't divorced, but he was no longer living with his wife. As a separated man, he spent his weekends keeping busy. Sometimes, when a long list of tasks was neatly stacked in his head, as it was that Saturday morning – trim hedge, wash car, fetch groceries, call on Mum – he could almost pretend that Pam hadn't made her announcement on that bright Sunday four months ago.

He stood in the kitchen, watching the clock made out of a china plate, and felt again the nausea that had washed through him when Pam had said those words. *I'm leaving you.* Not just leaving, but leaving *him*, Jim Shepherd. For a long time, he'd believed she was testing him, that if he could be nice enough about it all and pretend to understand, she'd come back. His mother told him to be patient, saying Pam was just having a wobble. An irresponsible, selfish wobble, but a wobble all the same. All he had to do was wait. He could do that, surely.

Sweat broke on his forehead and at the base of his spine. To steady himself, he filled the kettle and watched it boil, letting it puff steam into the room. He drew moist air into his lungs, pressed his knuckles into his eyes, and counted to twenty. Back to today's list. What was next? The supermarket. He knew this wasn't the best time; it would be much better to go around four in the afternoon, when most families and couples would have finished their shopping, leaving the aisles free for youngsters picking up barrels of Watneys for Saturday night and middle-aged singles rootling through knocked-down syrup sponges and cottage pies. But he had to get out of the house, right now.

It was a relief to walk through the automatic doors and into the bready fug. Now he had a clear task. Jim blinked in the bright lights and swerved his trolley left to avoid women's clothing and records, sections which might provoke memories of his past life. Over the last few months, he'd learned that if you didn't look at anyone it was less likely you'd be spotted, so he kept his gaze low and pushed on to fruit and veg. Rather than struggle with the plastic bag dispenser, he swiped up a net of oranges, one of onions and a small bag of spuds and dumped them in the trolley. He'd never eat them all but Meg would see he was looking after himself and might relay this information to her mother.

Onwards to canned goods. It was his weekend with the kids but they weren't arriving until tomorrow as Pam wanted them to celebrate her mother's sixtieth birthday today. There was a plan for a trip to a National Trust garden, followed by a new steak house in Oxford. On the phone, Jim had paused expectantly when Pam had explained these plans, but his invitation had not followed.

Reaching for a tin of frankfurters, he heard his name and looked up to see Phyllis Murphy grinning at him, her trolley blocking his way. Lillian had worked for Phyllis at the hairdressing salon years ago.

Phyllis was pretty made-up, for the supermarket. Some shimmery substance was on her lips and her hair looked enormous: inflated yet solid. She was what his mother might call, with a gentle grimace, a *handsome woman*.

'Phyllis,' he said.

'How are you, Jim?'

Cradling the tin to his chest, he said, 'Just finding my way around the supermarket!'

Phyllis eyed the contents of his trolley and Jim wished he'd selected more vegetables. 'Isn't it a *maze*?' she said. 'And they keep moving things! I've spent the last ten minutes scouring the place for Colin's Radox. Why he always has to have the same bloody bubble bath is beyond me. Husbands! Who'd have them?'

'Hmm.'

Jim watched her face fall as she seemed to realise what she'd said. 'Oh,' she said. 'Jim—'

'It's all right.'

'I was terribly sorry to hear about you and Pam.' She was frowning slightly from the ostensible depth of her concern. Jim hoped she wouldn't touch his arm. He remembered Phyllis as a touchy sort of woman. If she touched his arm now, his eyes might become wet.

Then her eyes lit up. 'I don't know if you've heard that Lillian's back in the area?'

Jim's heart squeezed and then released. He stared at Phyllis, dumbly.

Phyllis lowered her voice. 'Apparently she came into some money.'

Before he could stop himself, he asked, 'Is Mick with her?'

'Shouldn't think so!' She shook her head, holding his gaze but not – thankfully – touching his arm. Jim didn't dare ask more.

As Phyllis said goodbye and moved off, Jim watched her shoulders swaying in time with her hips and remembered she'd been a dancer, like him.

It felt important, after that, to avoid the awkwardness of

seeing her again, and to give himself time to absorb the information about Lillian. So he pushed his trolley as slowly as he could down every aisle of the supermarket and spent a long time choosing between two brands of finger rolls, almost enjoying himself now he could mull over the fact of Lillian's reappearance. It had been fifteen years. And while it wouldn't have been true to say that Lillian had been in his thoughts every day since she'd left, his memories of her had only grown stronger. While helping Meg into her coat for school, he'd often thought of Lillian's duffel coat folded about her as she knelt on the pavement, one ear to the ground, listening to the culvert. Showing his son Francie how to pump up the tyres of his bike, his mind had sometimes slipped to the times he'd pushed his own bicycle along the river path, Lillian beside him. His most treasured memory – one that he allowed himself to unfold only in the dark, when his wife was asleep beside him – was the kiss they'd shared in the gardens of the asylum, with the radio playing the Everlys. It had seemed possible, then, that he might be the one to take her away from that place. He hadn't thought of leaving Pam, exactly, but he'd imagined some future with Lillian in it.

Since she'd disappeared from Abingdon, he'd told himself that he had to forget, that he must – for Pam's sake, and for the children – pretend that Lillian Wells wasn't still tugging at his thoughts. But he'd lived, daily, with questions. Where the hell was she? What was she doing *right now*? And had she forgiven him for failing to pick her up from Longbrook? A few months after Francie was born, Jim had received a short note from her.

> *I'm writing to let you to know that I am all right. And that I won't forget your kindnesses. I hope to see you again, but I'm sure you'll understand that I cannot be in Abingdon now.*

A York postmark. No forwarding address. No mention of Mick, who, Jim had heard, had a new job in Coventry. Which was confusing. And hopeful.

At the till, the checkout girl didn't look at him when he thanked her, and he heard himself mutter, *Dunno why I bother*, but still Jim felt cheered as he wheeled his trolley into the car park.

The following teatime, Jim was in his Maestro, peering through the October gloom at the red-bricked houses on the new estate just outside Abingdon. Pam had said it was better for him not to come inside her mother's house, so he parked the car round the corner from Val's place to drop the kids back. Usually it went smoothly: a peck on the cheek from Meg, an awkward hug from Francie, and then he was away, putting distance between himself and his desire to run up Val's path and demand to see his wife. But now Meg turned to her father and said in a low voice, 'Can't you drop us at the house? It's so embarrassing.'

'What's embarrassing?'

'Francie tripping over all his stupid bags. Everyone seeing us and knowing we're the children of stupid divorced parents.'

'She's being *melodramatic*,' said Francie, who liked new vocabulary. His achievements at school sometimes left Jim feeling ashamed of his own academic shortcomings.

Jim said, 'Your parents are not divorced. It's a trial separation.'

'Have you ever heard of a trial separation that ends in people getting back together, though?' Meg sounded tired, more than anything. 'I mean, in real life, does that actually ever happen?'

Jim had no answer. His daughter was looking at him with what he realised was pity, as though she were the older, wiser party who understood the ways of the world. And it wasn't the first time he'd seen that look on her face. She stepped from the car without offering her cheek.

In the back seat, Francie's lips were pressed together and Jim realised his son might cry. So he said, 'Your sister doesn't know what she's talking about. Go and see your mother.'

As Francie was leaving the car, Val strolled into view. She was wearing some sort of embroidered scarf that looked more like a shawl. She ruffled Francie's hair as he passed, then waved to Jim.

He let her knock on his window before he rolled it down.

'I've a message,' she said, 'from Pam.'

Jim waited, watching his son lollop along the pavement, one side of his body weighed down by his holdall.

'She wants to talk to you.'

'So tell her to ring me.'

'She wants to meet. You could pop by tomorrow? I'll be out, of course.'

Not wanting to satisfy her with an immediate answer, he asked, 'How was your birthday?'

A concerned pleat appeared between her eyebrows. 'What shall I tell her, Jim?'

'Tell her I'll meet her up The Boundary. Wednesday evening. Tell her that.'

Val nodded and looked relieved. 'And how are *you* doing?'

'Smashing, thanks,' he said, starting the engine.

He arrived early at The Boundary House. The pub was under new management and had recently undergone a refurbishment: the walls were papered in burgundy stripes and cardboard menus were propped proudly on every table. Jim carried his pint and a glass of white wine over to a table slotted into the bay of one of the windows. He hoped the wine would impress his wife, though she rarely drank it, preferring the odd gin and slim. Sitting with his back to the window, Jim felt horribly on display. He snatched up a menu and frowned at it without reading a word as he supped at his beer.

He'd barely caught a glimpse of Pam over the past months. After the *announcement of her intentions* (a phrase he used when thinking of her leaving, to avoid the word *leaving*, or the word *divorce*) it had been amazing how easily his wife had slipped from view. That Sunday morning in June, she'd taken his hand in the front room and almost smiled as she said she had something to tell him, as though she were about to announce a pregnancy or a new job. Throughout her speech, she'd stared at the curtains and kept her voice mild. It was as though she'd switched on a tape player and the words were spooling into the room, spoken by some other woman. *There's no one else*, she'd said. *I want you to know that. I just haven't been happy for a long time, and I don't think you have, either.* It was this last statement that had most enraged Jim. Even if it was true, how could she claim to know what he felt? Jim had understood, straight away, that though Pam talked of *thinking about* taking the children and staying at her mother's for a bit, it was all planned. Val had been expecting her.

Now he picked up his damp beer mat, wiped it on the cushion beside him, then replaced it. At the table opposite, a family were silently attacking dishes of ice cream. A girl around Meg's age was serving. Every time she passed, Jim smiled and she failed to respond. He wondered if he should go and stand at the fruit machine, in order to relieve his face of the strain of it all.

Then his wife appeared.

To Jim's dismay, she'd had her hair streaked even blonder and she looked better than ever. Barely glancing at him, she slid into the seat opposite and blinked at the glass before her.

'Is that for me?'

Jim nodded. 'It's dry. Apparently.'

'I don't think it's a good idea for me to drink it, Jim. I'll ask for a coffee when the girl comes over.'

'No problem,' said Jim. 'All the more for me. I'll order some cake. We can share.'

Pam shook her head and smiled a small, knowing smile which irritated the hell out of Jim. 'What?' he demanded. 'Am I supposed to stop looking after my wife?'

'I don't know what you're supposed to do,' she said quietly. Then she signalled to the waitress, who took her order for a coffee and Jim's for a slice of Black Forest Gateau with extra whipped cream.

'Thanks for meeting me.' Pam placed both hands on the table, and he noticed she was not wearing her wedding ring.

To stop himself from shouting he took a long drink of beer, then said, 'You don't have to thank me for meeting you. I'm your husband.'

Pam briefly closed her eyes. 'That's what I want to talk about. I think we should divorce. It feels like the only option, to me. I'm so sorry, Jim.'

Her chin dipped and her mouth twisted. Recognising the physical signs of his wife being about to cry, and unable to respond to her words, Jim nodded, silently. Then he stared at the roots of her hair for a long time but she did not look up.

Eventually, he reached for her hand, which was cold. 'Let's not . . . rush into anything,' he said.

She'd talked, that Sunday morning, of not knowing who she was any more, of needing a break. And she'd also said that she felt as though Jim had never really loved her. He'd protested that was ridiculous, that he could show her how he felt, if she'd let him. But as soon as those words were out of his wife's mouth, it had been difficult not to doubt his own feelings.

The name *Lillian* had never been mentioned.

Pam folded her hand back into her lap and thanked him for remaining calm.

'You need to stop thanking me.'

'Are you OK?' she asked, brushing the hair from her eyes.

'Of course I'm not bloody OK,' he said quietly.

There was another long silence, during which Jim considered getting up to leave. Slamming his wedding ring on the table and walking out. He didn't want to have this conversation at all, let alone in a public place. Then Pam said, 'Meg told me something happened, at the weekend.'

He blinked, thrown for a minute: did Meg know about Lillian's return?

'You found out about Kevin? Meg's boyfriend.'

So she already knew about the boy – or perhaps man was more accurate – that Meg had slipped off to meet almost as soon as she'd arrived on Sunday. Francie had told him the lad worked at the cobbler's in town, but Meg had refused to offer any further information. This was how it was going to be, now, Jim thought: him always on the outside. As long as they were separated – divorced – his children wouldn't come to him first. He'd always be catching up.

'He's nice. It's been going on for a while,' said Pam.

With all his beer gone, Jim risked a sip of wine. It tasted like mouthwash but he managed a few more sips, then a gulp.

'And he's older,' he said.

'A bit . . .'

'And you think that's OK, do you?' His voice was too loud, and the woman on the next table glanced across, plucked eyebrows raised.

Pam lowered her voice. 'She's sixteen, Jim. I wasn't much older, when we first met.'

'Things are different now.'

'Are they?'

'They certainly look different,' said Jim, 'from where I'm sitting.'

'That would be a good thing, wouldn't it?'

'Not to me. Not at this precise moment.'

Pam just nodded and looked pitying, which was annoying enough to make Jim ask, aware he sounded like a truculent child, 'Did you ever really love me?'

Though the woman at the next table was no longer looking in his direction, her whole family had stopped eating and were sitting very still. This did not stop Jim from adding, loudly, 'Or did you say yes just because of Meg?'

Pam raised her voice now, too. 'Did you propose just because of Meg?'

The family at the next table also seemed to be waiting for his answer. He hung his head and gave a soft laugh. Then he leaned towards her, grasping her hand once more. 'I can do better, you know.'

Pam took her hand away. The waitress was delivering their order. They both gazed at the cake. It resembled a slice of mud, freshly dug from the ground, topped with a glacé cherry, and its frill of whipped cream was already dissolving.

Pam took up Jim's fork and handed it to him. 'Here,' she said. 'For God's sake, have some cake.'

He did as he was told, stoppering his mouth with sponge.

The following weekend, Jim stood at the window in the front room to watch Pam's mother park outside his house. He was relieved when his children stepped from her car without Val getting out. Having the woman on his doorstep would not be the best start to what already promised to be a difficult day.

After they'd met at The Boundary House, Pam had telephoned and used her mild voice to inform him she'd contacted a solicitor and had told the children about the divorce. It would be good for them to have certainty about what was going on, she said. Certainty, she added, would be better for everyone.

Now his children, the children of about-to-be-divorced parents, were coming up the front path, and it didn't seem to Jim that certainty improved anything about this situation.

Meg and Francie kept their heads down. Francie carried the sports holdall he sometimes took to school but Meg, Jim noticed, had nothing more than a large yellow handbag, a can of hairspray protruding from the zip. Jim resisted the urge to fling open the front door and embrace his children outside the house, instead moving to the hallway to listen for the double-clunk of the back door opening – first the handle going down, then the door's edge catching the frame. Realising he hadn't heard that sound for a week, he suddenly wanted to cry.

He didn't, of course. He went into the kitchen, having arranged his face into a smile, meaning to offer them a glass of Lilt, which he'd bought specially for their visit. But when they stood before him, his children seemed to have grown in just one week and they were both staring at him – Meg with her blue lashes and Francie with big wet eyes – as though unsure how to greet their father. This new, divorced version of their father. Jim didn't quite know, then, what his face was doing, but it had lost its arrangement. Meg dropped her handbag and held him, tightly. He inhaled his daughter. The scent of Val's house was all over her – astringent cleaning fluids, some expensive perfume – but he felt the familiar bones of her shoulder blades and her curls tickled his nose as she said, quietly, with what Jim recognised as deep relief, 'Hello, Dad.'

He held on. Francie, ever the practical child, set himself to the task of filling the kettle.

When Jim let Meg go, he tapped his son on the shoulder and Francie turned, his face tight. 'You're all right,' said Jim, swallowing. 'It'll be all right. I'm still here. I'm still your dad.'

Francie threw his arms around him and Jim let him hold on

for a minute or so before he gently but firmly removed himself from his son's grip.

It was Francie's suggestion, a few weekends later, that they go to the art museum in Oxford. His teacher had told him he should, apparently. Jim agreed to the plan because it wasn't a place with a whiff of Pam about it. As far as he could recall, they'd never been inside an art gallery together. Besides, where else were they going to go on a rainy afternoon, now that his daughter had announced she couldn't join them because she was meeting Kevin?

Though he remembered promising to take Lillian there once, he'd never actually been to the Ashmolean. He let his son lead the way through the drizzle. Jim nodded towards the Randolph Hotel, saying that Richard Burton and Elizabeth Taylor had stayed there. Francie, something of a film buff, responded with an interested 'huh', as though he might actually be impressed.

They crossed Beaumont Street and were suddenly faced with a steep sweep of steps and four huge columns holding up the porch to a building that seemed very unBritish – Greek, Roman or perhaps French, Jim wasn't sure. Even with the noise of the traffic and the clouds low in the sky, as they mounted the steps he was struck by a feeling of light and space opening up before him.

The revolving door, taller than three men standing on one another's shoulders, spat them into a hushed hall. A long corridor lined by white statues led one way, a wide staircase swept up the other. Between these was a desk, at which sat a woman in a blue nylon overall like the one Jim's mother wore to do her housework. Jim approached, opening his wallet, and with a small smile she told him it was free to come in but they could buy a guide for twenty-five pence, which Jim did. It was flimsy and all in black and white.

When he glanced back, Francie was already mounting the stairs.

'Shouldn't we look at this first?' Jim asked, unfolding the leaflet and frowning at the tiny print.

'Let's just explore,' said Francie.

So Jim stuffed the guide in his pocket and followed, marvelling at the way his son took the stairs as though they belonged to him. When Jim peered down from the top, he saw the white plaster heads below and felt a little dizzy. But his son strode ahead. On the second floor, Francie plunged through a pair of wooden doors into a room with tapestries bigger than Jim's whole front room. Francie pressed on, the wooden floor creaking loudly with every step, and Jim had to repress the urge to shush his son. The whole place seemed to sing and shift like a ship as they walked. Somewhere a clock began to strike intricately, then another, then another, which made them both stop and exchange smiles.

'Three o'clock, then,' said Jim.

'Evidently,' Francie replied.

Jim opened his leaflet, but Francie was off again, through another set of doors and into a room with pink walls and fancy upholstered benches. To Jim's confusion, Francie didn't pause before every painting, instead dismissing some with a quick glance and honouring others with a long gaze. Jim tried to keep up, though he was tempted to read all the information cards, feeling that otherwise he wouldn't receive the full experience.

He wasn't sure what Pam would have made of the place. Mummies and dinosaurs were things you went to museums for; you knew where you were with the really ancient things: the wonder being, obviously, that they were so *old*. With paintings and cabinets and clocks you weren't on nearly such solid ground. What, exactly, was he supposed to be seeing? It wasn't at all clear in the dark canvases of elaborate flowers and fruit, or the tall portraits of military men in armour or hats with feathers, and certainly not in the black-clothed Dutch people (he read that on the sign: *Dutch School*) with white ruffles around their necks that made them look like strange dolls.

Francie came to a standstill in front of another dark painting. This one, though, was wide and thin. The size and shape of a bath panel. Jim squinted at the label: *The Hunt in the Forest*. From afar the canvas had looked more like a pattern than a painting, but now he was up close he could see the brown and black was enlivened with red slashes that described the hunters' jackets and the horses' bridles. The hunters' backs were arched like metal warping in fierce heat as they chased through trees into darkness. And there were dogs everywhere, leaping. It was, Jim suddenly thought, a noisy painting, crammed with springing shapes and hollering trumpets and bodies getting lost in the forest.

'Why are they hunting at night?' he asked.

'Good question,' said Francie.

Jim fished the leaflet from his pocket. 'The painting can be read as an allegory for love,' he read aloud.

Though he suspected Francie might fully understand that statement, Jim couldn't admit to having no idea what an allegory was, and he certainly didn't want to have a conversation about love with his son. So he just *hmm*-ed in what he hoped was a wise way. But as he gazed at it, he felt the picture did have something to do with love. He spotted only one hunter who'd actually been successful; a deer lay across his shoulders like an expensive stole, or a wounded loved one, and he didn't look at all happy about his conquest. Peering closer, Jim began to think the hunters' raised hands made them look as though they were drowning. There was something here about the hide-and-seek of love. The hunters bending into strange shapes. The dark hood of trees hanging above. The blood, and the leap of the heart. The chase through the night. The loss.

'Good, isn't it?' said Francie, grinning.

'It is,' said Jim.

They sat together on the velvet-covered seat a while longer, looking at the painting. Two students wearing backpacks planted themselves behind them, speaking loudly in another language. Jim was about to get up to leave when a woman in a blue overall walked into the room, her dark head inclined slightly to the side, her hands in her pockets, her tread determined and quick.

Lillian Wells. He would recognise her anywhere.

Jim found, then, that he could neither speak nor move, and he was glad that Francie seemed still to be engrossed in the painting. He watched Lillian walk across the room, the floor creaking as she went, and he was eighteen again, observing her stride down Mason Road, his heart rising. The fact of her, there, was undeniable. The space she took up, the style of her, was exactly the same. He couldn't look away, and kept gazing at the far door long after she'd walked through it, though he wasn't exactly surprised by her presence; he'd almost been expecting her. For fifteen years, he'd been aware that at any moment she might step back into his life.

No one spoke of Lillian's time at Longbrook.

Eventually, after a few drinks at a pub not far from Gwen's student digs, Lillian told Gwen what she knew of her mother's experience. She repeated Ernie's words about the river, about Longbrook, and her 'attacks of the nerves'. She also told her what Daphne had said about ECT.

'She had depression,' said Gwen, who didn't seem very surprised by any of it.

Lillian said she supposed that was what it was. And she was relieved to have a single word for it. But even Gwen, in whose tiny terraced house Lillian had lived since turning up in York that November day, liked to say that Lillian had done an excellent job of moving on. 'The future,' she'd say, whenever they raised a glass of cider together in her damp kitchen, 'that's the thing.'

Gwen's parents had bought the house on Glendale Avenue and were letting it to their daughter and her housemate, Helen, for a greatly reduced rent. It was a Victorian two-up two-down, with a weed-choked yard out back, a front room made cheerful by Mrs Chadwick's throws and cushions, and a kitchen in which mould bloomed around the bin and the twin tub. Soon after Lillian had arrived, Helen moved out to live with another girl whose flat was closer to her boyfriend's place, and Gwen suggested Lillian take the back bedroom; she could begin paying rent once she'd found a job. The window was furred with dirt, and the first thing Lillian did on moving in was fetch a bucket of soapy water and a cloth to give it a good wash. As she wiped at the glass, the warm suds running into her sleeve, she thought of the hospital windows with their view of the cedars, the lawn, the allotment beyond, the men at the brazier, and was pleased to have this new view before her.

She was surprised, though, to find herself missing the ward routines and chatter. She missed, too, Akal's kind eyes and consoling words, and Jim's visits. She'd dumped the medication she'd been prescribed, telling herself she was facing a clean slate, which meant avoiding her mother's habits at all costs. She'd run from the home-going the hospital had imagined for her, as well as the one Mick had. She wasn't sure if Jim had any kind of plan for a future with her in it, but even if he had, his new family made it an impossibility. She'd made it here, alone. Though the days stretched terrifyingly ahead, unscheduled and filled with the possibilities of food, she was surviving.

She got a job cutting hair at a salon called 'Hair Affair'. Every evening, Lillian either went back to Glendale Avenue to sketch whatever was around her – the view from her window, plates of half-eaten sandwiches on the drainer, coffee mugs and milk bottles on the table – or escaped to Kelman's in the centre of town, where she sat with a frothy coffee and a bun, which did well enough for an evening meal, and drew the scene before her until the café closed. Young couples bickering over money while sharing a plate of chips. Middle-aged men emptying packets of sugar into their tea and stirring it disconsolately, first this way, then that. To her surprise she found that, rather than making her vulnerable, the sketchbook acted as a kind of armour. With it, she looked busy, as though she had purpose, and it seemed OK to be alone. Certainly no one tutted or wolf-whistled.

She often wondered what Jim Shepherd was doing, back in Abingdon. Several times she wrote to him, outlining the details of her new life in a chirpy tone (*Hair Affair is just the same as*

Michael John, only without your mother!) and asking as nonchalantly as she could why he hadn't turned up that day (*I hope nothing bad happened? Perhaps you were kidnapped?!*). But when she read them back she found the letters so dull that she tore them up and threw them away, telling herself it didn't matter, and that Jim had chosen to avoid participating in her life, even as a friend.

She wrote to Ernie to let him know her new address and that she was all right. He occasionally sent her a postcard of Abingdon with a few words scrawled on the back, saying she should let him know if she needed money, and Lillian, resigned to the fact that Ernie was never going to offer her anything more than that, did not write back.

She also sent a note to Mick's sister, Ida, asking her to forward a letter to Coventry. She kept the letter brief and factual, informing Mick she was living in York with Gwen and had no plans to return. He didn't reply, or come to find her, but he did forward the invitations from Longbrook to regular meetings with ex-patients. On one he printed in neat capitals: HOPE YOU'RE KEEPING WELL, LILYBUD.

It was almost three years before she received a letter from a Coventry solicitor, informing her of her husband's intention to divorce her. She knew, then, that Mick was marrying someone else – why bother with the expense, otherwise? She signed the papers and slipped her wedding ring in the envelope before returning them. Later, when she told Gwen, they toasted her freedom with a brandy and went to the pictures to see *The Way We Were*. Gwen said it was capitalist twaddle but had to admit it was worth it for Barbra Streisand. Though she was glad to be free of Mick, Lillian wept through much of the film. She missed his body in bed, his way of calling her *Lilybud*. She missed having someone to miss.

To cheer her up, Gwen insisted they go to a house party with some of the gang from the new radical magazine her friend Sheena had got her involved with. Everyone who worked on it was sick to death of the status quo, Gwen said. The publisher, an older academic named Clive, greeted them at the door with a wet kiss on both cheeks and an offer of his homemade elderberry wine. In the kitchen were lots of men with beards and suede jackets who smoked pipes, but there were also a few women – Gwen introduced her to Claire, June, and Sheena herself. Claire had cooked something with lentils that she urged Lillian to eat, since no one else was, and Sheena talked about the need to support local working-class women. Lillian wasn't sure if she counted as working-class, as she lived in the nice house on Glendale Avenue with Gwen, who'd recently started work as a school teacher. But a man without a beard, who'd been listening to their conversation, told her that as she was a hairdresser she most definitely did. He poured her some more wine, which tasted like cough syrup, and kissed her by the fridge, still holding a bottle of beer in one hand. His name was Ken, and he had a soft voice and tanned forearms. After they'd had nice enough sex in Lillian's single bed he traced her hairline with a tobacco-stained forefinger and told her that though he was really into her, she should know that he needed his freedom.

Freedom. It was a word she heard a lot during those first few years in York. Freedom was something everyone seemed to be reaching for; something that was prized above all else. One evening, at another party in Clive's basement, Sheena had a row with Ken, telling him that men's freedom always came at a price, and the price was usually paid by women, who were expected to pick up men's dirty Y-fronts and cook their tea while they fucked off in the name of freedom. And don't even get her started on looking after the kids. Remembering the 'Home Group' in Longbrook, and the men's response to her chucking leaves on the brazier, Lillian wanted to cheer. But Ken laughed, called Sheena a drag, and asked if she needed a shag to loosen her up.

After that, Lillian avoided him whenever he rang the bell at Glendale Avenue. He didn't stop appearing until she eventually opened the door and told him that they were both free, which was why she'd started sleeping with someone else.

It was a lie, but it did the trick.

There was never a day during which Lillian didn't monitor what she ate, aware of having to avoid not so much the food itself but the regret and self-loathing that followed eating a plate of chips or more than one slice of toast. In the fridge there was always one tub of low-fat margarine and one of cottage cheese, together with a few celery sticks. There was, also, always black coffee, which she now drank in great quantities.

Only sometimes did she dream that she was struggling to remain asleep in the swimming-pool-green of the curtained bed, under Akal's watchful gaze. She would wake dry-mouthed, with an urgent sense of needing to find her mother. Once her heart rate had slowed, she would check her hipbones: still protruding.

Gwen reduced her hours at the school, enrolled part time at the university and began a PhD. She told Lillian that she could do something similar: why not apply for an art course? Though she was tempted, Lillian didn't feel ready to face a full-time course, so she began to attend life drawing classes at the local technical college. Every week she looked forward to Thursday evening, when she focused entirely on the human form. The tutor, a woman in her fifties who loved Michelangelo, was circumspect but encouraging.

It felt to Lillian that she'd gained a precious equilibrium which must be protected. And though she knew that this domestic arrangement couldn't go on for ever – she and Gwen were both approaching their thirties – she was determined not to be knocked off balance. So she kept her head down. Kept working at the salon. Kept having occasional sex with one man or another from Gwen's circle of friends while insisting on her freedom. Kept eating the same small meals at exactly the same times. Kept drawing the same things. And survived.

Then, in the late spring of 1983, Gwen received an offer to teach at Oxford Polytechnic and announced her intention to take it up. Her parents had recently divorced, and the house in York needed to be sold. Lillian tried to think of a way around this. Perhaps she could buy the house? Impossible, on her wages. Perhaps she could live in Oxford with Gwen? But Gwen had not suggested the idea. She would have to begin looking, soon, for somewhere to rent. Alone.

She had a few viewings for flats lined up when she received a letter with an Abingdon postmark. In it, Daphne informed her that Ernie had been suffering from lung cancer for the last few months. 'I'm sorry to tell you that dear Ernie has passed on,' Daphne wrote. 'Please come to see me as soon as you can.'

The smell of the brewery was thick as Lillian walked from Park Road, where she was staying with Gwen's mother, to Ernie and Daphne's house. Trying to remember when she'd last heard from Ernie, she realised his final postcard must have arrived over a year ago. They hadn't let her know he was ill. But then, she hadn't asked. After reading Daphne's letter, Lillian had thrown it to the floor. How dare the man die before she'd asked him everything she needed to know? Then she'd clapped a hand to her mouth and succumbed to a short, sharp bout of weeping. Ernie had been what was left of her mother and number 25. His bear hugs. His big body stumping down the path as he checked for onlookers. His penny pressed into her hand.

Approaching Daphne's house, though, she found it hard to think of Ernie without remembering his visit to Longbrook and his refusal to offer her much more than money.

When Daphne opened the door, her hair was grey; she no longer wore make-up, which made her eyes seem smaller, but they were still piercing as she gazed at Lillian. 'Thank goodness,' she said. 'You're here.'

She led Lillian down the hall and into the kitchen, where she gestured towards a tray of biscuits.

'Have one. I've not long made them. Cheese. Ernie's favourite. They were all he'd eat, at the end.'

Lillian took a biscuit and examined its charred edges as she said, 'I was so sorry to hear about . . . your loss.'

Daphne stood at the sink, looking out of the window onto the garden. The back door was open, and Lillian could see a lawn, brightly green in the May sunshine, lined with rose bushes. A long silence passed. It was as though Daphne were not quite awake. Lillian nibbled on the burned biscuit, wondering how long it would take Daphne to get to the urgent matter. She still felt uneasy in Daphne's company, and couldn't help worrying that merely by stepping foot in the house she had again betrayed her mother in some way.

'You're keeping well?' Daphne asked, eventually, in a far-off voice.

Lillian said that she was.

'There's not much point to me, now, without my Ernie. That's the truth of it,' said Daphne, and Lillian got the feeling she'd been saying this for quite a while, now.

The walk had made Lillian thirsty and she longed for a glass of water, but Daphne was still gazing out of the window. She began to speak again, using the same far-off tone as before. 'Well. I suppose I may as well get on with it now you're here. I've wanted to tell you something for years.'

Then Lillian knew why Daphne had asked her here, and what she was about to say, and although it wasn't exactly a shock her heart gave a deep thud.

'There's no easy way to put it, so here it is. Ernie was your dad. But I suppose you'd worked that out already.'

Lillian felt as though all the blood had drained from her body. She swallowed down a hysterical laugh. She'd half-known as much for years, but now the fact of it had been spoken aloud it felt both enormous and ridiculous.

'He tried so hard, to do the right thing. We weren't long married, you see, when the thing with your mother . . . when it happened,' Daphne continued, still looking out of the window. 'He'd known her since they were children, of course, and she was very . . . reluctant to let him go. He always said he loved both of us, but I came first. And I felt that in my bones. I really did. So we just . . . carried on. And then your mother did that bloody stupid thing after she had you, which made everything a mess. Ernie couldn't just leave her – or you – in the lurch. And, well . . . you know the rest.'

'I need to sit down,' Lillian said.

Daphne turned, then, and dragged a chair from beneath the table. Lillian sank onto it and Daphne, seeming to have woken somewhat from her trance, said she would make her a cup of tea with a tot of something, for the shock. It seemed that all her words had been used up, and she boiled the kettle, scalded the pot and found the brandy from the larder in silence.

With the toe of her shoe, Lillian rubbed the crumbs from her biscuit into the rag-rug, trying to think of a way to respond to what Daphne had told her. Her head felt hot and empty but her skin had gone cold.

'Anyway,' Daphne said, 'he's left you money. We had a bit put away and he – and I – wanted you to have it.' She opened the drawer beneath the sink and produced a fat envelope, which she placed before Lillian.

Lillian gazed at the envelope, then found herself saying, 'Mum always said my dad was Maurice. She never said it was Ernie. Why did she lie?'

Daphne sat on the other side of the table and poured the tea. 'He told her not to tell you,' she said.

'He *told* her not to?'

Daphne sighed. 'He was a proud man. He didn't want you or anyone else thinking that he hadn't done right by you.' Then she added, 'And – you know how it is. Once you tell one secret, all the others tend to come out.'

'Why didn't *you* tell me, then? You could have said something that day I came here—'

'I wanted to. It wasn't my place. It had to come from Ernie.'

'Every Friday he sat there eating Mum's steak and kidney and he said absolutely bloody nothing!'

There was a small silence before Daphne said, 'I thought he'd say something when he came to see you at the hospital that time. He hinted that he might. But I suppose he felt it'd be too much for you, just then. And you know how men are. They just – get on with things. God forbid they'd have to have *feelings*. But I know he suffered, Lillian. Some nights he'd wake up howling.'

Just like Mum, then, Lillian thought. Except, of course, no one would have put Ernie in a mental hospital.

Daphne wiped her eyes with the back of her hand. 'I told him, all those years ago, that we could keep you. I would've loved to have had you. And it would've been easy, with Winnie in that place. But Ernie said your mother needed you. So that was that. And he was probably right.' She sniffed.

Lillian touched the envelope. Money, again. 'I can't take this,' she said, pushing it in Daphne's direction.

Daphne reached across and caught Lillian's chin in her hand. She held on, forcing Lillian to return her intense gaze. 'Now don't be silly about this. Please. I know he wasn't good at showing it, but Ernie loved you, in his way. You take that money and you do something for yourself with it, Lillian. And you don't ever need to come back here again if you don't want to. I'd understand. But if you do, then it's like I always said. I'll be so pleased to see you. You're always welcome in this house.'

In the warmth of the afternoon sun, Albert Park was as neat and orderly as it had ever been, its pale path lined with labelled shrubs and its iron benches freshly painted. Lillian walked around it slowly, going over what Daphne had told her. The envelope of money in her trouser pocket creased against her thigh with each step. Ernie was her father. Of course he was. But what did it mean? What difference did it make to her life now? She tried to imagine how things might have been, if the truth had been out in the open. What else might she have asked Ernie for, if she'd been able to call him *Dad*? Perhaps she could have demanded he take more responsibility for Winnie, so that she could go to art school. But it was all too late. He would never be her father in any way that mattered. To her, he'd always be Ernie.

It was Daphne who'd changed, she thought. Daphne, who had confirmed this truth. Daphne seemed different now.

Still, Lillian suspected she wouldn't visit Daphne again. The house made her too uneasy, and what she needed to do, she thought to herself, was what Gwen said: look to the future. Which meant leaving Ernie and his wife behind her.

★

After a few rounds of the park, she sat at the kitchen table while Gwen's mother, who now insisted on being called Rebecca, gave her iced water in the same rough-hewn mug Lillian had drunk from when she first visited the house. Lillian took off her dusty shoes and planted her bare feet on the kitchen tiles. The room smelled of yesterday's curry. Just inhaling it was almost like eating it, which pleased Lillian, who'd left half of what was on her plate last night. Eating half and leaving half was, she felt, a good balance. A way to survive. Rebecca said she enjoyed cooking with spices now that her husband, David, wasn't there to complain. He'd moved out months ago and was living in Jericho with one of his *mature students* – a phrase she uttered with undisguised contempt.

Lillian, who'd blurted most of the story as soon as she'd entered the house, said, 'I feel so *betrayed*. By all of them!'

She wasn't sure if this was what she felt, exactly, but it seemed a reasonable claim, and there was something about Rebecca's open gaze that made her able to say such things.

Rebecca placed a plate of Digestives on the table and sat opposite. Since Lillian had arrived two days ago, Rebecca had said nothing about her eating habits, but she never missed an opportunity to put food before her.

'Presumably,' Rebecca said, 'his wife – Daphne, was it? She knew all along? And didn't prevent Ernie from seeing you and your mother?'

'I suppose so.'

'That strikes me as quite the act of kindness.'

'It would have been kinder to tell me,' said Lillian.

Rebecca nodded. 'But what would have happened then?'

Lillian thought about this. Would Ernie have left Daphne and moved into number 25? She doubted it. She couldn't see her mother and Ernie getting along for more than a few hours at a time, anyway. And where would that have left Daphne?

'At least I would have known the truth,' said Lillian, though she could see that perhaps her mother and Ernie had tried not to inflict more damage than was necessary.

Rebecca helped herself to a biscuit. 'It's a shock for you, of course. But it's so important to find something to *do*, don't you think? To take action. Especially when you've been wounded.'

Rebecca's action, after David left, had been to join the local Women's Group. Of course, she'd said, a lot of it was sharing stories about how disappointing men were. But some of it was really quite practical. Women helping each other with childcare, job applications, problems at work. Someone at the group had been talking, she said, about the Ruskin School of Drawing in Oxford, and she'd thought of Lillian. You could get a grant, as – she smiled wryly at the term – a *mature student*.

'Of course,' she said, brushing biscuit crumbs from her jumper, 'what action you take all depends on what you want.'

Lillian said, 'I wouldn't mind your house.'

Rebecca laughed. 'I'm afraid that's promised to Gwenny and her sister—'

'Not like that. I mean, I'd like to have the *feel* of it, you know? I've always liked it.'

She didn't know precisely what she meant by this. Something to do with the freedom she felt in the place. She could imagine herself at home here.

Rebecca took another biscuit and looked at her seriously. 'You can have what you want, Lillian. But you might have to reach for it.'

She could never fully think of Ernie as her father, but she could make use of his money. She bought herself an old Escort and learned to drive. She rented a flat in East Oxford, not far from Gwen. At the bottom of her road there was a community theatre and at the top was an Asian mini-market. In between were terraced houses, not unlike Gwen's in York, containing teachers, social workers, Bangladeshi families and students. Her flat was the top floor of a house in the middle of the street, and she had it almost exactly as she liked it. The room at the front had a large bay window looking out onto the silver birches that lined the pavement and the telephone wires that criss-crossed the sky. In the mornings it was flooded with light, and Lillian liked sitting at the table, monitoring the movement of the leaves. Rebecca had offered her any item of furniture from Park Road as a house-warming gift, and Lillian had chosen the white rug from David's study. *Good riddance to that thing*, Rebecca had said when she picked it up. She had, too, her mother's peep-toe shoes beneath her bed, and the photo of the two of them in the Abbey Meadow up on the wall.

She also won a place on the BA in Fine Art at the Ruskin. All that sketching of half-eaten toast, cups of tea and men grappling with sugar packets had gone down well at the interview. Plus they were keen on mature women students. For that was what she was now, apparently.

And she got a new job, working part time as an invigilator at the Ashmolean Museum.

The Saturday that Jim Shepherd appeared, she was in her second favourite room: the Italian Renaissance. Her absolute favourite was the Western Art Print Room on the top floor, where few people ever ventured and she could lose herself in drawings by Toulouse-Lautrec and Leonardo and Palmer. There was something appealing about the blank page being part of those images. Even in Palmer's overflowing *The Valley Thick with Corn* it was possible to find space and air, to claim your own place in the picture.

She was crossing the gallery on her way to her next post when she spotted him. He was sitting with a teenage boy – unmistakably his son, though his posture was quite different to Jim's – frowning at the Uccello. Upright, head and shoulders held at a precise angle, as though he might be about to get up and dance across the parquet.

She needed to reach the Music Room by the allotted time or the invigilator waiting to change over, an old-hand named Charlie who always asked her about her boyfriends, might be irritated. But it wasn't just this that prevented her from greeting Jim. Those few steps across the room seemed too great a distance to cross. She had no clue what she might say to him after all these years. And the sight of him, to her surprise, gave her a tightness around the ribcage, an agitation in her arms. She found that she so wanted to touch him. To stride towards him and smile, to say hello and ask a direct question, so she might feel him turn his attention towards her once more. She'd lost her mother, and, she supposed, her father, too. But Jim, who knew her and had loved her, was right there. Just across the room.

She wasn't ready. She walked on.

Part of her homework was to draw as many people as she could, so she asked Gwen to the flat to sit for her. While her friend found a position on the settee, Lillian made coffee, then fetched her sketchbook and pencil.

'Clothes off or on?' asked Gwen.

Lillian pretended to consider the question seriously. 'On this time. Off next.'

Gwen sat, hunched forward, elbows to her knees, chin balanced on one fist.

Lillian perched on the chair opposite. 'Good pose. Very dynamic.'

'Miss Hardy would be proud.'

Lillian began to mark out her friend's shape and contours. The fluffy maroon jumper she wore made her outline rather indefinite, but her face had become more angled with age and she now wore her curls scraped back into a tight bun. To Lillian she looked thrillingly capable, as she always had.

'I don't think you've ever drawn me before,' Gwen said. 'Not even in all that time we lived together.'

Lillian realised this was true. But then, she hadn't drawn anyone she'd loved. Not her mother. Not Mick. Not Jim. She'd drawn landscapes, and objects, and strangers at her life drawing class. She wondered, now, if she hadn't been able to risk getting her loved ones wrong on the page.

After a while, she said, 'I saw Jim Shepherd today.'

Gwen dropped her hand from her chin.

'No breaking the pose.'

'*And?*' said Gwen, taking a swig from the mug Lillian had placed on the floor. 'You saw Jim Shepherd where exactly? *And then what?*'

'Not until you put your hand back on your chin.'

Gwen put down her cup and did as she was told.

'He came into the museum. I pretended I hadn't seen him.'

'You didn't say anything?'

'What was I going to say?'

'How about, *Hello*? How about, *How are you, old friend*? How about, *Did I tell you I found out who my real dad was*?'

Lillian blinked. 'It just didn't seem like the right time.' She sketched in Gwen's wrists, focusing on the curves where her sleeves fell away from her arms, the way her watch-face sat flatly on her freckled skin.

'If he comes in again, for God's sake say something to him. I want to know the gossip. Presumably he's still married to what's-her-name?'

'I thought you didn't like him.'

'Did I ever say that?'

'You said he was *orderly*.'

Gwen laughed. 'Well, I was right. But so are you, with

your regular meal times and your sharp pencils. It's all an act, though, to cover up the fire inside. I know.'

Lillian didn't look up from her sketch as she smiled.

Half past three the following Saturday. Rain pattered softly on the skylight of the Aegean Room. Lillian removed the small sketchbook from her pocket and, hoping her manager wouldn't appear, chose the view directly ahead. The sloping glass cabinet, flanked by two huge urns. The polished floorboards, on which her own feet rested, stretching towards the open doors, and beyond that a hushed gloom, disturbed by the occasional figure passing. Quickly, she began to sketch it out.

Then Jim Shepherd strode into the picture. He looked directly at her, his smile a little fixed, something a little wild in his eyes, as he approached. Lillian sat straighter, the sketchbook still balanced on her knees, and looked back at him. She saw the panic grow in his face, felt him hesitate about where to place himself on that polished floor. Where did they belong, now, in relation to each other? She wondered if he would turn right around and walk away rather than speak to her, and, feeling a great tenderness towards him, she took Gwen's advice and said, 'Hello, Jim.'

Once she'd broken the silence, his panic seemed to lessen. 'Hello,' he said, standing a couple of feet from her, hands in his pockets. 'I thought I saw you here, last week. But you were hard to find today!'

His hair and the shoulders of his jacket were dark with rain.

'Well, here I am.'

He nodded. He was thinner and looked as though he hadn't slept for a while. He cleared his throat and rocked back on his heels.

'What are you doing here?' she asked.

'I might ask the same of you.'

'I work here.' She glanced at her page, then, unable to hold his searching gaze any longer.

Jim said, 'I want to apologise. For not turning up that day. I would have been there. But Pam went into labour.'

Lillian looked up.

'He's fifteen, now. My boy. Francie.'

Of course. 'I saw him,' she said. 'Last Saturday.'

A moment passed. Lillian, glad that Jim didn't question her on why she hadn't spoken to him then, said, 'You must be very proud.'

'Oh yes. Francie's . . . unique. He's almost as tall as me, now.'

'And your daughter?' Lillian asked.

At this he smiled broadly. 'She's wonderful.'

'I remember.'

Then Jim said, quickly, as though it had just occurred to him, 'Listen, what time do you get off? Maybe we could have a drink or something?' Before she could reply, he added, quietly, 'I've separated from Pam. In case you were wondering.'

He was just the same, she thought. Decent. Solid. Open to her. And with a new directness to him. But she still couldn't answer his question.

He glanced at her page, shifting his body to get a better view. 'Still drawing?'

She didn't try to keep the pride from her voice when she said, 'I've just started an art degree. At the Ruskin.'

'Great!' said Jim, grinning. 'Good for you! I always knew you'd do something really special.'

'Did you?'

'Never a doubt in my mind.'

She laughed, then, and realised that it had been a very long time since she'd done so.

'I get off at five,' she said. 'I could meet you on the steps?'

'On the steps,' he said, beaming. 'Perfect.'

Jim waited on the step. He'd chosen one halfway down so he could see both the Randolph Hotel opposite and the doors to the museum, though he trained his glance away from them, not wanting to allow his heart to lurch at the sight of every single body emerging from the revolving doors. He should have planned somewhere to take her. He had no idea which bar or tearoom or pub would please her best. Then he remembered: they could simply walk. Lillian loved to walk. They could head to Christ Church Meadow and walk along the river.

He looked to the sky. Perhaps the weather would be kind.

Lillian took the concrete steps up from the basement staff room quickly, calling a goodbye to Charlie, who asked if she was meeting a nice young man tonight. She smiled and said nothing.

In the museum entranceway she stopped. Through the revolving glass door she saw that the drizzle had eased and the sky was patched blue and deep grey. The pavement was busy with people folding their umbrellas, checking the air with empty, upturned hands, looking first doubtfully, then hopefully, at the sky.

She waited for the gap in the doors to present itself before slotting her body into it. She'd learned it was no good to rush this. You had to travel at exactly the speed at which the doors wished to revolve. They span steadily, at the pace of a solemn procession, and pushing would only make them stall, trapping you between two plates of glass. It was warm there, and quiet; sealed from the street and the museum, she took a moment to tell herself: *He is waiting for you, and perhaps it will have been worth the wait.*

She walked down the steps, to where Jim was. He leaned in to kiss her cheek, and she turned her face so their mouths met.

Some months of near-bliss followed for both of them.

Every other Saturday, when it wasn't his weekend with the kids, Jim waited for her on the museum steps. From there, they walked to the Botanic Garden, then crossed the High Street and ducked into Rosie's Tea Room to sit close together, knees touching, sipping from willow-pattern cups and kissing, which felt vaguely transgressive in a tearoom. Then they headed up the Cowley Road towards Lillian's flat.

As they walked, they talked. Lillian listened as Jim told her about his divorce. He downplayed his shock at Pam's decision to leave but did admit that he should have seen it coming. He told her about his grief at no longer living with his children ('Nights are the worst thing,' he found himself saying, 'because I can't go and check on them in their beds'). He mentioned, too, his promotions at work. And Jim listened as Lillian told him about her time in York with Gwen, about drawing in cafés, and about finding out that Ernie was her father. He had no idea what to say to that, eventually plumping for, 'It was obvious he cared about you. When I told him you were in hospital, the poor man looked like I'd punched him in the guts.'

To which Lillian only said, 'Hmm.'

Jim knew this Lillian was a different Lillian. She was Ms Wells, now, a mature art student at Oxford University. *Oxford University!* He repeated that often, especially when he was stopped by tourists wanting him to take their photograph. Jim was only too pleased to accept the camera and instruct the group of friends, whatever their nationality, to repeat the word *cheese.* Handing the camera back to the group's leader (always a man, usually of his own age), he'd clasp Lillian's shoulder and say, 'This one's an actual student, you know, of the university here. She's an *Oxford University* student.'

Lillian rolled her eyes, but she looked pleased.

Her flat took up the top floor of an Edwardian terraced house, but the first time he went there what he noticed was its modernity – she'd painted every room white, hung her favourite artworks in clip frames on the walls, and placed several brightly coloured lamps about the place. 'Well,' he said, 'this is all very *you*. Very Ms Lillian Wells.'

She gave him a puzzled look.

There were blinds in primary colours instead of curtains, and a microwave in the kitchen. On her bedroom wall hung drawings of some pillows, which Lillian told him were famous. 'Six studies of pillows by Albrecht Dürer,' she said. 'I love them.' Jim agreed that they were good, but asked why someone would spend a lot of time on something so . . . mundane? Lillian laughed and said that ordinary things could be fascinating, and beautiful. She picked up his hand and examined it. 'Like your fingers,' she said, kissing each one in turn.

In bed, too, Lillian seemed determined that everything should be light and, Jim couldn't help thinking, modern. She looked him in the eye and smiled as she unbuttoned his shirt and he wanted to whoop for joy. To his surprise, they laughed a lot together. She teased him about his underwear ('No one wears Y-fronts any more, Jim. I'll buy you some boxers'), and his habit of balling his socks together as soon as he removed them. After sex, he sometimes blew raspberries on her stomach or tickled the back of her neck with his eyelashes. He particularly loved the back of her neck, exposed by her short hair, its curve, its sensitivity to his touch, and its smell, which was all Lillian's own.

After a while, Lillian realised she hadn't seen Jim fully naked. He liked to remove the boxers she'd bought for him under the duvet and always slipped them back on before standing up. So one evening, after they'd made love, she said, 'You know, I've never seen all of you.'

He looked surprised. 'Do you want to?'

She nodded, and he stood for her by the side of the bed. In his clothes, Jim looked respectable, and rather slight. Out of them, she saw his compact body was muscled – a dancer's, of course. But coupled with this was a fragility she hadn't really seen before: it was there in the awkward way he looked down at her, waiting for permission to cover himself. In the paint-splatter shape of the mole on his thigh. In his nipples, which were soft and furred, like, she thought, the pointed snouts of mice. It moved her deeply, this combination of strength and vulnerability.

'Can I draw you?' she asked.

'If you want,' he said.

So she fetched her sketchbook and her pencil and he stood like that for twenty minutes while she tried to get him down on paper. When she showed him what she'd done, he looked astonished and said, 'Blimey. You made me almost beautiful. Thank you.'

She loved him, then.

At the Ruskin, she studied life drawing, perspective, composition, colour theory. She had a personal tutor named Gregory

Nichols, a young painter – younger than her, she suspected. In his office were two wing-backed armchairs and a sideboard on which stood a cut-glass decanter of something alcoholic. He told her that her drawing looked like knitting, which Lillian knew he didn't mean as a compliment, but she saw he was right: her work was dense, often small-scale, tightly patterned, and she liked that.

There were two other mature students in her year. One, Paula, was older than Lillian with grown-up children. Paula wore an Alice band and liked to talk about 'Keeping up with Tabitha', her daughter who had gone to Central Saint Martins and done terrifically well. The other was a man named Mark, a Communist who often challenged the tutors ('Don't you think composition is a waste of time, in this age of nuclear chaos?'), and though she knew he spent a lot of energy seducing the younger female students, Lillian liked talking to Mark in the common room, where they discussed the habits of their personal tutors. He said his was crazy about *Titian, for fuck's sake!*, and he also told her Gregory Nichols was an alcoholic; not in the way most of the tutors were alcoholics, more in an about-to-be-kicked-out-on-his-arse way. Lillian got the sense that, though they were both in their mid-thirties, Mark viewed her as a motherly figure. Sometimes he asked her what she was having for her tea that night, as though wanting to pick up tips, or merely reassure himself that someone, somewhere, had a plan.

She made friends, too, with a young man from Liverpool named Scott, who wore black eye make-up and scarves with silver thread running through them. Scott told Lillian that her haircut – largely unchanged since the mid-sixties – was 'absolutely iconic'. He also wanted to know how she stayed so marvellously thin. After only a moment's hesitation, Lillian decided she may as well tell the truth, and said she'd suffered from anorexia. It was the first time since Longbrook that she'd uttered the word aloud, and it felt both frightening and freeing. Scott's response was a dark look and the words, 'How horribly profound.' Then he'd embraced her and insisted she come with him to a wine bar in Jericho. Some Fridays, she found herself there, sipping house red beneath the fairy lights strung above the bar, alongside Scott, his boyfriend Tommy, and their friends Nicky and Tolly, who were students at other colleges. But she really preferred to go to the cinema alone with Scott, who adored what he called 'old movies' and could make her howl with laughter just by saying the name *'Brick'* in his Elizabeth Taylor voice.

It was hard to imagine Jim meeting Scott, Paula, or even Mark.

In her final year at the Ruskin, she began a project called *Mason Road*. From memory, she drew as many houses as she could picture, each with a slightly different kind of hedge, or gate, or curtains, or door knocker. In every house she placed herself and her mother. In some, they were both in the front garden, looking at, or past, one another. In other houses, Lillian looked down from a bedroom at Winnie, who stood by the gate. In still others, this was reversed. She wanted the picture to be an exploration of her place, and her mother's place, in the road. From one window, she drew Monty Clift, waving. Outside one house was Ernie, standing by his Austin, looking to the side. She drew Jim pushing his bike along the pavement, heading for the end of the street. She drew a skeletal representation of herself, in the car with Dawn, on the way to Longbrook. She painted the people in colour but left the street as a pen and ink line drawing.

Unlike her other work, *Mason Road* was not small scale. The picture grew and grew, and the version she exhibited at her degree show was twelve feet long and a foot wide. She liked that anyone viewing it would have to walk its length to see the whole thing. In her evaluation of the piece, she wrote that her intention had been to meld the real Mason Road, and her memories of it, with Uccello's *The Hunt in the Forest*, Festive Road from *Mr Benn* and David Hockney's *Mulholland Drive: The Road to the Studio*. She didn't mention that, while she was working on the project, she'd thought a lot about Ernie, driving up to number 25 every Friday and then pulling away, and it had struck her that she hadn't been responsible for all her mother's sadness. Ernie had been the source of at least some of it, too. It crossed her mind, then, that she should really visit Daphne sometime. *Later*, she thought. Perhaps later she would be ready to face her again.

For a long time, it seemed easier to pretend that it was just the two of them, there on the steps of the museum, in the hothouse of the Botanic Garden, in the flat with the branches of the birch trees tapping at the front window. Though they spoke on the phone during the week, Jim stayed the night at Lillian's on alternate Saturdays only. In the morning he made them breakfast, bringing her toast and marmalade in bed. He'd bought his own butter from the corner shop, early on, and always kept a block in Lillian's fridge. He never suggested she make them a meal, or that they go out to dinner, for which she was glad.

After they'd been seeing each other for two and a half years, Jim mentioned that Pam was planning to re-marry. She'd met a man at her new job in the Midland Bank. Seeing his sadness, Lillian suggested that he could come to the flat more often, if he liked, and he began turning up on Wednesday and Thursday evenings. But Lillian never made the trip to Abingdon.

Then, one sunny Sunday morning in May, Jim presented

Lillian with her toast along with the words, 'I'd still like you to be my wife, you know.'

The bells from the church a few streets over had just ceased. She drew the duvet up to her chin and said nothing for a while. To see the hope on his face was terrible, but to watch it fade was more terrible still. If only she could go back to before the bells had begun to ring, and prevent the statement from coming from his mouth.

Jim, who was standing above her in his boxers, holding the breakfast tray, bent to put it on the floor. While she couldn't see his face, Lillian said, 'I don't want to be anyone's wife, Jim. Not again.'

'Not anyone's,' Jim said. '*Mine.*'

Lillian wished she had at least a nightie on for this conversation.

'But I love how we are,' she said. 'Why change things?'

When Jim looked at her, his expression was so dark that she feared he'd pick up the tray and throw it. 'What will it take?' he demanded, clenching his fists. 'What do I have to *do*?'

'You don't have to do anything.'

'For Christ's sake!' he shouted. It was the most he'd ever raised his voice to her, and the sound of it rang around the room. For a moment he stood with his hands on his hips, staring at her. She could think of nothing else to say.

He reached for the ball of his socks. Lillian stayed where she was, clutching the duvet, watching him dress. Socks first. Then trousers. Then belt. Then shirt. He took his watch from the bedside table and buckled it tightly to his wrist.

'Let me know,' he said, 'if you ever change your mind.'

Then there was the slamming of doors, his footsteps on the stairs, and the sound of his car's engine starting. Lillian drew the covers over her head and moaned.

★

She distracted herself with preparations for her degree show and tried not to think about Jim's departure very much until it hit her, while holding a plastic cup of warm punch at the private view, that it was too late for him to appear. She'd sent him the invite, hoping he'd had enough time to forgive her second refusal and begin to understand. But now it was half an hour until the show closed, and it was clear that Jim wasn't going to arrive, grin, hold her shoulder, and say, 'You did it. I always knew you would.'

She stood before *Mason Road*, held her head up, and told herself it was for the best. Marriage was not for her, and if that was what Jim insisted on demanding, she couldn't give it to him.

In the weeks that followed, she felt weary and at a slight remove from everything, as though something she couldn't quite focus on was irritating her, like a lash caught behind her eyelid. Though she'd taken on more shifts at the museum and was busy submitting her CV to various agencies, she put it down to the double loss of the structure of the course and Jim's visits. But by late summer, her missed periods told a different story.

As soon as she found out about the pregnancy, Lillian longed for her mother. After the doctor told her the test was positive, he asked if she meant to be a single mother – or was she planning on marrying the child's father? Lillian was too shocked to answer. The doctor handed her some leaflets, and advised her to think things over very seriously.

Lillian threw the leaflets in the bin without reading them. For the first time in years, she drove straight to Abingdon and, sitting in the car outside number 25 Mason Road, she wept. It was a Thursday lunchtime and the road was empty save for a woman pushing a buggy with one hand while trying to control a large and barking dog with the other. Number 25 looked very different: it had a new double-glazed door, a driveway where the front garden had been, and a wire fence where Winnie's hedge used to grow. In her mind's eye, Lillian reinstalled the red curtains and pictured her mother leaning out of the bedroom window, waving. She had no idea who lived there now.

She imagined, too, letting herself in the back door and screwing up the courage to tell her mother about the pregnancy. Though her mother had always warned her about not getting herself *into trouble*, now she suspected that, in reality, Winnie wouldn't be nearly as upset about this as she'd been about Lillian's plans for art school. She pictured her mother, after dishing out a scolding for Lillian's carelessness, making them both some sweet tea, producing a slice of cake, and saying that she was not to worry: they would face this together. And just think! A *baby*. How lovely.

Lillian wiped her face and started the engine. Before going home, she drove slowly past Jim's house, half-hoping he'd appear. He did not.

She kept the secret inside her, and tried to resume her life. She went to work at the museum and sent off her CV again. She kept all her rejection letters in a folder. Frequently she felt nauseous – it was like being stuck on that coach to Southsea, years ago – and she was always tired. Her skin turned grey. There was a taste in her mouth that reminded her of pencil shavings. She told herself that if Jim contacted her she would speak to him about the pregnancy. But actually calling him to break the news seemed impossible. She found it hard to believe there was a baby growing, right there in her own body. If she mentioned it to Jim, it would all become too real. She feared he would try to persuade her to marry him, and, in a moment of weakness, she would say yes, just because it might be easier that way. She imagined the ring on her finger. A ring would have the power to fend off questions such as the doctor had asked.

Gwen came over one Saturday evening. They sat together on the sofa, and Lillian told her the news. Gwen went pale for a moment, then squeezed her hands and said she would help her, whether she wanted to keep the child or not. Lillian had been avoiding making this decision, but as soon as Gwen mentioned the word *abortion*, Lillian knew she couldn't do that, and said so. Gwen poured them both a small glass and raised hers. 'How exciting,' she said. 'You'll be a single mother. The scourge of polite society. The *bête noire* of the Tories.'

Lillian tried to smile.

Over the following weeks, she slept, and she worked, and she ate. She began to think of the secret inside her as a child, and to feel that it was a girl. Though she still could not imagine herself as a mother, in her mind she called the child Rachel, in tribute to Miss Hardy. After four months, she found she wanted to eat almost all the time, and was glad to have this undeniable reason to feed herself. It was not her appetite, she told herself, but the child's. She must eat for her daughter's sake.

Gwen said Jim had a right to know and could at least provide some money, but Lillian refused to tell him. Not now, she said, not yet. She felt that she had to get to know Rachel, just a little, before she shared anything with Jim. And she needed to be ready for the possibility of saying no to him for a third time.

Gwen was with her at the hospital for most of the birth, which was thirty-eight hours of pain. The moment when Lillian screamed the loudest came when, waking after a short nap, she believed herself once again at Longbrook, trapped in the swimming-pool-green of her curtained bed. Gwen gripped her hand and told her to hold on. By the time the doctors had used forceps to tug Rachel free, Lillian felt herself to be somewhere on the ceiling, looking down at a red, screaming woman with a wound that would never heal.

It wasn't until the baby was handed to her that she came down from that ceiling. The surprise of it was huge: a new life, right there in her arms. A new life that needed her protection.

It was six months before Lillian told Jim he had a daughter.

She'd taken Rachel to Tots and Toddlers, where most of the other mothers were younger than her. No one had actually asked a question about Rachel's father until that morning when, over a mug of coffee with greasy clumps of whitener floating on the top, a woman named Sophie enquired what Rachel's father thought of her recent introduction to solids. Sophie, who had tired eyes and expressive hands, was struggling to get her little boy, Joe, to take anything other than milk, and she leaned close to hear Lillian's response. 'I don't know what he thinks,' Lillian said. Flustered, she added, 'I'll have to ask him.' Sophie sipped her drink, slid her eyes to Lillian's third finger, and said no more about it.

Walking home through the rain with Rachel asleep in the buggy, Lillian saw that she could no longer pretend there were only two of them in this story. The money from Ernie was running out and her social security barely covered the essentials. She could certainly do with Jim's help financially. But, more than this, Rachel needed to know her father. Whatever Sophie or anyone else thought, Rachel had a father. And Lillian couldn't deny her daughter this vital information, as she herself had been denied.

Jim received the letter from Lillian when he came home to Mason Road one blustery evening in July. He was used, now, to returning to an empty house, but he still left the hallway light on while he was at work so that he wouldn't have to face an unlit home even in summertime. He picked up the mail and, recognising Lillian's hand immediately, was tearing open the envelope even before he'd shut the front door.

He carried the letter into the kitchen, flicked on the light, and sat down to read.

Dear Jim,

I need to share something with you. It's too important for a letter or phone call. Would you please come to the flat on Saturday morning? Any time is fine.

Lillian

He almost picked up the phone to ask her what the hell was going on. Was she ill, or in some kind of trouble? Had she changed her mind about his question? He doubted she had. Ever since he'd taken the risk of again raising the subject of marriage, he'd regretted it. Maybe it was as she'd said, years ago in the grounds of Longbrook: if he hadn't mentioned it, she wouldn't have had to say no. The two of them might still be together. Many Saturdays, he'd driven into Oxford, walked to the steps of the museum, spent a few moments gazing at the revolving door, then turned around. Many times, too, he'd invented a script for the phone call he'd make to her. It usually went a bit like this:

JIM: I'm so sorry. I was selfish. I wanted too much.
LILLIAN: Can you understand why I don't want a husband? It's not that I don't want you.
JIM: I know. And I want you.
LILLIAN: (After a short pause) Then what are we waiting for?

But he'd been afraid that she would veer wildly from the script, so he hadn't picked up the phone. And he didn't pick it up, now. Instead, he told himself that he only had to get through one more day before he would see her again.

It rained all Friday night. Jim lay awake, listening to it sluicing down the window. He got up at six, washed, shaved and dressed carefully (boxers, not Y-fronts, and a new shirt) and was ready to leave by seven, but he delayed himself, rereading the letter, making another slice of toast which he didn't touch. At eight thirty he left the house and drove through the wet streets, making a short detour to the new Tesco supermarket to buy a bunch of chrysanthemums. He'd recently been promoted to Deputy Head of Sales at Morland, and as a result had treated himself to a nearly new Ford Sierra. He knew this wouldn't impress Lillian, but as he parked it on her street and climbed out, he couldn't help but feel slightly buoyed by the deep blue sheen of its paintwork.

He rang her bell and tried to arrange his face.

When she opened the door, she had a baby in her arms. A pink, fat baby girl with wisps of fair hair and a frown on her brow. Jim had never seen Lillian holding a child before, and his first thought was that the baby must be Gwen's, or perhaps some other friend's. But then he saw Lillian lightly kiss the child's head, and it was such a casual and obviously habitual gesture that he understood the baby to be hers.

'Come up,' she said, ignoring the chrysanthemums and taking the stairs.

Jim stood for a moment, dumbfounded. He looked at the blue of his new car, considering climbing back into it. Then he heard the child yelp with joy, and the sound made him follow Lillian upstairs to the flat.

Lillian stood by the window, jiggling the baby on her hip, making the girl's legs waggle.

'This is Rachel,' she said.

Jim crossed the rug and put the flowers on the table. He placed both hands on the back of a chair and inhaled deeply through his nose. 'Rachel,' he said.

'Yes.'

'And who is Rachel?'

'She's my daughter,' said Lillian.

Jim asked, 'And is she mine, too?'

Lillian said, 'She's ours.'

'Ours,' he repeated.

Jim looked at this child who was his new daughter. She was, of course, perfect. *His new daughter.*

'I'm sorry I didn't tell you sooner,' Lillian was saying. 'It's taken me a while to get used to it. But I should have told you.'

'Yes,' said Jim. 'You bloody well should have.'

He took his hands from the chair and shoved them deep in his pockets.

'I appreciate this is a shock,' said Lillian.

Jim spent some time pacing up and down on the rug, stealing glances towards Rachel. The girl kept pointing to him, laughing, swivelling her big head to look back at her mother, then pointing to him again.

'I am sorry, Jim,' Lillian said, catching Rachel's hand in hers and kissing it. 'Really I am.'

Rachel pointed and laughed again.

Eventually Jim said, 'It doesn't matter, now, does it? What matters is what we do about it.'

Lillian nodded, her head dipping low, and he noticed how tired she looked. 'Are you all right?' he asked.

'Yes,' she said. 'It's not easy. But I'm all right.'

'I can help. Money. And everything. If you want?'

Lillian sat on the sofa, where she propped Rachel up with a couple of cushions and handed her a yellow plastic tractor, which the child sucked on. Then Lillian ran her hands through her hair. 'You can help by making me a coffee,' she said.

Jim got to work, his hand shaking as he spooned out the granules. In the few moments that he had his back turned to her, his shock began to turn to hope. Everything had changed. For the two and a half years they'd been together after meeting again, he hadn't once felt that Lillian actually needed him. Liked him, yes; wanted him, yes; enjoyed his company, yes. Loved him? Maybe. But she'd been this new, independent Lillian. Now there was a chance that she actually needed him. Their child – *their child!* – certainly did.

He put the coffees on the small table by the sofa and sat next to Rachel.

'Thanks,' said Lillian, adding, quickly, 'I need you to understand some things.'

Jim offered his fingers to Rachel, who grabbed hold of them, stuffed them in her mouth and bit down with her gums, hard, making him wince. Removing his fingers, he offered her the tractor instead, but she batted it away and reached for him again. He asked Lillian if it was all right for him to hold the child, and she said he could, if he liked. He took Rachel on his lap and gave her his balled fist to chew. The warm weight of her was instantly calming, and he found himself closing his eyes and smelling the top of her head.

'Look,' said Lillian. 'I don't want a husband, OK?'

'I think you made that very clear last time I saw you.'

'But I do want Rachel to have a father. So I'd like us to work out an . . . arrangement. I was thinking you could come here for a few hours on Saturdays while I go back to work at the museum. She could get used to you, then maybe you could have her at your place sometimes? And we could share things a bit. We'll see how it goes. I want her to know you. But Rachel's home would, obviously, be with me.'

Jim took a deep sniff of his daughter. She was earthy and sweet. He held her tighter. 'I'm sure we can work something out,' he said.

Lillian picked up her coffee and blew on it. 'Good,' she said. 'Because I'm exhausted.'

For the next few years, Jim came to the flat to look after his daughter on Saturdays while Lillian worked at the museum. As Rachel grew, a few hours on a Saturday turned into every other whole weekend.

When Rachel was thirteen, Lillian took her to the accident and emergency department of the John Radcliffe Hospital. Rachel had been awake all night with terrible pains in her stomach, which had shifted to her left-hand side in the early hours of the morning, when she'd also begun to vomit. Once she'd been assessed by a nurse and was on a bed behind a curtain, Lillian called Jim from a hospital phone box.

He arrived within an hour. Rachel, yellow-skinned and sweaty, grasped his hand when he found them, and Lillian saw, for the first time, the need she had of her father, who smiled and spoke smoothly, telling his daughter that the doctors would sort this little thing out in no time at all.

In fact it took all day for the doctors to decide to operate, which they did late that night, leaving Lillian and Jim alone in an overheated waiting room. They'd been told it would take around an hour. When Lillian half-heartedly suggested that Jim go home and get some sleep, he said, simply, 'I can't do that.' Instead, he fetched them some scalding coffee in plastic cups from the vending machine and they sat on the hard seats, sipping and listening to the wall clock's tick. Lillian tried to absorb what he was saying when Jim told her that, statistically speaking, operations on appendices were the most successful in the world, and the John Radcliffe was one of the best hospitals in the country. It might be a blessing, in fact, he went on, for Rachel to have this thing out: no one knew what they were for and she'd be better off without it.

But these facts – how did he even know them? – seemed to Lillian too nebulous to grasp. What was true, at that moment, was that her daughter lay anaesthetised on an operating table. Her daughter's middle was being cut into by the surgeon's knife. Her daughter's appendix might have burst, which could cause what the doctor had termed 'complications'. Possibly life-threatening complications.

Closing her eyes, Lillian said, 'It would really help if you were to hold my hand.'

Jim did that, and after a while she turned to him and he embraced her fully. She smelled the brewery on him, and it was comforting. He held her for a long time. With her head on his shoulder, she said, 'Thank you.'

'For what?'

'For giving me Rachel.'

He stroked her hair, and when she looked at him she saw him wipe his eyes.

'She's going to be fine,' she said.

Jim nodded, and blew his nose.

Then the doctor appeared, and told them everything had gone well. They could go and see their daughter, now.

2005

When she arrived back at her flat from Gwen's, the phone was already ringing.

It was Jim. 'I wanted to speak to you before tonight,' he said. 'Just to make sure we're all on the same page. I don't know what Rachel's told you already—'

Lillian, sweaty from the climb up the stairs into the airless flat, her stomach curdling from the wine she'd drunk the night before, reached over to throw open the window. Then she sat at the table. *On the same page.* Jesus. The brewery had closed down a few years ago, when Morland had been bought by a bigger company, and Jim had wept at the loss of his job. He now worked for a friend, doing the admin and teaching some sessions for a small dance studio in town, but here he was speaking as though he were still Head of Sales.

'Lillian?'

'Have you even noticed?' she demanded. 'Have you even noticed what she's doing?'

'Sorry?'

'Patting her neck. And *blinking*! One, two, three! As if she's counting!'

'Of course I'd noticed, but—'

'So many bloody tics! She's riddled with them! It's driving me insane!'

After a moment, Jim said in a low voice, 'She holds on to the door handle before she opens it, too.'

Lillian, a little defeated by Jim's knowledge of their daughter's behaviour, said nothing.

'And you're worried,' Jim stated. 'Understandably.'

'I'm not sure she's ready for uni.'

'She'll be fine. She's just worried you won't be OK without her.'

Lillian wanted to rip the phone from the wall and throw it out of the window then. It was what Gwen had said, too. How could everyone – even Jim – have known this all along? Why was everything her fault? And why was he so calm?

She said, 'Since you know so much about it, perhaps you can tell me this. Do you think she's going down the same route?'

'The same route? What does that mean?'

Lillian gazed out of the window at the hazy sky. The telegraph wire bounced as a few starlings landed, then took off, chattering.

'The same way as me. And Mum. All the way to Longbrook.' She slumped in her chair, cradling her forehead with one hand. She was so tired. And so bloody hot.

Jim said, 'Lillian—'

'I know it's not the same, but it's similar, isn't it? All this . . . keeping control of herself. Or losing control of herself. I don't know which it is. Years ago, the doctor suggested I take her to some unit that was part of Longbrook. But that place is not what she needs!'

The ache behind her eyes had become a thudding pain. She scrabbled in a pot on her desk for paracetamol and threw a couple of tablets in her mouth, swallowing them with the cold coffee she'd abandoned the morning before.

Jim said, 'Let's not get ahead of ourselves. These tics. You used to have a few, didn't you?'

Lillian made an exasperated sound. 'What are you talking about?'

'You used to hold the back of your neck. And your wrist.'

He'd noticed that, too, then.

'She's been seeing a counsellor, actually,' Jim continued, 'and she's promised me she will again, once she gets to UCL, if she needs to—'

'Wait. *Rachel*'s been seeing a counsellor?'

'For a few months now. Every time she comes over here. I take her. She likes it.'

'But she told me that *you* were the one in therapy.'

Jim laughed. 'Me? Not bloody likely.'

'Why didn't she tell me?'

Jim said quietly, 'I expect she didn't want to worry you. So she worried me, instead. Which is fine. Since I'm her dad.'

There was a long silence, during which Lillian felt very lonely, but slightly lighter.

Then Jim said, 'Are you going to talk to her, Lillian? About what happened to you? And about . . . your mother, and Ernie, and . . . everything?'

Lillian swallowed.

'I know it's hard. But it will be good, I think. For both of you.'

Silently, she nodded.

After a few moments, Lillian asked if there was anything she could bring, and Jim said, 'Just your lovely self.'

Jim put the phone down and went to the kitchen window. Beneath the cherry tree at the bottom of his garden Rachel was sitting on a lounger, plastering her legs with suncream. He'd told her early that morning that her mother was coming tonight, and she'd already prepared a lot of the ingredients for the family dinner – there was something pungent and green sitting in the blender. The dirty chopping board and all Jim's sharp knives had been abandoned in the sink. He checked his watch. Ten thirty. He needed to pop in on his mother, then get to the studio by twelve to lead Ballroom for Mature Beginners. He hadn't realised, that lunchtime in Pam's flat behind the brewery years ago, how much he'd enjoy teaching. It wasn't just that all eyes would be on him for an hour as he moved expertly through the music; it was the feeling he got, when he helped someone to master a step, that he had enabled their happiness.

He filled a glass with ice from the freezer and topped it up with orange juice, then he went outside to present it to Rachel, meaning to ask her to wash up while he was gone.

She was flicking through the album she'd found at Daphne's house, and reached up to accept the juice in silence. She didn't even take a sip before placing it on the grass. Jim saw, then, that his daughter was upset. Her brow furrowed sharply and her eyes were slightly glazed as she looked past him.

He sat on the edge of the lounger, almost toppling it. In silence, they both shuffled into positions that allowed the thing to balance. Jim had learned long ago that it was no good quizzing Rachel when she was like this. Questions only made her retreat further into herself.

Eventually she closed the album and said, 'Am I being ridiculous?'

'About what?'

She gave him a slightly exasperated look. 'Expecting Mum to share stuff with me.'

Jim examined his hands. He knew Rachel wanted his version of events. And it would be easy enough for him to fill her in on lots of things about her mother's life before her birth. But he felt, very strongly, that this was not his story to tell.

'You're not being ridiculous,' he said carefully. 'But you may have to be patient with her.'

'How serious was it?' Rachel asked. 'Mum's mental health problem? I mean, it's clear she has some sort of eating disorder. She never eats anything other than what's on her plate. And that's always a tiny amount. But when did it start? And how bad did it get?'

Jim looked at the sky. It was white with heat. Sweat was beginning to seep through his socks.

'It was fairly serious, love. But she's all right, now—'

'*Fairly* serious?'

Feeling the strength of Rachel's stare, Jim could only nod.

'What does that mean? Devastating, or just inconvenient?'

'You'll have to ask her about it.'

'Devastating, then.'

He touched her forearm. She'd always seemed, he thought, a sturdy girl. Ready for anything. A lot of that, he knew, was down to her mother's careful, steady nurturing. Lillian had told him, early on, that she didn't want Rachel to be afraid of anything. But now Rachel was afraid. Jim could see it in her face. The word *Longbrook* wouldn't make her blood run cold, as it once had his. He knew, though, that Lillian's experience would come as a shock to Rachel; it would shift her view of her mother, and perhaps of herself, too. But he felt that his daughter was strong enough to weather these changes.

'She'll tell you, when she's ready.'

Rachel patted the back of her neck and, in his mind, Jim counted with her. *One, two, three.*

There was a pause. Rachel sipped her drink, then offered the glass to Jim. The juice was so sweetly cold he had to stop himself from gulping the lot.

'Have you got everything,' he asked, 'for the dinner? I can pop to Tesco on my way back from work.'

'Everything's ready,' Rachel said with a wry smile, 'for her majesty's arrival.'

Mrs Shepherd, now in her mid-nineties, still lived in the house opposite number 25. After a fall a few years back, Jim had tried to persuade his mother that the new care home on the other side of town might be a good idea, but she'd flatly refused to budge. 'You'll have to crowbar me out of this place,' she'd said, adding, 'How could I live somewhere Reg had never been? He wouldn't know where I was.' Jim had been so taken aback by this mention of his father that he'd said no more about it.

As he walked up the path he waved at the window, behind which he knew his mother would be sitting in her armchair. Then he let himself in the back door. The kitchen was spotless. The home-help must have been in earlier.

'All well?' he called, filling the kettle then flicking it on.

'Tickety-boo, dear,' came her reply.

He went into the front room, taking the comb from his back pocket. Though his mother was still just about able to feed and dress herself, she could no longer reach the back of her head, so it was Jim's job to comb her hair each day.

She was dressed in her tabard and slippers, despite the heat. He bent to kiss her cheek and smelled stale face powder.

'Warm today,' he said.

'I don't feel it.'

She leaned forward in the chair, and he began to run the comb through her white waves.

'Gently,' she warned, as she always did. Jim went a little slower, as he always did.

'How's Rachel?' she asked.

She'd always got on well with her second granddaughter. Meg had made a habit of answering her grandmother back and making a mess in her bedroom, but Rachel, as Jim's mother liked to say, was a very respectful girl. Plus, she had real *gumption*. Rachel had been the one to call the ambulance when her grandmother had got her feet tangled in the kitchen mat and had fallen. Jim had been mowing the back lawn and had heard nothing until Rachel told him the paramedics were on their way. He wasn't to worry, she'd said; she'd put Gran in the recovery position and the signs were that nothing had been broken.

'Rachel's fine,' said Jim. 'I expect she'll pop over, later.'

'She's a good girl. And her mother?'

She liked to call Lillian 'Rachel's mother' rather than use her name.

'Lillian's coming over for dinner with me and Rachel, later,' said Jim, trying to pat his mother's hair into some sort of shape.

He slotted the comb back into his pocket. 'I'll get your tea.'

Before he could move away, his mother clasped his hand, stilling him. Her fingers were cold, though slightly swollen.

'I've never understood why she doesn't eat with you *every* night,' she said. 'Surely it would be much easier if you were all together.'

Jim was tired of having this conversation. He was tired,

too, of thinking about it himself. After his second proposal, he hadn't dared suggest marriage to Lillian ever again, but occasionally he'd pointed out how much easier and cheaper things would be if they lived together, if not as man and wife then as parents. Lillian wouldn't hear of it, saying she was settled in her own place and just could not imagine returning to Mason Road. Not wanting to drive her away, he hadn't pressed her.

He sighed and said, 'It's not going to happen, Mum.'

She tutted. 'But it's confusing, Jim. What is the woman, exactly? Your *girlfriend*?'

Jim tried not to laugh. His mother often asked this. 'She's not my girlfriend,' he said. 'It's not like that.'

'What is she, then?'

'She's Ms Lillian Wells,' said Jim.

'Who?'

'She's my friend, Mum. And she's Rachel's mother.'

There was a pause before his mother squeezed his hand. 'Well. Whatever she is, Jim, I'm glad the three of you have each other. And I know you'll miss Rachel when she's gone.'

Jim nodded, and, feeling suddenly choked, escaped to the kitchen, where he stood at the sink, catching his breath.

His mother was right. He would miss Rachel terribly.

Once the shock of finding out about her birth had passed, he'd felt lucky to have been given this new chance. He'd made a mess of his early relationship with Lillian, but something good had come of it. Perhaps mess was too strong a word, he thought. Muddle might be better. He'd made a muddle of it all. But it had seemed to Jim then, and it still seemed to him now, that Rachel and his new relationship with her mother were the most unexpected, extravagant gifts he had ever received in his life.

He took his mother's pot from the shelf, poured hot water on tea leaves, and waited for them to brew.

Lillian tidied her desk. *Super Granddad* was almost finished; she'd even got him to look as though he was flying, albeit in a low and ungainly way. It had helped to depict him crashing into a few chimneys, his belly brushing tiles from rooftops. Then she showered and scrubbed at her muddy toes, digging yesterday's dirt from the riverbank from beneath her nails. She put on her good summer top – blue silk with embroidered birds on the shoulders – and threaded a pair of silver hoops through her ears. Her hair needed a cut, but it would do.

From the cupboard in her bedroom, she took down a scroll of paper, slightly soft around the edges and held in place by a fraying elastic band. She didn't have to unfurl it: she knew what it was, and remembered every detail. *Mason Road*, the project she'd completed for her degree. It would be a place to start her conversation with Rachel. While she didn't yet know how much she would tell her daughter, she had at least a sense of the shape of her story. Much of it would remain hers alone. But she would answer Rachel's questions as honestly as she could.

She drove with the windows down, enjoying the feeling of the warm wind battering her hair, her ears. She couldn't know, yet, if she would be broken by Rachel's departure. She knew only that she wanted to care for her daughter over this final week or so. And that included turning up at Jim's house and eating his food.

Though there was no longer a diversion, on the way to Abingdon she found herself taking the turning for Longbrook. As she approached the new housing development where the hospital had been, she held her breath. When she saw the sign advertising NEW APARTMENTS FOR SALE she let it out. There it was – the biscuit-coloured building, the immaculate lawn. It would always live inside her. But perhaps, next time, she would be able to pass this spot and breathe normally.

She drove on.

Rounding the corner into Mason Road, she wondered why Jim had never moved. He'd taken a cut in salary after Morland had closed, but surely now that Meg and Francie had long had independent lives, he could afford it. It was difficult, though, to imagine Jim anywhere else but right here.

She parked outside his house. On the back seat of the car was her artwork, together with a cake, a layered sponge filled with lemon curd and buttercream, housed inside a cardboard box. That afternoon, after staring out of the window for a very long time, she'd walked to the Covered Market to buy it. All the way back to the flat, she'd cradled it beneath her arm, saliva filling her mouth at the thought of the taste of it.

Stepping from the car, she was greeted by a slight breeze and the smell of approaching rain. A dog barked somewhere and a couple of kids swerved their bikes to avoid her. Glancing up the street she saw, very clearly, her mother come battling into view, blonde beehive unmoving, heels clicking, and she smiled.

Then Lillian reached into the back seat and took out the scroll and the cake box. Tucking one beneath each arm, she looked again for her mother, who had disappeared.

She made her way up Jim's path and round to the back of his house. In the far corner of the garden a sprinkler arced over a patch of parched grass. There was a handful of daisies, already wilting, in a vase on the patio table and embroidered cushions on the metal chairs. The sky was a dusty pink, and the air felt low and close, but there was no thunder. Without knocking, she let herself in the back door.

In the kitchen, there was an odour of onions and garlic. Rachel, Jim's apron on and hair loose, was stirring a pot on the stove. Lillian put the scroll and the cake on the table. They could wait. For now, she needed to kiss her daughter.

'Hello,' she said, her lips touching Rachel's cheek.

Rachel hugged her briefly. 'I've made Thai curry.'

'It smells amazing. And I brought pudding.'

Rachel raised her eyebrows. 'Mum. You never do pudding.'

Lillian said nothing to that.

Then Jim appeared in the doorway, wearing a shirt that looked fresh from the packet. The creases were still deeply scored and stood up in odd places, on his chest and upper arms. He touched her shoulder and looked into her face. 'You came,' he said. 'Smashing.'

'Oh my God,' said Rachel, 'who says *smashing* any more?'

Lillian smiled, then kissed Jim's cheek, too. 'Your father does,' she said.

Jim touched the place where her lips had been and glanced towards the table. 'I told you not to bring anything.'

'It's just some things for Rachel.'

Rachel looked at her. 'For me?'

'I'll show you after dinner,' said Lillian. 'It's a picture I made, at art school. I thought it might help us to talk about . . . some things.'

Rachel blinked. One. Two. Three. 'Really?'

'Yes.'

'Can't I look now?'

'Later.'

Rachel let her spoon drop into the saucepan and embraced her mother tightly. 'Thank you,' she said. Lillian held on, feeling the reach in her daughter's arms, savouring this brief moment in which all was safe and all was well.

2006

Lillian is waiting for her daughter, and she is hungry.

In her new study, which used to be Ernie and Daphne's bedroom, she sits at the table, looking out of the window at the river. A neat line of geese land on the water, deftly parting it so it laps at the banks. Before her are some preliminary sketches for a new picture. She's thinking of calling it *Portrait of the Artist as a Hungry Woman*. It will depict a woman sitting on the floor of the room where Lillian slept as a baby, the room Daphne kept intact, eating a cake as big as her body from a cardboard box. She hasn't managed much work this morning, but she'll have time in a couple of weeks, when the Easter holidays are over and Rachel has gone back to university.

She walks the house, a lightness in her step at the thought of showing all the changes to Rachel, who hasn't seen it for a few months. The smell of new paint is still strong, so she opens the window in her bedroom. She's kept the toy duck with the umbrella beneath its arm and the frilly coverlet but has taken the rest of the stuff to the dump. The room looks out onto the back garden, long, thin and overgrown, though Ernie's rose bushes are beginning to sprout new leaves. Gwen has promised to help her get it all in order. She's already talking about a pond and a pergola.

At first it was strange to sleep again in this room. More than once she woke and felt an urgent need to find her mother. But now she feels not only Winnie's but also Daphne's presence whenever she is in the house, and if she finds herself imagining the two of them at loggerheads – *That bloody snob; Your poor mother* – she sternly tells them both to be quiet and, to her surprise, so far they have been.

Downstairs, she goes into the kitchen. She's cooking a family dinner tonight for Jim and Rachel: pasta with asparagus, a salad, some crusty bread. Jim, who is picking Rachel up from the station, has promised to bring a pudding. Lillian takes a bread knife and cuts into the fresh loaf she bought earlier in the town, then smears it with cold butter from the fridge.

She carries her slice into the hallway and, clamping the bread between her teeth, shrugs on her new coat, which has pockets big enough for a pencil, a rubber and a pad. She takes a bite of her bread. It is deliciously soft and salty. She checks her watch. Eleven thirty. Even if the train is on time, it will be at least half an hour before Jim arrives with their daughter. Their beautiful, busy, clever daughter, who is still holding on to door handles and patting the back of her neck – *one, two, three* – is coming to stay, if only for a little while.

Lillian swallows, then takes another bite of bread, and another, and another, until it is gone. She licks her fingers, picks up her sketchbook from Daphne's telephone table, then opens the front door. There is plenty of time, she thinks, for a walk along the river before her daughter comes home.

Acknowledgements

Peter Agulnik, Ruth and Martin Carter, Debra Doggett, Johnny Highsmith, David Kennard, Scott Mandelbrote, Bob Osborne and Mary Parslow all shared their experiences and/or expertise with me while I wrote this book, for which I offer heartfelt thanks. Thanks to my agent, Véronique Baxter, for her insight and determination, and to Molly Slight and Clara Farmer at Chatto. For their input into an early draft, I thank the wonderful writers Kate Worsley and Hannah Vincent. Thanks, too, to my husband, Hugh, and my son, Ted, for their love and support. And to Mum, for her Abingdon stories and her love.

Bethan Roberts has published five novels and writes stories and drama for BBC Radio 4. Her books include *The Good Plain Cook*, which was a Radio 4 Book at Bedtime; *My Policeman*, the story of a 1950s policeman, his wife and his male lover (now a major Amazon Original film starring Harry Styles and Emma Corrin); *Mother Island*, which received a Jerwood Fiction Uncovered Prize; and *Graceland*, which tells the story of Elvis Presley and his mother, Gladys. She also writes short fiction, for which she has won the Society of Authors' Olive Cook Prize and the RA and Pin Drop Short Story Award. Bethan has taught Creative Writing at Chichester University and Goldsmiths, University of London. She lives in Brighton with her family.